Never Fear – Phobias

Heather Graham   F. Paul Wilson

Thomas F. Monteleone   E. McCarthy

Laura Harner   Lance Taubold
Elle J Rossi   Michael Koogler
Crystal Perkins   Richard Devin
Connie Corcoran Wilson   Mathew Kaufman
Aidan Russell   Ed DeAngelis
Jeff DePew   Don Marlowe
Holly Prentiss   Casey Parsons
Jason Possezzere

13Thirty Books
Print and Digital Editions
Copyright 2015

Discover new and exciting works at www.13thirtybooks.com

Print and Digital Edition, License Notes

DEDICATION

To all who fear.

CONTENTS

Astraphobia by F. Paul Wilson   3
Thanatophobia by Jeff DePew   39
Spectrophobia by Elle J Rossi   63
Oneirophobia by Connie Corcoran Wilson   75
Coulrophobia by Michael Koogler   95
Atychiphobia by Casey Parsons   121
Aichmophobia by Richard Devin   135
Taphophobia by E. McCarthy   147
Phobophobia by Lance Taubold   159
Chiroptophobia by Don Marlowe   175
Thantophobia by Thomas F. Monteleone   187
Logizomechanophobia by Holly Prentiss   195
Necrophobia by Laura Harner   209
Agateophobia by Mathew Kaufman   237
Merinthophobia by Jason Pozzessere   251
Cyprianophobia by Ed DeAngelis   269
Chronophobia by Crystal Perkins   291
Iatrophobia by Aidan Russell   305
Toxiphobia by Heather Graham   323

ACKNOWLEDGMENTS

To an amazing group of authors.

1

ASTRAPHOBIA

FEAR OF LIGHTNING

F. PAUL WILSON

"Please, signor," the corporal says in fairly decent English, shouting over the rising wind. "You are not permitted up there!"

I look down at him. "I'm well aware of that, but I'm all right. Really. Get back inside before you get hurt."

The patterned stone floor of the Piazza San Marco beckons three hundred feet below as he clings to one of the belfry columns and leans out just far enough to make eye contact with me up here on the top ledge. His hat is off, but his black shirt identifies him as one of the local Carabinieri. Hopefully a couple of his fellows have a good grip on his belt. I can tell he's used up most of his courage getting this far. He's not ready to risk joining me up here. Can't say I blame him. One little slip and he's a goner. I've developed a talent for reading faces, especially eyes, and his wide black pupils tell me how much he wants to go on living.

I envy that.

Less than an hour ago I was just another Venice tourist. I strolled through the crowded plaza, scattering the pigeon horde like ashes until I reached the campanile entrance. I stood on line for the elevator like everyone else and paid my eight thousand lire for a ride to the top.

The Campanile di San Marco--by far the tallest structure in Venice, and one of the newest. The original collapsed shortly after the turn of the century but they replaced it almost immediately with this massive brick phallus the color of vodka sauce. Thoughtful of them to add an elevator to the new one. I would have hated climbing all those hundreds of steps to the top.

The belfry doubles as an observation deck: four column-bordered openings facing each point of the compass, screened with wire mesh to keep too-ardent photographers from tumbling out.

The space was packed with tourists when I arrived--French, English, Swiss, Americans, even Italians. Briefly I treated myself to the view-- the five scalloped cupolas of San Marco basilica almost directly below, the sienna mosaic of tiled roofs beyond, and the glittering, hungry Adriatic Sea encircling it all--but I didn't linger. I had work to do.

The north side was the least crowded so I chose that for my exit. I pulled out a set of heavy wire clippers and began making myself a doorway in the mesh. I knew I wouldn't get too far before somebody noticed and, sure enough, I soon heard cries of alarm behind me. A couple of guys tried to interfere but I bared my teeth and hissed at them in my best impression of a maniac until they backed off: Let the police handle the madman with the wire cutter.

I worked frantically and squeezed through onto the first ledge, then used the mesh to climb to the second. That was hairy--I damn near slipped off. Once there, I edged my way around until I found a sturdy wire running vertically along one of the corners. I used the cutters to remove a three-foot section and left it on the ledge. Then I continued on until I reached a large marble sculpture of a griffin-like creature set into the brick on the south side. I climbed its grooves and ridges to reach the third and highest ledge.

And so here I am, my back pressed against the green-tiled pinnacle as it angles to a point another thirty feet above me. The gold-plated statue of some cross-wielding saint--St. Mark, probably-- pirouettes on the apex. A lightning rod juts above him.

And in the piazza below I see the gathering gawkers. They look like pigeons, while the pigeons scurrying around them look like ants. Beyond them, in the Grand Canal, black gondolas rock at their moorings like hearses after a mass murder.

The young national policeman pleads with me. "Come down. We can talk. Please do not jump."

Almost sounds as if he really cares. "Don't worry," I say, tugging at the rope I've looped around the pinnacle and tied to my belt. "I've no intention of jumping."

"Look!" He points southwest to the black clouds charging up the coast of the mainland. "A storm is coming!"

"I see it." It's a beauty.

"But you will be strike by lightning!"

"That's why I'm here."

The look in his eyes tells me he thought from the start I was crazy, but not this crazy. I don't blame him. He doesn't know what I've learned during the past few months.

***

The first lesson began thousands of miles away, on a stormy Tuesday evening in Memorial Hospital emergency room in Lakeland, Florida. I'd just arrived for the second shift and was idly listening to the staff chatter around me as I washed up.

"Oh, Christ!" said one of the nurses. "It's her again. I don't believe it."

"Hey, you're right!" said another. "Who says lightning doesn't strike twice?"

"Twice, hell!" said a third voice I recognized as Kelly Rand's, the department's head nurse. "It's this gal's third."

Curious, I dried off and stepped into the hallway. Lightning strike victims are no big deal around here, especially in the summer – but three times?

I saw Rand, apple shaped and middle aged, with hair a shade of red that does not exist in the human genome, and asked if I'd heard her right.

"Yessiree," she said. She held up a little metal box with a slim aerial wavering from one end. "And look what she had with her."

I took the box. *Strike Zone*™ *Early Warning Lightning Alert* ran in red letters across its face.

"I'd say she deserves a refund," Rand said.

"How is she?"

"Been through x-ray and nothing's broken. Small third-degree burn on her left heel. Dr. Ross took care of that. Still a little out of it, though."

"Where'd they put her?"

"Six."

Still holding the lightning detector, I stepped into cubicle six and found a slim blonde, her hair still damp and stringy from the rain, semiconscious on the gurney, an IV running into her right arm. A nurse's aide was recording her vitals. I checked the chart when she was done.

Kim McCormick, age 38, found "disrobed and unconscious" under a tree bordering the ninth fairway at a local golf course. The personal info had been gleaned from a New Jersey driver license. No known local address.

A goateed EMS tech stuck his head into the cubicle. "She awake yet, Doc?"

I shook my head.

"All right, do me a favor, will you? When she comes to and asks about her golf clubs, tell her they was gone when we got there."

"What?"

"Her clubs. We never saw them. I mean, she was on a golf course and sure as shit she's gonna be saying we stole them. People are always accusing us of robbing them or something."

"It says here she was naked when you found her."

"Not completely. She had on, like, sneakers, a bra, and you know, panties, but that was it." He winked and gave me a thumbs-up to let me know he'd liked what he'd seen.

"Where were her clothes?"

"Stuffed into some sort of gym bag beside her." He pointed to a vinyl bag under the gurney. "There it is. Her clothes was in there. Gotta run. Just tell her about the clubs, okay?"

"It's okay," said a soft voice behind me. I turned and saw the victim looking our way. "I didn't have any clubs."

"Super," the tech said. "You heard her." And he was gone.

"How do you feel?" I said, approaching the gurney.

Kim McCormick gazed at me through cerulean irises, dreamy and half obscured by her heavy eyelids. Her smile revealed white, slightly crooked teeth.

"Wonderful."

Clearly she was still not completely out of her post-strike daze.

"I hear this is the third time you've been struck. How in the..?"

She was shaking her head. "It's the eighth."

I grinned at the put-on. "Right."

"'S'true."

My first thought was that she was either lying or crazy, but she didn't seem to care if I believed her. And in those half-glazed eyes I saw a secret pain, a deep remorse, a hauntingly familiar loss. The same look I saw in my bathroom mirror every morning.

I held up her lightning detector. "If that's true, you should find one of these that really works."

"Oh, that works just fine."

"Then why--?"

"It's the only way I can be with my little boy."

I tried to speak but couldn't find a word to say. Stunned, I watched her roll over and go to sleep.

***

No way I could let her leave without learning what she'd meant by that, so I kept looking in on her during my shift, waiting for her to wake up. After suturing the twenty-centimeter gash a kid from the local supermarket had opened in his thigh when his box cutter slipped, I checked room six again and found it empty.

The desk told me she'd paid by credit card and taken off in a cab, lightning detector and all.

I spent the next week hunting her, starting with her Jersey address; I left messages on the answering machine there, but they were never returned. Finally, after badgering the various taxi companies in town, I tracked Kim McCormick to a Travelodge out on 98.

I sat in my car in the motel parking lot one afternoon, gathering courage to knock on her door, and wondering at this bizarre urge. I'm not the obsessive type, but I knew her words would haunt me until I'd learned what they meant.

It's the only way I can be with my little boy.

Taking a deep breath, I made myself move. August heat and

humidity gave me a wet slap as I stepped out and headed for her door. Nickel clouds hung low and a wind-driven Wal-Mart flyer wrapped itself around my leg like a horny mutt. I kicked it away.

She answered my knock almost immediately, but I could tell from her expression she didn't know me. To tell the truth, with her hair dried and combed, and color in her cheeks, I barely recognized her. She wore dark blue shorts and a white Lacoste --sans bra, I noticed. I hadn't appreciated before how attractive she was.

"Yes?"

"Ms. McCormick, I'm Dr. Glyer. We met at the emergency room after you were--"

"Oh, yes! I remember you now." She gave me a crooked grin that I found utterly charming. "This a house call?"

"In a way." I felt awkward standing on the threshold. "I was wondering about your foot."

She stepped back into the room but didn't ask me in. "Still hurts," she said. I noticed the bandage on her left heel as she slipped her feet into a pair of backless shoes. "But I get around okay in clogs."

I scanned the room. A laptop sat on the night stand, screen-saver fish gliding across its screen. The bed was unmade, two Chinese food containers in the wastebasket, a Wendy's bag next to the TV on the dresser. *The Weather Channel* was on, showing a map of Florida with a bright red rectangle superimposed on its midsection. The words "Severe Thunderstorm Warning" crawled along the bottom of the screen.

"Glad to hear it. Listen, I'd... I'd like to talk to you about what you said when you were in the ER."

"Sorry?" she said, cocking her head toward me. "I didn't catch that."

I repeated.

"What did I say?" She said it absently as she hurried about the room, stuffing sundry items into her gym bag, one of which I recognized as her lightning detector.

"Something about being with your little boy."

That got her. She stopped and looked at me. "I said that?"

I nodded. "'It's the only way I can be with my little boy,' to be exact."

She sighed. "I shouldn't have said that. I was still off my head

8

from the shock, I guess. Forget it."

"I can't. It's haunted me."

She stepped closer, staring into my eyes. "Why should that haunt you?"

"Long story. That's why I was wondering if we might sit down somewhere and--"

"Maybe some other time. I'm just on my way out."

"Where? Maybe we can go together and talk on the way."

"You can't go where I'm going." She slipped past me and closed the door behind her. She flashed me a bright, excited smile as she turned away. "I'm off to see my little boy."

I watched her get into a white Mercedes Benz with Jersey plates. As she pulled away, I hurried to my car and followed. Her haste, the approaching storm, the lightning detector... I had a bad feeling about this.

I didn't bother hanging back--I doubted she knew what kind of car I was driving, or would be checking for anyone following her. She turned off 98 onto a two-lane blacktop that ran straight as the proverbial arrow toward the western horizon. A lot of Florida roads are like that. Why? Because they can be. The state is basically a giant sandbar, flat as a flounder's belly, and barely above sea level. Roads here don't have to wind around hills and valleys, so they're laid out as the shortest distance between two points.

Ahead the sky was growing rapidly more threatening, the gray clouds darkening; lightning flashed in their ecchymotic bellies.

The light had dimmed to late-dusk level by the time she turned off the blacktop and bounced northward along a sandy road. She stopped her car about fifty yards from a small rise where a majestic Nelson pine towered over the surrounding scrub. She got out with her gym bag in hand and hurried toward the tree in a limping trot. Wind whipped her shorts around her bare legs, twisted her hair across her face. A bolt of lightning cracked the sky far to my left, and thunder rumbled past a few seconds later. I gaped in disbelief as she pulled off her shirt and shorts, stuffed them into the bag, and seated herself on the far side of the trunk.

"She's crazy!" I said aloud as I gunned the engine.

I pulled past her car and stopped as close to the tree as the road would allow. Amid more lightning and thunder, I jumped out and dashed up the rise.

"Kim!" I shouted. "This is insane! Get away from there!"

She started at the sound of my voice, looked up, and threw her free arm across her breasts. Her other hand gripped the lightning detector, its red warning light blinking madly.

"Leave me alone! I know what I'm doing!"

"You'll be killed!" I picked up her gym bag and held it out to her. "Please! Get back in your car!"

Her face contorted with fury as she slapped the bag from my hand, then covered her breasts again. "Get out of here! You don't understand and you'll ruin everything!" Her voice rose to a scream. "Go *away!*"

I backed off, unsure of what to do. I debated grabbing her and wrestling her to safety, but did I have the right? As crazy as this seemed, Kim McCormick was a grown woman, and very determined to be here. A daylight-bright flash, followed instantaneously by a deafening crash of thunder and a torrent of cold rain decided it. I ducked back toward my car.

"Keep your windows closed!" I heard Kim shout behind me. "And don't touch any metal!"

Drenched, I huddled on the front seat and did just that. The storm roared in with maniacal fury, lashing the car with gale-force winds and rain so heavy I felt as if I'd parked under a waterfall. I couldn't see Kim--couldn't even see the big Nelson pine. I hated the thought of her getting soaked and risking electrocution out there in the lightning-strobed darkness, but what could I do?

Mostly I resented feeling helpless. I fought the urge to throw the car into gear and leave Kim McCormick to her fate. I had to stay... *needed* to stay. I felt tenuously bound to this peculiar woman, by something unseen, unspoken.

The lightning and thunder finally abated as the storm chugged off to the east. When the rain had eased to a steady downpour, I lowered the window and squinted at the pine, afraid of what I'd see.

Kim was still huddled against the trunk, looking miserable: hair a rattail tangle, knees drawn up, head down, but seemingly none the worse for the terrible risk she'd taken.

I stepped out and tried not to stare at her glistening, pale skin as I approached. She glanced up at me. The bright excitement of an hour ago had fled her eyes, leaving a hollow look. I reached into her bag and pulled out her shirt. I held it out to her.

"*Now* can we talk?"

***

Kim pointed to a pink scar that puckered her right palm. "This is from the first time I was hit."

I'd followed her back to her motel, waited while she took a quick shower, then brought her here to Cajun Heat, my favorite restaurant. She'd seemed pretty down when we were seated, but a couple of Red Stripes and an appetizer of steamed spiced shrimp had perked her up some.

"That one was an accident," she said. "I was visiting my sister in West Texas last year. She and her husband and I had been fishing on White River Lake when it started to get stormy. We came ashore and I was standing on the dock, helping unload the boat. It hadn't even started raining yet, but somehow I took a direct hit." She rubbed the scar. "I had a fishing rod in my hand, my palm against the reel. That's all I remember. Karen and Bill were knocked off their feet but they told me later they saw me fly twenty feet through the air. I broke my forearm when I landed. My heart had stopped. They had to give me CPR."

"You were lucky."

"Yeah, maybe." She stared at her palm with a rueful smile. Her wet hair was pulled back and fastened with an elastic band, making her look younger than her thirty-eight years. "Karen still jokes about how she thinks Bill was maybe a little too enthusiastic with the mouth-to-mouth."

I said, "So the first strike was accidental. After what I saw today, I gather the next seven were anything but. Dare I ask why?"

Kim continued staring at her palm. "You already think I'm nuts. I don't want you thinking I'm a complete psycho."

"Try me."

"Hmm?" She glanced up. "Sorry. I'm a little hard of hearing, especially when there's background noise."

"I said, Try me."

She looked me in the eye, then let out a deep sigh. "Immediately after that first strike, I saw my son Timmy. I could see the lake and the dock and the boat, but they were faint and ghostly. I was standing right where I'd been when I got hit, but I could see my body sprawled behind me. Karen and Bill were running toward it, but slowly, like they were swimming through molasses, and they too looked faint, translucent. Timmy, though--he looked perfectly real and solid, but he was far away, hovering over the water, waving to me. He looked healthy, like he'd never been sick, but he was so far. He kept beckoning me closer but I couldn't move. Then he faded away."

The pieces fell into place, and there it was, staring me in the face. Somehow I'd sensed it. Now I knew.

"When did he die?"

She blinked in surprise, then looked away. "Almost three years ago." Her eyes brimmed with tears but none spilled over. "Two years, eleven months, two weeks, and three days, to be exact."

"You had a very vivid hallucin--"

"No," she said firmly, shaking her head. "He was *there*. You can't appreciate how real he was if you didn't see him. I'm a hard-headed realist, Doctor Glyer, and--"

"Call me Joe."

"Okay. Fine. But let's get something straight, Doctor Joe. I'm no New-Agey hollow-head into touchy-feely spirituality. I was an investment banker, and a damn good one--Wharton MBA, Salomon Brothers, the whole nine yards. I dealt with the reality of cold hard cash and down-and-dirty bottom lines every day. As far as the afterlife was concerned, I was right up there with the big-time skeptics. To me, life began when you were born, you lived out your years, then you died. That was it. Game over, no replay. But not anymore. This is real. I don't know what happened, or how it happened, but for an all-too-brief time after that lightning strike, I saw Timmy, and he saw me, and that changed everything." She closed her eyes. "I thought I was getting over losing him, but..."

No, I thought as her voice trailed off. You never get over it. But I said nothing.

"Anyway, at first I tried to duplicate the effect by shocking myself with my house current, but that didn't work. I concluded I'd need the millions of volts only lightning can provide to see. So I went back to Texas and hung around that dock during half a dozen storms but I couldn't *buy* another hit."

"Are you trying to die? Is that it?"

She tossed me a withering look. "I have a Ruger nine-millimeter automatic back at my motel room. When I want to die, I'll use that. I am *not* suicidal."

"Then what else do you call flirting with death like you did today? And you've been hit *eight* times? The fact that you're still alive is amazing--you've had a fantastic run of luck, but you've got to know that sooner or later it's going to run out."

The waitress arrived then and we dropped into silence as she set steaming plates of jambalaya before us.

"You don't know much about lightning, do you?" Kim said when we were alone again.

"I've treated my share of--"

"But do you know that it's usually not fatal, that better than nine out of ten victims survive?"

Truthfully, I hadn't known the survival rate was that high. "Well, you're closing in on number ten."

She shrugged. "Just a number. The first shock on that dock in Texas should have killed me. The usual bolt carries a current of ten thousand amps at a hundred million volts. Makes the electric chair look like a triple-A battery. Of course the charge only lasts a tiny fraction of a second, but that first one was enough to put me into cardiac arrest. If Karen and Bill hadn't known CPR, we wouldn't be having this conversation."

She dug into her jambalaya and chewed for a few seconds.

"Good, isn't it," I said.

She nodded. "Delicious."

But she said it with no great conviction, and I got the feeling that eating was something Kim McCormick did simply to keep from feeling hungry.

"But where was I? Oh, yes. After failing to get hit a second time in Texas, I started studying up on lightning. We still don't understand it completely, but what we do know is fascinating. Do realize that worldwide, every second of every minute of every day there are almost a thousand lightning flashes? Most are cloud to cloud or cloud to air. Only fifteen percent hit the ground. Those are the ones I'm interested in."

This was the most animated I'd seen her. I leaned across the table, drawn by her enthusiasm.

"But you're from Jersey. You were first struck in Texas.

What are you doing here?"

"It's where the lightning is. The National Weather Service keeps track of lighting--something called flash density ratings. According to their records, Central Florida is the lightning capital of the country, maybe the world. You've got this broad strip of hot, low-lying land between two huge, cooler bodies of water. Take atmospheric instability due to wide temperature gradients, add tons of moisture, and *voila*--thunderstorm alley."

"Seems you've been pretty successful around here--if you can call getting hit by lightning success."

She smiled. "I do. I started up around the Orlando area because of all the lakes. Being out in a boat during a storm is the best way to get hit, but I started thinking it was too risky, too easy to get knocked overboard and drown. Or take a direct hit from a positive giant."

"A what?"

"A positive giant. They originate at the very top of the storm cell, maybe fifty thousand feet up, and they can strike thirty miles ahead of the storm. You've heard of people getting struck down by a so-called 'bolt from the blue'? That's a positive giant. I don't want to get hit by one of those because they're so much more powerful than a regular bolt. Almost always fatal." She pointed her fork at me. "See? Told you I'm not suicidal."

"I believe you, I believe you."

"Good. Anyway, I settled on golf courses as my best bet. The landscapers take down a lot of the little trees but tend to leave the really big ones between the fairways." She showed me a pink, half-dollar-size scar on her right elbow. "That's an exit burn from the strike at Ventura Country Club." She parted her hair to reveal a quarter-size scar on her right parietal scalp. "This one's an entry at Hunter's Creek Golf Club. I could show you more, but not in public. I've got other scars you can't see. Like a mild seizure disorder, for instance--I take Dilantin for that. And I've lost some of my hearing."

I was losing my appetite. This poor, deranged woman. "And did you see...?"

"Timmy?" She smiled. Her eyes fairly glowed. "Yes. Every single time."

Kim McCormick was delusional. Had to be. And yet she was so convincing. But then that's the power of a delusion.

But what if it wasn't a delusion? What if she really...?

I couldn't let myself go there.

"One of these times..."

"You're right, I suppose.

And I'm prepared for it. I've got a solid will: How I'm to be cremated, where my ashes will go, and a list of all the charities that'll share my assets. But I stack the deck in my favor when I go out. That's why I get under a tree. Odds are against taking a direct hit that way. You get a secondary jolt--a flash that jumps from the primary strike point--and so far that's worked just fine for my purposes. Plus I keep low to the ground to reduce my chance of being thrown too far."

"But why do you undress?"

"I figure wet skin attracts a charge better than wet fabric."

I shook my head. "How long are you going to keep this up?"

"Until I get closer to him. He seems nearer here than he was in Texas, but he's still too far away."

"Too far for what?"

"I need to see his eyes, hear his voice, read his lips."

"Why? What are you looking for?"

A lost look tinged with terrible sorrow fluttered across her features. Her voice was barely audible. "Forgiveness."

I stared at her.

"Don't ask," she whispered before I could speak. "Subject closed." She shook herself and gave me a forced smile. "Let's talk about something else. Anything but the weather."

***

I stand alone on a rotted wharf, engulfed in fog. The stagnant pond before me carries a vaguely septic stench. No sound, no movement. I wait. Soon I hear the creak of wood, the gentle lap of a polished hull gliding through still water. A dark shape appears, with the distinctive curved bow of a gondola. It noses toward me through the fog, but as it nears I notice something unusual about the hull. Its classic glossy black, like all gondolas, but the seating area is closed over. I realize with a start that the hull is a coffin... a child's coffin... and bright red blood is oozing from under the lid. I shout to the gondolier. He's gaunt, the traditional striped shirt hanging loose on his bony frame. His face is hidden by his broad straw hat until he lifts his head and stares at me. I scream when I see the scar running across his left eye. He grins and begins poling his floating sarcophagus away, back into the fog. I jump into the foul water and swim after him, stroking frantically as I try to catch up. But the gondola is too fast and the fog swallows it again, leaving me alone and lost in the water. I swim in circles, my arms growing weaker and weaker... finally they refuse to respond, dangling limply at my sides as I slip beneath the surface... water rushes into my nose and throat, choking me...

I awoke gagging and shaking, dangling half on, half off my bed. It took me a long time to shake off the aftereffects of the nightmare. I hadn't had one like that in years. I knew why it had returned tonight: my afternoon with Kim McCormick.

***

Over the next few days I realized that Kim had invaded my life. I kept thinking of her alone in that motel room, eating fast food, her eyes glued to *The Weather Channel* as she tracked the next storm, planned her next brush with death. The image haunted me at night, followed me through the day. I found myself keeping *The Weather Channel* on at home, and ducking off to check it out on the doctors lounge TV whenever I had a spare moment.

I guess my preoccupation became noticeable because Jay Ravener, head of the emergency department, pulled me aside and asked me if anything was wrong. Jay could never understand why a board-certified cardiologist like myself wanted to work as an emergency room doc. He was delighted to have access to someone with my training, but he was always telling me how much more money I could make as a staff cardiologist. Today, though, he was talking about enthusiasm, giving me a pep talk about how we were a team, and we all had to be players. He went on about how I hardly speak to anyone on good days, and lately I'd barely been here.

Probably true. No, undoubtedly true. I don't particularly care for anyone on the staff, or in the whole damn state, for that matter. I don't care to make chitchat. I come in, do my job--damn efficiently, too – and then I go home. I live alone. I read, watch TV, videos, go to the movies--all alone. I prefer it that way.

I know I'm depressed. But imagine what I'd be like without the forty milligrams of Prozac I take every day. I wasn't always this way, but it's my current reality, and that's how I choose to deal with

it.

Fuck you, Jay.

I said none of this, however. I merely nodded and made concurring noises, then let Jay move on, satisfied that he'd done his duty.

But the episode made me realize that Kim McCormick had upset the delicate equilibrium I'd established, and I'd have to do something about her.

Just as she had researched lightning, I decided to research Kim McCormick.

Her driver license had listed a Princeton address. I began calling the New Jersey medical centers in her area, looking for a patient named Timothy McCormick. When I struck out there, I moved to Philadelphia. I hit pay dirt at CHOP--Children's Hospital of Philadelphia.

Being a doctor made it possible. Physicians and medical records departments are pretty tight-lipped about patient information when it comes to lawyers, insurance companies, even relatives. But when it's one doctor to another...

I asked Timothy McCormick's attending to call me about him. After having me paged through the hospital switchboard, Richard Andrews, MD, pediatric oncologist, knew he was talking to a fellow physician, and was ready to open up. I told him I was treating Kim McCormick for depression that I knew stemmed from the death of her child, but she would give me no details. Could he help?

"I remember it like it was yesterday," he told me in a staccato rattle. "Sad case. Osteosarcoma, started in his right femur. Pretty well advanced, metastatic tumors to the lung and beyond by the time it was diagnosed. He deteriorated rapidly but we managed to stabilize him. Even though he was on respiratory assist, his mother wanted him home, in his own room. She was loaded and equipped a mini-intensive care unit at home with around-the-clock skilled nursing. What could we say? We let her take him."

"And he died there, I gather?"

"Yeah. We thought we had all the bases covered. One thing we didn't foresee was a power failure. Hospitals have back-up generators; her house didn't."

I closed my eyes and suppressed a groan. I didn't have to imagine what awful moments those must have been, the horror of utter helplessness, of watching her child die before her eyes and not being able to do a thing about it. And the guilt afterward... oh, lord, the crushing weight of self-doubt and self damnation would be enough to make anyone delusional.

I thanked Dr. Andrews, told him what a great help he'd been, and struggled through the late shift. Usually I can grab a nap after two a.m. Not this time. I sat up, staring at *The Weather Channel*, watching with growing unease as the radar tracked a violent storm moving this way from Tampa.

I called Kim McCormick's motel room but she didn't answer. Did she guess it was me and knew I'd try to convince her to stay in? Or was she already out?

As the clock crawled toward six a.m. I stood with keys in hand inside the glass door to the doctor's parking lot and watched the western sky come alive with lightning, felt the door shiver in resonance with the growing thunder. So *much* lightning, and it was still miles off. If Kim was out there...

If? Who was I kidding? Of course she was out there. And I couldn't leave until my relief arrived. I prayed he'd show up early, but if anything, the storm would delay him.

Jerry Ross arrived up at 6:05, just ahead of a pair of ambulances, and I dashed for my car. The storm was hitting its stride as I raced along 98. I turned onto what I thought was the right road, fishtailing as I gunned along, searching for that Nelson pine. I almost missed it in the downpour, and damn near ditched the car as I slammed on the brakes when I spotted it. I reversed to the access road and kicked up wet gravel as I headed for the tree.

The sight of her Mercedes offered some relief, and I let out a deep breath when I spotted the pale form huddled against the trunk. I barely knew this strange, troubled woman, and yet somehow she'd become very important to me.

I skidded to a stop and ran up the rise to where she sat, looking like a drowned rat. Halfway there the air around me flashed noon bright and the immediate crash of thunder nearly knocked me off my feet, but Kim remained unscathed.

"Not again!" she cried, not bothering to cover her breasts this time. She waved me off. "Get out of here!"

"You can't keep doing this!"

I dropped to my knees beside her and tried not to stare. I

couldn't help but notice that they were very nice breasts, not too big, not too little, just right, with deep brown nipples, jutting in the chill rain.

"I can do anything I damn well please! Now *go away!*"

I'd been here only seconds but already my clothes were soaked through. I leaned closer, shouting over the deafening thunder.

"I know what happened--about Timmy, bringing him home, the power failure. But you can't go on punishing yourself."

She gave me a cold blue stare. "How do you–?"

"Doesn't matter. I just know. Tell me--was there a storm when the power went off?"

She nodded, still staring. The red blinker on her lightning detector was going berserk.

"Don't you see how it's all tied together? It's guilt and obsession. You need medication, Kim. I can help."

"I've *been* on medication. Prozac, Paxil, Zoloft, Effexor, Tofranil, you name it. Nothing worked. I'm not imagining this, *Doctor*. Timmy is there. I can feel him."

"Because you *want* him there!"

More lightning--so close I heard it sizzle.

"Damn you!" she gritted through clenched teeth during the ensuing thunderclap. I didn't hear those words, but I could read her lips. She closed her eyes a second, as if counting to ten, then looked at me again. "Do you have any children?"

I didn't hesitate. "No."

"Well, if you did, you'd understand when I say you *know* them. I *know* Timmy, and I know he's *there*. And since you've never had a child, then you can't understand what it's like to lose one." Her eyes were filling, her voice trembling. "How you'll do anything--risk everything--to have them back, even for an instant. So don't tell me I need medication. I need my little *boy!* "

"But I do understand," I said softly, feeling my own pain grow, wanting to stop myself before I went further but sensing it was already too late. "I--"

I stopped as my skin burst to life with a tingling, crawling sensation, and my body became a burning beehive with all its panicked residents trying to flee at once through the top of my head. I had a flash of Kim with strands of her wet hair standing out from her head and undulating like live snakes, and then I was at ground zero at Hiroshima...

...an instant white-out and then the staticky blizzard wanes, leaving me kneeling by the tree, with Kim sprawled prone before me, flaming pine needles floating around like lazy fireflies, and a man tumbling ever so slowly down the slope to my right. With a start I realize he's me, but the whole scene is translucent -- I can see through the tree trunk. Everything is pale, drained of color, almost as if etched in glass, except...

...except for the tiny figure standing far across the marsh, a blotch of bright spring color in this polar landscape. A little girl, her dark brown hair divided into two ponytails tied with bright green ribbon, and she's wearing a yellow dress, her favorite yellow dress...

...it's Beth...oh, Christ, it can only be Beth... but she's so far away.

A desperate cry of longing leaps to my lips as I reach for her, but I can make no sound, and the world fades to black, my Beth with it...

I sat up groggy and confused, my right shoulder alive with pain. I looked around. Lightning still flashed, thunder still bellowed, rain still gushed in torrents, but somehow the whole world seemed changed. What had happened just now? Could that have been my little Beth? Really Beth?

No. Not possible. And yet...

Kim's still white form caught my eye. She lay by the trunk. I tried to stand but my legs wouldn't go for it, so I crawled to her. She was still breathing. Thank God. Then she moaned and moved her legs. I tried to lift her but my muscles were jelly. So I cradled her in my arms, shielding her as best I could from the rain, and waited for my strength to return, my mind filled with wonder at what I had seen.

Could I believe it had been real? Did I dare?

***

Still somewhat dazed, I sat on Kim's motel bed, a towel around my waist, my clothes draped over the lampshades to dry. When she'd come to, we staggered to my car and I drove us here.

The room looked exactly as before, except a Hardy's bag had replaced the Wendy's. Kim emerged from the bathroom wearing a flowered sun dress, drying her hair with a towel. She was bouncing back faster than I was--practice, maybe. She looked pale but elated. I knew she must have seen her boy again.

I felt numb.

"Oh, God," she said and leaned closer. "Look at that burn!"

I glanced at the large blister atop my left shoulder. "It doesn't hurt as much as before."

"Oh, Joe, I'm so sorry you caught that flash too. I feel terrible."

"Don't. Not as if you didn't warn me."

"Still...let me get some of the cream they gave me for my heel. I'll make you--"

"I saw someone," I blurted.

She froze, staring at me, her eyes bright and wide. "Did you? Did you really? You saw Timmy? Didn't I tell you?"

"It wasn't your son."

She frowned. "Then who?"

"Remember by the tree, just before we got hit, when you asked me if I had any children? I said no, because... because I don't. At least not anymore. But I did."

Kim stared, wide-eyed. "*Did?*"

"A beautiful, beautiful daughter, the most wonderful little girl in the world."

"Oh, dear God! You too?"

My throat had thickened to the point where I could only nod.

She stumbled to the bed and sat next to me. The thin mattress sagged deeply under our combined weight.

"You're sure it was her?"

Again I nodded.

"I didn't see her. And you didn't see Timmy?"

I shook my head, trying to remember. Finally I could speak. "Only Beth."

"How old was she?"

"Eight."

"Timmy was only five. Was it...?" Her own throat seemed to clog as she placed her hand on my arm. "Did she have cancer too?"

"No." The memory began to hammer against the walls of the cell where I'd bricked it up. "She was murdered. Right in front of me." I held up my left arm to show her the seven-inch scar running up from the underside of my wrist. "This was all I got, but Beth died. And I couldn't save her."

Kim made a choking noise and I felt her fingers dig into my

arm, her nails like claws.

"No!" Her voice was muffled because she'd jammed the damp towel over her mouth. "Oh-no, oh-no, oh-no! You poor... oh, God, how...?"

I heard a sound so full of pain it transfixed me for an instant until I realized it had come from me.

"No. I can't. Please don't ask. I can't, I can't, I can't."

How could I talk about what I couldn't even think about it? I knew if I freed those memories, even for a single moment, I'd never cage them again. They'd rampage through my being as they'd done before, devouring me alive from the inside.

I buried my face against Kim's neck. She cradled me in her arms and rocked me like a baby.

***

"What about Timmy's father?" I said, biting into my Egg McMuffin. "Does he know about all this?"

After clinging to Kim for I don't know how long, I'd finally pulled myself together. We were hungry, but my clothes were still wet. So she took my car and made a breakfast run to Mickey D's. I sat on the bed, Kim took the room's one upholstered chair. The coffee was warming my insides, the caffeine pulling me part way out of my funk, but I was still well below sea level.

"He doesn't know Timmy exists. Literally. We never married. He's a good man, very bright, but I dropped him when I learned I was pregnant."

"I don't follow."

"He'd have wanted to marry me, or have some part in my baby's life. I didn't want that." My expression must have registered how offensive I found that, because she quickly explained. "You've got to understand how I was then: A super career woman who could do it all, wanted it all, and strictly on her own terms. I went through the pregnancy by myself, took maternity leave at the last possible moment, figuring I'd deliver the child--I knew he was a boy by the third month--and set him up with a nanny while I jumped right back into the race. I saw myself spending a sufficient amount of quality time with him as I molded him to be a mover and a shaker, just like his mother." She shook her head. "What a jerk."

"And after the delivery?" I'd guessed the answer.

She beamed. "When they put that little bundle into my arms, everything changed. He was a miracle, by far the finest thing I'd ever done in my life. Once I got him home, I couldn't stop holding him. And when I would finally put him into his bassinet, I'd pull up a chair and sit there looking at him... I'd put my pinkie against his palm and his little fingers would close around it, almost like a reflex, and that's how I'd stay, just sitting and staring, listening to him breathe as he held my finger."

I felt my throat tighten. I remembered watching Beth sleep when she was an infant, marveling at her pudgy cheeks, counting the tiny veins on the surfaces of her closed eyelids.

"You sound like a wonderful mother."

"I was. That's no brag. It's just that it's simply not my nature to do things half way. Everything else in my life took a back seat to Timmy, I mean *way* back. It damn near killed me to end my maternity leave, but I arranged to do a lot of work from home. I wanted to be near him all the time." She blinked a few times and sniffed. "I'm so glad I made the effort. Because he didn't stay around very long." She rubbed a hand across her face and looked at me with reddened eyes. "How long since Beth...?"

"Five years." The longing welled up in me. "Sometimes I feel like I was talking to her just yesterday, other times it seems like she's been gone forever."

"But don't you see?" Kim leaned forward. "She's not gone. She's still here."

I shook my head. "I wish I could believe that."

The lightning episode was becoming less and less real with each passing minute. Despite what I'd seen, I found myself increasingly reluctant to buy into this.

"But you saw her, didn't you? You *knew* her. Isn't seeing believing?"

"I don't know. Sometimes believing is seeing."

"But each of us saw our dead child. Can we *both* be crazy?"

"There's something called shared delusion. I could be–"

"Damn it!" She catapulted from the chair. "I'm not going to let you do this!" She yanked my pants from atop the lampshade and threw them at my face. "You can't take this from me! I won't let you or anybody else tell me--"

I grabbed her wrist as she stormed past me. "Kim! I *want* to believe! Can't you see there's nothing in the world I want more? And that's what worries me. I may want it too much."

I pulled her into my arms and we stood there, clinging to each other in anguished silence. I could feel her hot breath on my bare shoulder. She lifted her face to me.

"Don't fight it, Joe," she said, her voice soft. "Go with it. Otherwise you'll be denying yourself--"

I kissed her on the lips.

She drew back. I didn't know where the impulse had come from, and it was a toss-up as to which of us was more surprised. We stared at each other for a few heartbeats, and then our lips were together again. We seemed to be trying to devour each other. She tugged at my towel, I pulled at her sun dress, she wore nothing beneath it, and we tumbled onto the unmade bed, skin to skin, rolling and climbing all over each other, frantic mouths and hands everywhere until we finally locked together, riding out a storm of our own making.

***

Afterwards, we clung to each other under the sheet. I stroked her back, feeling guilty because I knew it had been better for me than her.

"Sorry that was so quick. I'm out of practice."

"Don't be sorry," she murmured, kissing my shoulder. "Maybe it's all the shocks I've taken, but orgasms seem to be few and far between for me these days. I'm just glad to have someone I can feel close to. You don't know how lonely it's been, keeping this to myself, unable to share it. It's wonderful to be able to talk about it with someone who understands."

"I wish I did understand. Why is this happening?"

"Maybe all those volts alter the nervous system, change the brain's modes of perception."

"But I've never heard of anything like this. Why don't other lightning strike victims mention seeing a dead loved one?"

"Maybe they *have* seen them and never mentioned it. You're the only one I've told. But maybe it has to be someone who died during a storm. Did Beth--?"

"No," I said quickly, not allowing the scene to take shape in my mind. "Perfect weather."

"Then maybe it has to do with the fact that they both died as children, and they're still attached to their parents. They hadn't let go of us in life yet, and maybe that carries over into death."

"Almost sounds as if they're waiting for us."

"Maybe they are."

The temperature in the room seemed to drop and Kim snuggled closer.

***

Later, when we went back to pick up Kim's car, we walked up to where the lightning had struck. The top of the Nelson pine was split and charred. As we stood under its branches, I relived the moment, seeing Beth again, reaching for her...

"I wish she'd been closer."

"Yes." Kim turned to me. "Isn't it frustrating? When I took my second hit, up in Orlando, Timmy was closer than he'd been in Texas, and I thought he might move closer with each succeeding hit. But it hasn't worked that way. He stays about fifty yards away."

"Really? Beth seemed at least twice that." I pointed to the marshy field. "She was way over there."

Kim pointed north. "Timmy was that way."

I swiveled back and forth between where I'd seen Beth, and where Kim had seen Timmy, and an idea began to take shape.

"Which way were you facing when you saw Timmy in Texas?"

She closed her eyes. "Let me think... the sun always rose over the end of the dock, so I guess I was facing northeast."

"Good." I took her shoulders and rotated her until she faced east. "Now, show me where Timmy was in relation to the end of the dock when he appeared in Texas."

She pointed north.

"I'll be damned," I said and trotted down the slope.

"Where're you going?"

I reached into my car and plucked the compass from my dashboard. Sometimes at night when I can't sleep I go out for long aimless drives and wind up God knows where. At those times it's handy to know which direction you're headed.

"All right," I said when I returned. "This morning Timmy was that way – the compass says that's a few degrees east of north. If you followed that line from here, it would run through New Jersey, wouldn't it?"

She nodded, her brow furrowing. "Yes."

"But in Texas--where in Texas?"

"White River Lake. West Texas."

"Okay. You saw him in a northeast direction. Follow that line from West Texas and I'll bet it takes you--"

"To Jersey!" She was squeezing my upper arm with both hands and jumping up and down like a little girl. "Oh, God! That's where we lived! Timmy spent his whole life in Princeton!"

It's also where he died, I thought.

"I think a trip to Princeton is in order, don't you?"

"Oh, yes! Oh, God, yes!" Her voice cranked up to light speed. "Do you think that's where he is? Do you think he's still at the house? Oh, dear God! Why didn't I think of that?" She settled down and looked at me. "And what about Beth? You saw her... where?"

"East-northeast," I said. I didn't need the compass to figure that.

"Where does that line go? Orlando? Kissimmee? Did you live around there?"

I shook my head. "No. We lived in Tampa."

"But that's the opposite direction. What's east-northeast from here?"

I stared at the horizon. "Italy."

***

A week later we were sitting in the uppermost part of Kim's Princeton home waiting for an approaching storm to hit.

She had to have been earning *big* bucks as an investment banker to afford this place. A two-story Victorian--she said it was Second Empire style--with an octagonal tower set in the center of its mansard roof. One look at that tower and I knew it could be put to good use.

I found a Home Depot and bought four eight-foot sections of one-inch steel pipe, threaded at both ends, and three compatible couplers. I drilled a hole near the center of the tower roof and ran a length through; I coupled the second length to its lower end, and ran that through, and so on until Kim had a steel lightning target jutting twenty-odd feet above her tower.

The tower loft was unfurnished, so I'd carried up a couple of cushions from one of her sofas. We huddled side by side on those. The lower end of the steel pipe sat in a large galvanized bucket of water a few feet in front of us--the bucket was to catch the rain that would certainly leak through my amateur caulking job at the roof line, the water to reduce the risk of fire.

I heard the first distant mutter of thunder and rubbed my hands together. Despite the intense dry heat up here, they felt cold and damp.

"Scared?" Kim said

"Terrified."

My first brush with lightning had been an accident. I hadn't known what was coming. Now I did. I was shaking inside.

Kim smiled and gave my arm a reassuring squeeze. "So was I, at first. Knowing I'm going to see Timmy helps, but still... it's the uncertainty that does it: *Is* it or *isn't* it going to hit?"

"How about I just say I don't believe in lightning? That'll make me feel better."

She laughed. "Hey, whatever works." She sidled closer. "But I think I know a better way to take your mind off your worries."

She began kissing me, on my eyes, my cheeks, my neck, my lips. And I began undoing the buttons on her blouse. We made love on the cushions in that hot stuffy tower, and were glazed with sweat when we finished.

A flash lit one of the eight slim windows that surrounded us, followed by a deep rumble.

"Almost here," I whispered.

Kim nodded absently. She seemed distant. I knew our lovemaking had once again ended too quickly for her, and I felt bad. Over the past week I'd tried everything I knew to bring her through, but kept running into a wall I could not breach.

"I wish–" I began but she placed a finger against my lips.

"I have to tell you something. About Timmy. About the day he died."

I knew it had been tough on her coming back here. I'd seen

his room--it lay directly below this little tower. Like so many parents who've lost a child, she'd kept it just as he'd left it, with toys on the counters and drawings on the wall. I would have done that with Beth's room, but my marriage fell apart soon after her death and the house was sold. Another child occupied in Beth's room now.

"You don't--"

"Shush. Let me speak. I've got to tell you this. I've got to tell *someone* before..."

"Before what?"

"Before I explode. I brought Timmy home from the hospital to a room that was set up like the finest ICU. All his vital signs were monitored by telemetry, he had round-the-clock skilled nursing to give him his chemotherapy, monitor his IVs, draw blood for tests, adjust his respirator."

"Why the respirator?" I couldn't help it--the doctor in me wanted to know.

"The tumor had spread to his lungs – he couldn't breathe without it. It'd also spread to many of his bones, even his skull. He was in terrible pain all the time. They radiated him, filled him with poisons that made him sicker, loaded him with dope to ease the pain, and kept telling me he had a fighting chance. He *didn't* have a chance. I knew it, and that was why I'd brought him home, so he could be in his own room, and so I could have every minute with him. But worse, Timmy knew it too. I could see it in his eyes when they weren't glazed with opiates. He was hanging by a thread but no one would let it break. He wanted to go."

I closed my eyes, thinking, Oh, no. Don't tell me this... I don't want to hear this...

"It was the hardest decision of my life. More than anything else in the universe, I wanted my little boy to live, because every second of his life seemed a precious gift to me. But why was I delaying the inevitable? For him, or for me? Certainly not for him, because he was simply existing. He couldn't read, couldn't even watch TV, because if he wasn't in agony, he was in the Demerol zone. That meant I was prolonging his agony for *me*, because I couldn't let him go. I *had* to let him go. As his mother, I had to do what was right for him, not for me."

"You don't have to go on," I said as she paused. "I can guess the rest."

Kim showed me a small, bitter smile. "No, I don't think you can." She let out a deep shuddering sigh and bit her upper lip. "So one day, as a thunderstorm came through, I dosed a glass of orange juice with some ipecac and gave it to Timmy's nurse. Ten minutes later, while she was in the bathroom heaving up her lunch, I sneaked down to the basement and threw the main breaker for the house. Then I rushed back up to the second floor to be with Timmy as he slipped away. But he wasn't slipping away. He was writhing in the bed, spasming, fighting for air. I... I was horrified, I felt as if my blood had turned to ice. I thought he'd go gently. It wasn't supposed to be like that. I couldn't bear it."

Tears began to stream down her face. The storm was growing around us but I was barely aware. I was focused on Kim.

"I remember screaming and running back down to the basement, almost killing myself on the way, and resetting the breaker. Then I raced back upstairs. But when I reached him, it was too late. My Timmy was gone, and I hadn't been there. He died alone. *Alone!* Because of me! I killed him!"

And now she was sobbing, deep wracking sounds from the pit of her soul. I took her in my arms and held her tight against me. She virtually radiated pain. At last I understood what was fueling the engine of this mad compulsion. What an appalling burden to carry.

"It's all right, Kim," I whispered. "What you saw were muscle spasms, all involuntary. You did the right thing, a brave thing."

"*Was* it right?" she blurted through her sobs. "I know it wasn't brave--I mean, I lost my nerve and changed my mind – but was it *right*? Did Timmy really want to go, or was it me just thinking he did? Was his suffering too much for him to bear, or too much for me? That's what I've got to know. That's why I have to see him close up and hear what he's trying to say. If I can do that, just once, I swear I'll stop all this and run for a basement every time I hear a storm coming."

As if on cue, a blast of thunder shook the little tower and I became aware again of the storm. Rain slashed the windows and the darkened sky was alive with flashes. I stared at the steel pole a few feet before me and wanted to run. I could feel my heart hammering against my ribs. His was insane, truly insane. But I forced myself to sit tight and think about something else.

"It all makes sense now," I said.

"What?"

"Why we're seeing Beth and Timmy... they didn't give up their lives--life was taken from them."

Kim bunched a fist against her mouth. She closed her eyes and moaned softly.

"Through love in Timmy's case," I said quickly. I cupped my hand behind her neck and kissed her forehead. "But not in Beth's."

Kim opened her eyes. "Can't you tell me about it? Please?"

She'd shared her darkest secret with me, and yet I couldn't bring myself talk about it. I was about to refuse her when a deafening blast of thunder stopped me. I was dancing with death in this tower. What if I didn't survive? Kim should know. Suddenly I wanted her to know.

I closed my eyes and opened the gates, allowing the pent-up past to flow free. A mélange of sights, smells, sounds eddied around me, carrying me back five years...

I steeled myself and began: "It was the first time in years I'd allowed myself more than a week away from my practice. Twelve whole days in Italy. We were all so excited..."

***

Angela was first generation Italian-American and the three of us trooped to the Old Country to visit her grandparents – Beth's great-grandparents. While Angela stayed in Positano, yakking in Italian to all her relatives, Beth and I dashed off for a quick, two-day jaunt to Venice. Yes, it's an overpriced tourist trap. Yes, it's the Italian equivalent of Disney World. But there's not another place in the world like it, and since the city is supposedly sinking at the rate of two-and-a-half inches per decade, I wanted Beth to experience it without a snorkel.

From the day she was born, Beth and I shared something special. I don't think I've ever loved anyone or anything more than that little baby. When I was home, I'd feed her; when I wasn't on call, I'd get up with her at night. Most parents love their kids, but Beth and I *bonded*. We were soulmates. She was only six, but I felt as if I'd known her all my life.

I wanted her to be rich in spirit and experience, so I never passed up a chance to show her the wonders of the world, the natural and the man-made. Venice was a little of both. We did all the touristy stuff – a gondola ride past Marco Polo's and Casanova's houses, shopping on the Rialto Bridge, eating gelato, crossing the Bridge of Sighs from the Doge's palace into the prison; we took boats to see the glassblowers on Murano and the lace makers on Burano, snagged a table at Harry's Bar where I treated her to a Shirley Temple while I tried a Bellini. But no matter where we went or what we did, Beth kept dragging me back to Piazza San Marco so she could feed the pigeons. She was bonkers for those pigeons.

Vendors wheel little carts through the piazza, selling packets of birdseed, two thousand lire a pop. Beth must have gone through a dozen packets during our two-day stay. Pigeons have been called rats with feathers, and that may not be far off, but these have got to be the fattest, tamest feathered rats in the world. Sprinkle a little seed into your palm, hold it out, and they'll flutter up to perch on your hand and arm to eat it. Beth loved to stand with handfuls stretched out to both sides. The birds would bunch at her feet, engulf her arms, and even perch on her head, transforming her into a giggling mass of feathers.

I wasn't crazy about her being that close to so many birds-- thoughts of the avian-born diseases like psittacosis that I'd studied in med school kept darting through my head--so I tried to limit her contact. But she got such a kick out of them, how many times could I say no? I even went so far as to let her talk me into doing her two-handed feeding trick. Soon, holding my breath within a sea of fluttering wings, I was inundated with feathers. I couldn't see Beth but I could hear her distinctive belly laugh. When I finally shook off the pigeons, I found her red faced and doubled over with laughter.

What can be better than making a child laugh? The pigeons grossed me out, but so what? I grabbed more seed and did it again.

Finally it was time to leave Venice. The only flight we could book to Naples left Marco Polo at 6:30 the next morning, and the first public waterbus of the day would make a number of stops along the way and get us to the airport with only a few minutes to spare. Since I didn't want to risk missing the flight, I had the hotel concierge arrange for a private water taxi. It would pick us up at five a.m. at a little dock just a hundred feet from our hotel.

At ten of five, Beth and I were standing by our luggage at the end of Calle Larga San Marco. The tide was out and the canal smelled pretty rank. Even at this hour it was warm enough for short sleeves. I was taken with the silence of the city, the haunted emptiness of the dark streets: Venice on the cusp of a new day, when the last revelers had called it quits, and the earliest risers were just starting their morning coffee.

Beth was her usual bossy little self. As soon as she'd learned to string words together, she began giving directions like a sergeant major. She had no qualms about telling us what to wear, or what to buy in the supermarket or a department store, or setting up seating arrangements--"You sit there, Mommy, and Daddy, you sit there, and I'll sit right here in the middle." We called her "the Boss." And here in Venice, without her mother around, Boss Beth took charge of me. I loved to humor her.

"Put the suitcases right there, Daddy. Yours on the inside and mine on the outside so that when the boat gets here we can put them right on. Now you stand right over here by me."

I did exactly as she told me. She wanted me close and I was glad to comply. Her voice trailed off after that and I could see her glancing around uneasily. I wasn't fully comfortable myself, but I talked about seeing Mommy in a few hours to take her mind off our isolation.

And then finally we heard it--the sputtering gurgle of an approaching *taxi acquei*. The driver, painfully thin, a cigarette drooping from his lips, pulled into the dock – little more than a concrete step-down – and asked in bad English if we were the ones going to the airport. We were, and as I handed him our two suitcases, I noticed the heavy drop of his left eyelid. My first thought was Bell's palsy, but then I noticed the scar that parted his eyebrow and ridged the lid below it.

I also noticed that he wasn't one to make contact with his good eye, and that his taxi didn't look to be in the best shape. A warning bell sounded in my head--not a full-scale alarm, just a troubled chime--but I knew if I went looking now for another taxi, we'd almost certainly miss the plane.

If only I'd heeded my instincts.

Beth and I sat together in the narrow, low-ceilinged cabin amidships as the driver wound his way into the wider, better-lit Grand Canal where we were the only craft moving. We followed that for a while, then turned off into a narrower passage. After numerous twists and turns I was completely disoriented. Somewhere along the way the canal-front homes had been replaced by warehouses. My apprehension was rising, and when the engine began to sputter, it soared.

As the taxi bumped against the side of the canal, the driver stuck his head into the cabin and managed to convey that he was having motor trouble and needed us to come up front so he could open the engine hatch.

I emerged to find him standing in front of me with his arm raised. I saw something flash dimly in his hand as he swung it at me, and I managed to get my left arm up in time to deflect it. I felt a blade slice deep into my forearm and I cried out with the pain as I fell to the side. Beth started screaming, "Daddy! Daddy!" but that was all she managed before her voice died in a choking gurgle. I didn't know what he'd done to Beth, I just knew he'd hurt her and no way in hell was he going to hurt her again. Bloody arm and all, I launched myself at him with an animal roar. He was light and thin, and not in good shape. I took him by surprise and drove him back against the boat's console. Hard. He grunted and I swear I heard ribs crack. In blind fury I pinned him there and kept ramming my right forearm against his face and neck and kneeing him in the groin until he went limp, then I threw him to the deck and jumped on him a few times, driving my heels into his back to make sure he wouldn't be getting up.

Then I leaped to Beth and found her drenched in blood and just about gone. He'd slit her throat! Oh Lord, oh God, to keep her from screaming he'd cut my little girl open, severing one of her carotid arteries in the process. The wound gaped dark and wet, blood was everywhere. Whimpering like a lost, frightened child, I felt around in the wound and found the feebly pumping carotid stump, tried to squeeze it shut but it was too late, too late. Her mouth was slack, her eyes wide and staring. I was losing her, my Beth was dying and I couldn't do a thing to save her. I started shouting for help, I screamed until my throat was raw and my voice reduced to a ragged hiss, but the only replies were my own cries echoing off the warehouse walls.

And then the blood stopped pulsing against my fingers and I knew her little heart had stopped. CPR was no use because she had no blood left inside, it was all out here, soaking the deck and the two of us.

I held her and wept, rocking her back and forth, pleading with God to give her back to me. But instead of Beth stirring, the driver moved, groaning in pain from his broken bones. In a haze of rage as red as the sun just beginning to crawl over the horizon, I rose and began kicking and stomping him, reveling in the wonderful crunch of his bones beneath my soles. I shattered his limbs and hands and feet, crushed his rib cage, pulped the back of his skull, and I relished every blow. When I was satisfied he was dead, I returned to Beth. I cradled her in my arms and sobbed until the first warehouse workers arrived and found us.

***

Kim clutched both my hands; tears streamed down her cheeks. Her mouth moved as she tried to speak, but she made no sound.

"The rest is something of a blur. An official inquiry into the incident – two people were dead, so I couldn't blame the Venice authorities for that--revealed that the killer had overheard the hotel arranging our water-taxi ride. He borrowed a friend's boat and beat the scheduled taxi to the pick-up spot. The court determined that he was going to kill us, steal whatever valuables we'd bought or brought, and dump our bodies in the Adriatic. They suspected that we weren't his first victims.

"I was released, but then came the nightmare of red tape trying to return Beth's body to the States. Finally we brought her home and buried her, but my life was changed forever by then. The world was never the same without Beth. Neither was my marriage. Angela never said so, but I know she secretly blamed me for Beth's death. So did I. Angela and I split a year later. She couldn't live with me. Who could blame her? I could barely live with myself. Still can't."

"But you're *not* to blame."

"I had a chance to back off before we stepped onto that water taxi, but I didn't take it. And Beth paid for it."

We sat in silence then, each mired in our pools of private guilt. Gradually I realized that the flashes outside were less frequent, the thunder not quite so loud.

"I think it's passed us by," I said.

Kim glanced around, frowning in disappointment. "Damn.

We'll have to wait for another storm. That could be next week or next month around here." She pointed to the steel pole. "Oh, look. It's wet."

Fine rivulets of water were coursing down the surface of the steel.

"So much for my caulking skills. I'll see what I can do tomorrow."

Kim got on her knees and leaned forward to touch the wet surface and--

--the tower seemed to explode. I had an instant's impression of a deafening *buzz* accompanied by a rainbow shower of sparks within a wall of blazing light; boiling water exploded from the galvanized bucket as multiple arcs of blue-white energy converged from the pole onto Kim's outstretched arm. Her mouth opened wide in a silent scream while her body arched like a bow and shuddered violently, and then a searing bolt flashed from her opposite shoulder into me...

...the whiteout fades, as do the walls of the tower, leaving ghostly translucent afterimages, and I know which way to turn. I spot the tiny figure immediately, still in her yellow dress, standing so far away, suspended above the treetops. Beth! I call her name but there is no sound in this place. I try to move toward her but I'm frozen in space. I need to be closer, I need to see her throat... and then her hand goes to her mouth, and her eyes widen as she points to me. What? What's the matter?

I realize she's pointing behind me. I turn and see Kim's ghostly figure on the floor... so still... too still...

I came to and crawled to Kim. Her right arm was a smoking ruin, charred to the elbow, and she wasn't breathing. Panicked, I struggled upright and kneeled over her. I forced my rubbery arms to pound my fists on her chest to jolt her heart back to life – once, twice – then I started CPR, compressing her sternum and blowing into her mouth, five thrusts, one breath... five thrusts, one breath...

"Come on, Kim!" I shouted. I was so slick with sweat that my hands kept slipping off her chest. "Breathe! You can do it! Breathe, damn it!"

I saw her eyelids flutter. Her blue irises had lost their luster, but I sensed an exquisite joy in their depths as they fixed on me for a beseeching instant... the tiniest shake of her head, and then she was gone again.

I realized what she'd just tried to tell me: *Don't... please don't.*

But it wasn't in me to kneel here and watch the life seep out of her. I lurched again into CPR but she resisted my best efforts to bring her back. Finally, I stopped. Her skin was cooling beneath my palms. Kim was gone

I stared at her pale, peaceful face. What was happening in that other place? Had she found her Timmy and the forgiveness she craved? Was she with him now and preferring to stay there?

I felt an explosive pressure building in my chest, mostly grief, but part envy. I let out an agonized groan and gathered her into my arms. I ached for her bright eyes, her crooked-toothed smile.

"Poor lost Kim," I whispered, stroking her limp hair. "I hope to God you found what you were looking for."

Just as with Beth, I held Kim until her body was cold.

Finally, I let her go. I dressed her as best I could, and stretched her out on the cushions. I called the emergency squad, then drove my car to the corner and waited until I saw them wheel her body out to the ambulance. Then I headed for the airport.

I hated abandoning her to the medical examiner, but I knew the police would want to question me. They'd want to know what the hell we were doing up in that tower during a storm. They might even take me into custody. I couldn't allow that.

I had someplace to go.

***

I arrived in Marco Polo Airport without luggage. The terminal snuggles up to the water, and the boats wait right outside the arrival terminal. I bought a ticket for the waterbus--I could barely look at the smaller, speedier water taxis--and spent the two-and-a-half mile trip across the Laguna Véneta fighting off the past.

I did pretty well leaving the dock and walking into the Piazza San Marco. I hurried through the teeming crowds, past the flooded basilica on the right--a Byzantine toad squatting in a tiny pond--and the campanile towering to my left. I almost lost it when I saw a little girl feeding the pigeons, but I managed to hold on.

I found a hotel in the San Polo district, bought a change of clothes, and holed up in my room, watching the TV, waiting for news of a storm.

***

And now the storm is here. From my perch atop the Campanile di San Marco I see it boiling across the Laguna Véneta, spearing the Lido with bolts of blue-white energy, and taking dead aim for my position. The piazza below is empty now, the gawkers chased by the thunder, rain, and lightning--especially the lightning. Even the brave young Carabinieri has discovered the proper relationship between discretion and valor and ducked back inside.

And me: I've cut the ground wire from the lightning rod above me. I'm roped to the tower to keep from falling. And I'm drenched with rain.

I'm ready.

Physically, at least. Mentally, I'm still not completely sure. I've seen Beth twice now. I *should* believe, I want to believe... but do I want it so desperately that I've tapped into Kim's delusion system and made it my own?

I'm hoping this will be my last time. If I can see Beth up close, see her throat, know that her wound has healed in this place where she waits, it will go a long way toward healing a wound of my own.

Suddenly I feel it--the tingle in my skin as the charge builds in the air around me--and then a deafening ZZZT! as the bolt strikes the ungrounded rod above the statue of St. Mark. Millions of volts slam into me, violently jerking my body...

...and then I'm in that other place, that other state... I look around frantically for a splotch of yellow and I almost cry out when I see Beth floating next to me. She's here, smiling, radiant, and so close I can almost touch her. I choke with relief as I see her throat--it's healed, the terrible grinning wound gone without a trace, as if it never happened.

I smile at her but she responds with a look of terror. She points down and I turn to see my body tumbling from the tower. The safety rope has broken and I'm drifting earthward like a feather.

I'm going to die.

Strangely, that doesn't bother me nearly as much as it should. Not in this place.

Then in the distance I see two other figures approaching, and as they near I recognize Kim, and she's leading a beaming tow-headed boy toward Beth and me.

A burst of unimaginable joy engulfs me. This is so wonderful... almost too wonderful to be real. And there lies my greatest fear. Are they all--Beth, Kim, Timmy--really here? Or merely manifestations my consuming need *for this to be real.*

I look down and see my slowly falling body nearing the pavement. Very soon I will know.

2
THANATOPHOBIA

FEAR OF DYING

JEFF DEPEW

The apartment had one of the best views on the Las Vegas Strip. With the electric shutters raised, the panoramic windows on three sides commanded views from Mt. Charleston to the west to Boulder City and Arizona in the east, and the entire Las Vegas Valley, including the strip, in between. The casinos, new and old, the expensive towers, the giant observation wheel. Flashing lights shone through the windows, blended and altered the bluish light from the flatscreen TV, bouncing off the ceiling and creating eerie shadows on the walls.

Normally, the traffic on the Strip could not reach up here. Residents were supposed to feel as though they were removed from the rest of the world. The sliding glass door to the balcony was open, however, and the shrill cries of sirens echoed through the room. Sirens. All the time now, it seemed.

Logan Barnett sat on the arm of the couch, staring blankly at the TV screen. He held the remote and pushed the channel up button repeatedly. It was the same on most channels. If the station wasn't showing the same footage of the president being quickly led from his helicopter to a motorcade, it was showing scenes of civil unrest, cities in flames, rioting, looting. Exhilarated newscasters reported on mass rioting, governments toppled, panic in the streets.

The crawls at the bottom of the screen varied from "The End of Days? ...The White House calls for Martial Law... Paris in flames... Experts Have no Answers... " and on and on and on... He thumbed the TV off. How had it gone so wrong?

He shut off the TV and went out to the balcony. He stood beside a chair that lay on its side and leaned on the railing.

The sirens were much louder here, more insistent. He could also hear voices; screams, really. And figures running through the streets, dodging cars, fighting. Some, he could just make out, were looking at him, pointing and gesturing. Others were lying down. On the sidewalks, in the streets. But they were all moving. They were all alive.

Three Days Ago

The room was bare of furniture, hardwood floor gleaming in the shimmering light of several dozen candles placed throughout the room. Large diagrams and circles within circles painted across every surface of the room. Symbols, runes, letters, in Latin, Aramaic, even Aklo, among other older languages along with unrecognizable inscriptions and figures, covered the walls and ceiling. Writing over writing. Patterns crossing over onto other designs. The closet door was closed and painted over, continuing the patterns. A stepladder stood leaning against the window, which was covered with newspaper and then painted over. Beneath lay several cans of spray paint.

A large circle was spray painted in the center of the floor. It was surrounded and accented by writing and ancient symbols. Barnett, wearing only a pair of sweatpants, was on his hands and knees, an ancient tome in one hand and a piece of red sidewalk chalk in the other. The pages of the book were patch-worked with sticky notes: pink, yellow, blue, white. Pages were marked with more sticky notes, napkins, newspaper clippings, highlighted Xerox copies and other makeshift bookmarks. He stared intently at the pages, his lips moving soundlessly, then drew a symbol, looked at it, back at the book, added a line, looked at it again. He picked up another book from a stack on the floor, undid the metal clasp, leafed through it briefly, and located a specific page. He read, looked back at what he had written, nodded, placed the book and chalk down, stood up, his arms pushing in the small of his back, and stretched. He glanced at his Rolex. Ten–fifty. Plenty of time. He had been at it for three days, barely sleeping, barely eating. Tonight should be it.

Picking up the chalk and the book, he looked around the room one last time. He grabbed a plastic trash bag and tossed in the cans of spray paint, leftover chalk and wadded up towels. No distractions. Everything neat and orderly. He looked around again. Nodded. It was time.

Closing the door behind him, he walked past a small bathroom, a laundry room, through a connecting door, and into a modern, expansive kitchen. The bedroom and bathroom off the kitchen were originally intended as a maid's quarters, but he had a different purpose for them. Barnett dropped the trash bag beside a chrome trash can and continued up a flight of spiral stairs and entered a master bedroom. It contained a king-size bed and a dresser. Nothing on the walls. Barnett stripped off his paint- and chalk-smeared sweatpants and stepped into the shower. The cold water blasted his back and he shuddered, but stayed beneath the stream. If he couldn't handle some cold water, how would he deal with what he had planned?

After his shower, he toweled off and pulled on a pair of jeans and a white Oxford shirt. He rolled the sleeves up and tucked it in. In all his research, Barnett had been unable to determine if what he wore made any difference. He knew that some of the ceremonies called for particular robes, or often, nothing at all. Since he had not found anything specific, he decided it didn't matter, so he might as well be comfortable. As he finished getting dressed, he glanced down at his cell phone on the floor, plugged into a charger. He paused, debating whether or not to check his voicemail, but left it. No distractions.

In the kitchen, he threw a frozen pizza in the top oven and poured himself a large bourbon. Only one. He was nervous, but he needed to keep his wits. His head began to throb and he looked through a selection of pharmaceutical bottles on the counter. He found what he was looking for and swallowed several Tramadol. He twisted open a plastic water bottle, chased down his pills and topped off his bourbon. He walked to the window and stared out at the lights.

It was nearly midnight when he approached the adjoining door and opened it. He was carrying a butane lighter and a battery-powered lantern which he placed by his feet. He stepped inside and carefully closed the door and shot the deadbolt. He looked around to make sure everything was as it should be. A couple of candles had gone out, so he quickly relit them. With a piece of chalk, Barnett made some quick additions to several of the diagrams, solidifying a line here, thickening a line there, and he was ready. So much time, so much effort, so much money had gone into this... project. Time to see if it had all been worth it.

Midnight.

Barnett opened the book to a page he had marked with a *7-11* receipt. He placed three bells on the floor by his feet. They were small, roughly made and very old. It had taken him two years to find all three of them.

He began to read aloud, softly at first, finding his rhythm, and then with more power and ferocity. He felt something in the room change and he stumbled over a word. The room had grown noticeably colder. He looked around before continuing. One of the candles flared suddenly, revealing for a moment a shadowy figure in a corner of the ceiling. He heard a flapping sound for an instant, as if enormous wings were beating. He glanced upward nervously and then winced and put his hand to his temple. His headache was back.

Barnett continued reading, chanting, reciting. He could see his breath as the room grew steadily colder. He grew hoarse and he cursed himself for not having the foresight to bring one of his water bottles upstairs. His voice cracked and the flames danced. He knelt and picked up the first bell and rang it gently. The apartment shook for an instant. Another candle flared and he saw the outline again before it disappeared and the candle went out. This time, the shadow seemed more... solid. Barnett picked up the pace. He rang the second bell and recited the words. *It's working.* A candle flamed up and the figure appeared again. Only this time it stayed. And the candle did not go out.

Barnett stopped reading and stared at the dark shape in the center of the circle. It seemed smaller than he was expecting. It was hard to make out exactly what it looked like. It was somewhat amorphous, but human shaped. It moved, but it was still. It was dark, but he saw flashes of white. Without taking his eyes off the figure, he knelt down and rang the third bell, said the words. The figure coalesced into a solid, discernible shape.

"By the power and word of--" Barnett began and the rest of the candles popped out, all at once. The room was plunged into darkness. He took an involuntary step back, and then another, backed into the door and cried out. The book tumbled from his grasp. Kneeling down, crawling forward in the darkness, he desperately felt around for the lantern. His fingers fumbled and found the power switch and twisted. Harsh white light filled the room. Barnett grabbed the book and clasped it to his chest.

He leafed through the book, looking for the page where he had left off. He continued: "By the power and word of--" and began listing gods and beings whose names had not been spoken aloud for thousands of years, if ever at all.

Release me, said a voice (in his head, in his ears--it was impossible to tell where it had come from.)

This was hard. He was more frightened than he expected. *Deep breath. Be strong.* He closed his eyes, his face screwing up in concentration. *Deep breath in. Hold it. Now out. Focus.* He continued reading, reciting the words. He read carefully, hitting all the syllables and the harsh, discordant consonants.

"Release me," repeated the voice. (This time it was in his ears.) The figure glided toward him. As it moved, it seemed to clarify, to grow more solid. *It looks like a kid!* He had time to think before it reached the edge of the circle. A bright flash. The building shook or maybe it was just the room. He heard something crash to the floor in the kitchen. Blue light shot around the floor, tracing the circle he had drawn on the floor. The dark figure stumbled back and righted itself. The room smelled like burning plastic. The circle continued to glow blue for a moment, then went back to its original red.

"*What have you done?*" came the voice again, but this time it was clearly audible. The voice was soft, speaking softly accented English. *Or is that just what it sounds like?*

A boy stood in the center of the room. He looked to be about fourteen or fifteen. He was dark, with sharp cheekbones and large black eyes. His hair was short with tight curls. He wore dark pants and coat with a white shirt, open at the collar, tie loosened. His feet were bare. He stared at Barnett. His face showed nothing. No pleading, no anger.

"*Let me go. This should not be happening.*"

Barnett strode towards the barrier, feeling more confident with every step. He turned back to the book and continued.

The boy winked away and in his place stood an ancient, horrible woman, hunched over, dressed in filthy rags. She gnashed her teeth together, which made an odd clanking sound. By the glare of the lantern, he realized her teeth were iron, filed to a point. Eyes, white and milky, regarded him hatefully. She held a broom in one claw-like hand, and pointed a bony finger at him with the other. Her nails were long and broken and filthy.

Dat' mne svobodu. Her voice was a husky rasp, barely audible. A thread of saliva hung from her tongue, which dangled over her black and blistered lower lip, as if there was only room in her mouth for those terrible teeth but nothing else.

Barnett was horrified, but held his ground. He had been warned that this could happen. He turned back to the book. *Don't think. Just read.*

The crone leered at him and licked her cracked black lips. More drool fell to the floor. It pooled blackly beneath her.

Then she was gone and in her place stood a great, tall figure, clad entirely in a heavy black shroud and carrying a scythe. Its face was a bleached skull, eye sockets blazing with internal flame and the empty jaw gaped at him. Despite the absence of any sort of breeze, the shroud was waving and fluttering.

RELEASE ME! blasted through his brain, intensifying his headache.

He looked away and kept reading the words; the alien, somehow *wrong,* words that left an oily taste in his mouth. He sensed, rather than heard something change. He looked up.

Thick, writhing tentacles crawled from beneath the robes. They moved with a purpose, like enormous greedy worms, searching for something. They were covered with suckers, each ringed with what looked like dozens of tiny hooked teeth. The shape slid across the floor toward him. The scythe was gone, and beneath the hood, instead of a skull, there was… nothing. Just an emptiness, a void, leading… nowhere? Everywhere? It was beautiful.

He forced himself to look away. Continued to read.

Logan. A woman's voice. Soft, seductive, with a hint of an accent.

He turned back, cautiously. A stunning young woman stood before him. She wore a black fur cape, which she held close at her throat. Her dark red hair framed an elegant, seductive face. Her mouth was half curled in an amused smile. Looking at him as if he was a child. Green eyes looked him up and down, then stared boldly at his own eyes.

Gi meg min frihet, she said softly, still smiling and toying with the clasp on her cape.

Without realizing it, Barnett took a step forward. The woman released her cape and it fell silently to the floor, exposing her nude body. Barnett's eyes traced down her neck, shoulders, firm, small breasts, taut stomach, but--from the waist down her body was withered and grey, the desiccated body of a corpse. He could see ropy muscle and tendons move through ragged tears in her flesh. She held her hands at her sides, palms open, offering herself to him. He looked up at her and she met his horror-struck gaze, mouth still curled in a smile. A wave of nausea surged through him as he stared, horrified, at her corpse-half. He fought back the urge to run. He had to breathe through his nose to avoid vomiting.

The boy reappeared.

Let me go. You do not know what you are doing. You are making a mistake.

Barnett read the last word, pronounced the last syllable. He let out a breath and closed the book. Walking around the circle, he looked closely at the marks and lines on the floor. The boy's gaze followed him but he remained silent.

Satisfied, Barnett paused at the door and looked at the boy. "You are uh... forbidden to leave that circle, right?"

The boy nodded, just barely. His eyes never left Barnett. *Yes.*

"Good."

Barnett nodded, satisfied. He took one last look around the room and left.

The figure of the boy stood in silence, unmoving.

***

Barnett's older brother had died of cancer five years ago; he was only forty-five. Barnett was there at the end, in his private room. He would like to say that he had been holding Robert's thin, skeletal hand, comforting him at the end, but he hadn't. He couldn't.

He had stood as far away as he could, pressing his handkerchief to his mouth and nose. The smell. The smell of death and sickness. He couldn't bear it and had almost passed out. If he hadn't taken several Xanax beforehand, he would have.

He had looked at Robert, once so strong and alive, now brittle and weak. His face was a mask of skin drawn tightly over his skull. His eyes were dull and clouded. His skin was grey with sickness. A vein weakly throbbing in his temple.

He had seen the pain that Robert was going through, the pain his wife and daughters were going through. Barnett had done what he could. He paid the medical bills, had flown him from clinic to clinic, found Robert the best care, but it didn't matter. Robert had gotten sicker and sicker, closer to death every day. And eventually the cancer won. Just as it had with their father.

So when Barnett was diagnosed with inoperable brain cancer, he did what he always did when faced with a problem; he set out to solve it, one way or another. He was not going to die, not going to turn into that… "thing" that Robert had become.

He was not going to go out like Robert. Robert was weak at the end, and he had given up. Barnett was different. He was a survivor. Money was no object.

When he had first been diagnosed, he had gotten a second opinion. Had flown to Tokyo for a third. But it was always the same. "I'm sorry, Logan, but there's nothing we can do… " or "… the cancer is very aggressive… " What could they do? Nothing, except make his last days "comfortable". Like Robert's? Sure, he was *comfortable*. He had been so drugged up he had not recognized his own girls. Is that any way to go? Looking like a skeleton? Where's the dignity? Where's the final goodbye? And the smell...

It was not just the cancer. It was death. Blackness, emptiness. Rot, decay. He was not a religious man; he never had been, and the concept of death scared the shit out of him. He had no aspirations about heavenly gates and all that. The lights go out and that's it. You're just a hunk of meat, cold and empty. What about all that you've accomplished, all that you have yet to do? "Oh Logan, your legacy will live on long after you are gone." Fuck his legacy. Life was for the living and no way was Logan Barnett giving in so easily. No way was Barnett going out like that. It's not fair. Fuck death. And while we're at it, fuck those doctors. They were great at telling you what you already knew. But as for helping you? As the old saying goes: "The gods help those who help themselves." Whether they like it or not.

***

Barnett collected occult items; he'd always been interested in the occult even as a boy--but it was a secret--his stockholders, and the media, must never know. And only a few of his inner circle suspected. What would they think about a CEO who collected books that had been owned and purportedly destroyed by the Vatican? Molitor's *De Lamiis et Pythonicis Mulieribus, The Diary of Aleister Crowley* and *Clavicula Salomonis Regis* were a few of the better known books in his collection. And that one he had "borrowed" from Miskatonic University--the one that had caused such a stir back in the thirties.

It was more than a hobby; he actually believed that the right combination of words, in the perfect circumstances, should be able to produce something... what? Wonderful? Amazing? Impossible? He owned too many books, had traveled to too many places, spoken with too many mystics to decide it was nonsense. Why did the lore and knowledge still exist after tens of thousands of years if there was nothing to it? Was yoga nonsense? Or meditation? And both of those had been around for thousands of years. And magnetism? Used for cheap parlor tricks and "magic" in the 19th century. And now look at it. So why not this? There's got to be more to the world than what we sense with just our eyes and ears.

He spent hours poring over ancient books and scrolls, turned crumbling pages while wearing white cotton gloves, frequently watched by nervous curators. He flew to Nepal, to Bremen, to Paris, Boston, and sought out certain individuals who "knew things", for lack of a better term. He spoke with professors, museum curators, historians and, for a generous donation, a patient in a New England mental hospital. He took copious notes and bought books. Always the books. His assistant Katya hated the books, and more importantly, the money he spent on them. If she only knew... But it was his money, not the corporation's, as he told her several times.

And that would usually shut her up for a few weeks. And so he kept looking.

And eventually he found what he needed to do.

Barnett owned real estate all over the world. Several years ago, during the housing crash, he bought a luxury high-rise in Las Vegas that had been built and then sat vacant. Barnett never planned on using the building, having bought it solely as an investment, planning on holding on to it until the market righted and then unloading it for a nice profit. Neither his name nor his company's name was anywhere on the lease. He used it from time to time, when he wanted to discreetly entertain certain visitors. To keep up appearances, he had sold several of the apartments on the lower floors. He had never met the other tenants and didn't want to.

His personal suite, on the top floor, had two stories, a private pool and three bedrooms with the smaller, attached maid's quarters and an adjoining door in the kitchen. That's where he would perform the ritual. The only way in (or out) was through his suite. He'd had the unit's separate entrance sealed off when he moved in.

***

He sat in the empty parking garage, the engine of his car idling. Another one of his little secrets. Along with his apartment he had a car, paid for in cash and registered to an employee who had died last year.

He silently cursed himself for not planning this out better. He should have gone to an animal shelter and bought a cat or dog. It would have been easier. Now he had to go out and find a test subject.

He knew what he had to do now, but he did not want to. The first reason was that he didn't want to leave that... kid, thing, whatever it was, unsupervised for long. But if what he had read was true, and he had to assume he done everything right, it would not be able to leave the circle without his permission. He had said he couldn't leave. Could he lie? Barnett didn't think so. Not based on what he had read.

The second reason he didn't want to do this was because he had never killed anyone before. But if everything had gone as it should (and so far so good), nobody would die. So with that thought, he put the car in drive and headed out.

He headed away from the Strip, toward a more unpopulated area. At this time of night, the Las Vegas Strip was packed and in full party mode, but these back streets full of office parks and low rent apartments were more or less deserted. He drove slowly, his window down, searching the sidewalks and shadows. A stray dog. A stray person. Either one would do.

Finally. He spotted a figure sitting beside a shopping cart behind a darkened office building and slowed to a stop.

He stopped the car just outside the reach of the parking lot lights. He got out and looked down the street, both directions. Nothing. He had passed only one car a while back, going the other way. No one around. It's now or never.

Barnett reached into his pocket and brought out a pair of thin leather gloves, which he pulled on. From his inside pocket he pulled out a small pistol, a Taurus 709 Slim 9mm. More than enough, he had been told, for what he wanted to do. The gun was virtually untraceable. The serial number had been filed down and the bullets had been made in a garage somewhere in Idaho.

Breathing deeply, he strode quickly toward the bum, his gun was held down at his right side.

The man could have been anywhere from thirty to sixty. His face was dark and lined from sun, wear and tear, and bad decisions. He blinked up at Barnett and looked around warily.

"Yeah? What you want?"

Barnett shot the man five times. The first three shots tore into his chest, but the gun jerked up slightly and one bullet hit him in the throat, while the last bullet ricocheted off the cement behind him. The bum rolled sideways against the side of the building and slid to the ground.

Barnett tentatively approached him and looked down. He still held the gun out in front of him, not sure if he had another bullet or not. His mind flicked back to the iconic scene in *Dirty Harry* and he couldn't help smiling.

The bum was stirring. Moaning, he slowly pushed himself up to his hands and knees. Blood pumped steadily from the wounds in his throat and chest, pooling on the concrete beneath him. He groaned again and gagged. He hacked up a red wad of tissue the size of a golf ball that splatted on the ground.

Yuh shuh muh!" His voice was raspy and he wheezed as he

struggled to get up. He clutched at the shopping cart, pulling himself up slowly.

Barnett sighed and shot him in the head. A hole blossomed in the back of the man's skull. He let out a grunt and his weight pushed the cart forward, away from him and he collapsed. He coughed up another clump of blood along with something pink and white.

"Fuh--!" The bum gurgled through a mouthful of blood. "Uh hur... plz... "

He turned to look up at Barnett, who was struggling to eject the magazine and shove another into the gun. He finished and stepped forward, pointing the gun at the man again. He paused. He already had four holes in his chest, one in his throat, and one in his head. He was still bleeding. He couldn't (shouldn't?) be alive... but he was. It worked.

"Hlp muh... " begged the man, crawling toward his cart. His face was gray and one of his eyes was filled with blood. Blood was flowing freely through the jagged hole in his throat.

He slowly dragged himself up the side of the shopping cart and leaned on it. He could barely stand. "Puh--c... no." His one good eye stared helplessly. Barnett, holding the gun in front of him--like a talisman--backed away until he reached the door. He shoved it open, and gagging, ran for the car. He stopped and leaned on the trunk and vomited a thin stream onto the asphalt. Before getting back in the car, he glanced over at the man he had shot. He was now on his feet, walking unsteadily toward Barnett's car. He was still trying to speak.

Barnett drove without headlights back to his building. He hit the remote, drove beneath the rising metal gate, screeched to a stop, leapt out of the car and punched the up button on the elevator. His mind was racing with exhilaration and excitement.

Back in the apartment, he hurriedly unlocked the door, pounded down the hallway, unlocked his apartment door and went into the kitchen. He unlocked the deadbolt, the latch and the padlock.

The boy was still standing there, waiting.

"It worked, didn't it? I caught you and there's nothing you can do!"

"Have you seen enough?"

"What? No. You're not going anywhere. With you in here, I'm not going to die. Right? Nothing can die."

Nothing can die, repeated the boy. *Is that really what you want?*
"Yes. Yes it is." Barnett slammed the door behind him. In the
kitchen, he poured himself a bourbon and headed out to the balcony.
The view was more spectacular than usual. He held up his glass and
saluted the heavens. He was flooded with...what? Hope? Euphoria?
Invincibility? He polished off his drink and debated having another.
The adrenaline rush was abating and he felt weary. His headache was
gone but he was utterly exhausted, physically and mentally. Sleep
sounded fantastic.

He went back to the kitchen and checked the door to the
maid's quarters. Locked. He took a couple of sleeping pills and
headed up the stairs to his bed.

The next afternoon, he sat on the couch with a mug of
coffee, switching between news channels.

"...officials have not commented, but there are scattered
reports of people remaining alive and conscious after devastating
injuries."

"...some type of disturbance at University Hospital..."

"...absolutely incredible, but the proof is irrefutable. People
who should be dying are remaining alive. They are conscious and
alert and doctors have no explanation as to-"

He pushed the off button and silenced the TV. All the
channels were the same. People weren't dying.

Barnett glanced over at his cell phone and checked the time.
He scrolled through his messages. The phone rang in his hands. He
looked at the name. Katya. Of course. He thumbed the "answer"
button.

"Hey, Katya."

"Oh my God, Logan, where are you? I've been calling you for
over an hour! Are you okay? Everyone is trying to find you. The
investors have been calling all day. We need to call a board meeting.
How soon can you get here? "

By "here," she meant San Francisco, home of his main office.
Her tone alarmed him. Katya was many things: she was extremely
organized, able to juggle phone calls and a web conference with ease,
all while texting and drinking a cup of coffee.

"I'm fine, Katya. Everything is fine. You sound worried.
What's going on? "

I don't even know! No one seems to know. People say that

no can die anymore, and some are saying it's the Rapture, if you can believe it. But one thing--"

He cut her off. "What do you think is going on?" She was smart and he wanted her take on this.

When she replied, her voice was faint, unsure.

"I don't know what to think. It's too soon to know for sure. Whatever is happening, it's scary. People are getting freaked out."

"I'm planning on coming in first thing tomorrow. But right now I'm tired and need some breakfast."

"It's three o'clock."

"So lunch. But don't worry. I'll be there tomorrow."

"You can't make it until then?"

I'm exhausted, Katya. I haven't slept in a couple days. I mean, really slept. I'm gonna hole up in Vegas for the night. I'll get there when I get there."

"Vegas? How long have been in Vegas?"

"A couple of days. I'm looking at some properties."

"You're in Vegas." Her disapproval oozed out of his earpiece.

"Looking at some properties."

Silence from Katya.

"Jesus, Katya, relax. I'll fly out in the morning. Try to be in by ten or eleven. How's that?"

"All right. Do you want me to call the airline?"

"No, you set up the meeting. Schedule it for one tomorrow. I'll call Stuart and have him book the flight. And Katya--"

Yes?"

It's going to be okay. It's going to be great."

She started to say something, but he hit "end call". He loved Katya, but she could be such a worrier.

He slept most of the rest of the day, waking up occasionally to look in on "The Kid" as he was beginning to think of him. The Kid never moved. Just stood there, gazing blankly at Barnett each time he opened the door.

He finally decided to get going around eight. He was well rested, hungry and it was time to start celebrating. The sun was just setting over Mount Charleston and the hotels and casinos were starting to come alive. There were even some people walking on the sidewalk in front of his building. He stood on the balcony, watching the lights, chasing two pain pills with an energy drink. He was feeling good now, excited. His headache was just a dull throb in the back of his head. Catching up on sleep was all he needed.

After a quick shower and shave, he grabbed his phone, pocketed his car keys and headed out.

He spent the next several hours celebrating.

A massive headache woke him up. His throat and mouth were raw, as though they had been scoured and sandblasted. He couldn't breathe through his right nostril. He sat up, holding his head and surveyed his surroundings. He was in his bedroom at the apartment, but according to the lingerie on the floor, he wasn't alone. He turned his head and softly grunted from the pain. He turned his head more slowly.

There was a girl in the bed. All he could see was the top of her head. Brunette. He struggled to remember what had happened last night. He recalled heading to his favorite nightclub, meeting his local source, scoring some cocaine and buying drinks for a large group of people. He vaguely remembered drinking and dancing with a beautiful brunette, but after that... he carefully lifted up the sheets. She was naked. But so was he.

He stood up slowly and with great difficulty and effort, was able to pull on a pair of sweatpants. He made his way out to the living room, holding on to the wall for balance. He stopped twice because his head was swimming.

The light was too much for him, so he hit the switch and the shutters came down, filling the room with soothing darkness. He grabbed an energy drink out of the fridge and chased a couple of pain pills. His head was pounding; every beat of his heart was a vise being cranked tighter and tighter on his temples.

He leaned against the counter with his head down, waiting for the pain pills to take effect.

"Morning."

The girl had gotten up. *Laurie? Carol?* She was wearing his shirt, not quite buttoned up all the way. She was dark haired and way too young for him.

"Hey," he managed weakly, turning to greet her.

"Oh, are you hung over? Poor baby," as she hugged him. Her breasts pressed against him through the thin cotton, and despite his head, his body responded. *No. I have to get her out of here.* She moved away and opened the fridge.

"I'll call you a cab…" he began.

"Why's it so dark in here? That view was so amazing last night. Oh my god, I would love a Starbucks right now. Let's go get some. Your fridge is empty and I'm literally starving." She faced him and whispered conspiratorially, eyes wide. "Hey, do you have any more coke?"

Barnett stared at her. Where to begin? He tried to remember her name. Something with an *S?*

"Uh, okay. Sure."

He went to the wall switch and metal shutters began to rise. The light wasn't so bad this time. He walked to the window and gazed outside. He heard sirens.

"Hey, where's this go?" the girl asked from behind him.

Barnett slid open the door to the balcony. Fresh air was good for hangovers, he had read somewhere. He put his hands on the waist-high railing, took a deep breath and leaned over. Two police cars raced past, sirens screaming. Some people stood on the sidewalk outside the apartment, just milling around. They seemed to be looking up him. *That's odd.*

He could hear sirens now, but could also smell smoke. In the neighborhoods beyond the strip. A plume of dark smoke rose into the afternoon sky.

"Oh my god!" the girl cried out. Lisa! That was her name! He walked through the living room and saw that the door to the maid's quarters was wide open. *Oh shit, I forgot to lock it!* He had time to register. He turned, expecting the worst. He raced through the door, down the short hallway, stopped in the doorway of the room. *The room.*

"What is all this? This is awesome!" Lisa was just inside the doorway, looking around, an amazed smile on her face. The Kid stared impassively at her.

Barnett watched her warily. She hadn't reacted to the Kid. *Maybe she can't see him?* But when she stepped too close to the circle Barnett yanked her away.

"Hey! What the fuck?" She rubbed her arm where he had grabbed her.

"You need to leave. Now." Not angry. Not yelling. Firm. No need to create a scene.

"What is all this?" Lisa asked, ignoring him. "Are you a

musician?" She held up her cell phone and started snapping photos.

"No!" screamed Barnett, snatching for her phone with one hand and clutching a fistful of shirt with the other. A button popped off and spun through the air. He tugged her out of the room into the hallway.

"You need to leave."

"Let go of me!" Shrieking, spinning away from him. "Don't you fucking touch me!"

"All right, all right, just calm down!" Barnett held up his hands in a placating gesture, but she pushed him away.

He quickly looked back in the room. The Kid was still standing there, staring at him. Barnett closed the door. He followed Lisa into the kitchen, locking the door behind him this time. It felt as though an iron spike was being jammed into the base of his skull. All he wanted was to go back to bed. But first, he had to deal with this.

In the living room, Lisa had a cell phone out. Now she was texting. *Shit!* Barnett lunged toward her and slapped the phone out of her hand. It skittered across the floor. His head was throbbing.

"Just wait a minute," he started, "You can't--"

"Get away from me!" she screamed, chasing after her fallen phone. "Don't you fucking touch me!"

She scooped it up and went out to the open balcony door, still pushing buttons.

"Wait a minute! You have to delete those pictures!" Barnett shouted, going after her. Lisa turned her back, shielding the phone with her body.

Barnett's head was pounding and it was difficult to process what was happening. *Get her phone. No pictures.* That would ruin him.

He lunged for her phone again. She spun away from him and her free hand reached out and raked her nails across his face.

"Shit!" He was blinded, in pain and enraged. This idiot was going to ruin everything.

He grabbed her in a bear hug, his hands trying to wrench the phone away from her. He lifted her but she got her feet up on the balcony railing and pushed. She was stronger than she looked and Barnett stumbled back into a chair, knocking it over, but didn't release her.

"Will you just listen for a second?" he gasped.

"Let go of me! Help!"

His ankle tangled with the leg of the chair and he lurched forward, sending them both off balance. Lisa slammed into the railing and let out a *whoosh* as it collided with her midsection. The sound reminded him of air being released from an air mattress. She kicked her heels back, landing a solid shot in his nuts and he instinctively pushed her away. He stumbled back and landed on his butt. Lisa went over the railing.

Oh shit.

He scrambled to his feet and looked down, although every part of him warned him not to.

She lay in a small heap. The white shirt stood out in the dark street. One of her hands was outstretched, perhaps reaching for her phone. The people down there didn't seem to notice. None of them went to her. They were just looking up. At him.

As he watched, in horrified fascination, she twitched and began to move. She struggled to her feet, fell back and began crawling toward the sidewalk. And he wasn't sure, but he thought she looked up at him.

He thought now might be a good time to head back to California.

After half an hour, Barnett threw down his phone in frustration. Not only was Stuart not picking up, but he couldn't even make a reservation himself. All the flights from McCarran Airport were grounded. Nothing in, nothing out. Whatever was happening was being treated as a National Emergency. Cable news reported that there had been several suicide bombings in the last few hours, including several in Washington DC. The country was on lockdown. But of course they weren't really "suicide" bombings any more, were they?

He'd have to drive. Eight hours. Along with all the other unlucky folks driving back to California because they couldn't get flights. Make it twelve hours.

After double checking all the locks, he headed out.

The building was roughly T-shaped. The elevator was located at the junction of the top bar of the T. The two shorter ends led to stairs.

Barnett stepped around it and hurried to the elevator at the end of the hall. He pushed the down button. It lit up. He looked around nervously. Nothing had changed. The light above the elevator indicated it was on the fourteenth floor. Twenty-six more to go.

A door slammed shut and Barnett jumped. A figure was approaching from the end of one of the long corridors. Female, long hair.

"What the hell are you doing up here?" Barnett shouted. She ignored him, kept walking. There was something odd about the way her head moved. It bounced with each step she took.

"Hey! I'm talking to you!"

"Logan Barnett," she said, her voice faint and raspy. "You've done something you should not have."

"Get the fuck out of my building!" He started towards her, but then he saw her. Really saw her.

Her pale face was slack, her eyes wide and unfocused. The pale pink silk nightgown she wore was covered in blood. Her throat had been slashed from ear to ear. She staggered closer and closer and he backed up. "Why did you do this?" Her voice was soft, full of pain. "Please. It hurts. This is your fault." She started towards him.

"No, I never--" Barnett wasn't sure what he was going to say he had "never" done, because at that moment the elevator bell went off and the doors slid open.

He sensed, rather than saw movement from the corner of his eye and ducked away from the grasping hands. Off balance, he stumbled away and fell to one knee, and desperately crawled away from whatever was coming out of the elevator. Even without looking, he knew what it was. Scrambling to his feet, he headed for the stairs.

"Why? Why did you do this?"

"Look what you did to me!"

"Whuh yuh Wn?"

"Why? Why did you do this?" came the haunted voices of the dead, alive.

"Only you can help us!"

He pounded down the stairs two at a time. Just get out. He ran madly, heedlessly down the stairs, almost falling. He caught himself and he leaned against the wall, gasping. The stairwell door slammed open up on the fortieth and the voices above called down. Asking him why, why?

"LEAVE ME ALONE!" he roared. He tried the nearest door (thirty-second floor), and it opened. He entered the hallway warily and headed toward the nearest elevator.

He punched the down button and looked around. All quiet.

The elevator arrived. It was blessedly empty. He hit the "G" button and leaned against the side of the car. His head was still throbbing.

The elevator stopped on the third floor. Barnett braced himself against the back wall. The doors pinged open.

He waited.

Nothing.

No one.

Electrical glitch?

The doors shut.

He exhaled. The doors opened again at the garage level. He ran to his car, but stopped. There were people in the garage. Several figures tottered towards him. Two men and a woman. *How did they get in?*

"Barnett," hissed one of the men. His voice sounded mushy, wet. He moved under a yellowish light. He was wearing a bright orange vest and a tool belt. Broken walkie-talkie hung from a lanyard around his neck. His lower jaw was missing and Barnett could see all the way down his throat. His chest was covered in blood.

The other two were a barefoot woman wearing a hospital gown and a shirtless fat guy wearing green pajama pants.

"Help us, Logan", said the woman.

Barnett walked sideways, keeping his car between himself and the three. He felt sick, lightheaded and avoided looking at their faces. *Got to get out of here.* He used the remote to unlock the door and quickly got in his car. He backed up, felt a solid thud as he hit the undead woman, knocking her down. He instinctively braked, rethought it, shifted into drive and headed for the exit. He was about to hit the button to open the garage door when he slammed on the brakes. The screeching tires echoed through the empty garage. He stared, unbelieving, through the windshield.

The lower garage floor was constructed of cement poles connected by horizontal metal struts about one foot apart. They were far enough apart that the natural light was enough to see by, but too narrow for trespassers to squeeze through.

A crowd of people was clustered around the outside of the metal garage door. The bottom right corner was pushed up at an angle, creating a small space, and a man wearing a dark suit was crawling underneath it. The mob behind him was rattling and shaking the door. They were calling out to Barnett.

Barnett gunned the engine and accelerated, slamming into the dark suited man and the garage door. That should stop them from coming in, he thought, shifting to reverse. But when he tried to back up, he pulled the door open further. The car was somehow snagged on the door.

Cursing, he leapt out of the car and headed back to the elevator.

There was a street level fire exit, but that, too, was clogged with people calling, begging him. *What do they want me to do?* Nowhere to go but back up.

Looking behind to make sure no one was coming after him, he ran right into pajama pants man.

The man said, "Why did you do this? What do you want?"

When Barnett was seven, he and his brother Robert found a dead fox out in the fields behind their house. Logan had hung back but Robert, fascinated, had grabbed a stick and pried the stiff fox up and over. He had loosened something, tearing the fox open, exposing wriggling maggots and decaying flesh. Both boys had run home screaming. Logan had nightmares for a week. He never forgot that smell of death and rot.

This guy's breath smelled like that. His lips were dry and cracked, and his mouth was awfully close to Barnett's face.

Gagging, Barnett turned his head away and pushed away.

"Get the fuck off me!"

There were some lengths of rebar piled off to one side and Barnett lunged and picked up a length about three feet long. He hefted it. It was heavy, but lethal.

"Keep the fuck back," he warned, wielding the rebar like an abnormally long baseball bat.

Orange vest was now approaching. He and PJ pants stood side by side. The woman was creeping weakly behind them.

The orange vest guy stepped forward and Barnett swung the rebar with all his strength which, due to the adrenaline surging through him, was prodigious.

The bar slammed into the orange vest and the man staggered to his knees and collapsed. Then he got back up.

Barnett threw down the rebar and ran for the elevator.

He got off at the floor below his own and made his way up the stairs. He slowly opened the stairwell door and peeked down the hallway. There was a knot of the people outside the elevator, not trying to get in, not talking, just waiting.

He quickly made it to his apartment door and pulled out his keys, trying to find the right one. The group turned at the jingling sound and started toward him.

"Logan," asked a thin woman in a torn black dress. "What do you want with us?"

"I don't want anything with you," he said, keeping his distance, trying not to make eye contact. Fiddling through at his keys. *Where is it, God damn it?*

"Then why did you keep us from our rest?" asked a short man with what looked like a bullet hole in the side of his head.

"It hurts," a man with severe burn wounds all over his face and chest murmured through blackened lips. "It hurts so bad." He smelled like burnt bacon, and Barnett's stomach was churning. And his headache was back.

"Look, I'm sorry, but there's nothing I can do." He found the key and quickly unlocked and entered his apartment. Slamming the door, he bolted the locks and stepped back. He thought for sure they would try to get in, but they only scrabbled at the door with their dead fingers, nothing more.

He threw his keys on the counter, and headed for the balcony. He looked over the edge and groaned. There were now dozens of figures milling about on the sidewalk and street around his building. Most were standing, but a few were crawling. He saw a couple of police cars across the street, but the cops were standing and watching. It's not a crime to stand on the sidewalk, even if you are dead.

A TV van was out there as well.

He took the last of his painkillers. He drank the last of the bourbon. He had no food left in his apartment.

He tried his cell phone, but there was no signal.

He looked through the peep hole in the door. They were still gathered in the hallway. More had joined them. Lisa was out there. Apparently, they had managed to find another way into the garage.

He was trapped.

He sat back on the couch and closed his eyes. His head was throbbing.

Now

He walked back in from the balcony, avoided looking at the front door. It was getting louder out there. He was afraid to see how many there were now. He picked up his phone. No signal. He had to hold it at an angle because he couldn't seem to see through his left eye.

He went through the kitchen, running one of his hands along the wall to guide him until he stood outside *The Room*.

He opened the door, entered and closed the door.

He put his back to it and slid down until he was sitting on the floor, his legs stretched out before him.

The Kid slowly sat down as well, cross-legged. *Is it everything you wanted? Immortality?*

"I can't see out of my left eye."

Your cancer is very aggressive. And very much alive. Barnett nodded. "I kind of figured that out."

You said it yourself. Nothing can die. Not you. Not them (arm sweeping out, indicating the dead) *and not your cancer.* "This isn't what I wanted," Barnett said, weakly, petulantly. "I don't want to die."

Few do. Barnett weakly waved an arm, indicating the walls and floor. "But I did all this. For what? I can't die."

And you won't. No one will. Nothing will. And your cancer will continue to spread. "What will happen then? When I die?"

That's up to you. Barnett put his hands to his face. The room was silent. Just his breathing. And the muffled shouts from the hallway. They were pounding on the door now.

"What do I have to do?"

Just set me free. Let me do what I am meant to do.

Logan reached out and wiped his hand across the chalk circle, smearing and erasing part of it.

Death stood up and stepped out of the circle. He looked taller now. He stood over Barnett and held out his hand. Barnett gazed weakly up and let the darkness take him.

It was awful.

NEVER FEAR - PHOBIAS

3
SPECTROPHOBIA

FEAR OF MIRRORS

ELLE J ROSSI

"Come on, Vanessa. Stop being a chickenshit."

I rubbed my sweaty palms on my jean-clad thighs and shot my best friend a wry glare. Cool and calm Olivia with her sleek blond hair, big brown eyes and pouty lips; nothing ever got under her skin. If I didn't love her, I'd hate her.

I wasn't being a chickenshit, per se. That would imply I was only mildly scared, when in fact I was terrified to the point my muscles were refusing to move. Stepping foot into a funhouse wasn't something I did. Ever.

On the off chance calliope music started drifting on the wind, I'd probably shit my pants.

Granted my fears were irrational and stemmed from childhood nightmares that could rival the best horror movie out there, but they were very real to me. And Olivia knew it.

I blew out a breath and tried to clear my head, but the memory refused to remain locked.

I woke, startled by a chorus of whispers close to my ear. Grabbing Rosie, my pink bear, I hugged her to my chest and squeezed my eyes shut. But the whispers called and they were mad. They made me look. Lip trembling, I slowly opened my eyes and hissed in a sharp breath. I squeezed my legs together to keep from wetting the bed, but some of it leaked out anyway.

Mama gave me the white mirror for my birthday. Five years old. Big girls don't wet the bed. She'd said it was an antique floor mirror and very special. An heirloom, she'd called it. I'd loved it. Until... Until...

I shivered out of the memory, dragging my focus back to the present.

For as long as I could remember, I'd avoided mirrors at all costs and with good reason. Mirrors were so much more than reflective glass. Mirrors were gateways to Hell; a never-ending, living Hell.

Public restrooms were a bitch. I'd learned the hard way to keep my head down and aim for the stall. Driving had brought a new set of challenges, but I'd conquered those too. The mirrors in my car were all pointed away from me. I'd practically become a contortionist when it came to keeping an eye on the traffic. And thank God for technology. If it weren't for the camera on my phone and computer, I'd no doubt look like a frazzled nut on a daily basis.

"Helloooo?" Livvy waved a hand in front of my face.

"Just go in without me. If you hurry you can catch up with Adam and Chase." They were no doubt waiting for a prime opportunity to jump out and scare the mess out of us; yet another reason I wasn't going inside. I liked Chase, I really did. But sometimes his juvenile antics were enough to make me reconsider our status. Of course, then he'd say something in that sexy southern drawl and I'd find myself lost in his mesmerizing baby blues and flip the coin to the other side.

Livvy grabbed my elbow and tugged me along. The beam of her flashlight bounced around, illuminating things I really didn't want to see: reflective animal eyes at the edge of the clearing, splatters of unknown substance, a ripped sweatshirt hanging from the drooping branch of a dead tree.

I fixed my gaze on one spot, which happened to be the thin layer of dust on my brand new Chucks. I dug my heels in, but the truth was, I didn't want to stay out here alone any more than I wanted to go in, so I ended up trailing after her like a puppy learning to walk on a leash.

"What kind of best friend would I be if I didn't help you face your fear? Come on, girl." Livvy turned and looked me dead in the eye. "You can do this."

Her expression was so serious, I almost believed her. But if fifteen years of therapy hadn't cured me, I doubted her method would work.

I stared at the broken lights haloing the giant clown mouth at the entrance and nearly tripped over my thumping heart. This was stupid. We shouldn't be here.

Here being a carnival ride graveyard smack dab in the middle of absolutely nowhere. When Chase had said he had something exciting planned for tonight, I sure as hell didn't think it'd be something as warped as this.

Chase had moved to Indiana three months ago. The wickedly handsome Georgia boy had immediately deemed our state and all its cornfields boring. He was an adrenaline junkie and he'd lured Adam, Livvy, and me into his world by dangling the idea of fun mixed with a bit of danger in front of us-not to mention his breath-taking looks. I had no doubt if he put his mind to it, he could sell crack to a priest. Usually, I went along with his adventures. I wasn't about to be the odd man out. A ghost hunt had led to climbing the tallest water tower, which led to driving on the back roads at midnight with the headlights off, which led to jumping off the ledge at the quarry... blindfolded. Yeah, we'd done it all and somehow lived through it.

Tonight was different though, and I could feel trepidation tightening the muscles in my neck.

I should have stayed in the car. But we'd passed the last of the streetlights about five miles back, and then the wind started whistling through the trees and I got all girly.

A screech owl's shriek tore through the silence of the night like a banshee. I screamed loud enough to stumble from the force of the colliding sounds.

"What the hell?"

Ignoring Livvy, I pointed my flashlight toward the sky, sweat beading on my upper lip as I swept the beam back and forth like a deranged woman until I spotted the enormous bird sitting on a dangling car at the top of a massive, rusted Ferris wheel. He stared right back. As if he'd suddenly found his prey, he spread his wings and dive-bombed, swooping low enough that I ducked down and covered my head with my hands. I probably screamed again but I couldn't hear anything over the pounding in my ears.

Livvy barked out a laugh. "Jesus, you are so freaked out. You better not piss your pants. It's a long ride back."

"Shut up." I clenched the flashlight tight enough that my knuckles cracked. "You know what? I don't want to do this."

"Yeah. You've said that." She blew out a breath while her gaze ping-ponged between the fun house and my trembling limbs. "Look, nothing is going to happen to you. If it were ten in the morning rather than ten at night, you wouldn't be so scared."

"Not true."

Livvy blinked at me, a technique she probably learned in her psych class. "True. Come on, don't you want Chase to protect you from whatever creepies you think are inside? I know I can't wait for Adam to guard me." She lifted one blond brow and smiled. "All of me."

She had no idea what the *creepies* were capable of, but I did. Besides, if Chase had wanted to score tonight, he probably shouldn't have ditched me at the car. At this point, I didn't really care if he ever put his hands on me again. I just wanted to be done with it. "Whatever. Fine. I'll go in, but I'm not going into the room with mirrors."

Livvy flashed a victorious smile. She and Adam had been dancing around each other for months now. I couldn't believe she'd chosen tonight to seal the deal. Just thinking about them doing the nasty in a place like this made my skin crawl.

"I mean it, Liv. No mirrors." I took a deep breath and marched up the steps. Jaw clenched, I crawled through the barrel, expecting it to spin and dump me in an ungraceful heap. The drum didn't move. How could it? There was no electricity out here to power anything. I briefly wondered if I'd feel better if everything had been lit up before discarding the thought. Nothing, aside from getting back in the car and driving home, could make me feel better.

Livvy shoved my butt. "Keep going."

I swiveled my head and shot her a don't-mess-with-me look. "I'm going. Just give me a second." *Hello? Major panic attack ensuing here.* I rolled out of the barrel and stood, whacking my head on the low ceiling. "Ouch."

"You okay?"

"I'm fine." I rubbed my scalp. "Watch your head. The ceiling is really low in here." I took a step and promptly fell on my ass. And the floor moved. Awesome.

With a curse, I shoved off the ground and struggled to remain upright. Every step I took tipped the section beneath me and I never knew which direction it would go. Liv started giggling. This time, her laughter was laced with a tinge of nerves. I didn't even bother to hide my smile, which wasn't very nice of me, but I wasn't feeling especially magnanimous at the moment.

"It's so quiet in here," she said, her voice taking on a tone I'd never heard from her before. "I wonder where they are?"

So, the unflappable Olivia wasn't so fierce after all. Noted and filed away for future reference. One never knew when they'd need to blackmail their best friend.

I took another step and my knee buckled as the black and white checkered floor slid to the right. I busted one hell of a *Twister* move and caught myself with both hands. I was so unsteady on my feet, I couldn't stay balanced enough to point the flashlight to see how much farther we had to go to get out of this room. Or which room of tricks would be next. Maybe I'd luck out and this funhouse wouldn't have any mirrors. With the way my night was going, I figured the chances of that happening were slim to none.

"I don't know where they are, but you're going to have to go around me." She owed me. The least she could do was go first and play scout.

Breathless, Livvy crouched next to me and plastered her cheek to mine. A flash of light temporarily blinded me. She gave me a smacking kiss on the same cheek and pulled back.

"What are you doing?" I squinted into the darkness as dots danced around my vision and saw her typing on her phone. "Uh uh. No way. You are not posting that." I wiped the sweat from my forehead with the back of one hand and reached for her phone with the other.

"Already did." She smiled and slid her phone into her back pocket. "If we're going to die I want my last update to be a picture of you and me."

How sweet. "We're not going to die." But even as I said the words my heart dipped to the pit of my stomach. In my dreams, I always died in a place like this… in a room full of mirrors. "Maybe we can just wait here for them to come back out."

My suggestion fell flat. When she didn't answer, I lifted my flashlight and illuminated her face.

Livvy sat there, one brow lifted, sporting a full on pout. "What kind of fun would that be? Come on." She moved past me. "You can be my wing-man. But when we find them, distract your boy so I can be alone with Adam. Those two drive me nuts with their bromance."

"I can't believe you're really going through with this. Don't you want your first time with him to be somewhere a little, hell, I don't know, cleaner and less creepy?"

"I'm a modern woman, Vanessa. Who needs romance when they can have excitement?"

I had a feeling there was a lot more to it than that. Like the fact that they might not really like each other if it weren't for all of the amped-up shenanigans. My opposition stuck in my throat when Livvy shrieked.

I froze. My gaze darted but all I saw were shadows. No Livvy. Her scream echoed and then faded as if she were falling through a rabbit hole. She erupted into a fit of giggles somewhere in the distance and relief swept through me.

The laughter abruptly stopped on something that sounded a lot like a gasp followed by a moan.

"Liv?"

Silence.

I scooted forward. "Where are you?"

My foot caught on a ledge and I pitched forward. I scrambled for purchase and lost the battle and my flashlight. Momentum careened me over the edge and, the next thing I knew, I was whizzing head first down a steep incline. I landed in a pit of balls and might have laughed if I weren't being suffocated by half-deflated, mildew-saturated balls.

Flailing like a fish out of water didn't help. I forced myself to calm down, breathed through the sea of darkness attempting to pull me under. I hoped to God no one caught me on camera. I would never live this down. After several grunts and some awkward maneuvering, I managed to right myself. Moonlight filtered in through the broken windows allowing me to see enough to know that I was alone in the pit surrounded by about ten thousand rainbow colored balls. Finding my flashlight would be nearly impossible.

"Livvy?" Where the hell was she? "Chase? Adam? Come on, guys. This isn't funny anymore." Never had been.

Not one of them answered my call.

I jumped at the sound of whispers coming from my right. It had to be them because the possibility of it being anyone else wasn't something I wanted to consider. I had no problem believing Chase and Adam would punk me, but Livvy? That stung. If I thought I could climb back up the slide, I'd leave the way I came and wait for them to grow up. The incline was too steep and I'd never make it. I turned a full circle, looking for another way out, which proved futile. I had to go through the door on the right.

My breaths came out fast and shallow. I had no idea what trick the next room would bring.

"Mama?" I could barely hear myself. I cleared my throat and tried calling for her again. "Mama, help me."

The whispers turned into laughter. Goosebumps covered my arms and I pulled the blanket tighter around me.

Fog poured out of the mirror and filled my room. Mean faces swirled in the fog. I quietly slid Rosie under the blanket to protect her.

The fog disappeared and I saw a bony hand reach out of the mirror and crook a finger at me.

I clamped my eyes shut and screamed until my throat hurt.

Then the blood came and Mama went away.

Even now, all these years later, the fear I'd felt latched on to my heart and squeezed. Pursing my lips, I slowly blew out a breath. And then another until the paralysis eased.

I basically swam through the ball pit, latched onto the ledge and dragged myself up. With noodly legs, I inched toward the door as bead after bead of sweat raced down my spine. Nothing but darkness beckoned from the other side of the door. Something brushed against my ankle and I jumped. I looked down expecting to see a rat or a snake. Nothing.

Fighting off a case of major heebie-jeebies, I swallowed hard and stepped through the doorway. My back hit the wall and strong hands gripped my shoulders. Without thinking, I twisted and jerked my knee straight up, and met a whole lot of air.

"Fuck, Vanessa. I need my balls, babe."

I had to blink back tears before I could respond. For the first time tonight, I was happy to be shrouded in darkness. Falling apart wasn't something I wanted my boyfriend to see. "You want to keep your balls?" I asked, faking bravado. "Don't sneak up on people, Chase. Not cool." I couldn't keep the quivering out of my voice.

He trailed his fingers down my arm. "I was just having a little fun." He leaned in. "You remember how to have fun, don't you?"

I couldn't deny the effect he had on me. I compartmentalized and labeled it a mixture of relief that I was no longer alone and the fact that Chase could be alluringly persuasive when he wanted to be. His lips found mine and I sank into his kiss, clutching his shirt in my fists. If we kept kissing, I could forget about everything else. His heart thumped hard in his chest, a mixture of adrenaline and hormones no doubt.

He broke the kiss and pulled me deeper into the room.

"Wait. Where are we going?"

"We haven't seen everything yet."

I let him drag me along until I came back to my senses. I wrenched my hand from his and stopped. "I'm done. Take me home, Chase." The room was so dark I felt like the walls were pressing in on me. I shouldn't have been so hasty in moving away from him.

"Not yet."

I whipped around. How had he moved behind me and I hadn't heard him? "Knock it off."

"Come on, Vanessa. Aren't you even the least bit turned on by this?"

I turned again and bumped into him. He wrapped his arms around me and held on. "You don't get it," I said softly, leaning my forehead against his chest. "I've been up for everything we've done this summer, but… I can't do this, Chase."

He tugged me closer and I thought he was finally beginning to understand.

"What the hell is taking so long? Hurry up and get the fuck in here, bro."

Adam.

Chase hoisted me over his shoulders and took off. I pounded on his back. "Put me down!"

"It's just one more room, babe." He stumbled but caught himself before we both went down. "You can do this."

If one more person said that to me…

Chase turned a corner and stopped. My breath stuck in my

throat as I slid down his body until my feet touched the floor.

I squeezed my eyes shut but I'd already seen too much.

"Breathe, babe," Chase whispered in my ear.

I wanted to breathe but the air kept getting lodged in my throat.

"Olivia told us about your mirror issues."

My eyes flashed open and I searched the room for the person who was supposed to be my best friend. All I saw were reflections of me, trembling hands, mascara streaks on my pale cheeks. Candles were everywhere, the light playing tricks in tandem with the warped mirrors.

Anger mixed with fear and I nearly passed out from the intensity of it all. They'd set me up. All of them.

Chase walked up behind me. "Say it, Vanessa."

My lips trembled but I couldn't look away. "Say what?"

He smiled and his blue eyes twinkled in the candlelight. "The five words. Say them and you won't be afraid anymore."

What was he talking about? To them this was just another stupid game, a crazy way to get high. To me it was so much more.

"Here," he said. "Let us help you."

Adam appeared next to Chase. He pulled a rag from his back pocket and wrapped it around his hand. Then he slammed his fist into one of the mirrors.

I nearly choked on fear. The mirrors wouldn't be happy. They'd get retribution. They always did.

Chase picked up a shard of glass and sliced it across his left palm.

I shook my head. "What... what are you doing?"

He leaned in and kissed my temple. "I'm fixing you."

Fixing me? I wasn't broken. I blinked hard and saw Livvy standing next to Adam. How could she have done this?

"I only wanted to help you. Don't be mad."

I shook my head again. Her voice didn't sound right.

Chase dipped his finger in the blood pooling on his palm. "Five words, babe. Just five words."

He reached out and swirled his finger over the mirror in front of me, then stepped back and grinned like he'd just solved all the problems of the world.

Mirror, mirror on the wall

The bloody letters blurred until I could hardly make them out. Tears streamed down my face and my veins grew cold. "You don't know what you've done," I choked out.

"Just say the words."

Adam laughed and Chase clapped him on the back. Livvy looked nervous and I wanted to scream. But screaming hadn't helped before. They'd come for me then and I knew they'd come for me now.

"Fine," Adam said. "If you won't say it, we will." Nodding, he glanced at Chase and Livvy.

"Don't." I swiped at the tears running down my cheeks. "Don't do it. Please," I begged.

"Just forget it, guys. She doesn't want to."

"We always finish what we start, Liv," Adam said. "Mirror, mirror on the wall. Mirror, mirror on the wall."

Chase squeezed my hand and joined in. "Mirror, mirror on the wall."

I snatched my hand away and stepped back, my heart slamming against my ribcage. Fog rolled in and swirled around my legs. Didn't they see it? My panicked gaze flicked to Livvy. She offered an apologetic shrug then laced her fingers through Adam's and spoke the words.

"Mirror, mirror on the wall."

"What the--"

A hand shot out of the mirror, grabbed Adam's shirt and pulled him through the glass. Livvy stumbled after him.

I bit down hard on my fist but couldn't contain the scream. It was happening again. The mirror would take us all.

"Jesus, Vanessa." Chase whipped his head toward me, eyes wide. "Did you see that? Where the hell did they go?"

I pointed to the mirror then pulled my hand back when a face appeared. The eyes were nothing but black holes, the mouth wide and deep.

The fight-or-flight response is a peculiar thing; an in-between state that is based purely on fear and adrenaline with just enough confusion thrown in to make your head spin and your heart erupt through your throat. I wanted to curl up in a ball and pretend this messed-up situation was nothing more than a nightmare vivid enough for the big screen.

I heard Livvy screaming, begging someone to help her. I couldn't move, couldn't look away from the face swirling in the mirror.

The mouth formed an 'O' and sucked in the fog. I lurched backward, away from the vacuum. But Chase got caught in it. He reached for me, struggling to stay on his feet. The mirror took no pity, dragging him through the glass as he screamed.

I covered my ears, but I would never forget the horrific sounds. They would meld with the others that haunted me.

Come to me...

I jerked away from the whispers, stumbled and fell, catching myself on all fours. Pain shot through my entire body. I swore I could feel my mind splintering into bits so small I'd never be able to put all the pieces back together. The mirror's laughter slid over my skin like a million leeches, sucking out my blood through microscopic straws, draining all the warmth from my body.

Come to me...

Frantic, I crawled over broken glass, ignoring the pain as the shards lodged in my knees and palms. No matter which direction I went, I couldn't get away from all the mirrors; away from the screams. The candlelight danced and flickered as if it were mocking me.

Another face emerged. Chase. Oh, God.

His face, contorted with fear and pain; his hands, clawing at the mirror. He called to me, shouting my name over and over. Pleading for me to help him.

I couldn't see Livvy, but I could hear her sobbing. Adam was silent and I feared something even more terrible had happened to him.

Every fiber of my being screamed at me to turn and run away. But how could I leave them? I shook my head, pounded on the floor until my knuckles were dripping blood.

Mind and soul fracturing, I reached out for Chase's hand and tumbled through the mirror.

Falling.

Falling.

Falling.

I landed with a thud, my legs twisted in unnatural angles, my wrists tethered to the floor.

The face moved toward me, leaned close. I couldn't speak. Couldn't move.

Black eyes glistened and the face spoke to me.

"Vanessa, it's time for your medicine."

4
ONEIROPHOBIA

FEAR OF DREAMING

CONNIE CORCORAN WILSON

The machine gun fire was deafening.

Two groups of men, clad in camouflage, approached. Black masks. Three men in each group. They ran in a half-crouch towards the confused employees in the plant lunchroom.

"What the fuck?" Gregory Chandler shouted at co-worker Brad Clemens. "What's going on?" Recognizing imminent danger, Greg shouted, "Hit the floor!" Both men dove beneath the cafeteria lunch table. Just an ordinary day at the John Deere Harvester Works in East Moline, Illinois, where combines were assembled.

Until now.

Be quiet!! Lie Still! Play dead! These thoughts raced through Gregory Chandler's head as he watched the boot-clad gunmen come closer.

Brad was hit. A red stain slowly spread across his chest. He lay there beneath the table, facing Gregory Chandler. Slack-jawed. Eyes glazed. A thin rope of drool suspended from his lower lip. The hot dog he'd been eating fell to the floor. A ketchup stain on Brad's cheek simulated the blood now gushing from wounds in his neck and torso. A surprised look reflected in Brad's blue eyes, pupils dilated in death. A sickening smell wafted towards Greg; he tried not to inhale.

Just barely breathe. Don't look at Brad. Quiet. Play dead. Greg's eyes were shut tight. He hoped his eyelids didn't flutter and give him away. He prayed that the killers wouldn't shoot more rounds of ammunition into the two men lying face-down under the cafeteria table, both of them now drenched in Brad Clemens' blood, as the pool widened and stained them both.

The strangers came closer. Cubans armed with automatic weapons--machine guns. The assailants had just mowed down half of the first-shift workers sitting in the gigantic cafeteria eating a peaceful lunch. A veritable cacophony of percussive noise. Screams echoed from the tiled walls. The employees had no more chance than the theater goers at the showing of "Batman: The Dark Knight Rises" in Aurora, Colorado when a psychotic red-haired gunman named James Holmes fired into their midst, killing twelve and wounding seventy. Innocent casualties were everywhere. Confusion and chaos reigned.

***

A hand grabbed Greg's shoulder.

"GREG! GREG! WAKE UP!"

Cynthia Chandler was shaking Greg. Concern clouded her features. "What's the matter? You were muttering and shaking and screaming!" Cynthia was upset.

Still groggy, the dream still fresh in his mind, Greg tried to respond.

"I--I was at work..."

"Yes...?" she said, her tone indicating she wanted her husband to continue.

Still too groggy to articulate clearly, Greg said, "Cubans. Cuban assassins."

"What?" Cynthia wasn't tracking. For that matter, neither was Greg Chandler. It was so REAL. It seemed as though it was actually happening! The sound of machine gun fire still echoed in his brain. The smoky haze. The odor. Brad's dead body.

"What's this about Cubans?" Cynthia asked, puzzled.

"They--they were in the cafeteria. They were armed. They

shot us."

"O--kay." Cynthia did not sound as though it was okay. She sounded like she was humoring her husband. She cocked her left eyebrow quizzically.

"Never mind. Just hold me. Hold me a minute," Greg said, moving his head to rest on Cynthia's ample bosom. He tried to calm his rapidly beating heart, to slow his respiration and bring it back to normal.

Cynthia snuggled Greg's head against her breasts. She said, "Okay, but remember: I saved your ass from certain death." She hugged him tightly, smiling to herself. "Don't you dare get yourself killed in a dream. Leave that to me when there's a good reason." She chuckled. "You know I'm gonna' kill you if you die on me at forty-six. The kids and I are counting on you." She kissed the top of his head with genuine affection.

Eventually, both Greg and Cynthia drifted off into fitful slumber.

Tuesday morning.

The Chandlers' cheery kitchen. Greg Chandler looked like he'd had a rough night. Cynthia Chandler poured Greg a steaming hot cup of strong black coffee. She offered it to him, holding the coffee mug at arm's length, when he entered the room. As Greg stretched his right hand out to receive the cup, he ran the fingers of his left hand through his thick, dark, tangled hair, ruffling it into a messy pile that looked like a small bird's nest. The slight blonde and the tall, dark, forty-six-year-old Brad made a handsome couple.

"Honey--you were just having a nightmare. Nobody shot Brad. Nobody's shooting at you." Cynthia paused and then added, almost as an after-thought, "Who's Brad, anyway? Do I know him? And why Cubans?"

In the harsh glare of daylight, the previous night's dream seemed silly. Stupid. Greg felt slightly embarrassed to still be talking about armed Cubans in the cafeteria.

"Uh… I dunno. I just knew they were Cubans--somehow." Greg's simultaneous sipping of his coffee confused his articulation of the sentence. It came out half-gibberish, all muddled together. He seemed to want to drop the subject.

"Honey--do you even *know* any Cubans?" Cynthia appeared amused. She chortled.

"Well--there was Desi Arnaz," Greg answered. Slowly. Dully. Even *he* smiled at his answer and the length of time it took him to respond. He was tired.

"R-i-i-i-g-h-t," said Cynthia. "Very timely. A Cuban who appeared on *I Love Lucy* in the fifties. What were you doing in this dream? Time traveling backwards?" Cynthia still sported a slight smile. She sounded like she, too, was suffering from the lack of a good night's sleep.

"Well, I didn't know I was limited to only *current* Cuban celebrities in my dreams," Greg said, trying to amuse. "I could have said Gloria and Emilio Estefan, if you had explained the conditions of my nightmares to me beforehand. But Gloria and Emilio don't sound too menacing." He took another sip and added, "Gloria would have to sing me to death." Greg smiled. He grabbed Cynthia around the waist, breaking into song: "Rhythm is gonna' get you." He laughed, and then resumed, in a more serious tone. "These guys were scary, Cyn'. And they were after *me*. I know they were. They were whispering my name."

"Whispering?"

"Yeah. You know: *Greg-oh-ree! Greg-oh-ree!* But softly."

"So, let me get this straight: these 'Cubans' are shooting machine guns at random Deere employees in the plant cafeteria at lunchtime, but they're whispering your name while they're doing it? What are you...the patron saint of cafeteria workers or something?" Gloria smiled, knowing she was being a smart ass. Then, seeking equal time, she sang the next verse of Gloria Estefan's famous song: *"At night, when you turn off all the lights, there's no place that you can hide."* Both of them joined the upbeat rhythm chorus Greg had sung earlier. The pair laughed when they finished singing the "rhythm" part, with Cynthia pretending to be shaking maracas and her booty simultaneously. It would be the last time that they would find anything amusing about Greg's nightmares. And they wouldn't be doing any more singing of upbeat songs over morning coffee.

Greg looked sheepish. "Yeah. I mean... I don't know. They were just scary as shit. And they were after me. I *know* they were after me. And, yes, they *were* whispering my name." Greg was adamant, détente or no détente.

"If they were whispering it, how could you hear them over the noise of machine gun fire?"

"Damn! The woman can be maddening when she wants to be! Greg thought.

Greg remembered the second verse of Gloria Estefan's song. He realized it was exactly what he had done in his dream. "In bed, throw the covers on your head. You pretend like you are dead."

Greg had always liked that song.

Until now.

The cheerful, upbeat rhythm belied the menacing message. *What was "the rhythm?" Why was it out to get him?* This thought, following on the heels of their recent duet popped into his fatigued brain.

"I don't know, Cynthia. I just know that this group of big scary Cuban guys was out to get me. And they *DID* get Brad." Sipping his coffee once again after blowing on it to cool it, Greg added," You should know Brad. Remember the Christmas party? The blond guy with the glasses? I told you about him. Before Christmas vacation he left work to get a vasectomy. He came back to work the same day. Passed out in the parking lot next to his car. Security had to haul his unconscious ass into the building and take him to the infirmary."

As he finished telling this old story, which both of them had laughed about at the time, Cynthia and Greg laughed for real. Their last laugh for days. It defused the tension in Greg's voice. But not in his brain.

Lunchtime: John Deere Harvester Works, East Moline, Illinois, Wednesday Noon.

When it was time for lunch, Greg avoided the Killing Ground. He could still see every detail of the cafeteria the way it had been in his nightmare: smashed French fries on the floor. Half-eaten hot dog. Spilled Coca Cola. Bullet casings. Blood. Slack-jawed corpse of Brad Clemens, blood oozing from his mid-section, saliva dripping from his open mouth. Shocked look on Brad's face.

Instead, Greg walked to the machines near his office that held bags of chips and pre-made sandwiches. He wondered if he'd be able to enter the lunchroom tomorrow or the next day, days after his nightmare. He knew today was too soon. The previous night's dream lingered in his consciousness. He could not snap out of the feeling of impending doom.

I could stand to lose a few pounds, anyway, he reasoned, defending his cowardice with a more logical excuse for chickening out.

Evening, Day Three, Wednesday:

As the evening wore on, Cynthia and Gregory Chandler watched a recorded episode of *The Walking Dead*. They followed that up with a *Game of Thrones* replay. Greg dozed off occasionally. That was normal after a long day at work. The gore quotient of the shows they watched was high. The Red Wedding episode. Smashed zombie heads.

At one point, as they ate their food on TV trays, Cynthia said, "They ought to call this show 'Smashing Pumpkins II' or something. Why does every show have to have zombies getting their heads brutally smashed with a rifle butt, and always while I'm eating?"

Cynthia was not as big a fan of *The Walking Dead* as Greg. She objected to viewing really gruesome shows while dining, but she traded *Modern Family* for zombies. She was definitely more squeamish than Greg. Most of the time, Cynthia was the only one awake to watch anything, as Greg habitually dozed off. Especially tonight.

Greg was feeling less and less happy about turning in. He had to be at work by 7:30 a.m. Middle management supervisory duties had its perks, but it also had its drawbacks. Arriving before the rank-and-file for early morning meetings was one of the duties.

Greg routinely went to bed at 10 p.m. in order to try to get eight hours of sleep. But tonight, he couldn't make himself turn off the television set. He wasn't ready to knit up the day's raveled cares in the arms of Hypnos, the Greek god of sleep.

"Aren't you coming to bed, Hon?" Cynthia was holding her toothbrush, fully lathered, in her right hand as she peered from inside the master bathroom door that opened onto the family room.

"In a minute," Greg said, looking and sounding preoccupied.

In reality, Greg was dreading dreaming, fearing sleep.

Zombies. White Walkers. Cubans. Who will try to kill me tonight?

Midnight. One A.M. Two A.M. Three A.M. Finally, Greg couldn't keep his eyes open. He watched Jimmy Fallon. Seth Meyer.

Carson Daley. Repeats of *The Today Show*. He had no idea what the programs were about. The steady drone of voices anesthetized him from thinking about his nightmare. It didn't stop him from worrying that a NEW dream might await him tonight.

As he finished washing his face and spat a final bit of toothpaste into the bathroom's double sink, Greg thought, *If I encounter Cubans again tonight, I'd better find a more current Cuban celebrity when I tell Cynthia about the dream.* He smiled wryly. *Is Andy Garcia still considered famous? Will he be good enough for Cynthia when I freak out? How about Mark Cuban? 'Shark Tank'? I'm really losing focus now. Getting loopy. And I know it.*

He looked at himself in the bathroom mirror. Apprehensive. He accidentally bumped the mirror that jutted out from the wall while leaning over to place his toothbrush back in the holder. Swore wearily. Muttered aloud, "I keed, Greg. I keed." Bad Cuban accent.

He crawled into bed, exhausted.

***

The first shot grazed his ear. He reached up. Felt something warm. Blood. It was blood.

Shit! They're back!

The Cubans weren't in the cafeteria. It wasn't even lunchtime. It was morning. Bright. Sunny. Cheerful. Greg was in his corner office. Sunshine was streaming through the windows, bathing the Berber carpeting in light. It refracted from the beveled edge of a glass door of the bookcase in the room. Rainbow-colored reflected rays of light were shining in his eyes, preventing him from getting a good look. He couldn't see the men coming down the hall because of the glare. One of them had managed to shoot through the glass of his office window. That bullet had brushed his ear.

Greg clapped a hand over his right ear to stop the bleeding, but he seemed incapable of any other movement. He was paralyzed with fear.

Although he couldn't see the men, he could hear them. They grew louder as they came closer to his office door, whispering his name with increasing volume: *Greg-oh-Ree! Greg-Oh-Ree! GREG-OH-REE!*

Panic. Short, choppy breaths. Heart beating like a

hummingbird. His tongue felt like a dry brush in his mouth. Hands sweating. He couldn't think clearly. *Am I having a heart attack?* Greg dropped to his hands and knees. Collapsed, really. He crumpled into the knee-space beneath his desk. He hoped he could control his bladder and bowels. Brad had lost that ability in death. But Greg was very much alive and as frightened of the next few moments as he had ever been afraid of anything in his life.

Maybe they won't know I'm here. Maybe they won't see me. Maybe they won't kill me. WHY do they want to kill me? He prayed that his breathing wasn't as loud as it sounded in his own ears.

They were coming for him…whoever "they" were. They were calling…well, whispering…his name. When they reached the door, he'd know who "they" were, but what good would that do him? They had already shattered the glass in his office windows with a stray bullet. He had no weapon. He was no match for men with guns.

Greg began to whimper: *No! No! No! No! No!*

***

This time, Cynthia jabbed him sharply in the back as he lay there, curled in the fetal position (*facing away from her*), moaning, chest heaving, his breathing rapid and shallow. Hyperventilating.

"Stop it! Stop it! You're dreaming again!" Cynthia sounded alarmed, but not as sympathetic as the first night, now four nights ago.

Greg woke much more quickly. He had, after all, only been in bed for three hours. It was six in the morning.

He rose. Rushed into the master bathroom. Splashed cold water on his face. He noticed that his right ear was wet. Wet with blood. He took the washcloth, blotted the nicked ear, washed away the red stain. It wouldn't stop. It just kept oozing blood. *Did I cut myself?* He had been so tired at bedtime that he couldn't remember. Nightmare and reality were merging and becoming seamless. Things that happened in his dreams seemed to be happening in his real life.

Now that he was awake, Greg couldn't get back to sleep. He decided he might as well get ready for work. He had to be there by 7:30 a.m., anyway. That was only an hour and a half away.

When he entered the kitchen this time, Cynthia was

considerably less cheerful. No outstretched mug of hot coffee to greet the prodigal husband this day.

"Cubans again?" she asked. Her voice had a tone somewhere between annoyance and empathy.

Greg just nodded.

Cynthia spoke the words, "Rhythm is gonna' get you." She sounded tired. Sarcastic. She turned and left the kitchen.

Greg rummaged for a stale bagel, some juice and the remaining hot coffee. He prepared to face another day at the plant with both the cafeteria and his once-safe office now threatening places to be avoided at all costs.

Fortunately, Greg had a meeting in the large conference room at the opposite end of the plant. The meeting lasted until nearly lunchtime.

At lunchtime, one of the other visiting Supervisors from the John Deere plant in Waterloo, Iowa suggested they go get lunch out somewhere. The Waterloo plant was the largest in the company; it had recently laid off 460 workers. But John Hearn, the visitor to the Harvester Works, was not one of them. He had been sent to East Moline for this meeting concerning staffing levels and a collaborative project. He wanted to see a little bit of the second-largest metropolitan area in the state of Illinois, after Chicago.

John said, "Hey, Greg. Let's go out somewhere nice for lunch. You know the Quad Cities. I don't." John winked and grabbed his coat.

This was fine with Greg. In fact, it was more than fine. Greg didn't want to go back in the plant cafeteria. Now he wasn't keen on going back to his office, either. And he was tired. So very tired. It was four days since he had slept soundly, going on five. Greg suggested Johnny's Italian Steakhouse and the pair set off to drive to John Deere Commons in Moline where it was located.

Three hours of sleep is not enough to think straight, Greg thought. *I wonder if it's enough to think crooked?*

He cracked the bad joke to himself and smiled inwardly.

***

That night, when Greg got home, Cynthia waited, primed to have a serious discussion.

"Can't you take something to help you sleep through the night, Honey?" She interrupted herself to ask, "What happened to your ear?"

Greg had put a Band-Aid on the outer curve of his right ear before leaving for work. The ear just wouldn't stop bleeding. "Maybe you should call Dr. Jenkins and see if he can prescribe something? Or, if you don't want to take anything that is prescription strength, try melatonin over the counter or extra-strength Tylenol PM or *something*. It's not that I don't love you, dear, but I'm going to sleep across the hall tonight in the guest room. I haven't had a good night's sleep since that first night...going on five days ago."

Tell me about it! Greg thought.

He responded, "But, Cynthia, I can GET to sleep. The problem is that I keep having these nightmares after I go to sleep and they wake me up."

"I know, Greg, but they also wake ME up. And you look like hell. You need to find a way to sleep through the night. Maybe there is somebody you can talk to about different sleep techniques?"

***

So it was that Greg found himself walking down the hall to the factory infirmary to consult with Dr. Jenkins, the plant doctor.

Dr. Jenkins looked up, slightly startled, when Greg entered.

"Hi, Greg! What can I do you out of?" (*The doctor was a well-known jokester.*)

"I've been having some trouble sleeping through the night, Dr. Jenkins. I can GET to sleep all right, but I've been having some really troubling nightmares that wake me up. When I'm awake, I can't get back to sleep."

"How long has this been going on, Greg?"

Greg looked at the ceiling and counted silently in his head. "Well...let's see. This is about the fifth day that I've not had a whole lot of sleep."

"How much is 'not a whole lot'? Bigger than a breadbox? Longer than an Infomercial? Shorter than '*War and Peace*'?" The doctor appeared legitimately concerned for his patient, but was searching for specific information and doing so light-heartedly.

"One night, I got three hours. Another night---the best

night…maybe five. Mostly a couple of hours for all of this week since Monday. It's Friday now and we have a chance at a nice weekend. I'm so tired I just want to sleep. But I'm afraid to. I've had two pretty weird nightmares. They were scary as hell. It's all over but the shouting, once I'm awake."

"Did you watch anything violent on television prior to going to bed? Eat anything strange or different from your normal eating patterns?" The doctor was starting with the obvious and being serious now. Greg hadn't given much thought to his viewing habits or his diet. He'd been more fixated on the effect of workday stress. He was responsible for supervising thirty plant workers, and he knew each of them personally. If the Harvester Works followed the path of the Waterloo Works, some of those friends that he supervised might soon be out of a job.

"The first nightmare just--happened. But, yes, I think we were watching 'The Walking Dead.' And we watched an episode of 'Game of Thrones' before the second one. 'The Red Wedding'."

"So, you've had at least two of these disturbing dreams, right?" The doctor was scribbling on a piece of paper on his clipboard. Doctor Jenkins looked up and added, "Knock off the gore fest before bedtime. Go with some comedy sit-com offerings. Don't eat anything that might upset your stomach, either. Nothing spicy or heavy. Other than that, I'd say you simply have an overactive imagination. You know all the Freudian bilge about daytime fears coming out in our dreams at night, right?"

"Of course. You don't sound like you believe old Sigmund was on the right track." Greg had no firmly held opinion of his own concerning dream theory and Freud, but he was interested to hear what the doctor would say.

Doctor Jenkins just shrugged dismissively.

"I think REM sleep is necessary for good health and dreams go along with that, but you've got to learn to relax and put the day's worries aside. You might try some meditation or yoga or the traditional glass of warm milk before bedtime. Something like that. If I start you on pills…well, it's a slippery slope. Sometimes, people taking the really strong ones become addicted. A few of them can even cause hallucinations and side effects that are worse than the nightmares you're having. It's sort of like all those commercials you see on TV that tell you how great this or that drug is going to be for some illness. Then, at the end of the ad, they rattle on about twenty-five to thirty things that sound far worse than what you had in the first place and will kill you. Makes you want to err on the side of caution. My vow is 'First, do no harm.' Do you think you could alter some of those R-rated shows as an experiment?" Doctor Jenkins was smiling. Acting like this wasn't a Big Deal. Just a little speed bump for old Gregory Chandler.

"Okay. I can do that," Greg agreed. "And, as for the nightmares, they were just so REAL! Two of them. But I thought about those nightmares all the next day...all week, in fact. They were so vivid in my mind. Disturbing. One night, after I woke up, I even saw that my ear was bleeding. I think that was in the dream. A couple of nights I couldn't remember the nightmare, afterwards. They were so frightening, I think I blocked them out."

The doctor shook his head, agreeing. "Yes, it's quite common to have a nightmare, wake up, but not be able to recall what the dream was about. Nothing unusual about that."

"I don't sleep well normally," said Greg, "and now this. My wife is pretty upset with me. She moved across the hall into the guest room. When I have one of these dreams, I hyperventilate. I cry out. I wake her up. Afterwards, I talk nonsense." Greg looked at Doc Jenkins, self-conscious that he was admitting all this to a medical professional. "Then, after I wake us both up, neither one of us is worth a shit in the morning. Or all day."

The doctor shook his head sympathetically. "I see. She works, too, doesn't she?"

"Yes. English teacher at the high school. She really wants me to get something to help me sleep--*anything* to stop these dreams. It's not just *me* that ends up being disturbed. It's her, too. To be honest, I've never been as terrified in my life as I was during the first nightmare. Can you help me out with something, Doc?"

The doctor listened to Greg's fanciful tales of Cubans armed with machine guns. He didn't laugh, but he seemed slightly incredulous, all the same. Then Dr. Jenkins scribbled a prescription for Clonazepam.

"Take one of these at bedtime. It's a long-lasting benzodiazepine. It acts as a muscle relaxant, among other things. It's used to treat convulsions, sometimes.

You should be able to drift off if you take one. It's a low

dosage, though. If you don't find yourself being able to fall asleep, take two." He gave Greg a quick lecture on other side effects the drug might have.

Greg shook his head as though he understood even half of what the doctor had just said about the amnesiac and hypnotic properties of the drug. Then he said, very seriously, "Thanks, Doc. Thank you very much." Greg thought he was verging perilously close to prime-time Elvis with that expression of gratitude. "It's getting so I don't want to even *TRY* to go to sleep. Who said, 'To sleep, perchance to dream,' Doc? Shakespeare?"

"Don't know, Greg. Can't tell you. Ask the wife," said Dr. Jenkins, hand on the doorknob, ready to move on to examine his next patient.

Greg walked to the far end of the factory, trying to figure out a way to avoid both the cafeteria and his office. Those sites still spelled danger.

Then it came to him. He was a Supervisor of thirty workers. He hadn't been doing much "supervising" lately on the plant floor. The company had been having meetings about the lay-offs necessitated by market conditions and about new collaborative initiatives with the Waterloo Works, so he had been cooped up elsewhere all last week. He'd check out the activity on the plant floor and actually supervise the thirty workers he wrote up for performance reviews. He knew all of them by name. A familiar face would be a welcome sight.

"I'll get a good weekend's sleep and this Monday I'll earn my pay on the plant floor," he thought, turning over a new leaf.

But the weekend would prove to be as problematic as Monday through Friday had been. He hadn't been this tired since the twins, who were now sixteen, were infants and he and Cynthia took turns getting up in the night with them.

Greg made a hard right turn within the labyrinthine hallways. He headed for the floor where the gigantic combines were assembled--the most complex machine, in terms of moving parts, aside from the lunar landing module. The S690-S Series. Up to 45 feet wide. Half a million dollars to purchase just the main combine. (*Attachments optional, extra, necessary and expensive*).

Ninety acres under one roof. Operating since 1913. Over four million square feet...and East Moline's Harvester Works wasn't even the biggest of Deere's factories. (*That distinction went to the Waterloo Works*).

When Greg emerged on the plant floor, one of the line workers, Stan Sanchez, hollered, "Hey, Greg! What's up? Long time, no see." He waved. Greg waved back and smiled. Stan's parents had fled Havana after the 1959 revolution. His dad had been a mucky-muck in the Batista government. Stan had been working here twenty years, himself, always running the workstation with the big hammer.

Greg walked over to where Stan was operating the jackhammer. The jackhammer machine stood at least thirty feet in the air. A piece of molten metal would be placed on the stamping block below it. The jackhammer would come down with thousands of pounds of pressure and stamp out a combine door or some other part of the huge machine. The jackhammer did this over and over again, with a distinct tempo that was reverberating in both their ears right now.

Over on Stan's far right the grinders were welding various parts for the behemoth machines. Sparks flew.

The smell of molten metal was in the air. Although the plant was extremely clean and every effort was made to keep it cool and to remove noxious fumes, a particular odor filled the air. Anyone who has been in a foundry knows the smell. The smoke from the heat of the production process drifted through the factory, permeating the workers' clothing. Still, it was a far cry from "the old days," when Greg had worked on the line in the now closed Moline Malleable Works, working with nodular and gray iron. In those days, Greg would come home from work, hot, sweaty and filthy from the ironworks. Today's Harvester plant was quite a step up as a work environment.

"Haven't seen you out here for a while, Boss." Stan smiled.

"Yeah. I've been being meeting-ed to death," Greg replied. (*At least I don't have to admit that I've been worried about being sung to death by Gloria Estefan,* he thought, amusing himself with that.)

"Well, keep on keeping on," Stan said, reaching for the safety apparatus for the jackhammer. Pushing two buttons brought down a safety cage around the device. The buttons had to be pushed with the fingers on each hand. The metal safety cage would descend with a bang. The jackhammer stamped with a consistent deafening rhythm that Greg had heard in the background for all of his twenty-five-year work life. It was the specific sound of the factory in full operational mode. Sparks flying. Smoke drifting over the scene. Greg felt right at home and, although fuzzy from lack of sleep, better than he had felt in over a week.

"This thing is getting old. It wants to rest, I think," Stan said to Greg, with a grin, gesturing towards the jackhammer.

"What do you mean?" Greg asked. "Is something wrong with it?"

"Oh…it's just the tempo. The safety cage, when it descends, it seems to be slightly 'off.' One time it comes down immediately, going a mile a minute. The next time I push the buttons, it takes its own sweet time." Stan smiled as he shared the information.

"Reminds me of some workers I supervise," Greg joked as he walked away. "Let me know if it keeps doing it, and I'll take a look."

***

Greg's first stop after work was at the local pharmacy at Kennedy Square Shopping Center. The Jewel/Osco pharmacist, daughter of a life-long drugstore owner in nearby Silvis, knew him on sight.

"What can I do for you, Greg?" Karen asked.

"I need to fill this prescription for Clonazepam, one milligram," Greg answered, checking the scrip to make sure he had the right dosage.

"Okay. It'll just be a minute."

Karen quickly filled the prescription and then asked, "Do you have any questions?"

"No, not really. I guess I should ask if this is going to give me a morning hangover?" Greg said.

"Naaah. It's a small dosage. You'll be fine."

I hope so, he thought.

That night, Greg popped one of the little round green pills right after he brushed his teeth. He turned in at his normal 10 p.m. bedtime, even though tomorrow was Saturday. He lay there, tossing and turning.

After two uneasy hours, he got up and took a second pill. *After all, Doc said I could take more than one if I needed to*, he rationalized.

***

The first sound he was aware of was the rapid beating of his heart. The second was the whisper: "Greg-oh-Ree! Greg-oh-Ree! GREG-OH-REE!"

Greg began to whimper, although he didn't know he was making any sound. Cynthia was no longer lying next to him, prepared to "save" him.

The Cubans had on long coats this time. They wore slouched fedora hats with brims--like characters from an old Humphrey Bogart movie, their faces shrouded by the brims of the fedoras. Greg could not pinpoint the exact location where the men were standing. It looked like a street from a movie set. The shadowy streetlamp cast a dim light on the sinister figures clad in long coats. The Cubans were about twenty yards away. There were three of them. They were no longer running after him, guns blazing, but the long coats--dusters like cowboys wore in the old west…might be hiding those long guns. Mainly, Greg heard the men whispering. It grew louder. And Louder. And LOUDER!

Greg-oh-Ree! Greg-oh-Ree! GREG-OH-REE!

The sound of their voices was just as frightening as the unexpected shooting in the cafeteria that first night. It was unclear what they intended to do with him when or if they caught him, but it was quite clear that they wanted HIM. Not Brad Clemens. Not Stan Sanchez. HIM.

Greg grew frantic, suffering a full-blown panic attack. He woke in a cold sweat, heart racing. He rushed for the bathroom, where he promptly threw up what was left of last night's pizza.

Week Two

When Greg reached the plant for work on Monday, he was running on empty. His mind was foggy. His body ached. Once again, he avoided his office and took the long way around the plant that allowed him to avoid the cafeteria.

He decided to spend his time on the floor with the workers he was supposed to be supervising. It had been uneventful there, so far, and he really didn't want a return visit from the Cuban Killers, stalking him in the locations they'd already visited.

Greg stopped near Stan Sanchez's workstation, pulling his monogrammed handkerchief out of his back pocket to wipe his brow. Greg was old-fashioned in that he used a cloth handkerchief instead of Kleenex. It was a habit he attributed to his father, who had been a plant engineer running time studies in the old days, when a slide rule was the name of the game. In fact, some of Greg's monogrammed handkerchiefs (*GKC, Gregory Kevin Chandler*) had been his late father's (*George Kevin Chandler*).

"Hey, Greg!" Stan Sanchez called out.

Greg walked over closer to the burly man, so he could hear him over the din of production in the huge plant.

"Remember when I told you the cage was acting up?"

"Right. The safety cage for the jackhammer. You said it was erratic in its response time...right?"

Greg was mentally patting himself on the back that he had remembered anything at all from the Friday last week when he and Stan had spoken. He found himself having more and more difficulty with simple tasks of daily life. His nerves were frayed. Even something as elementary as knowing how he had cut his ear in the night eluded his failing memory. Lack of sleep was taking its toll.

"Let me take a look at it, Stan," Greg said, climbing up to Stan's perch, where Stan operated the gigantic jackhammer from a raised operator's platform.

Stan stepped aside. Greg climbed up three steps to join him at the controls of the huge machine, a jackhammer large enough and strong enough to smash molten metal into combine parts.

Greg examined the controls. He hadn't touched one of these things for at least fifteen years, back when he worked on the line, before he worked his way up to floor Supervisor.

He pushed the button with his right forefinger. Nothing.

"You have to push each one separately, Boss," Stan reminded him, "One with each hand." Stan was surprised that his superior did not seem to have much of a grasp of how to operate the machine. Everyone knew that Greg had worked at the plant all through high school and had gone to work there full-time as soon as he graduated from college at twenty-one. Gregory Chandler was widely viewed as knowledgeable and likeable, a second-generation engineer of the "Nothing runs like a Deere" culture.

"Oh. Right...First one button. Then the other...right?"

"Right," said Stan, relieved that Greg *now* seemed to know what he was doing.

Stan knew nothing of the fog of fatigue plaguing Greg for over a week now.

This was not a machine to fool around with. If it came down on you, it would definitely kill you. That was the purpose of the security cage: to prevent such deaths. It was also the purpose of the two buttons that had to be pushed individually with each separate hand in a pre-programmed sequence.

"So, what's it been doing?" Greg asked.

"Like I told you last Friday: it comes down slow or fast. Off-tempo. And now it isn't coming down at all." Exasperation was evident in Stan's voice.

Greg made a move to step onto the platform, the spot where the jackhammer would come down when it was operating properly.

"I don't think I'd do that, Boss," Stan said, uneasily.

Greg just looked at him blandly. Dully. Exhaustion showed on his face. He said, "Why not?"

At that precise moment, the recalcitrant machine crashed downwards to the exact spot where Gregory Chandler stood, crushing him instantly in a messy and horrifying display of brute machine power. It shocked everyone. The accident brought production on the line in the plant to a standstill (a Major No-No) as everyone on the floor rushed to the accident site.

Greg's bloody handkerchief, now stained red, lay relatively unscathed in the midst of the carnage, atop what had once been a human body…a small square of cloth, soaked red but still neatly folded atop a horrifying red mound of humanity.

All hell broke loose.

***

Hours later, when Stan Sanchez was, once again, explaining to the authorities how this floor death during work hours had occurred (a Huge No-No), voice cracking with emotion, tension running high, Stan said, "The rhythm was off. If you are on that spot when the jackhammer comes down, God help you! It'll kill you instantly. I feel so bad. Greg was a great guy." Stan paused, took a deep breath and added, "I thought he knew what he was doing; it just happened so fast. I tried to warn him. If the tempo of the jackhammer is off and you get into the stamping zone while the cage is up…if the safety cage is off-rhythm, it's going to get you." Stan was very upset. His Cuban accent…diminished after years of living in the United States…crept in as he relived the horror of the moment, saying, over and over again, " I feel like I should have done something more. It just happened so fast. It was over so quick!" His voice had a plaintive quality. He was obviously traumatized, as was everyone who had witnessed the accident and come running to the scene. (*There, but for the grace of God, go I…*)

Everyone, except OSHA (Occupational Safety and Health Administration), agreed that Gregory Chandler's death was a damned shame, but it wasn't anyone's fault but his own.

Deere was fined half a million dollars for the faulty cage apparatus by OSHA, a large portion of which went to Cynthia Chandler and her twin sons. The three were inconsolable at the funeral. The teen-aged boys had to literally hold Cynthia up at Greg's grave site. Rumors flew that Cynthia couldn't sleep…kept having a recurring nightmare. She was a basket case. The high school hired a temporary substitute teacher to take over her English classes; she wasn't capable of taking care of herself, let alone teaching.

Seemingly still in shock from the news of her husband's tragic death, Cynthia half-muttered something puzzling to Stan Sanchez after the funeral, back at the Chandler house after the burial. Stan was, once again, expressing his tremendous regret and remorse for not being able to stop Greg…not being able to save him. This had been an ongoing refrain from Stan since the day of the accident.

"I'm never going to be able to listen to that song again," Cynthia interrupted. She punctuated the curt remark by downing a pill, washed down with a big gulp of Chardonnay. Swaying slightly, she slowly crossed the room, walking away from Stan mid-sentence.

Stan…puzzled…didn't ask, "What song?" Curious, he wanted to ask, but Cynthia wasn't herself. Plus, she was gone as soon as she articulated the thought. Cynthia wasn't really making sense. She wasn't sleeping. Doped up with tranquilizers, leaning heavily, physically and emotionally, on her teen-aged sons, she seemed helpless and, strangely enough, guilt-stricken.

Stan Sanchez also felt tremendous guilt that Greg had died at *his* workstation. Stan had worked the hammer for two decades without incident. To tell the truth, Stan kept thinking, *that jackhammer's rhythm was 'off' for at least two weeks before Greg took a look at it. That could have been ME!*

The lingering vision of what remained of Greg Chandler after the jackhammer crushed his body kept Stan up that night.

And the next night.

And the night after that.

Stan just kept thinking of the consequences of human failure when operating dangerous machinery. Pilot error. With every nightmare, Stan lost more sleep. He experienced bad dreams, a victim of post-traumatic stress disorder.

At night he kept thinking: *The rhythm---if it's off---it's going to get you.*

***

Stan Sanchez' retirement party is next week, six months to the day the line shut down to scrape what was left of Gregory Chandler into a receptacle for his grieving widow.

Cynthia Chandler, his wife, now institutionalized for treatment, won't be attending.

5
COULROPHOBIA

FEAR OF CLOWNS

MICHAEL KOOGLER

A Quarter To Five

It was coming for him again. It was coming and he was powerless to stop it. Like before, he wanted to run, but he was never able to, and this time would be no different. Lying helplessly on the filthy and blood-stained mattress, he was bound with duct tape, his hands and feet wrapped tightly, as if enfolded in the sticky web of some monstrous spider that meant to feed on him. It would come to him with its teeth. And its claws. And the knife.

Always the knife.

And he could never escape it.

As before, he heard the plodding footsteps in the hall and his blood froze in his veins. It was almost here, and the end was always the same. The footsteps. The creaking of the door as it opened. The appearance of the monster. And his siren scream as the nightmare began to use the knife.

Another sound caught his attention and he turned his eyes toward the bathroom doorway, frightened beyond belief. Even as the door to the hall began to creak open to reveal the creature, another monster was already there, stepping into the room from the darkness of the toilet. It looked at him, its black fathomless eyes drinking in his terror. It lifted the long, gleaming knife and began to shuffle toward him.

The doorway to the hall opened wide and the monster stepped into the room, focusing its eyes on him just as the other one did. He wanted to scream, but nothing came out. Something had changed. Countless times before, it had come at him from the hall. Only the hall.

Now there were two.

And they both had knives.

As the abominations slowly approached him, the dirty window across from the bed slowly lifted, scraping upward on the rotted wooden frame. As his growing horror plunged him deeper into madness, he could see another creature's ghoulish face leering at him from outside. The knife, held in a clawed hand, pushed into the room first, the creature slowly following it in.

Three.

He heard a hard scrabbling sound beneath him and a ghoulish hand slithered out from under the bed. It reached up, clawing at the bed, slowly pulling itself out from underneath the mattress, desperate to bleed him like the others. The other hand emerged, its hideous fingers wrapped tightly around the handle of a knife.

Four.

The closet door, covered by a large tattered poster of a circus tent with happy, juggling clowns and soaring acrobats, slowly slid open, revealing the hideousness of the monster within. It stepped out, the knife held before it, its horrible teeth dripping red.

Five.

***

Devon Marler suddenly awoke, his silent scream of terror dying on his lips, the memory of the approaching horrors tattooed on the inside of his eyelids. They were there for him to see forever, no matter how tightly he shut his eyes.

Taking deep gulping breaths, he fought to slow his pulse, to regain his sanity, to embrace reality. He called up the mental checklist he had started using to combat the growing nightmares, something his psychiatrist, Dr. Staum, had taught him. He was back in his own bed, his wife sleeping beside him. Check. The clock showed a quarter to five. Check. He was awake. Check. He was safe from the nightmare. Check. The monster was gone. Check...er, no. Not just a monster. Monsters. Plural.

What did that mean?

It took him longer to calm himself this time, but who could blame him? All the other times he had the nightmare, there had been only one. This time?

There had been five.

He lay in bed for another hour before finally forcing himself to get up. He probably should have risen earlier. There was never any chance of him getting back to sleep after the nightmare. He always awoke at a quarter to five. Even if he set his alarm earlier, he would always fall back asleep and wake at a quarter to five. It was always the same.

A quarter to five was when he died.

Three hours later, Devon was in the kitchen, his thoughts scattered as he drank down the last of his orange juice. He stood up from the breakfast table, his hand shaking at the prospect of what the day intended for him, as well as the lingering terror of last night's dream. He was trembling so badly, the glass slipped from his hand as he was about to set it in the sink. It clinked loudly against the metal side, but thankfully didn't break.

"You know, you don't have to do this, babe," Michelle Marler said, as she struggled to get the little squirming animal that was strapped into her high chair, to eat her oatmeal. The feisty seven-month-old only shook her head back and forth, squealing with laughter, oblivious to her father's consuming dread.

"I need to do something, 'Chelle," he said helplessly, swallowing his nervousness and forcing a half smile. He bent and kissed his wife, then leaned over to plant one on his daughter's forehead. The baby immediately reached for him with oatmeal-covered hands, but Devon slipped away from her grasp. The baby chattered happily, thinking it a wonderful game.

"I still say we should've gotten a dog," he said with a better grin this time, pushing his fear to the back of his mind, where it lay quietly festering. Seeing his wife's look of disdain, he added, "Just kidding, babe. You know that." He leaned in and kissed her again and then turned away.

"What if it doesn't work?" she called out to him, voicing her own fears. Chelle Marler knew why her husband was agreeing to the radical new treatment. She just didn't agree with it at all. Had she known what he was truly getting ready to do today, she would have zip-tied him down and started her own therapy on him.

"Look, it'll work," Devon said shortly, but he was no longer certain of anything. "It has to," he added quietly. His wife didn't know exactly what today's phase of the treatment was going to be and he was fairly certain that if she did, she would blow a gasket. But he needed the treatment; needed relief from the constant nightmarish reliving of what happened to him in the past. He needed to sleep past a quarter to five.

And of course, they could use the money. Being a test subject for a radically new and potentially dangerous psychiatric treatment had its monetary advantages that would amount to five digits on the left side of the decimal point. "And it's just for a day. I'll be home tomorrow, noon at the latest. I swear."

Chelle handed the baby the oatmeal spoon and stood up to face him. As Bree immediately began smacking her new toy into the bowl, splashing oatmeal everywhere, Chelle put her arms around her husband and pulled him close. "You know that I want nothing more than for these dreams to go away and for the past to stay in the past," she said softly. "But virtual reality? Forcing you to face your fears in what amounts to a real world setting? Babe, your dreams have been worse than ever these past four weeks, ever since you started this treatment."

"Dr. Staum says that's normal," he argued half-heartedly, trying to back down her concern. "The treatment has brought everything to the surface, ready to be faced and purged one final time." But even as he defended it, he knew she was right.

Since he had started on the VR treatment, which put him in a virtual world with his terror, his nightmares had increased in intensity, and even his waking hours now had him sensing the monster lurking somewhere nearby. That had never happened before. And what was up with last night's fright-fest and multiple copies of the creature?

Yet, even though she was right, he still couldn't agree with her. Not yet anyway. Not when today's treatment had the potential to completely banish the demon once and for all; when a quarter to five would come and go and he would sleep blissfully beyond it. If today's treatment worked, according to Dr. Staum, he would finally be free of the thing that had plagued him since childhood. He would finally be able to exist without the ever-present specter of his nightmare looming over him.

He would finally be able to sleep past a quarter to five.

"This is it," he added. "Last treatment. They said that today's the breakthrough day. If it works, I'm cured. If it doesn't, then I'll find another way to deal with it."

She kissed him and pulled him close. "Promise me."

"Last one, Scout's honor," he agreed, kissing her back. Then he nodded toward Bree, who was happily offering her oatmeal-covered hands to Granger, their golden retriever. The big dog was licking as fast as she could dip her hands back in the oatmeal bowl. "Good luck, babe," he smiled and then turned away. "Kiss the munchkin for me!"

The last thing he heard as he slipped out the door was Chelle telling Granger to go outside and play.

***

Devon tried to stretch out in the patient chair, but he was too keyed up to get comfortable. Instead, he sighed for what had to be the hundredth time and looked back to the ceiling above him. The room he was in was not like the VR room he had been in during his past sessions. That room had been full of video monitors, surround-sound speakers, and a wide array of technical equipment, most of which he had never seen or heard of before. The VR room was designed to immerse him completely in his phobia and fuel his terror enough to push him to the brink of madness.

But this room was different…different in that it was almost empty. Except for the chair he was seated in and a padded doctor's stool nearby, the room was starkly bare. White metal walls and floor, marred only by small cameras mounted on the ceiling at each corner of the room, were the extent of the room's décor.

He'd been alone for almost an hour now, reclining in the

chair, an IV bag hanging on a hook above him, administering the solution contained within. As he looked at the milky gray liquid in the bag, now nearly three quarters empty, he shook his head, wondering not for the first time, why he had finally agreed to do this. Including his time in the chair, he'd been at the clinic now for upwards of three hours, having run through a battery of tests to make certain he was prepped accordingly. But all during that time, he had yet to see Dr. Staum, and the doctor's absence had fueled his questions and his lack of understanding about what was going to happen today.

During previous sessions, the doctor had told him, mostly in generalities, what to expect out of today's particular treatment. Other than the fact that today's appointment would positively be the last one, Dr. Staum had told Devon that it would be very intense, much more than his previous sessions. But most importantly, it was guaranteed to succeed. When Devon Marler walked out of the clinic today, he would finally be free from the terror that had stalked him for years. That was enough for him to overcome his nervousness.

Mostly.

He looked again at the armrests of the chair and briefly wondered at the three thick Velcro straps attached to each arm support. At the moment, they were not being used. The nurse that had cheerfully set him up with the IV had done nothing to immobilize him and hadn't bothered to explain what their function would be in the session. He wondered if they would strap him down for the procedure. Could it be that intense?

At that moment, the door opened and a short and pudgy bespectacled man walked in. Dr. Henry Staum was as serious as anyone Devon had ever known. The man was also thorough and complete, if he was anything. Over the weeks that Devon had been undergoing Staum's VR psychiatric treatment, the doctor had carefully explained everything that had been going on, including the official diagnosis, and recommended treatment options for Devon's phobia. The only thing Staum hadn't gone into depth about, was what was going to happen during today's final session. For that, because of proprietary agreements on what amounted to a brand new and highly secretive technology, Devon had agreed only to the barest of information and that golden promise of being fully cured when it was all over. All he had to do on his end was be willing to undergo the final session and show up for it, at which time he would be told everything and also be well-paid for his trouble.

That time had finally come and Devon was more than a little nervous.

"Good afternoon, Mr. Marler," Dr. Staum said as he entered the room, his normally monotone voice showing the barest hint of excitement.

That was new. Devon's thoughts slithered back to the nightmare and the five monsters, but he quickly tamped it down and concentrated on the doctor. "Morning, Doc," he replied, feeling the apprehension gnaw quietly at his insides. "So, this is it, right? We're really gonna do this?"

"Yes, Devon, this is it," Staum said, pulling the stethoscope from his neck and placing it on the crook of Devon's arm. He quickly inflated the blood pressure cuff the nurse had left in place and then listened silently for some seconds. "Your blood pressure is slightly elevated," he added, looking at the reading. "143 over 86. But it's well within operating parameters and not unprecedented. After all, this procedure has never been attempted before. I'm sure you may be a little anxious and probably have some questions about it."

"Sure do, Doc," Devon began. "Since I'm here, can you finally tell me more about the whole thing? I mean, VR was one thing, but you kept telling me that this is deeper. How?"

"You have signed all the proper forms, so I can indeed divulge more of the procedure now," Staum answered importantly. "When we last met and you agreed to this final step, I told you that it was a medical procedure designed to force you to face your fears in a wholly new and unique way."

"Yeah, but what exactly will it do? That's what I've been dyin' to know."

"In layman's terms, we will force you to become that what you fear most," Staum replied, patting his hand and offering what Devon thought was the first smile he had ever seen the man give. "Out of the virtual world and into the real world."

"How will you do that?" Devon questioned, feeling somewhat confused. "Do you dress me up or something?"

"In a matter of speaking," Staum said, smiling again as he unwound the cuff and shoved it into one of the pockets in his white lab coat. The stethoscope went back around his neck. "In your earlier treatments, you were forced to become a virtual representation of your fear," he went on. "We forced you to face that fear, as that fear, in a virtual environment. It is quite the revolutionary concept and has seen unparalleled success in treating phobias in a number of clinics now in the United States and around the world."

"And this?"

"We are breaking new ground today, Devon," Staum said, continuing to smile. The man was obviously excited about what they were doing and Devon felt himself go slightly cold at that thought, particular from a man who had been stoic during every other visit and treatment. "What this new treatment will do for you," Staum went on, "will take virtual reality and bring it into the real world. Today, you will experience your phobia as that phobia, but it will be real this time instead of VR."

"Real," Devon repeated, feeling his hands go numb.

"Yes, as real as it gets. You will physically become your fear and you will do so in the real world."

"You're going to really turn me into that monster?" Devon asked, feeling his blood pressure begin to rise. He silently wondered about the other four that had joined it in last night's dream, but he didn't voice his fear.

"Now, Devon," Staum assured him. "Take a deep breath. Remember what we have talked about before in all your other sessions. It wasn't a monster, at least not in a physical sense. It was a man--just a man that dressed the part to play on people's fears."

"Just a man," Devon repeated, trying unsuccessfully to convince himself. He had seen it. Regardless of what the police had said when it happened, he knew it was more than just a man, more than what Dr. Staum was claiming it was.

"Just a man," Staum nodded, pleased at how quickly his patient had settled down. Some of that had to do with the solution being injected into his veins, laced with a mild sedative to keep him calm. But he knew that would change once they ramped up what was now inside him.

"Then how come you can't just dress me up?" Devon asked. "Wouldn't it be easier to give me a makeup job and put me in some funny clothes?"

"Playing dress-up would be ineffective for several reasons, Devon," the doctor answered. "The biggest issue is that, even with makeup, you'll know it's fake. Your mind will know it isn't real, that you aren't real. It would be no different than an actor acting out the part in a play or a movie. It might be an intense experience, but it would still not be real. Deep down, you would know that." Staum walked around the other side of the chair, more animated than Devon had seen him in the past. "This procedure," the doctor went on, "makes it completely real. There is no makeup or costumes here; just real changes to your body. You quite literally become him."

Staum reached for Devon's carotid and checked his pulse, then looked at the IV insertion point, as he continued. "You fear this thing in your head, Devon, but no amount of Hollywood work could create that which is in your mind, no matter how carefully you explained it to me. This procedure makes it so you don't have to."

"Then how are you going to do it?" Devon asked, fearing what was to come. He knew he had to face his demon. He knew that he had to become the monster to finally be rid of it. That much, Staum had assured him of.

Staum reached over and engaged the first strap, pinning Devon's right wrist to the armrest. "Mr. Marler," he asked easily while he worked, "do you know what a nanite is?"

For a moment, Devon was silent, letting his mind sift through the things he'd heard about nanites. He wasn't much of a technical guy. Making a living as a carpenter…and a good one, at that…had kept him away from science and other technical advances. But nanites…he had heard about, at least a little. Chelle would know a lot more, but she wasn't here. "Aren't they little machines?" he answered.

"Yes," Staum nodded, tightening down the strap on his left wrist. He had done it so inconspicuously that Devon hadn't realized it until the doctor was working on the second set of straps, further immobilizing him. "Nanites are microscopic machines, programmable in any number of ways. They represent the key to so many discoveries for mankind, helping us heal the mind and body. In time, not to sound too grand in my optimism, they will likely even lead us to eternal life."

"I don't get it," Devon shook his head.

"Imagine having your body full of these machines, floating along in your bloodstream. You would never even know they were there, but they could effectively repair every injury, remove any disease, and basically keep your body in perfect and flawless condition."

"So, you wouldn't get sick or hurt or anything?" Devon asked, watching the doctor tighten down the last strap and then reach into his pocket and pull out a capped syringe.

"Mostly correct," Staum answered. "Oh, you could still get hurt, but if it wasn't a catastrophic injury, the nanites could repair the damage quickly. You might still get sick. You could even get cancer. But the nanites in your body could eradicate diseases, too. It's really quite an amazing technological breakthrough."

"And you're using them to help me?"

"Indeed," Staum answered with a smile, expertly tapping the syringe, preparing it for use.

"What's that?"

"This," Staum said, holding up the hypodermic, "is the catalyst. What we have been putting into your body for the past hour is a full matrix of nanites. Those nanites will be the building blocks of helping you face your fears. They will help you heal your mind, on both a physical and mental level, Devon. That is what's so exciting about this process."

"But why the shot?" Devon asked fearfully. "I don't much like shots, Doc."

"You have coulrophobia, Mr. Marler, not trypanophobia," the doctor answered with a touch of scorn. "It's just a needle, and I will inject this into your IV line, not your arm," he went on, doing exactly that as he spoke. "This solution will activate the matrix and allow us to manipulate it to achieve the desired effect. You will begin to feel warm inside, perhaps even hot. But it's completely harmless, so don't worry."

"Yeah…whoa," Devon said, feeling a flush of heat flood throughout his body. He tried flexing his arms, but the Velcro straps held him tightly down.

"What you are feeling is the activation of the nanites," Staum said. "The feeling of being hot will pass after about an hour, when the matrix will shut down."

"So, it won't last long?"

"Not long at all," Staum answered and then stood up. "It will last just long enough for us to complete the session. Once complete, the nanites will become dormant and eventually, your body will break them down and absorb them. You'll never even know they were a part of you." Staum paused briefly and looked at Devon. "Now, let us begin."

"But what if…"

Staum raised a hand and cut him off. "No more questions, Mr. Marler. The time has come to face your fear." The doctor reached into his pocket and withdrew a device that looked like a fancy TV remote. Devon saw him press several buttons and suddenly, his world went dark.

Immediately a set of familiar eyes appeared in the darkness, reflecting back to him from some distance away. Then another. Then three. Four. Five.

Six.

The eyes drew closer and panic began to rise up within him, but just as suddenly, the fear drained away. The lights came back on and he realized he was no longer in the lab. He was in what looked like a kitchen. It was disgustingly filthy, with empty fast-food boxes and dirty dishes piled everywhere. Flies could be seen buzzing between piles of rotting food, and cockroaches were in abundance, scurrying everywhere. The smell was horrific.

Devon wanted to recoil and rush out of the room, but his body wouldn't respond. Instead, it was moving on its own. As he watched through his own eyes, he shuffled around the kitchen table, ignoring the putrid garbage heaped on top of it. He could hear sirens in the distance and felt himself moving toward the kitchen counter. As the sirens grew louder, he pulled open one of the drawers and looked in. It was full of knives, each one clean, gleaming, and in pristine condition.

Taking a moment to scan the large collection, he selected one and pulled it out. It was a long-bladed butcher knife, the kind made famous when Michael Myers was chasing Jamie Lee Curtis around the house in the original Halloween movie. Ignoring his growing apprehension at the sirens, he carefully shut the drawer and walked through the kitchen and into the living room.

The living room wasn't much better than the kitchen. The room was filled with empty pizza boxes and fast food wrappers, buzzing flies, and crawling with cockroaches. He kicked aside a sack of garbage, sending rotted food, insects, and other putrefying items across the room, and began to mount the stairs leading to the bedroom. It dawned on him that he somehow knew the bedroom was his destination, that his victim was there waiting for him.

The top of the landing opened into a hall, with two bedrooms on one side and a bedroom and bathroom on the other. The end of the hall held a dirty and cracked floor-length mirror, and as he walked toward the rear bedroom, the mirror reflected his image back to him.

Inside his non-responding body, Devon Marler saw what he was and time seemed to freeze long enough for him to truly witness his own horrifying self. Many people in the world feared clowns, the very essence of coulrophobia. They feared Bozo and Ronald McDonald and Clarabell and the various clowns at the circus. But they were just clowns; people dressed up in bright colors and weird wigs under a whole lot of makeup. What many truly feared was the sensationalism of Hollywood and its plethora of terrifying depictions of clowns. That was what he was. And what he had become transcended simple fear and bore his psyche right into outright horror.

His face was made up like a clown, but the makeup was blood red and muddy brown. He knew immediately that the coloring was actual blood, some of it fresh and some of it old and crusty. His clown nose, a dirty red ball of foam, was pressed into a nasal cavity that was missing the actual nose. It was just a rotting hole eaten into his head by something. But in the hole, the foam had been shoved, giving it a misshapen appearance. His eyes were two glittering black orbs, surrounded by smears of bright red blood. They were piercing and deep, enough to drill straight into a person's very soul. But it was his mouth that riveted him, freezing his blood in terror. Oversized, it was filled with jagged teeth, each of them long and sharp. All of them were yellowed, where they weren't smeared with blood and other bits of gore.

Devon wanted to scream in terror at his visage, but his voice was frozen in his throat as he walked toward the mirror. He turned to face the door, giving him respite from the nightmarish image of what he had become. The sirens were right outside the house now and he could hear men shouting as he slowly twisted the handle on the door. He pushed it open and stepped into the room.

Where the rest of the house was filled with trash and rotting garbage, this room had only a ragged bed, covered with a blood-stained sheet. All atop the bed where numerous balloon animals, all shapes, colors, and sizes--animals he had created. A young boy, bound hand and foot with duct tape, cowered on the bed amidst the balloons, whimpering up at him as he approached. The boy was all too familiar to him. The boy was him. He was the victim, just as he was the monster. It was happening again, just like it had happened when he was nine.

On the bed, his childhood-self began to scream as he raised the knife. Inside his monster's body, his adult-self screamed right along with him. Through the monster's eyes, he watched the knife raise high and then plunge downward. His younger self abruptly stopped screaming.

Leaving the knife embedded in place, he began reaching for his child-self with clawed hands. It was time to make another balloon animal. Maybe he would make a lion this time. Behind him, there was a loud crash and he was suddenly assailed with thunderous booms. His body jerked spasmodically as invisible hammers began smashing into him. Pain bloomed behind his black eyes and his head tilted toward the old clock hanging on the wall near the closet.

It was a quarter to five.

And then a new scream pierced his ears. It was a high-pitched shriek of agony and terror, dissimilar to screams of his past victims-- children he had heard so many times before. No, this was the shriek of a man. His vision began to clear and the room came back into view…but he was no longer in the bedroom. This room was sparse, with white metal walls. It was almost completely bare, with only a large doctor's chair and a small stool as furnishings.

There was something familiar about the room and the chair, like he should be sitting in it. But his mind was muddled, almost as if he was adrift in a sea of black, and his thoughts quickly scattered. But his eyes saw clearly. And his ears heard perfectly.

A man was kneeling before him, a white-coated lab technician, screaming in unholy agony. At the moment, Devon was busy twisting the man's arm into a grotesque representation of a balloon animal--a lion, it looked like. But it might have been a dog. He wasn't sure. What he was certain about was the sound of the man's screams and the popping crack of bone as he mangled the man's arm.

All around him were other white-coated men, all of them shouting in panic, trying to pull the injured man away from him.

"Put him under!" a voice rang out over the chaos. "Put him

under now!"

Devon thought he recognized the voice, but like before, his thoughts slid back under the murk. As men swarmed around him, grabbing at his arms and sticking sharp objects into him, he continued to entertain as only he knew how. He reached for the man's face, digging long dirty claws into his nose, thinking about how much the children loved the game of, "I've got your nose." The mutilated man fell into garbled sobs as he tore the soft flesh away, opening up the nasal cavity.

"I've got...your nose," he said, his voice sounding like someone dragging rocks along the bottom of a pool.

He reached for the man's other arm, blood dripping from his fingers. Thinking he might make a giraffe this time--the kiddies loved giraffes...his own limbs suddenly began to feel heavy.

"More!" the voice shouted again. "We need to shut him down! We need to shut him down now!"

Blackness began to fill his vision and he tottered sideways.

"In the chair! Put him in the chair!"

The last thing Devon Marler remembered was falling backward. He landed hard in the chair and a moment later, he knew nothing more.

***

Dr. Henry Staum looked at the man, watching in amazement as the features of the horrible monster from just moments ago began changing back to those of his troubled patient. Behind him, one of his assistants was busy trying to staunch the flow of blood from the noseless technician, who was still wailing pitiably. Another lab tech was looking helplessly at the horribly broken arm, snapped in over a dozen places.

One of the senior doctors on the project stepped next to him, his eyes riveted on the now peacefully sleeping subject. "That wasn't a man, Henry," the doctor said softly, his voice almost a whisper. "That was something else. This is a catastrophic failure!"

"On the contrary, I think it was an astounding success, Joseph," Staum said calmly, his eyes still fastened on the sleeping patient. Devon Marler was himself again. The only difference from the man he had originally put under was that the man in the chair was

108

now spattered with blood and bits of flesh that hung from his now-normal fingers.

"Success?" the other doctor exclaimed loudly. Dr. Joseph Hiroto was a Japanese national, one of the very few people entrusted to work at this level on Staum's project. Hiroto had been with Staum from nearly the beginning, but even though he had knowledge of almost everything to do with the project, he had always thought there was more to it. Staum's uncanny calm only confirmed that for him. "This was supposed to turn him into a representation of the criminal that had abducted him, Henry! It was supposed to help him face his fear! You turned him into a monster!"

"He was turned into what he fears, Joseph," Staum assured him. "Nothing more. The procedure worked perfectly."

"I've seen his file, Henry," Hiroto went on angrily. "I've studied the police reports and everything we know about what happened. Arthur Dade was a man, just a man! He was a serial killer, a sick and twisted psychopath that hunted children, but he was still a man! He was shot to death by police after stabbing nine-year-old Devon Marler in the head, injuring him badly enough that Marler died on the way to the hospital and had to be resuscitated. There was nothing monstrous about the man beyond his actions."

"And you don't think that makes a man into a monster?"

"Did that look human to you?" Hiroto exclaimed. "That wasn't a man acting monstrously. That was a monster! That was a nightmare brought to life! This isn't what we were charged with accomplishing, Henry!"

"Now you listen to me, Joseph," Staum said, his own eyes blazing with anger. Grabbing the man by the arm, he steered him away from the carnage on the floor, his voice lowering. "You are as much a part of this project as I am and you know, as well as I do, that they want the monster in Devon Marler's head. They couldn't care less about Arthur Dade, the serial killer. They want Arthur Dade, the clown monster as seen through the eyes of a nine-year-old child!"

"And you condone this...this abomination?"

"What Mr. Marler projected is so much more than we could have ever hoped for," Staum answered. "Don't you see? We created something based on a dream, based on what his mind projected. Do you have any idea how deeply seated coulrophobia is in a person, particularly someone like Devon Marler? He created that monster,

Joseph. We merely pulled it out of his head."

"But why?" Hiroto asked helplessly. "Why create something so horrible?"

"To heal him."

"By turning him into a monster?"

"I see only a man seated before you who is sound asleep," Staum said calmly, nodding his head in the direction of the slumbering patient. The tragedy on the floor behind him was already forgotten, the success of the experiment beyond even his highest expectations. The general would be extremely pleased. "The man inside Mr. Marler's head was more terrifying than we had originally believed," he went on, "but it was a man none-the-less. We simply saw Devon Marler become that which has plagued him for years."

"This is wrong," Hiroto said, his voice cracking. "I can't be a part of this."

"You already are, Joseph," Staum warned him, "and you're long past the point of turning back."

Dr. Hiroto stared at his associate, hating what had just happened; hating Henry Staum for what he created. "Be honest with me, Henry," he finally said after a long pause. "Through all your sessions with Mr. Marler, did you ever expect this?"

"No, I expected something a little less Hollywood, if you want the truth," Staum replied with a shrug. "But regardless of what Mr. Marler metamorphosed into, the test was a success. It works, Joseph. The project works. We should be celebrating, not pouting."

"At the expense of that?" Hiroto said acidly, pointing back at the grievously wounded tech.

"Unfortunate, to be sure," Staum said without a trace of concern. "But nothing more than an accident."

"Is that what you'll tell them? That it was just an accident?"

"I'll tell them the truth, Joseph," Staum answered, then turned his eyes toward the observation window in the far wall. "Is there anyone else in the observation room?"

"No," Hiroto sighed, shaking his head. "It's just the five of us. When the project...when Marler went off the rails, standard safety protocol shut down all communication in and out of the lab and locked down the floor. We're quietly waiting for you to make the call and stand down the emergency."

"Excellent," Staum said, pulling out his cell phone. "I'll

inform the general." He turned toward the door, only to have Hiroto grab him by the arm and spin him back around.

"Henry, what are you doing?" Hiroto snapped. "We need to get Selken to the hospital! You need to give the all-clear so we can get him out. You can call the general later."

Staum glared at Hiroto, his gaze icy hard. It was enough for his partner to release his arm. "Stabilize Selken as best you can for the moment," Staum finally said, his voice betraying no emotion. "I will have a team on site in ten minutes to deal with what happened and take charge of our injured associate." He started to walk toward the door, but paused to look back. "Oh, and you might want to strap Mr. Marler back into his chair, too," he said coldly, holding up the remote with his other hand. "It would be terrible if he were to suddenly revert to his maniacal state." Leaving the threat unspoken, Staum exited the room, leaving Hiroto to quickly comply and do his best to calm his colleagues from the nightmare that had come to life.

***

Devon Marler sighed, stretched, and opened his eyes. Outside, the birds were singing and he took a deep breath, breathing in the spring air. The clock on the wall said it was nearly 9:00. Shocked, he quickly sat up and rolled his legs off the bed, planting his feet on the carpet. How had he slept so long? He hadn't slept past a quarter-to-five in years, ever since the nightmares began coming back.

The nightmares! A happy thought assailed him and he smiled. He didn't have a nightmare last night!

"Honey!" he shouted, standing up and running to the mirror. The handsome image of Devon Marler stared back at him, a lopsided grin on his face. His eyes still looked hollow, but not nearly as bad as before. He actually looked rested for once. Even better, he felt rested for the first time in months.

"Honey!" he shouted again, throwing open the bedroom door and hurrying into the hall. His wife did not answer his call. Puzzled, he poked his head into Bree's room. Her crib was empty. He checked the other rooms and then hurried downstairs. Chelle and Bree were nowhere to be found. He walked outside, looking around. The sun was out and the air was warm, but they weren't in the yard, either. But the car was still in the driveway.

Puzzled, he walked back in the house and into the kitchen. That's when he saw it. Fear growing coldly within his belly, he looked at the basement door. Four long gashes were clearly visible in the wood, as if someone or something had dragged sharpened knives across the wood. Knives.

Or fingernails.

His heart beating hard in his chest, he slowly pushed open the door and looked down into the blackness of the basement. Reaching for the wall, he switched on the light. The basement light flared to life for a moment and then with the pop of a burning filament, it went out.

That's when he heard it. Something was moving in the darkness. Something was down there.

Grabbing a flashlight from the kitchen junk drawer, he switched it on and began descending the wooden steps, each step an eternity of growing fear. He heard nothing more. Step by agonizing step, he reached the bottom and walked slowly into the main room, sweeping the light back and forth. He didn't have to search long.

Chelle was lying in the middle of the main room, her eyes open and unseeing. Her nose was missing, just a ragged and bloody hole in her face. Her arms and legs were mangled, broken and twisted into macabre shapes.

The sound came again, a horrible bubbling noise as the creature slid out of the darkness. The hellish clown stared at him through gleaming black orbs and cocked its ghastly head. Its forked tongue slid between a mouthful of jagged teeth as it rasped, "Welcome back to the circus, Devon. Do you like balloon animals?"

Devon Marler began to scream.

***

Thirteen weeks later, Dr. Henry Staum ushered the five military men down the long, antiseptic hall, going through not one, but two handprint and voiceprint activated steel doors. Inwardly, he was excited, although he kept his exterior cool and icy, matching that of the men that had paid him a lot of money to complete the project. This was the big reveal; the day he could show them what he had created; the day he would cement his legacy as the world's foremost researcher into nanite weapon technology. What the military did with it after today, he didn't care. This was the pinnacle. He was done. And he longed to leave it far behind.

They stepped into a room with a long glass plate comprising one wall. Large video monitors were on the walls next to it, each with in-wall control panels. Looking beyond the huge window into the next room, the men had to pause to let their eyes adjust. There were no direct lights, the only illumination provided by the soft white disks imbedded in the steel walls beyond the viewing window.

"Why is it so dark?" one of the visitors asked, a two star general by the stars on his army uniform.

"The subject is light sensitive," Staum explained, knowing the question would be among the first. "Full sunlight or direct artificial light will drive the biological process into dormancy."

"Meaning what?"

"Meaning, we can talk with the man he once was under current illumination," Staum answered. "Full darkness allows the matrix to manifest fully and that person then vanishes into the creature. The matrix takes over and it becomes that which I created."

"Can light harm it?"

"Not that I have discovered. It only allows the subject to revert to his human form for a brief time."

"Let's see it," another man said, as he stepped forward. There were four stars on the shoulder of his uniform. He was General McCalister, the lead man on the project, who had recruited Staum and had helped the doctor over the years to get to the point they were at today. His vision of the perfect weapon was about to be revealed.

"You'll have to look closely," Staum said, shaking his head. "If I increase the strength of light in the room, he'll become more of the human part of him. This intensity is actually the optimal setting for viewing. It keeps him between metamorphosis...and in doing so, manageable."

They all stepped closer to the viewing window, looking inward. The room was completely bare and fairly dark, but not enough that they couldn't see the patient. The subject was in the center of the room, slumped in a ragged heap--if it could even be referred to as human anymore. A number of smaller misshapen lumps of what appeared to be organic material were scattered around

it.

"What's his story?" another man asked. He was the only one of the group not wearing a military uniform. Instead, he was in a black suit and immaculate tie. If the other men's countenances were cold, his was downright glacier-like. Staum didn't know his name, but he had met him several times over the years as the project progressed. A high-ranking member of a government black ops agency, Staum didn't like him at all.

"The subject's name is Devon Marler," he explained, addressing the group with his back to the viewing window. "Over the years, as we moved into VR testing of phobias with nearly a hundred possible test subjects, Mr. Marler was eventually chosen to be ground zero for the transformation phase."

"What was he afraid of?"

"He had coulrophobia," the doctor answered. "He had a particularly terrifying fear of clowns, due to his encounter as a child with Arthur Dade, the serial killer. We treated him with Virtual Reality to help bring his phobia into focus, before we moved on to the final phase to give birth to that fear."

"I've read your lab reports," the man went on, stepping up to the glass and peering closer at the thing within. "Am I to understand that he actually became a monster during the test?"

"After his release from our facility, Mr. Marler was arrested for the murder of his wife and the disappearance of his six-month-old daughter," Staum replied. "When he was arrested in his home with the body of his wife by his side, his mind had broken. He ranted to police unceasingly about a clown being the murderer. Considering the man's childhood abduction, where he had nearly become Arthur Dade's eleventh victim, the conventional thought was that he had become that which he had feared and killed his wife."

"Do you consider the project a failure then?"

"Not in the least," Staum replied haughtily. "While the death of Mr. Marler's wife is unfortunate, the final goal wasn't to see if we could actually cure Mr. Marler. It was to see if we could birth the monster that was in his head. We did that."

"And this thing still resides within him?"

"See for yourself." Staum indicated the room beyond the glass. "Devon," Staum said a little louder, looking at the heap of biological mass on the floor.

The thing moved at his voice, but didn't look up.

"Devon," he repeated. "Can you hear me?"

"Cir...cus," the thing said, its face hidden under an arm, its voice gravelly and difficult to understand. "Time...to go...to..."

"Devon," Staum said a bit more forcefully.

This time, the creature raised its head. Over the weeks, Henry Staum had stopped being outwardly shocked and horrified at the transformation, although he could never suppress the involuntary shudder that ran through him every time he looked upon his creation. Devon Marler was a hideous mutation, caught somewhere between the man he once was and the monster that had resided in his head. The five men in the room with Staum, however, were obviously not familiar with this level of horror, and four of them took involuntary steps back, amid shocked gasps.

The fifth, the man in the suit, stepped closer, his eyes riveted on the creature in the room. "Absolutely fascinating," he said. "I assume the secrecy on the project is fully intact? Your colleagues are accounted for?"

"Yes," Staum replied cryptically. What he left unspoken at the moment was that only Hiroto was still alive, and he was currently undergoing his own personal metamorphosis. He would shortly have to explain that, though, and he hoped that the group saw it as an added benefit.

"And the press surrounding Mr. Marler? I'm certain murdering his wife was high profile."

"Naturally, we took control of him immediately after his arrest. All references to him and what happened in that house were purged from public record and those first responders have been...reassigned," Staum said smugly. "The details of the murder have never been released and, despite the few persistent rumors still circulating, Devon Marler has already been largely forgotten by the short-attention-span crowd over the past three months."

"Excellent," the man said, then shifted his questioning. "Tell me, doctor, what happens if you shut the lights off?"

"As I said, he will fully manifest," Staum said hesitantly.

"Can we see it?"

"I would not recommend it," Staum said, and his voice involuntarily rose an octave. This was the one thing he did not want to happen. Not yet anyway. At least not while he was still here.

"Why not?"

"Because fully manifested, Devon Marler displays traits we cannot even begin to document yet. He...or it, becomes quite large and is extremely strong."

"How is that a threat to any of us?"

"This glass wall you are looking through is eight inches of hardened plasteel," Staum said. "It's the strongest transparent substance known to man."

"You didn't answer my question."

"I was getting to that," Staum answered coolly. "This is the second plasteel wall we've installed. Marler broke through the first one during a full-dark test. Several of my employees were...injured in that event."

The black-suited man turned and cast a wary glance at the doctor, before looking back to Marler. "You mentioned traits, doctor," he went on. "What other traits does the subject show?"

"Besides taking on the full appearance of Mr. Marler's fear, it has the ability to...well, how should I put this..."

"Please don't mince words, doctor. Tell me what it does."

"It has the ability to infect others," Staum shrugged. "It's almost as if it is trying to propagate itself."

"Explain."

Without a word, Staum turned to one of the walls and activated the monitor. He keyed in several commands and brought up a live-feed of a similar room. In it, huddled in the corner was another biological mess. What once was a man was now a hideous combination of man and clown, similar to Marler in that it was monstrous, but it had different markings, eyes, and hair. "That is Dr. Joseph Hiroto," Staum explained. "He was once my associate and one of my best scientists. He was mauled when Mr. Marler broke through the original barrier. He was gravely wounded, but thankfully, he was not killed. However, less than twenty-four hours after the attack, he became that," he said, pointing to the feed. "He is similar to Mr. Marler in appearance, but smaller, weaker, with a greater intolerance for light."

"And the others that were injured in the attack?"

"They were killed, I'm afraid."

"Where are their bodies?"

"Do you see those organic mounds in there with Mr.

Marler?" Staum answered, reaching back and tapping the glass of the enclosure. There was no reason to explain further.

The man nodded in understanding. "Tell me, does Dr. Hiroto exhibit the same abilities that Mr. Marler does?"

"Do you mean, can he create copies of himself?" Staum clarified, before answering the question without waiting for a reply. "The answer is yes."

"And you have proof?"

"We have tested his ability to infect others on four separate subjects," Staum answered. "He is every bit as communicable as Mr. Marler."

"So as long as we keep them in the light, we are reasonably safe."

"Correct."

"And if the lights go out?"

"I have run the numbers already," Staum answered. This was the part that was both fascinating and horrifying. "If conditions were true dark and Mr. Marler metamorphosed and escaped, I estimate that the city would be overrun in twenty-three days, the state in less than three months. By then, the end would be inevitable."

"So if you turn it loose behind enemy lines, there is no cure for it? No hope for our enemies?"

"None."

"Then how do you kill it when it's completed its mission?"

"You don't," Staum answered softly. This was the part he wasn't happy about.

"What do you mean?"

"I mean exactly that, sir," Staum answered. "We have engineered a creature here that is impervious to damage, sickness, disease, and anything else we can throw at it. The nanite matrix is designed for rapid healing and does its job incredibly well. Simply put, you can't kill it fast enough to make its death permanent."

"What if you blow it to pieces?"

"Look inside the enclosure," Staum said. "How many of those small organic lumps do you see scattered around Mr. Marler?"

"Several dozen," the man replied. "Why?

"Three of those were employees," Staum said. "The rest were once part of Mr. Marler."

As the implication sank in, the man nodded appreciatively.

"And they're going to become like him?"

"Some already have," Marler said, coding a camera change into the control board on the wall again. The video screen switched to the live-feed of another room. It was literally filled with creatures; clowns of every shape, size, and disposition. All of them appeared to be dormant in the half-light. But only just.

"And you can't kill them?"

"No," Staum answered. "Bright light drives the nanite matrix into near dormancy, but that's the extent of it. Nothing will kill it. Even acid cannot break it down fast enough to defeat the matrix."

"And how do you know this?"

"Because for the past four weeks, that's all I've been trying to do," Staum answered. "I've tried explosives, acids, electrocution, even other matrixes. Nothing works."

"I thought the original program parameters showed that the matrix was designed to go dormant in twenty-four hours."

"Yes, yes," Staum said nervously. "Somehow the matrix has managed to deactivate the clock. We haven't yet discovered how."

"So really what you've done is create a monster," the suited man said quietly, smiling as he gazed at the creature behind the glass. "A monster that is indestructible and can make more of itself."

"Yes, sir."

"That's brilliant," the man said, reaching into his suit coat and pulling out a gun. "Pretty soon, everyone will be afraid of clowns."

He only needed five shots.

As the light faded from Dr. Henry Staum's eyes, the man holstered his weapon. He stepped over the blood-spattered bodies and gazed at the monster on the other side of the glass. Pulling his phone, he swiped a finger across the screen and had an immediate connection with his superior, even this deep inside the facility.

"*Sdelano,*" he said, speaking flawless Russian.

"*Vy mozhete upravlyat'?*" a voice replied, asking if he had control of the facility.

"*Klouny idut,*" he answered, before switching back to English. "The clowns are coming. Our enemies will be no more."

***

Early the next morning, a carefully created set of explosive devices took out the main generator and auxiliary power structure of the Meridian Government Medical Facility in Greensboro, North Carolina.

As darkness engulfed the building, the thing that was once Devon Marler woke up.

It was a quarter to five.

~~NEVER~~ FEAR - PHOBIAS

6
ATYCHIPHOBIA

FEAR OF FAILURE

CASEY PARSONS

"Jason," Marnie whispered quietly. "Jason," she said again, her voice strained. "Please wake up." She gently shook his shoulder and looked around the dark room. Jason blinked his eyes open and saw Marnie standing above him, her long dark hair fell disheveled around her shoulders, in stark contrast to her porcelain skin.

"Christ, what is it, Marn?" He rubbed at his face sleepily and started to sit up, when he saw her staring at him with wide, glassy eyes. "What's wrong?" he asked with concern, jumping out of bed and putting a hand on each of her shoulders. "You're shaking."

"There was someone in my room," she whispered.

"What do you mean there was someone in your room?" he asked with slight annoyance, despite her obvious panic.

"There was someone in the corner of my room. They knocked something off my desk and woke me up. I ran in here before they could get to me." Her voice started shaking as she spoke.

"Marnie, we've been through this night after night; there's no one in your room. You were dreaming." He sat back down on his bed and rested his head in his hands, sighing with exasperation.

"Please check," she begged him softly. In the dark room, her eyes shimmered with the tears she held back. Marnie had always been a brave and independent child. She was never prone to nightmares or other illogical fears. Jason found it a little unnerving dealing with it now that she was eighteen years old.

"Okay, stay here." Jason walked down the hall, hearing her footsteps close behind him. He turned the light on and stepped into her room. "Everything looks fine. There's nothing on the floor by your desk. There's never anything on the floor that doesn't belong there. It was probably the wind against the house. Stop leaving your window open at night; use a fan or something," he said with annoyance, knowing it was going to take him forever to fall back asleep.

"I didn't open the window," she muttered, looking down at her hands that worried the fabric of her T-shirt. She looked back up at him and his heart melted, as it always did every time his sister gave him that look. It didn't matter how old she was, she would always be his little sister. And he would always protect her from the monsters in the closet.

"Come on, you can sleep in my room," he said, the annoyance in his voice replaced with sympathy. "Actually, I'm not feeling all that tired anymore. We can watch some TV." He walked over to shut and lock the window, then led his sister back into his room. She didn't have a television in her bedroom. She had told him once that it distracted her from her schoolwork and had him remove it. There were times during her childhood that it was hard to tell which one of them was the grown up.

"I'm sorry, Jason," she said, crawling into bed next to him while he turned on the television.

"You know, Marn," Jason said hesitantly, trying to start a long overdue conversation. But as he turned his head, he saw she was already sound asleep next to him. He sighed and started flipping through the channels. Eventually, he would have to have a talk with her about these consistent nightmares, but not tonight. Lying next to him she looked so peaceful. He knew she was a lost soul right now. All her friends would be heading off to college in a couple months, and she would be left behind. She wasn't taking it well. Jason had tried to give her time to deal with things on her own, but each day she seemed to lose a little more of herself. He told her there was nothing wrong with starting in community college first, but losing out on the scholarship she had been counting on devastated her. He was watching his sister, the girl he had raised for the last ten years, slowly fade away over something as silly as a scholarship.

Jason's alarm went off at seven and they both groaned. He fell asleep watching the TV and still had the remote in his hand. He cringed as he moved to hit the snooze button, neck stiff from falling asleep at an awkward angle. Neither of them were morning people, but Marnie used to at least make a better effort than him. The second time the alarm went off she sleepily shoved at him.

"Go on," she said, her voice rough with sleep, and pulled the covers up over her head to block out the morning sun peeking through the curtains. Jason bitterly rolled himself out of bed and headed to the bathroom.

He stepped into the shower, closing his eyes while the hot water ran across his face. He didn't want to move and risk exposing his skin to the cool morning air. Just as he was considering reaching for the shampoo, he felt a cold chill. He pulled the curtain aside in time to see the door shutting. The bathroom was suddenly freezing. He stepped out of the tub to see the bathroom window wide open, cold morning air poured in and battled with the hot steam from the shower.

"Aren't we too old for this," he yelled, as he shut the window and rushed back into the water. But it was no use. The moment was over and the bathroom didn't seem to want to warm up again. "Just for that, I'm going to take my time. We'll see how you like taking a cold shower."

Jason came out of the bathroom wrapped in a towel and feeling proud of himself for using up the hot water. Marnie had laid back down in his bed and was feigning sleep.

"Hey," he called, pulling back the covers. "What happened to the girl that faced each day with renewed enthusiasm?"

"She's dead," Marnie said, grabbing the comforter and pulling it back over her head.

"C'mon, TGIF, right? You can't lay around here all day, every day. Get up, get ready, go do something." It was the same argument they had been having for months. She never left the house anymore. She never really went out often before that, always staying in to study. But there was always a friend or two hanging around, dragging her out of the house now and then. Since school ended, he hadn't seen a single one of her friends.

Marnie stood and glared at him as she walked next door to her room and closed the door.

Jason opened his closet, looking frustrated.

"Marnie, when's the last time we did laundry? I'm down to my back-up shirts here." By "we", he really meant her. It was rare that she wouldn't grab his clothes when she was doing her own. He looked over at the basket. It was empty. "Where are all my clothes?" he shouted, but received no answer. He pieced together a work outfit, thankful it was Friday.

"I'm leaving early, thought I would pick up donuts for the office," he said to Marnie's closed door, while he finished the knot in his tie. "Marnie, I know you're disappointed about not getting that scholarship, but you still have options. Just consider taking some classes at the community college, get the basics out of the way. Or maybe a part time job until you figure things out. We'll talk about it tonight after I get home. Me, you, maybe I'll invite Ellie, too. It's been awhile since the three of us hung out. Don't make plans. I'll pick up some pizza on the way home." He waited for a response, but received nothing. "In ten years, you'll look back at this as just a little bump in the road. I promise."

He jogged down the stairs to the kitchen and downed a glass of water. He could have sworn the orange juice was full yesterday, but this morning he pulled an empty container from the fridge.

"You're losing your touch, Marn. There was an empty juice container in the fridge." He yelled up the stairs. "I left some money on the table, in case you find the time to run to the grocery store between all of your moping." He turned to leave and tripped, his head smacking against the wooden door frame.

"Gah," he yelled, feeling the bump already forming on the side of his forehead.

"You might want to watch where you're going," Marnie said to him stoically from the top of the stairs. He looked down to see Marnie's old purple teddy bear laying at his feet before the front door. He hadn't seen that for years. When she first came to live with him it never left her sight, but they packed that away years ago with the rest of her kid stuff.

"Marnie, what is going on with you? I'm not finding these

practical jokes very funny. Pick this up and put it away. I think I'm going to have a bruise from that." He rubbed absently at the sore spot on the side of his head.

"I didn't put it there. I haven't played with toys for a very long time," she said as she turned and walked out of sight. He stepped over the stuffed animal and looked around the room. The rest of the house looked fine from what he could see--nothing out of place. Marnie never let anything get out of place. She had always kept the house immaculately clean, and not because he asked her. Usually, it was Marnie nagging him. *Damn,* he thought. He forgot to rinse his glass and put it in the drying rack. She hated when he left dishes out. It was one of her many pet peeves. How a young girl could be so meticulous about every aspect of her life had always confounded him. He sucked a breath in between his teeth, thinking of the many beratings she had given him over simple things over the years, like just picking up after himself. There were times he had to remind himself that he was the adult in this relationship.

"Marn, I'm sorry I left a cup out. I'll get it when I come home. And I love you," he said, before shutting the door and heading off. He knew it wouldn't be there when he got home. She wouldn't be able to bear seeing it sitting there.

Jason yawned as he pulled into the office parking lot and took another sip of the large coffee he had purchased at the donut shop. He felt like he had barely slept all week, between Marnie's constant nightmares and worrying about when he would have time to see Ellie. She used to be so supportive and helpful with Marnie. He could always count on her help, especially for girl specific things. Now, she barely wanted to talk about it and she never wanted to come over to the house. She wasn't going to be happy when he told her he was breaking their date tonight to stay home and be with Marnie.

"Hey," Rob shouted with excitement, as Jason walked into the break room and sat the box of donuts down. He grabbed a jelly-filled before the box had even hit the counter. "How's it goin'?" he asked around a mouthful of pastry. "Of course, no one can be unhappy around donuts."

"I'm alright, rough night, didn't sleep all too well. I was actually wondering if I could get some advice from you," Jason said, leaning against the counter.

"Sure, what's up?" Rob said, sitting the donut down on a

napkin at the table.

"Your sister, Lily, did she get rejected from any of the colleges she applied to?"

"Jason, man, I don't know," Rob said hesitantly.

"Look, I know it's a different set of circumstances. You're not her guardian or anything like that. I was just wondering if there was anything you could tell me. I just don't know what to do to make this easier."

"That was years ago, Jayce, I… I just don't know," he grabbed the donut and continued, changing the subject. "You and Ellie have anything special going on tonight? Cause I was thinking…"

"I actually I think I am going to stay home tonight. There are some things I need to talk to Marnie about," Jason said absent mindedly before his friend could finish.

"Ummm… yeah, does Ellie know about your plans?" Rob said looking uncomfortable.

"I was going to call her on my lunch break. Marnie had another incident last night and I just need to find a way to get through to her. I was actually hoping that Ellie would join me. I'm starting to feel a little lost here." Rob stared at Jason as he spoke, looking uncomfortable.

"Well, I'm sure you'll figure it out, man. Ummm, I think it's about time to get to work." He slapped his friend on the back, snatched up another donut and headed out of the room, effectively bringing their conversation to an end.

The day was crawling by, as it usually did on Fridays. Jason had been watching the clock for the last ten minutes, waiting for lunch. Finally, the clock turned noon and he closed up everything and walked outside and down the street toward food. While eating his second burger, his phone rang.

"Ellie," he said, answering the phone with a smile. "I was just about to call you."

"Hey, babe, how's work going?" The sound of her voice made all the stress Jason had been feeling melt away. More than ever, he just wanted to fix things, so everything could be like it used to be. He had been planning on proposing to her before Marnie left for school, but then everything changed. Marnie needed him right now, whether she admitted it or not. Unfortunately, it seemed like he and

Ellie were growing apart because of it. She had never seemed jealous of Marnie in the past, but now just the mention of Marnie's name seemed to set Ellie off.

"You know, it's Friday. I'm just counting down the hours until the weekend," he said happily, trying to avoid what he had to say next.

"Great," she said cheerfully. So, about the weekend; I think we should stay in tonight, maybe watch a movie?"

"That's exactly what I was thinking," he replied. "I think I need to face the facts. I really don't know how to get Marnie out of this funk she's in. I was thinking that maybe y…"

"Please tell me you're joking, Jayce." Ellie said, interrupting him.

"No, why? It will be like when Marn was younger. We'll have a movie night. I'll get a veggie pizza, like the two of you like, and then…"

"No." Ellie said flatly. Jason took a breath to say something, but she cut him off quickly. "Just no. I won't be a part of this." She hung up the phone, leaving Jason confused.

"Well, that went a little worse than I expected," he said to the phone in his hand. "I guess it's just me and Marnie tonight then." He would worry about this new thing with Ellie later, after he dealt with his sister.

Jason walked up to his house carrying a pizza box and found Ellie and Rob waiting for him on his front porch.

"Hey… guys…" he said with confusion. They looked at him nervously. "What's going on? I only got one pizza. I thought it was only going to be me and Marnie."

Rob and Ellie exchanged looks with each other for an uncomfortable moment, until the silent decision seemed to be Ellie would take the lead.

"Jason," she said lovingly, placing her hand on his chest. Her blue eyes met his hesitantly. "We're starting to get really worried about you. We can't keep going on like this, like nothing is wrong." Jason stared back at her, not knowing what to say.

"Jason, dude, the way you were talking about Marnie today… It's just getting too weird. People at the office are starting to talk," Rob said, stepping forward. "You have to stop with this."

"I know," Jason said, looking at his friends.

"You do?" Ellie said with a sigh of relief.

"I'm going to have a talk with her this weekend. It's time she stops moping around and gets over this scholarship thing. Then our lives can get back to normal. This is just getting ridiculous. I know she's a teenage girl, but--"

"No," Ellie said loudly, backing away from him. "Jason, you need help." She was nearly in tears, fighting back anger and frustration. Jason was speechless. He knew that things had been weird between them the last couple months, but he didn't understand her reactions to this. She had known Marnie since she was thirteen. There were times when Marnie confided in her. She looked up to her. Ellie had backed up to Rob and started crying into his shoulder, saying, "I can't do this again," over and over. Jason reached out to her, but Rob turned her away, putting himself between them.

"Jason, Marnie is gone. She's not coming back." Rob spoke slowly and carefully.

"What?" Jason said, looking at his friend like he was crazy.

"Marnie is dead, Jayce. You have to stop talking about her like she's still here," Rob said, placing a hand on Jason's shoulder. Jason shrugged it off.

"This isn't funny." Jason spat the words out angrily. "I think you should go." Ellie walked back up to him with tears in her eyes.

"You're right, it's not funny, Jason. It has never been funny. I lost that little girl that night too, and I can't imagine what it was like to be the one to find her. But you have to wake up," Ellie said softly. "It's time to stop acting like everything is fine. Why do you think we won't come in the house anymore? It's a mess. There's rotting food all over the kitchen. It smells. I clean it up. I stock the fridge, but it all ends up a mess again. You drop things or knock them over and just leave it, thinking she's going to pick up after you. And worst of all, her blood is still covering the upstairs. It's smeared all over the bathroom walls and sink. The bathroom window is still broken. You don't see any of it. You talk about how she crawls into bed with you at night, like she's still this little girl you're trying to protect. No one blames you, Jason. It wasn't your fault. But it's time to face it. It's been months. Every time I think you're getting better, you relapse. We've already done this. We've already been through this and I don't know how much more of this I can take." She reached for his hand, but he pulled away.

"I think you should both leave." Jason turned his back on them and opened the door to his house. He could hear Ellie crying behind him, trying to catch her breath. He rushed in the door and nearly tripped, as his feet got tangled in a small pink jacket. The pizza box flew from his hands and landed next to the purple teddy bear he had tripped on earlier. He picked it up angrily and yelled out.

"Marnie, I thought I told you to pick this up."

He picked up the jacket. It was the one she wore when she was eight. It had faded silver hearts on it. He looked back outside the open door to his friends watching him silently. When he looked back at the room, there were items all over the floor, spilling out from a box, the box he'd tripped on this morning that threw him into the door. It was a box of memories, items from Marnie's childhood he never could bring himself to get rid of. The jacket fell from his hands.

He took a deep breath and walked through the entryway toward the kitchen. As he reached the doorway, a rancid odor hit him. He stepped back, covering his nose with his forearm. There was a bowl of fruit on the kitchen table, all the pieces shriveled and moldy. And all around it were the piles of money he had been leaving for Marnie's grocery runs. *Had that really been there this morning? What have I been eating?* The countertop was covered in dirty cups and plates. Jason turned and quickly walked away, catching sight of his friends still standing at the open door. He turned and bolted up the stairs.

There was a brown stain across the carpet that traveled from Marnie's closed door to the bathroom. He followed the drips as the carpet turned to tile and the stain continued to smear across the bathroom floor and streak across the walls. He heard movement behind him, turning, he saw Ellie.

"This..." his words caught in his throat and were barely a whisper. "This wasn't here this morning." Ellie's eyes were red and glistening, but she held back her tears now, trying to be strong for the man she loved. Jason looked across the room. There were bloody handprints on the side of the sink and on the mirror. He looked back at Ellie, silently begging her for another explanation for what he was looking at. The window was broken, a cool evening breeze blowing in. Jason walked over and stared at it. He thought he had shut the window this morning? He remembered shutting the window. *It hadn't been broken, had it?*

"Remember, the officer said she was probably just delusional with blood loss. She was might have been trying to open the window for air and got frustrated. She broke it with a hairspray bottle, shoving her arm through it and cutting her up more." Ellie looked down at her hands, trying to not look at the horrible scene in front of her. "She had already lost so much blood..."

Jason heard a blood curdling scream, and turned from Ellie to see Marnie standing in front of the mirror. She was holding a towel to her left arm; it was soaked with blood. She looked right at Jason.

"I can't breathe. I can't..." she said, looking right into his eyes. She grabbed the can of hairspray sitting on the counter and turned, putting it through the old pane of glass. The broken shards sliced into her arm. Jason flinched, watching as she pulled her arm back through the broken glass, slicing through her beautiful pale skin. Blood gushed from the lacerations and pooled on the floor. The can fell from her hand and she grabbed the side of the sink, losing her balance. A small, panicked laugh escaped her lips, as her bloody hand slid against the porcelain. "This is going to be hell to clean up. Who's going to do it for you, Jason?" Her eyes looked menacing as she spoke to him.

Jason watched in horror, sucking in a shaking breath. He ran from the room, pushing past Ellie and back into the hallway. He opened the door to Marnie's room. It was a mess. He had never seen her room look like this before. *But it was pristine last night.* He remembered standing in this same spot with Marnie, checking the room. It was fine. But now there was blood everywhere. His head started pounding. He pressed the heels of his hands hard against his temples, shaking his head and taking deep breaths. He froze suddenly, seeing Marnie's body at his feet, face down in front of her bed, the carpet soaked with blood. He started backing up, until his back hit the wall in the hallway. In a flash, he remembered everything.

It was him that knocked the stuff off her desk. Marnie had been crying for days about not getting a scholarship, and without the scholarship she couldn't go to the big college she wanted to. Instead of being there for her, he wanted to go out and meet Ellie. He had tried to be sympathetic, but he had had enough.

"Get over it!" he had yelled, and pushed her books off her desk. "So you're not perfect. Surprise. None of us are. Life goes on."

Jason slowly walked back into the room, stepping over clothes and broken picture frames. Marnie must have gone manic after he had left that night. She tore her room apart. Her bookshelf was toppled over, books, DVDs and scrapbooks strewn about. Photos and colorful paper were torn up and crumpled everywhere. He bent down and picked up a book that said SENIOR YEAR in fancy letters below a plastic cover. It was empty inside, all the pages torn out.

"They said she used a crafting knife down the length of her arm. There's nothing you could have done. She cut right down the vein." Ellie said from the safety of the hallway. Jason looked back at her, anger in his eyes. "I'm sorry," she whispered, moving toward him.

"Sorry," he heard again, but Ellie's mouth had not moved. "I'm sorry." He turned into the room again and found himself face to face with his sister. Her skin was grey, eyes lifeless. Her dark was hair matted with blood, just like he had found her.

"Two days..." Jason whispered to himself. He looked at Ellie with wide eyes. "I was with you for almost two days while she lay here." Ellie's breath hitched in her throat. She couldn't hold back the tears any longer and they fell from her eyes despite her objections.

Jason remembered the note that was left, neatly written and sitting on top of Marnie's empty desk.

Jason,

I'm sorry you had to give up the best years of your life to raise me. It was not fair, but I have learned now that life never is. I tried to be the best that I could. I thought I had it all worked out. I would be someone important and be able to pay you back for everything you have done and all your sacrifices. You and Ellie would probably have been married by now with your own children if it weren't for me. I cannot stay here in this town and rot away. I cannot ask you to take care of me any longer. What has all my work been for? A GPA is worthless to me now. I watch you struggle every day, work hard to barely pay the bills. I'm already exhausted and I haven't even started yet. I struggled for so long with our mother's suicide. I thought she was selfish and questioned how she could just leave me behind like that, but now I get it. She knew something I didn't. Life is hard and unyielding. And no matter how hard I try there will always only be failure to look forward to. I understand now that I can never be perfect. Life can never be perfect. And I don't want to live in an imperfect world.

Jason sank to the floor, a sob escaping his throat. He never regretted taking Marnie in. He loved having her there with him. He never meant to make her feel like a burden. He remembered this feeling now. Ellie was right. He had done this before--many times before. Last night he was in here, pacing, causing more destruction, and in a moment of desperation he opened the window and sat on the edge, legs dangling. He tried to make himself understand, to feel what she felt. He wished it was a dream, but it wasn't--everything else was.

"You never once complained to me about raising her. Even when she was a hormonal pre-teen, you took it all in stride. You loved her, and she loved you, but there was something deeper... something dark she hid inside her, and hid well. None of us saw this coming," Ellie said, almost as if she was reading his thoughts. She was kneeling next to him, her arms wrapped around him, his head buried in her chest.

He remembered all of it. He had come home from spending the night at Ellie's, something he did often on the weekends. Marnie was eighteen and a good kid. He trusted her to be home alone; she never said it bothered her. In fact, she often remarked that it was easier to get her work done with him out of her hair. He could see it all now. The brown stains on the carpet had been red when he first saw them. Panic had taken over as he ran to Marnie's room and found her collapsed on the floor, covered in blood. One arm was sliced from wrist to elbow, on the other, the skin was jaggedly torn by the glass of the broken window in the bathroom. The side of her face that was visible was tear stained and smudged with blood and makeup. Worst of all had been her eyes, open, vacant and lifeless. He knew instantly she was gone.

"What happened to the girl that faced each day with renewed enthusiasm?" he had said this morning.

"She's dead," he whispered to Ellie. "She's dead."

"I know, baby. We both loved her so much. But she's gone and nothing is going to bring her back," she said, cradling his head, like you would comfort a crying child. "We'll get through this. I promise, no matter how long it takes." Jason raised his head to look at her, but only saw the bloody corpse of his sister standing behind her. Their eyes met.

"Don't go," he whispered to Marnie. "Don't leave me."

"I'm not going anywhere," Ellie answered, thinking he was

talking to her.

***

One year later, Jason sat at the kitchen table, nursing his morning coffee. Ellie came into the kitchen with a yawn.

"Look at you, already up and dressed on a Saturday morning," she teased, while she poured a cup of coffee for herself. He smiled at her. She looked adorable in one of his T-shirts that she had taken to wearing to bed.

"Well, you know, I wanted to get an early start. I've got a lot of things on my list today," he said, walking over and placing a kiss on the side of her neck. With one hand, he took the coffee mug from her grasp, and with the other he cupped her growing belly hidden under the oversized shirt. With a smirk, he dumped the cup in the sink and brought a bottle of juice over to her from the refrigerator. While she poured herself a glass, he went back to the sink and rinsed the mug, placing it in the drying rack, smiling proudly.

Upstairs, his feet padded softly against the hardwood floor of the hallway. He opened the door to his sister's room and stepped inside. The hardwood flowed into the room. Jason sat down on the floor where all the pieces of a crib were separated accordingly.

He looked at the bright yellow walls covered in fairy and flower decals. Marnie's room had been white. He never offered to paint it another color, nor did she ask. There had never been posters on the wall. She didn't have collections on display. Everything was always neatly put away.

"How'd that get there?" he said out loud, spotting Marnie's purple Teddy Bear high on one of the shelves he'd just put up.

"I put it there," Ellie said, walking in the room and moving to stand next to him. "I wasn't going to leave it sitting on the floor. I thought it was a good spot for it. I remember Marnie always carrying it around when she was little." He put his arm around her as she spoke. "It was a good idea you had."

"What idea?" he asked, looking down at her curiously.

"Getting the bear out for the nursery. I miss her, Jayce, and it made me smile thinking that a little piece of her could still be here, in this room, watching over her niece." She rested a hand on her small baby-bump.

"Yeah," he said quietly, smiling and a taking in a slow breath. "It does make it feel like a little part of her is still here."

He looked over at the disassembled crib and winked at Marnie, happily sitting on the floor waiting for him to get back to work.

7

AICHMOPHOBIA

FEAR OF SHARP OBJECTS

RICHARD DEVIN

I liked the cool feel of the knife in my hands. The weight was heavy, even for a smallish knife and kept it perfectly balanced on my palm. I gripped the knife tighter. I had complete effortless control of the blade.

I walked slowly toward the nursery, playing with the knife, tightening my grip on it, then relaxing my muscles. The knife would do the work. I paused at the nursery before pushing on the door. It slowly swung in. I followed, stepping into the room. Soft, deep carpet padded my footfalls. I looked around, ready. The room was empty. Nothing was out of place. It was, as the room always was, clean and organized. The only thing new was the decorations applied to the door. Red, smudged hand prints. When had she done that? The question slipped into my thoughts as I headed out of the nursery, taking the few steps down the hall toward the master bedroom. That door was open. I paused again, readying myself. The knife urged me on, cajoling me, mocking me. I capitulated and stepped in. This room was also undisturbed. Everything was in its place. All except for a trail of red footprints that led from the bathroom off a corner of the room, to where I was standing. I followed them with my eyes. They came toward me, near the doorway. The stains crossed over each other, and then faded, disappearing directly at my feet. I looked down. My bare feet were covered in blood.

***

Nickie watched as I swooped up my briefcase and headed toward the door leading from the kitchen to the garage.

Nickie followed me, putting a coffee cup in the sink on the way. "I hope not. The baby and I would like to spend some quality family time with…"

Her words were cut short by the--sleeping, now awake--baby's cries from the converted guest room down the hall.

"See? He agrees with me," she said.

"Oh that's what he's saying?" I gave her one more kiss to the cheek. "Give him a kiss for me." I stepped into the garage hitting the button attached to the wall at shoulder level to raise the garage door.

I took in the heavy, salty, damp air of the California coast as it swept into the garage, gave Nickie a nod and jumped into the Mercedes. I backed out, closing the garage door via the remote. I knew Nickie would wait until the garage door had nearly touched the cement flooring of the drive before she stepped back and headed for the nursery. She always waited to make sure the door had closed completely, a concern born from watching too many episodes of *Forensic Files*.

It took about twenty-five minutes to drive the five miles from the house, until I pulled into the parking space, clearly marked by a sign that read: "Reserved for Ad Lib Vice President," a perk that put a smile on my face every time I saw it.

"Hey CJ," I said, walking into the wall-less space that served as offices for most of the forty or so employees of the firm. I smiled again as I walked by the overstuffed chairs, sofas, pillows and a few draft-style desks that were spread throughout the space—a far cry from the office set-up I had been used to. But this was California.

CJ was curled up on a red velvet sofa, he looked up from his computer tablet. "Kurt."

"How you coming along on the project?" I asked him, stopping just outside of my office door.

"Great. Let me show you." CJ flopped off of the sofa and followed me into the office. He sat down on the slick, black leather chair that some designer had placed in the traditional location in front of my desk, long before I joined the firm.

I eased into the high-tech office chair positioned behind the desk, adjusted a pen that was out of place, leaned back in the chair, "Show me what you've got," I said.

CJ handed the tablet to me. He had a sly grin that spread across his square jawed face.

I took the tablet, glanced down at it as a slight rumble vibrated through the office. "Did you just feel that?" I looked around to see if anything was swaying.

"Nope." CJ looked to the same places I was looking, "What are we looking for? What did we feel?"

"I thought it was a quake."

"Probably just a big rig on the 5 shaking the place."

"Hope so."

"Happens all the time. Big rigs, probably over loaded, hit a bump in the road and the whole building shakes. I don't even notice it anymore. You'll get used to it too," CJ said.

"Hope so. Quakes were never a worry for me in upstate New York."

"Maybe so, but look at all you get if you're just willing to shake a bit every now and then." CJ grinned, shaking himself in the chair.

"Oh yeah, traffic and more traffic and…"

This time even CJ felt it. The building swayed slightly to one side and then back, righting itself. Then a rumble and hard jolt shook the building.

CJ jumped up and headed for the doorway. "Ok you're right."

I grabbed hold of the edge of the desk, hoping it would secure me to the spot.

The building swayed slowly in one direction then back and to the other side. Then once again before it righted itself.

"What the hell?" I said with a bit more volume than I had anticipated putting into my voice.

A picture frame on my desk followed the motion of the building, and like a chair on a swaying ship, slid from one side of the desk to the other before falling off. It was followed by a gold-plated letter opener. The sharp pointed tip fell directly into the center of the picture frame, cracking the glass and piercing the heart of the images in the picture: my wife, Nickie, holding our son. "Is it over?"

CJ let go of the door jam. "I think so. Most of the time they're quick like that."

"This building swayed like crazy. Are we safe?" I got up and moved to the window, taking a long look at the cars and people below. Traffic continued moving on the roadways, and people milled about and continued in and out of shops as though nothing had happened. "Fuck!" I let out a long breath.

"We're good. A lot of buildings are on rockers, like a rocking chair, so they sway rather than fall down."

"I'll take the swaying then."

CJ laughed, came up beside me at the window, slapped me on the back. "Welcome to your first earthquake, boss."

"Hope it's the last," I said and moved to the desk. "I'm going to check with my wife. Let's go through the campaign ideas later. To be honest, I'm kind of shaken up by this."

"Pun intended, I hope?" CJ laughed.

I didn't get it and raised an eyebrow in CJ's direction before it sunk in. I shook my head, picked up the phone and dialed.

Nickie answered on the first ring. "Hello?" The sound of a cooing baby filled the slight pause between the "Hello," and my response.

"Well you all seem to be fine."

"Why wouldn't we be?"

"Didn't you feel it then?" I moved the receiver from one ear to the other.

"Umm. That would be a no." Then she added, "Feel what?"

"There was an earthquake."

"It must have been little quake, the baby and I didn't feel a thing."

"Good then. I just wanted to check on you." I let out a long breath as if I had been holding it. Maybe I was?

"You ok?" There was a slight edge of concern in her voice. "No..." She paused in an attempt to find the right words, "...issues then?"

"No, I'm good. Just a little concerned and rattled."

"Earthquake humor?"

I hadn't even noticed that I had done it again. "I didn't mean to."

The baby's cooing turned to cries. "I'll see you tonight. The baby's hungry so let me go."

"Ok. I'll be home right after work." I held onto the phone, expecting a response. Only the silence of a dead line remained. I put the phone down into the cradle on the desk, then leaned back into the chair and closed my eyes.

***

No issues, she had asked.

"Issues," I whispered.

The panic had come out of nowhere. I was fine and then... I wasn't. Nickie and I had just entered a cutlery store on West 72nd Street after a great stroll through Central Park. It was our first trip to New York City and before moving to California for my new position with Ad Lib. We put together a quick itinerary and headed off on the first flight we could catch to New York.

The panic set in quickly. The air suddenly got thicker. I was having a hard time breathing. It wasn't like I couldn't get a breath, I could. I just couldn't get a deep breath and began to feel as though I was slowly suffocating. Nickie smiled at me as we stepped farther into the store. I hoped that she hadn't noticed anything *off* about me. I smiled a fake smile back and tried to take in a deep breath. Sweat started to bead up under my arms and above my lip. I casually wiped it away from my face with the back of my hand. Nickie picked up and examined a paring knife.

"We could use one of these," she said, then placed the knife down.

"Let's wait until we get to Cali before we buy too much and have nowhere to put it."

"You're right." She put her hand on my chest. "Kurt, what's wrong, you're sweating?"

"It's just warm in here." I tried to act nonchalant. It didn't work.

"Not really, Kurt. No, it's not. Are you sure you're feeling ok?"

I took in a deep breath, well as deep as I could, then let it out, "Sure, I'm fine. Ready to move on?" I wanted to get outside as quickly as I could. I wanted to run for the door. I wanted out, and I wanted out now.

"Sure, let's continue down the street."

I held on with all that I could muster. Blades gleamed in the floodlights. Black and silver, brass and gold. So many sharp edges, all around. I wanted to grab them, feel the razor edges slice through my skin. Cut me so deeply that only bone would stop the blade. I stuck my hands into the pockets of my jeans, safe from the blades.

We turned to walk toward the door, just as a group of Japanese tourists poured into the store, led by a young woman holding a small Japanese flag on a stick high above her head. The throng followed her into the store, blocking the way out. Nickie stepped to the side, allowing the group to parade by. My chest grew heavy. The air in the store felt depleted. The Japanese tourists were taking in all the oxygen and I began to suffocate. I bolted for the door, smashing into the little Japanese men and woman still streaming into the store. I pushed at them, not caring at all if they fell into shelves, or cursed at me with vowel-filled words. I needed to get out, and I needed to get out now. I could faintly hear Nickie in back of me calling my name. I couldn't stop. I reached the door and squeezed out shoving people as I did. I stumbled onto the sidewalk, gulping in great breaths of the silt-filled city air. I leaned against a street sign, closed my eyes, and a moment later, heard Nickie's voice. She was standing right next to me.

"Kurt? Kurt?"

I opened my eyes, looked at her. She was flushed with both concern and anger.

"What the hell was all that about?"

I breathed out, felt the weight lifted from my chest. "Sorry Nickie, I don't know. I just had to get out of there."

I saw the look on her face soften. "Kurt, you've got me worried."

"Don't' worry. It's just the stress of the move and the new job. It just got to me." I took hold of her hand and kissed it gently. "Come on we've got a lot more city to see." I held tightly to her hand as we moved away from the store, heading uptown. In the back of my mind I could hear the blades calling me back.

***

I walked in expecting Nickie with the baby in arms to be standing in the kitchen putting the finishing touches on dinner. I was wrong. "Nickie. I called out, expecting a response from the nursery just down the hall. I was wrong again. I closed the door behind me and walked through the kitchen into the family room and then down the hall toward the nursery. No one. I pulled my cell phone out of my back pocket--I had a terrible habit of carrying it there and I'd broken more than one screen by sitting on the phone--and hit *recent calls*. Before the phone could connect, Nickie called from the kitchen.

"Kurt?"

I came around the corner to find her holding the baby in one arm, a bag dangling from her hand in the other and one leg stretched back, keeping the door from closing fast. "Let me help you."

"Take the baby, my arm is going to break,"

I grabbed the baby from her arms, planting a kiss on his head as I did. "Where were you?"

"Oh, I took the baby for a walk around the block and we passed a garage sale," she said, coming into the kitchen and plopping a bag down on the counter. "I have one more in the garage." She retrieved it and return.

"So what's all of this?" I asked pointing to the bags. I set the baby in the playpen, handed him a favorite toy and brushed his head with my hand.

Nickie pushed a few sweaty strands of hair back from her face. "I don't know what got into me, I'm not really a garage-sale-girl, but I stopped to look at a stroller for the baby. I just couldn't buy it even though they offered it to me at a really good price. I got a bit skeeved thinking about the baby in someone else's stroller and not being sure if they kept it clean. Kind of stupid I know, but I'm a new mom, what do you want?"

She gave me a look that made me unsure if I was supposed to answer or agree. I remained silent.

"But I did get a really good deal on these," Nickie continued. "I thought we could use them and they're still wrapped." She pulled a cellophane wrapped wooden block from the bag and plopped it down on the counter. "Look." She spun the block around.

My face went flush as though all the blood that could rushed to it, and then just as quickly drained away. I took several steps back hitting a small table as I did. The vase that had sat atop the table, filled with dried flowers, tumbled to the floor. Only the thick carpeting kept it from breaking.

"Kurt? Kurt!" Nickie's voice was filled with question and concern.

"No. No!" I kept my voice soft and low at first. It sounded like I was strangling. "No! Go! Get that out of here. Get away. Get away." I turned and dashed out of the room without a second thought.

I could hear Nickie following. She came up behind me as I fell to the bed and buried my face into the comforter.

"What is up with you?" She sat next to me, softly rubbing her hand along my back. I could feel the cool damp fabric of my shirt press against my skin.

"I don't know." My voice was muffled by the comforter. "I took one look at the knives in that block and it just freaked me out."

"We have knives. They're in the drawer. Those don't bother you."

"I can't explain it Nick, but when I see them I want to run. I don't know how to say it." I paused waiting for the right words, "They want me to do... things."

"The knives? The knives want you to do things? What?"

Those weren't the right words. I should have chosen better, but that's how I feel. The knives try to take hold of me. Control me. I couldn't tell her that. "That's not exactly what I meant." I hated to lie to her. "I just don't think straight when I see them. That's all."

"Why? What do you think will happen?"

Immediately words filled my mind, trying desperately to escape, to be free from my thoughts, to be spoken. "Sharp." I held back as much as I could but that one word got by me. It came out slowly, almost growling. I felt the pressure alongside of me on the mattress easy up, and Nickie stood. She kissed me on the back of the head and left the room, closing the door behind her.

The room fell quiet, only the sound of my breathing accompanied me. I counted my breaths, trying to find a rhythm and comfort in the slow in and out of my breath.

The panic slowly dissipated. My heart beat steadied and my

eyes closed.

When I awoke, it was morning. I was still dressed in the clothes from the night before. I rolled to the side and almost fell from the bed. I hadn't even crawled into the covers. I awoke where I had fallen asleep.

"Nickie?" I spoke her name quietly as I stepped out of the bedroom. No answer. I stood, frozen for a moment in my own thoughts, before a sound from the kitchen brought me out of the stupor. Nickie was attempting to put the dishes from the night before into the dishwasher with as much stealth as possible. It wasn't working. "Good morning." I couldn't think of another way to let her know I was there. It felt stilted and I'm sure my words came out that way.

She turned to me, startled. "I didn't know you were up."

"I know."

A pause followed. When neither of us knew how to break the awkward silence. She gave it a try.

"Did you sleep well?"

It was an attempt. "Um, yeah," I responded.

"Feeling better too?"

I knew where this was going so I just went there. "I think so. I also think that I should see someone, you know, a doctor or psychiatrist." I waited a moment for her to respond, when she didn't I added, "Maybe I could get some meds or something?"

"I think that would be a good idea." She came over to me and wrapped her arms around me, laid her head on my chest and squeezed me. "You have me really worried."

I kissed the top of her head and hugged her back. "I'll make an appointment today."

***

The cold tiles of the shower stall chilled my naked body as I leaned my back onto them, then slid down to my hunches. I eased the paring knife up to my mouth. Then smiled as though a photographer was demanding, "cheese!" I slid the paring knife along the smooth surface of the tooth. The tip pierced the gum, slicing into it. I pushed on the handle; the knife point dug deeper. When I felt the blade hit bone, I eased the pressure and tilted the handle away from my face, causing the blade to pivot in between the fleshy bleeding gums and the roots of the tooth. I pushed down, prying the roots loose from their footing. The gums tore, blood dripped in constant droplets that threatened to turn into a stream. The blood covered my hands and my grip on the knife slipped. The blade fell from my hand, spun as it did and lodged into my thigh. I muffled a scream, pulled the knife from tightened muscles and muffled another scream. Breath came to me heavily, Sweat mixed with blood. The smell of fear and cooper. A pair of long-nose pliers lay just in reach, left behind from some forgotten task Nickie had asked me to complete. I grabbed at them, tightening my grip on the pliers in my left hand, spread them apart and pushed them closed several times. Then I raised the pliers to my mouth, reached in, with what reminded me of a heron's beak, and clamped down on the tooth and yanked. I strained, applying more pressure, and the tooth slipped out--actually a bit more easily than I had thought it would. I opened the pliers, dropping the tooth to the shower floor and went back in applying the same technique on the tooth next to the first, and it too slipped out. I felt the pliers scratch against an incisor and like the heron stabs at a frog or fish, the pliers took control grasping onto the tooth. I pulled, it didn't budge. I pulled harder, feeling a scream that came up from my gut, escape my mouth. Blood and spit sprayed out over the shower tiles. I pulled harder, this time twisting the pliers to the right and left as I did. The tooth ripped from my gums and the screaming stopped. Without emotion I examined the tooth, studying the roots, blood and tissue that clung to it. I tossed the tooth to the floor, reached in for the next, grasped it tightly. The tooth cracked and splintered. I turned my hand twisting the pliers and the tooth creating a gap between my gums and the root of the tooth. I tried to scream but blood and spit muffled the sound. I pulled. The tooth came out with a pop. The coppery taste of blood filled my mouth. I spat it out, and before the blood could fill my mouth again, gagging me, I went in for the next tooth. "Sharp," the word gurgled from my mouth. "Sharp." I could not stop. The knives would not let me. They commanded me. They controlled my thoughts and actions. They wanted to hurt me.

Blood streamed from my mouth, drooling onto my chest, then to the shower floor. I watched it pool there into a puddle that slowly trailed off toward the drain. "Sharp." The word was hardly recognizable, mangled by copious amounts of spit, blood and mucus. "Sharp. Run. Sharp."

Dazed, I walked into the kitchen, leaving the light off, the soft blue glow from the digital clock on the microwave gave the kitchen the look of a bad B movie. I pulled a knife from the butcher block allowing it to ease out, felt its weight and perfect balance in my hand. I held it a moment, then pushed it back into the slot carved in-between the pieces of the wood. It slipped into place easily, nearly without sound. I felt a shudder rush through my body. I reached for another. The handle was smaller, cold, smooth. I let it slide silently out of its resting place, examined it closely, admiring the shine and gleam in the light. I held it up, taking in my reflection--a toothless, bloodied grin. Crimson saliva dripped from my mouth where my teeth had once been. Once straight, white teeth, perfected from years of braces that had been firmly planted onto my teeth, were now gone. Blood dripped from my fingers, splattering droplets on the counter and floor. A glimmering trail of droplets followed me. *Sharp.* The word echoed in my mind. *Sharp.* It would not stop.

"Run!" Run Nickie," I screamed the words as loudly as my toothless mouth and lips would allow.

But no one could hear.

8

TAPHOPHOBIA

FEAR OF BEING BURIED ALIVE

E. MCCARTHY

"Everything you want is on the other side of fear."- James Canfield

Eric Broadview felt sick to his stomach, his palms sweaty. He had expected the cemetery to be hushed, a sacrosanct village of silent inhabitants, where wildlife skirted out of fear and the modern world left it alone out of respect. But as he and Natalie, his girlfriend, slipped inside the property from the back by the ravine, he heard the low hum of the expressway that cut down the west end, and the overhead roar of an airplane. There was also very clearly the angry barking of a dog in the yard of one of the cookie-cutter houses that soldiered the east perimeter. Suburbanites in search of their square of land and colonial house with granite countertops didn't mind abutting the cemetery when those lots came with a reduced price.

The owner yelled at the animal to shut up and the night air filled with the sound of Jimmy Buffet looking for his lost shaker of salt.

There was no romance in it.

Death had lost its ability to shock.

It wasn't exactly how Eric had envisioned this night, where he would be conquering his fear, Natalie hers. It should have been more gothic, atmospheric. Silent except for the cawing of a distant crow, and dark save a full moon. Instead the headstones were mostly illuminated by glaring fluorescent streetlights, and everywhere surrounding them was the volume of average, daily life. It was disappointing. There was never a damn raven when you needed one.

"This isn't fair," Natalie said, squeezing his hand tightly. "This is almost totally focusing on my fear, not yours."

"That's not true. Sure, you're afraid of the cemetery, but really, that's an irrational fear. I'm afraid of something that has to do with follow through. It's actually more likely to affect my daily life than yours is." Immediately he felt that was a poor choice of words. He sounded selfish. He didn't mean to discount her fear, even if he had a valid point.

"Fear of commitment is not something more debilitating than the fear of being buried alive!" she whispered, her voice rising to a shrill keen at the end of her sentence. "It's just more ordinary, but equally irrational."

He looked down at her, studying her beautiful face. "You're right." He cupped her cheek, stroking. She really was gorgeous. When he had seen her for the first time, at a Steelers' tailgate party, he'd thought she was out of his league. Blond, petite, tanned, bubbly and full of life, excited about her brand new shiny RN and her first job at the hospital. She could have had any guy, really, and most people would have assumed she would go for the muscle dude, who sold insurance and laughed too loud, and made misogynistic jokes that she was supposed to ignore.

Instead, she had chosen him, the quiet tech guy who sometimes struggled with the unspoken rules of large crowds, mating rituals, and the all-too-confusing modern bromance. But she had flirted until he had finally figured out she was attempting to mate with him, and she had stuck in there even after he had messed up things like her birthday party (he told her about the surprise her friends had planned, because really no one liked surprises, but in fact, she liked surprises) and his complete inability to display any interest whatsoever in the reality TV shows she religiously watched. She said it was because he was loyal. That he was her Lassie who would always be by her side and would tear apart anyone who threatened her.

Sure, he might metaphorically drop a dead chipmunk at her feet or get some mud on her skirt, but to her, it was worth it to know that he was there. He would always be there.

Which was why it was so ironic that he simply couldn't commit to her. He wouldn't have expected it to be so hard.

But that final step seemed impossible.

Which was why they were here, conquering their fears.

He bent down and brushed his lips over hers.

She sighed. "What's in that backpack of yours? Please tell me it's wine and candles and the engagement ring that I showed you three weeks ago. Because nothing else is worth being here for, honestly."

Eric swallowed hard. He felt the cold fear creep along his spine again and the mealy tang of his anxious sweat. It was almost like he could feel the weight of that ring in the backpack, a thirty pound stone, instead of three quarters of a carat, ready to yank him backwards with a Reaper's hand, and haul his flailing body down into death.

That's what marriage meant to him--the cessation of youth, of a promising life. The giving in to the weight of the reality of time, gravity and mortality. It wasn't about monogamy. It was about accepting the very ordinariness of his existence.

But he had promised Natalie. Promised himself. This was something he had to do. He had to push through and do it his way, so that he wouldn't be ordinary. It wouldn't be settling into a suburban manse and having pride over his ride-on lawnmower. "Shh," he told her. "I know you like surprises. Let's not ruin the surprise."

Her eyebrows went up. "That's all I get? I'm shivering in a cemetery. Throw me a bone, babe."

"I'll throw you a bone," he said with a smirk, because she would like the dirty joke.

She did. She giggled and reached out to feel across the front of his jeans. His body swelled accordingly. But he stepped back because if they messed around, it would just be an avoidance tactic on his part. He didn't want to do that to her. Well, he did want to do it to her, but it wasn't going to make either of their fears pass, and that was the goal here.

"Boo." She pouted.

Natalie was a glorious pouter. She could have gotten her degree in it, and sometimes when he watched her doing that, he was inordinately fascinated by the power women had over men. Nothing about that expression should be appealing or arousing, yet it was.

"Why do I feel a speech coming on?" she asked, as he took her hand and led her into the cemetery. "About how it's not in male genetics to settle into human-created institutions like marriage."

She knew him. Or somewhat knew him. He felt the urge to lecture on why marriage was doomed to failure as men were genetically hardwired to procreate with as many women as possible. But that really wasn't the issue he had with commitment. He was loyal, Natalie was right. He could easily be satisfied with just her physically for the rest of their lives. It was the finality of the thing that scared him. Finality.

He needed to stop being a pussy. "I promise that on tonight of all nights, I won't present you with the reality of science." He scanned the cemetery, finding what he was looking for. "Tonight it's all about you."

Natalie sighed. "I wish it could be all about me back at your apartment in bed."

He had no doubt. Natalie was used to getting her way and he had to admit she was a lazy lover. She wanted endless oral sex but could only muster up about thirty seconds with her mouth on him. But that wasn't a complaint he had either. She was beautiful and he was awkward and he was frankly lucky that she let him poke her pincushion on a regular basis. No, that didn't bother him.

"Tell me why you're afraid of graves," he said, starting to get a hard on. His nerves dissipated a bit as he thought about Natalie naked. Maybe he did need the distraction of sex after all.

He brought her to the edge of a freshly dug grave that was awaiting a funeral the following day. He had done extensive research and scouting to make sure the timing of this was accurate. In order for Natalie to conquer her fear, she had to step into the burial vault, the concrete box awaiting tomorrow's casket. There were chains around the vault for safety.

"I don't know." She was already hugging herself as they came up to the grave and stood there, staring down into the hole. "Maybe I saw that movie where Sandra Bullock was buried alive when I was way too young. But all I can think is that would literally be the worst thing that could ever happen to me. I'd rather be raped than trapped in a coffin."

Eric squeezed her hand in reassurance before opening his backpack and pulling out a bottle of red wine; a deep, rich Noir. Black as the night. It seemed fitting.

He almost laughed to himself. When had he become so goth-romance?

"Can you smell that?" he asked as he dropped to the ground and let his feet dangle over the opening. "Fresh turned dirt."

She reached down and grabbed his shoulder. "Don't sit that close! You'll fall in."

"I'm not going to fall. And if I do, it's only four feet deep. I'm six three. I can easily get out of the hole."

"I thought graves were six feet under."

"Not in modern times. Now they're only four feet deep because the burial vault prevents them from rising in heavy rain, and it prevents sink holes, so a six foot depth isn't necessary."

She laughed nervously and sat on the ground behind him. "Why do you know so much about graves?"

Looking back over his shoulder, he smiled at her. "Because I'm a nerd, remember?"

"You totally are." She grasped the wine bottle and handed it to him. "Open this for me."

"Sure." Sometimes he stopped to think about the fact that she was really damn bossy, but again, it didn't bother him. Pretty girls could be as nasty as they wanted, and despite the fact that she could be a raging bitch if she chose to be, she really wasn't. She was petulant and demanding, but she was funny, generous and caring. She genuinely loved nursing, which he found admirable. He had zero interest in wiping someone's ass.

So he opened the wine and poured them each a generous amount into the plastic cups he'd brought. He took a swallow and tried not to make a face. He preferred beer. Natalie took hers down in two gulps. That amused him.

"Are you doing shots or drinking wine?"

She stuck her tongue out at him. "So who goes first? Or am I done just because I'm here staring at this creepy-ass open grave."

"No, you're not done until you actually get in the creepy-ass grave. Let's go together. You get in the grave and I'll propose to you."

Natalie stared at him. "That's not how I want to get engaged."

"It's what we agreed to. We're moving past the fear together." He tried to explain. "I don't think I can do this unless it's weird, does that make sense? If I have to do some elaborate proposal video with photographers in the bushes and shit, I'm going to crack. I want you. I want this. I just need a... push."

The question was if her need to be engaged, to announce on social media that she had achieved ring status, was greater than her fear.

He could hardly wait to see.

There was a long pause where all Eric could hear was the ragged anxious breath of his girlfriend, the hum of the highway in the distance, and the echoing silence of his own thoughts. His mind was a curious blank of anticipation; peace washing over him; discomfit scurrying off into the night.

Natalie scooted closer to him and swung her legs over the side. "You'll lift me out, right? I mean, you're strong enough to haul me up, right?"

"Nat, you weigh two pounds. Of course I can pull you up."

She closed her eyes. He watched her. If she could do this, then he could stop beating around the bush and commit. He couldn't wimp out or change his mind.

Her eyes popped open and she lifted the chain up with one swift motion and slid down into the vault. She landed with a soft thump.

Now that was sexy.

But immediately she started to panic, muttering, "Oh, God, oh, God, I can't do this. Eric, help me up!"

"You're fine, baby. You're fine." He reached into his backpack and pulled out the ring box. "Stop clawing at the walls, you'll break your nails. Step back so I can ask you something."

She looked wild in her irrational fear but she did quiet down and stare at his hands, eyes wide as saucers. Her chest heaved up and down and it occurred to him that his fear had been as unwarranted as hers. Tapophobia was ridiculous in modern times, with current science. And he had nothing to be afraid of either.

He opened the box and displayed the ring. "Natalie, will you marry me?"

Her hands went up to her mouth and she nodded. "Yes," she whispered.

She rushed toward him, to collect the ring.

He kicked her as hard as he could in the gut.

With a cry, she doubled over in pain and he brought his fist down on the back of her skull, dropping her like a stone. Barely even breathing hard, his heart pounding only from adrenaline, not exertion, he tossed the ring box into the vault on top of her unconscious body. Then he stood up and carefully eased the lid down into place so he wouldn't disturb the neighborhood.

Then he sat and waited for her to wake up screaming. He took a swig of wine and relished the idea. See, it wasn't so hard to commit to killing her after all.

Maybe he should have told her when they started dating that he was a sociopath who had been fantasizing about murder since he'd been old enough to strangle a backyard bunny with his own hands. But if a girl couldn't be bothered to ask, he wasn't obligated to share.

He had been hesitating for months to make Natalie his first kill because honestly, she was sweet and gorgeous and if he could love anyone he would love her. But that's why it was so fitting. If he was going to cross that line, it couldn't be with a meth addict hooker. That was so half-ass, so ordinary. Utterly lacking in style. Too easy. Prostitutes were basically asking to be killed. No, he had wanted to take the life of someone who had everything to live for, who would fight it.

Glancing around to make sure he was still alone, he marveled at how easy it was to make someone trust you. He'd given her no reason other than that he was willing to do what she wanted when she wanted. He let her dictate their plans, their sex life, their relationship as a whole. But passivity didn't equal sincerity. It was fascinating. He'd always found it fascinating that people let their phobias consume them, yet they were never afraid of what they actually should be--other people.

He chuckled to himself and took another swig of wine. It wouldn't be long.

As he enjoyed the Noir and the cool October night air,

sprawled out on his side next to the closed vault, he waited. Within five minutes he could hear her muffled groaning. Then a bang as she sat up. Then a scream. It was intensely satisfying, that deep feral panic she was emitting. He had thought he'd feel some guilt but there was none. He should have never been afraid that he would feel any. Hadn't his mother always said he had zero genuine emotion? She was almost right. He didn't have emotions regarding other people. But he certainly felt pride, satisfaction, excitement. They coursed through his veins now.

Pulling his cell phone out, he found Natalie under favorites, where she had placed herself, and called her. He could hear her scream cut off as she must have felt the phone vibrate in her pocket.

She answered with a sob. "Oh my God, what happened? Where are you? Help me!"

Didn't she remember him kicking her? Most likely she did, but she was still unwilling to accept he was responsible for her predicament. This was why he didn't understand people. They refused to accept the obvious. It had always puzzled him.

"You need to stay in there, babe. How else will you get over the fear?"

There was a pause, Natalie panting into her phone. "Are you kidding me? This isn't funny, Eric! Let me out!"

He wasn't laughing. But he *was* grinning a little, then felt a slight sense of shame for it. That wasn't nice. "Just lay down quietly for a little while. I'll let you out in an hour, I promise. Before you start to run out of oxygen."

That was the truth. He did have to let her out because he couldn't explain tomorrow when the family of the dead dude arrived for a funeral and they opened the vault to find Natalie. He would be a suspect, his fingertips and fibers all over the place. He wasn't stupid. No, he was merely going to leave her in the vault long enough to have her begging him. To see if he could draw the crazy out in her eyes, and take Natalie from ordinary to extraordinary. The plan to kill her was to wait until she was teeth-chattering, freaked-the-fuck-out, then let her out. Take her home. Feed her pills as he hugged and soothed her.

Walk out long before she actually died. It wasn't exactly hard core and not what he preferred but given she was his girlfriend he had to be careful about police looking too closely at him.

There would be evidence that he called her and they talked for a few minutes. He would say they argued, say he stopped over there, told her he did not want to get married. He would take the ring back. He had debated a whole suicide note thing but that seemed like it could potentially bite him in the ass. Instead, he was going to go home, tell his roommate they had broken up and that she had threatened to kill herself, which she did every time they fought. That was the truth. Numerous people had heard her go crazy on him at parties when she thought he wasn't falling over her feet fast enough. She threatened to kill herself at least once a month, usually with witnesses.

People might still speculate that she didn't seem suicidal at the moment but there would be no evidence of foul play.

Natalie was crying in his ear. "This is insane. Why would you do this? I can't see anything. I'm going to have a heart attack."

God, he hoped not. He'd have to haul her corpse across town and that sounded like a bitch to finagle.

"Beg me," he said, and he was shocked to hear his true inner voice, the one he never really allowed to speak out loud. He hadn't heard it since he was fifteen and he'd gutted a live cat in the woods, giving it a running commentary on which organs he was currently removing while the cat yowled and thrashed. He'd learned to control those urges, to wait, to plan, to pretend. Pretend to be normal.

Then the fear had tenuously crawled in, surprising him. He had been afraid to commit to taking a human life. He had hesitated and in doing so had become so very ordinary, so very staid. So "suburban guy with a golf cart."

Not anymore.

"Please," she murmured, tentative. She didn't know this Eric and she was frightened into a stunned silence, the word hesitant.

"That's not trying hard enough."

"Please let me out. Please!" Her voice got shrill.

"No." He hung up the phone.

He expected her to call him back but she didn't. One minute went by, then five. He started to get concerned that she had fainted. Or run out of oxygen. He called her again. The call connected but she didn't speak.

"Are you okay?" he asked, puzzled, wary. Concerned. It couldn't be over this soon. He didn't want to her die in the hole. Not before he saw her eyes.

"Can't. Breathe." She was wheezing. She sounded weak and hoarse, air rattling in and out of her lungs.

Maybe he'd overestimated the time she could be underground. Maybe he hadn't accounted for the presence of radon or something, hell, he didn't know. "Natalie, stay with me. I'm going to crack the lid, just so you have a bit of air, okay? You're going to be fine."

There was nothing but silence. Even her breathing seemed to have stilled.

The cemetery seemed to press in on him, yet at the same time he suddenly felt fully exposed. Something wasn't right. This wasn't as fun as he'd been expecting it to be. It was like he actually cared about the stupid bitch. It didn't make any sense. He knew he shouldn't open the vault, but he couldn't resist the compulsion to check on her, make sure she hadn't suffocated already.

He lifted the lid two inches, fully expecting to see her eyes blink in fear and recoiling from the sudden moonlight. But there was no sign of her. He lifted the lid even further, its springs creaking obnoxiously. He had the lid halfway up when she sprang on him, the sudden searing pain in his chest shocking and confusing. He let out a roar before he was flat on his back, the light from above disappearing as the lid fell back in place. What the hell? He tried to sit up, but Natalie was pressing on his chest with one hand, not looking like it was a strain at all, even though he was frantically pushing up with all his strength.

Her eyes were glowing in the dark. Not with fear, but with disappointment, amusement. "Really, Eric? I never took you for the theatrical type. It's one of the things I appreciated about you. This was insanely melodramatic."

He stopped fighting, not sure what was going on. He gripped her wrist with his hand and tried to shift her off of him, but she didn't budge. He started to sweat again, like earlier, the cold fingers of fear tickling up his spine. "I don't understand," he said, stupidly.

"You're not the only one with secrets." Her free hand stroked his cheek in the dark and he shuddered, the tight fit in the vault unnerving, her demeanor even more so. She sounded like a different person.

Her true inner self?

"You wanted to know why I have a fear of being buried alive? It's because I was put into a coffin every night, night after night, for two hundred years." Her cold lips teased across his. "I was so glad when I aged out of that shit. It gave me a fear of small spaces. Of coffins, graves, cemeteries. Which is ironic, considering I can't die."

The illogic of that jerked Eric back to his senses. "That's ridiculous. Everyone dies."

"Not vampires."

"Vampires don't exist. Plus you go tanning," he said, which was a ludicrous statement.

"I like having color," she said, before clamping down hard on his bottom lip. "I feel healthier."

He tasted blood.

"I'm annoyed with myself for not realizing who and what you are," she murmured, before sinking her teeth into his upper lip.

It stung and he couldn't move. Nothing in his body worked. He was frozen, pinned by her single hand. "I feel the same way," he said, accepting that he was going to be killed instead of getting to kill.

"I won't ask you to beg. Just remember the only thing you have to fear is fear itself."

She jabbed into his neck with her teeth, the blood pulsing and gushing straight out of him. It felt like it was drawing up and out all the way from his toes. The air was thick with the tangy sweetness.

"No," he managed to say. "The only thing you have to fear is other people."

Or vampires.

She drew back, the glow of her eyes hypnotic.

Then while he screamed out loud or maybe just in his own mind, she tore his flesh apart, burying her face inside his chest cavity, ribs cracking, muscle shredding. Natalie growled as she fed and he lay there dying in agony.

Her fangs sank into his heart and he bled all over the vault, faster than she could lap it up.

He hoped she would keep the ring he'd planned to return and think of him fondly.

9

PHOBOPHOBIA

FEAR OF BEING AFRAID

LANCE TAUBOLD

The lights were on.

They were all seated before him. A murmur of whispering voices could be heard as everyone settled, made themselves comfortable.

Waiting.

They're all here for me. Me. They want to hear my story: all the guts and glamor. Well, I'll give it to them: the whole truth. Then they'll all know how brave and fearless I really am.

"I started out in the Marines. My parents encouraged me. We're the best and brightest the military has to offer. Always on the front lines. Always ready to serve. We are trained to kick ass--and we did. Twice they called me up to go to Iraq. And twice my orders were cancelled. It sucked. I wanted to go defend our country so bad after what those Muslim fuc... sorry, freaks did to New York. To the whole country. Hell, to the whole world.

"You'll have to forgive my language. I get so passionate, sometimes I forget when I'm in polite company. That's the Marine in me: tough but rough.

"Anyway, after my orders got cancelled the second time, I started to rethink my life in the military. My time was up in the Marines and I needed to think about my future. I wanted to serve my country still, but I needed an education too. The Marines only had a tuition assistance program for getting a degree. But the National Guard would pay for everything, tuition, books, etc.

"So, I joined the Guard, which made me part of the Army, of course, and they would pay for school as long as I stayed in. The Army's awesome--and they're tough too. Great guys. This would also give me the opportunity to study to become what I'd always thought of becoming: a surgeon--you know; save lives. I knew it would be a lot of school and studying, but I don't mind hard work--never have. I grew up in a pretty small town; there wasn't a lot to do, so I studied hard and read a lot, didn't hang out like a lot of kids did. Not a lot of friends, which was fine. So studying wasn't new for me. Bring it on.

"I went for three months to medic school--Fort Sam Houston in San Antonio, I figured it would be great to do that, you know, in case my unit got called up to go to Afghanistan, which they said was really unlikely, but a guy could hope. But if I did go, I would be there to help if any of my guys got injured. 'Cuz that's what it's all about, keeping my guys safe and protected.

"It wasn't long 'til I got out of medic school--and not to brag--but I was top of my class. I loved it. Met some great guys and women too who were there.

"Anyway, then it happened. I still remember the day we all got called into the Drill Hall on our day off. A Friday. The company commander announced, "Gentlemen, we're going to Afghanistan."

"I heard lots of guys around me swearing, and mumbling things about how they couldn't go and what were they gonna tell their girlfriends. But not me. I was stoked! I think I punched my fist in the air. Finally, I was going to get my chance. Of course, I was going to have to put school on hold for a year, but it was worth it. Freaking Afghanistan!

"Then, things got even better. It turned out where we were going in country was a very strategic place for us and we were going to have a four-man sniper team. And, they needed a medic. I was a great shot. I'd grown up with guns and would go out shooting all the time back home, not that there was any danger where we lived, but you never know, you know."

He laughed and gave his audience a chance to laugh with him, before he continued.

"So, I put in to be the team's medic. I would be there to back them up and take care of them if they were wounded. But I had to shoot too. Which, as I said before was no problem. I didn't know these guys at all, but everyone said they were the best and I wouldn't have anything to worry about. Hell, I would probably just be on the sidelines most of the time, but I told them I wanted to be in on the action too. And they told me, who was going to take care of me if *I* got hurt. Which made sense, so I didn't push it. They needed me and I would do whatever they wanted. Our group would be special and reserved for special assignments, so I wouldn't really be with the rest of the guys, as such. There were other medics that could handle it. It felt great to be part of that elite group, knowing that I would be doing something really worthwhile.

"I was prepared though, just in case. I carried three weapons: two pistols and my rifle, and of course, my knife. I also figured if one of the guys needed a backup weapon, they could use one of mine.

We trained for three months. The whole time I was worried, and kept expecting to hear them tell us our tour was cancelled.

"But it wasn't. We left in August last year. It took forever to get there, stopping in Germany, then Kyrgyzstan. But I'd gotten smart. Every time I flew--even in the states--I would take something to knock me out-- Well, not really knock me out. It was just something to make me drowsy so I could sleep, you know. So I wouldn't have jet lag.

"It was funny, when we landed in Germany--our stopover-- my buddy, Gary, woke me up and punched me. I guess I fell asleep on his shoulder. But he didn't know it either, 'cuz he was passed out too. Hey, I was comfy."

He paused to let everyone laugh again.

"Oh yeah, he also said I talked in my sleep; something about getting shot or shooting somebody. Yep, I was ready to see some action!

"So, we get to the Baghram Air Field--our last stop--before we head out to our COP, you know, our combat outpost.

"Let me tell you, this place was no Marriott--not even a Holiday Inn--not even a Motel 6! This was bare bones minimum. Except it had a gym. Which was awesome. As you can see, I love to work out. And when I was there, I was jacked! I mean I'm okay, now. The ladies seem to like how I look. Guys, too--just kidding. Besides, it was war, a military thing, guys help each other out. I mean... what I mean is: the guys all liked me, they'd tell me how ripped I was and ask me for workout tips.

"But over there even the gym was pretty bare bones: all free weights--which I love--It makes you bigger, faster--a couple of benches, bars, mats. Oh, they did have a couple of leg machines, not that I really needed it. My legs are huge from all the ruck marches we did, so that way I could really focus on my upper body. We had a lot of down time and I spent most of it in the gym. I'm 5'9" and I was 195--all muscle. Big traps and delts. Got my arms to 18". I had the Afghani guys that were with us take a lot of pictures of me.

"I was eating, like, 3500 calories a day. I'd ordered online a bunch of supplements, protein powder. No anabolics though! It was all natural. Protein, three to four hours a day of hard workouts, and it paid off. The Afghans were all afraid of me 'cuz I'd gotten so big. They'd ask me to help with their workouts and shit, sorry--stuff, and I'd give them some pointers. They liked to spot me on the bench when I needed it. Didn't want to get hurt, tear a rotator cuff or anything. Then I couldn't support my guys. I'd be useless to them. But bein' jacked was really all for them, you know, so I could carry guys if they needed it--which they didn't, thank God. I don't know what I would have done if they'd gotten injured or killed. I can't think...

"I mean, I... I woulda done what needed to be done. Whatever! I could do it, you know?

"I'm trimmed down now--a buck 80 to 85, depends on the day. Lean, mean muscle. Nobody's gonna mess with me. I know you can't tell through what I'm wearing really well, but I've got great pecs and arms.

"It's kind of hot in here. Is the AC on? My forehead's sweating and I know I've got bad pit stains.

"Well, I guess you all want to hear about my time in country, where the action really is.

"We went on patrols most days into the villages in the surrounding area. I guess you heard how I used to give out toys to the kids in the villages; that was my idea. I figured it would take the Afghans off guard, Then they'd think we came in peace. I'd carry an extra pack filled with stuff for the kids and my guys would distribute them. We still carried our weapons, of course, to let them know if there was any funny business from them, we would take 'em down.

"There was this one time, right around Christmas, we went into this village--where we'd been lots of times before--and it was all quiet-like. No kids came yelling for treats. There were a few animals around, but that was it. Some of the guys got scared, but I told them everything was all right; probably a holiday or something. It made them feel better. But everything wasn't all right.

"Can I get some water please? It's still pretty hot and my throat's kind of dry from all the talking."

He swallowed.

"That's better. Thanks.

"So I sent one of the guys to go ahead a little and he walked about thirty yards or so, while we scanned the area--and that's when it happened. *Blam!* Sorry, didn't mean to make anyone jump. But it made *us* all jump and hit the ground hard. Those bastards had placed an IED in the middle of the road! A fucking bomb! I... I...

"I don't know... I ran... I hid... I... yelled... I... black... screamed... gun... *Motherfuckers!... blood... blood... Pauly... dead... dead...*"

Silence.

"Oh yeah, sorry, just trying to remember everything so I tell it right. It happened pretty fast. So then I got the guys together, tried to calm them down and told them to get it together; that we needed to get out of there, see who was hurt. I was fine. My HMMWV-- Humvee--was in the center of the formation at the time the IED went off, but I had to check on my other guys. They depended on me: their Doc.

"Oh, this is kind of funny: one of the guys who was injured, Slater, needed me to give him a sedative so when I went to stick him, I missed the stick three times before I got it in the right spot. Me, the doc, missed the stick. Hey, it happens, you know? So I'm not perfect after all.

"Anyway, we medevaced him out with the two other guys who were injured. They were all checked out back at the base in Baghram, recovered, and were back in action a couple of weeks later. Yeah, I'm not sure where they were reassigned, but I heard they were okay.

"But it just goes to show you, you can't trust the Afghans. They'll smile and take gifts from you, then turn around and stab you in the back--or blow you up... nasty fuckers... crazy dune coons... raping little boys... selling their daughters... should blow *them* up...

"Can I get some more water please? It's hot; kind of stuffy too.

"That's great. Thanks.

"Oh yeah, I got another good one for you. We were driving to the base to get supplies for the week--nice little convoy, MRAPs... Oh yeah, that's Mine Resistant Ambush Protected..., HMMWVs, I think six... that was pretty standard--six to eight.

"Well, this time there were six. We'd been driving about a half hour. The roads were hardly roads--dirt paths, rocks, boulders. Let me tell you, after one of these runs, I was issuing naproxen and ibuprofen to my guys like they were jellybeans. All that bumping and jarring fucked your back up for days. And your ass. It wasn't fun. Of course we couldn't take their, quote--unquote--roads. IEDs everywhere. But those sneaky fucks were not as stupid as we thought. This time they'd planted one on the route we'd taken a couple of times before. This was my first run. They wouldn't let me go before in case I was needed back at the COP, you understand.

"So, we're bumping along, laughing, joking, ragging on each other, talking about girls, when suddenly the MRAP in the front position hits a *fucking IED*. And this had to be a big motherfucker, 'cuz the mine roller on the front hit that pressure plate and BOOM! It rocked the MRAP straight up in the air onto its two back wheels. Freakiest fuckin' thing I've ever seen! The mine roller was toast. Ripped metal everywhere. The MRAP wheels were spinning in mid-air. The rest of the convoy slammed their brakes on. Guys were running to the MRAP, opening the side doors and the gun turret to get our guys out.

"Everyone was yelling... screaming... I... got my... They were... yelling... I couldn't find my... yelling..."

Silence.

"I got my bag and ran to the MRAP. My guys had gotten the injured soldiers out of the vehicle and I took over. I did triage and worked on the guys that were hurt the most first and I assigned other guys to help the couple of guys who were only shaken up bad. I applied a tourniquet to one guy whose leg was bleeding pretty bad.

Then treated the other injuries: a dislocated shoulder, busted wrist, bruised ribs.

"So I took care of them, did my job, you know. The helo got there, took 'em out.

"When we finally got back to the COP, we were all affected by what had happened, but I was good. Except that night, I must have eaten something bad at the mess hall, 'cuz I was sick--sick as a dog. Sick as one of those nasty flea-bitten strays that hung around camp and annoyed the fuck out of us until we had to shoot them. Nasty things always barking and howling, you know.

"So anyway, I was sick for a couple of days, throwing up my guts. All I could do was lay in bed; I couldn't eat anything. Even water came back up. The guys felt bad for me. Nobody else got sick, which was weird, but I was glad they didn't. I dropped like five pounds, which I got back fast and got back into action as fast as I could.

"The guys from the IED incident all healed fine and got reassigned.

"My guys all said I probably saved Albano with the tourniquet I put on him. They said I definitely earned my CMB-- Combat Medic Badge. I never did get it though--some messed up paperwork or something. Didn't matter though. I was just happy I could help them. Just doin' my job. I don't need badges or medals.

"That was my last supply run. The guys didn't want to risk me being in a blown-up vehicle. I understood. That was cool.

"But then right after that incident, the powers-that-be decided to cancel our sniper team op. No real reason. I mean, we were all ready to go. I was shooting every day. I'd gotten real good. Maybe not as good as the others, but pretty damn close. I gotta be honest here; I was real down. I wanted to do something important... Not that what we were all doing wasn't important, but you know, a sniper team... yeah, well, that's how it goes sometimes. I did have my guys to take care of.

"And they all loved me. Well, almost all of them. There was this one other medic, Nelson... I never did anything to him. I *liked* the guy. Really. But he had it in for me. I think he might have been jealous, me being on the sniper team and all. He would say shit about me to the other guys all the time. How I didn't know my shit and I didn't want to get my hands dirty. He told the guys I was gay and I only got on the sniper team 'cuz I was blowing them. That's all I was good for. And if one of the team did get injured, they'd probably die, because I'd be hiding out behind some rocks somewhere. When I heard that--that he called me a *coward*--I snapped.

"That was it. That prick could call me a loser or say I was gay; I didn't care. But that fuck calling me a coward... *ME!* That was it. I mean after everything I'd done, all my training... I know my guys didn't believe it for a second. I mean, who would? Right? Damn straight!

"But I had to do something about it.

"I wasn't afraid of him. He was a pretty big guy, six-two, 220-225. In the gym a lot. He always worked out when I wasn't there; or he'd leave if I showed up. I think he was afraid of me. He talked behind my back, but was afraid of confronting me. So this one day, not long after the IED mess, I'm in the gym trying to put my mass back on after being sick. I'm on my last set, and in walks Nelson with two other guys: Richter and Price--both kind of douches too. They followed him around like puppy dogs. I finished my last set and I'm sittin' on the bench drinking my post-workout drink. The three of them walk over and surround me, like they were trying to intimidate me or something. Then Nelson says, 'I hear you fucked up on the supply run and you're tryin' to tell everybody what a hero you are.'

"I didn't say anything at first. I mean, what a joke. I had witnesses.

"Then he says, 'I hear they cancelled the sniper team 'cuz you're such a fuck-up. Can't put on a simple tourniquet? Yeah, Mobley told me *he* had to do it. And then Slater the other time; you couldn't even do a goddamn stick without breaking--what was it?-- five, six needles?'

"I saved them, I told them.

"*Bullshit!*' he yelled at me, and knocked my drink out of my hand and shoved me on the bench.

"I kinda saw red, I think. There was a dumbbell next to me on the bench and I picked it up and kinda swung it to get him out of the way. He backed up... and he must have tripped 'cuz he fell back and hit his head on the quad machine.

"Richter grabbed me and tried to hold me down and then Price tried to take a swing at me. But I got away from them. They came at me but I was ready for them. All my training came into play and when they started throwing punches I--"

"Mr. Banner--" said an older man sitting directly in front of him.

"It's Sergeant Banner, sir. And I'll take questions after."

"No, Mr. Banner, we've heard enough."

"I'm not done--"

"Yes, you are. Now please, let us talk. Otherwise, the attendants will be forced to take you back to your room." The man removed his glasses and looked at Banner. "Do you understand, *Mister* Banner?"

Banner nodded meekly and squirmed a little in the straitjacket confining him.

The man confronting Banner spoke to the three other gentlemen seated at the long table. "Dr. Kent, Dr. Geetay, you have heard from Mr. Banner over these past months of his residence here at the hospital, but Dr. Hunter, this is all new to you and we felt it best if you had no foreknowledge of the patient's case in hopes that you could shed, perhaps, a new light on the situation. Banner has not improved--if anything he has gotten worse and regressed into his own world. If you choose to accept his case, we will, of course, provide you with all of his records, documentation, therapy sessions etc. Now, I know this protocol is a bit unusual and we thank you for indulging us, but we are at our proverbial wit's end with Banner. If you would, indulge us a little further, and please, give us your initial assessment."

"Thank you, Dr. Scolini, I will be happy to and I would like to thank you all for entertaining my idea to join your staff. I hope I can prove my worthiness. With that being said..." He cleared his throat. "From a purely analytical standpoint, I would say this man suffers from delusions of grandeur--I've always enjoyed that term-- and it is certainly apt here." He smiled before continuing. "In addition, he has acute paranoia and a severe case of phobophobia, the fear of being afraid. For example, this phobia, as many other phobias demonstrate, manifests itself in sweating, nervous energy, tics, nausea, tendencies to overcompensate. Here, Banner's excessive need for firepower--three or four weapons at all times. His fanaticism with marksmanship is obviously for self-preservation, and the false sense of feeling that having those said weapons on him will make others fear him, so that *he,* in turn, won't be afraid. This phobia drives every action he makes, I'm going to assume, throughout his life. I would need to see his history to learn of the emergence of the phobia, the catalyst, and for how long it has existed.

"To continue, his joining the National Guard, so as not to be deployed but still maintaining the outward appearance of being a "hero" and defending his country. Being in the military is as insular a vocation as he can get. It is a group of its own--an exclusive society. A brotherhood. It gives a sense of belonging to something. And it is a society that *protects* its own. Vastly important to someone with this fear. It gives him more control, only having to deal with other military personnel. Becoming a medic--an admirable and heroic duty, saving others' lives. Yet a medic is a revered position and one that is more apt to be protected by others. *And* is most unlikely to see combat, made more so by always needing to be at the ready, but if he does see combat, he knows he will be protected more so than anyone else.

"The superficiality of the extensive workouts to, ostensibly, make him stronger for 'his soldiers' is, in and of itself, another intimidation tactic in order to ensure that no one will, as he puts it, 'mess with him.'

"When one has a phobia this severe, the victim of it will go to any lengths--*any lengths*--to avoid confronting it. The perfect example of this being Banner's reaction after the second incidence of the IED explosion. Not only did he crumble under the pressure, he subsequently was ill afterwards, supposedly from food poisoning, but I'm certain it was from the realization that it could have been his *own* vehicle which was blown up.

"I am certain I have merely brushed the surface here. This man is deeply disturbed. Dr. Scolini, gentlemen, I have dealt with many cases--"

"Dr. Hunter, *that* is the express reason for asking you to meet with us. Almost to a word, Banner's story is pure fabrication. And we believe that after the months we, and several other doctors, have been working on this case, that perhaps as a doctor with your credentials and experience dealing with phobia cases, you might be our last resort to helping Banner come back to some degree of normalcy. I'm sure you are not aware of this, but the altercation between Banner and Sgt. Nelson was not an accident--"

"*Yes it was! It was!*" Banner screamed and threw himself from the chair, sending the small table in front of him flying as he hit the floor. The larger of the two attendants held Banner on the ground, while the other attendant pulled out a syringe from his coat pocket and injected it into Banner's neck.

Banner struggled for a few moments, while the drug took effect.

Banner stopped moving. The attendants released him and stood to either side of him.

"We knew at some point he would snap, which is why we let him remain," Scolini said. "We wished you to see this and know exactly his potential for violent behavior. Banner will be out for a few minutes now, allowing us time to discuss his case."

"Exactly how did Sgt. Nelson die?" Hunter said.

Dr Geetay spoke, his Indian accent surprisingly pronounced. "If I may…"

"Of course, Doctor," Scolini said.

"Mr. Banner was indeed finishing up his workout; the other two soldiers there gave corroborating testimonies to this. It seems that Sgt. Nelson *was* impugning Banner's capabilities as a medic and as a man. Banner's phobia came to the fore. He was surrounded by three soldiers and being confronted. It proved to be too much for him. I am thinking it was similar, but on a more pronounced scale, to what you just witnessed. Banner swung the dumbbell and hit Sgt. Nelson in the temple. He then proceeded to pounce on Sgt. Nelson and bash his skull in with the dumbbell before the other two soldiers could even move. They said they were both so dumbstruck and that it happened so fast; I believe Private Richter said that Banner was like the 'Tasmanian Devil' from cartoon lore, a blinding whirlwind of action, and they did not have time to react before it was too late. When they did finally try to stop Banner, he turned and tried to attack both men. On interviewing the two soldiers, I got the impression that both men were very frightened of Mr. Banner's crazed actions and were hesitant to react initially.

"We do not expect a miracle here and we understand what we are asking, and your undoubted reticence to take on this precarious case, But to be honest, Doctor, we are receiving pressure about several cases at the hospital--this being one of our most difficult--that show no progress. If you cannot help, there is a great probability of Mr. Banner being institutionalized permanently."

Hunter sat in silence for a few moments. "I have a couple of more questions."

"Of course, please," Dr. Scolini said.

"His family," Hunter began, "Have they been forthcoming with any information?"

Dr. Kent, a short balding man in his fifties, raised his hand and spoke. "Banner's father passed away while he was in Afghanistan. His mother is hesitant to speak of her son's childhood, other than to say that Banner was a quiet child with no friends. He read a lot and kept to himself. He left home at seventeen and joined the Marines; she having no problem signing off on his being underage. They had little contact, no visits. She has not been to see him here and from my inference from our conversations, she seems to be relieved that he *is* here--locked away so to speak. She knows more than she is willing to tell, and I fear she will never tell."

"That sounds ominous," Hunter interjected.

"Indeed. From what we have gleaned from his school records," Dr. Kent continued, "he was an average student, showing some aptitude in mathematics and computers, but nothing exceptional. His father dabbled in the computer area before he became ill. There may be some link there, but with his father being deceased, it is another dead end. Sociopathism is Doctor Geetay's and my conclusion, and combined with his phobophobia, Banner becomes an enigma. A dangerous one."

"And your conclusion, Dr. Scolini?" Hunter asked.

"I was not going share my experience with Banner, but I feel you need to know the complete story," Scolini said, massaging his square jaw before continuing, deciding what to say. "I was the first doctor to deal with Banner and it was not a pleasant experience, which was my reason for bringing in these gentlemen. Banner displayed an extreme dislike for me from the beginning, including violent vocal outbursts and several physical attempts as well, whereby he needed to be put in restraints on more than one occasion. I discovered the source of his anger against me to be his equating me with his father, something about my appearance or voice, I suspect. At the last session I had with him, a particularly violent one, he raged about being held here against his will and how he was a hero, and should be honored not imprisoned. During his rant, he called me by his father's name several times, threatened me with bodily harm...

and he threatened to kill me. I realized at that point further sessions with me would prove fruitless and likely injurious to his possible rehabilitation."

"So there is a definite paternal issue," Hunter said.

"That was my conclusion," Scolini said. "As to the conclusions of our two doctors here, I concur. We are hoping that your expertise in dealing with phobias can shed some light and ultimately give us a useful course of action."

"Doctors, this is an unusual situation, granted. I have seen milder cases of phobophobia in my experience and have helped patients to deal with it. Banner's is by far the most extreme, especially with the resultant murder of Sgt. Nelson. This heinous and evil act is, in itself, reprehensible. Banner will never be brought to justice for this: insanity or post-traumatic stress syndrome will be cited, I'm sure. As a case study, it is fascinating, and perhaps it will give us some insight into the workings of the phobic mind so as to prevent something as tragic as this from happening in the future; for there are definite warning signs with any phobia.

"Unfortunately, with this particular phobia, the victim of it is reluctant to acknowledge it as it plays right into his phobia, by making him appear there is something wrong with him, making him feel weak and propagating the fear: a catch-22.

"With past cases, I have found the best way to approach it is through a back door technique which never addresses the phobia overtly, but instead, addresses the symptoms and possible ways to avoid their manifestations. As soon as the phobophobic person feels these symptoms coming on, they trigger other symptoms, and tragically, as with Banner, the symptoms compound, until sedation or force is required. I have encountered one or two cases where the victim has caused bodily harm to himself but never to the extreme we are dealing with here.

"I know you are dealing with pressures from higher up but this particular case may require quite a bit of time to see any results, as you doctors have witnessed. I would be willing to put together a possible treatment plan for Banner that you could present to the hospital board. Ultimately, we are dealing with the human mind, and I can't promise a satisfying outcome, but if I am given the time... I am willing to try."

Dr. Scolini nodded and said, "Thank you, Dr. Hunter. I

believe I speak for all of us when I say that your consideration and willingness to help is most appreciated. If you would put together your proposal, we will figure out a way to convince the board of its validity and urgent need. Once again, we thank you."

Kent and Geetay nodded their assents.

Scolini said, "I see our patient is beginning to stir, gentlemen-_"

"If I may, Doctors," Hunter interrupted, "I would like a few moments alone with the patient. I would like to observe his actions after this violent outburst. Having you all in here will cause him undue stress and anxiety, and, as I am unfamiliar to him, I will not pose as great a threat--something we wish to avoid. I assure you, I will be safe. You may leave the attendants outside the door."

Scolini looked at the other doctors. Both nodded. "The attendants will remain outside the door; call them if you require assistance and they will escort Banner back to his room when you are finished. We will leave a syringe of Haldol with you should you feel the need to sedate him again."

"Thank you, Doctor."

The men shook hands, and with the attendants left the room.

Banner was stirring and mumbling.

Hunter approached him and knelt down. "Can you hear me, Mr. Banner?"

Banner raised his head and nodded. Haldol was a powerful drug.

"Good. I have something to show you and if you start to scream, I will immediately inject you again and have you removed. Do you understand?"

"Yes." It was barely above a whisper.

Hunter reached into his jacket pocket and withdrew a small photo. He shoved it in Banner's face. "This *was* my nephew, my sister's pride and joy, the love of her life... and mine as well. She lost her husband right after her son was born. He was all she had, and between the two of us we raised him. He became a strong, intelligent, fine man. A man to be proud of. And you... you with your pathetic phobia. Your weakness, your lying... You are *disgusting*. A worm of a human being: selfish, arrogant, despicable. And yes, most decidedly, yes... a *Coward!*"

Banner began to whimper and cry softly.

"You took his life. You *murdered him*. Denied him a wonderful, promising life. All because you couldn't face your*self!* How you ever were allowed into the Army is a travesty in itself. I intend to investigate that as well. You stole Alex's life from us. Yes, you parasite, his name was *Sergeant* Alexander Nelson. An heroic and proud member of the United States military. And now he's gone."

Hunter was unaware that tears were streaming down his own cheeks now. "And so is my sister. My beautiful sister, Laura. Laura Nelson. And all because of *you*. *You* took away her reason for living. You murdered her too!"

He leaned in so close now, his lips were brushing Banner's ear. "But now… now is the time for retribution. Now you're *mine*. *All mine Alan Banner.*

"You have no idea what fear is. Over the next few years--and yes, I do mean *years*--you will know all the depths and horrors of *true fear.*"

Banner was shaking hard now, mewling and sobbing.

Hunter's voice grew even softer. He blew into Banner's ear, causing him to jump violently. "Yes, Mr. Banner, show your true feelings. A small breakthrough, I'd say. I will have to inform the doctors that I believe there is hope."

He put his arm around Banner's head and drew him into his chest. "Perhaps, you should rest now, I know this has been quite draining for you."

Banner tried to pull his head away.

Hunter reached for the syringe that had been left on the small table.

He plunged the needle into Banner's neck. "Rest now, Mr. Banner." Hunter looked down on the floor where the photo of his nephew lay--a photo taken on the day Alex joined the Army. There they were the three of them, arms linked, smiling, Alex in the middle, displaying such joy and pride on his handsome face, his sister Laura's face mirrored Alex's. Hunter remembered that day and the pride and joy he also felt for the boy-turned-man and the promise of a bright future.

He looked at Banner--whose eyes were now starting to close, as the Haldol took effect-- with a look of contempt and utter malevolence. He began to smile.

"Until our next session, *Mister* Banner. "

~~NEVER~~ FEAR - PHOBIAS

10
CHIROPTOPHOBIA

FEAR OF BATS

DON MARLOWE

What was that sound?

I was trapped in the dark, but that wasn't the worst part. The worst part was that I wasn't alone. I could hear something moving. To a boy with a vivid imagination, what was here with me could be anything. Anything.

I am not even sure how I got in here. I was running through the woods as young boys love to do, and I guess I fell. I think I was knocked out for a while so things are kind of fuzzy. My knee hurts so it's tough to walk but it's so dark I can't see where to go anyway. And I don't want to walk right into the arms--or jaws, or claws--of whatever is out there.

I hope someone can hear me if I yell. But that might attract whatever is here with me; whatever is moving and making those sounds. I don't think I want to do that. Fear can affect every part of your being. Fear of being stuck here. Forever. Fear of dying. Fear of being eaten alive by whatever it is. All these run through my head, but as of yet they are not real. Just ideas of things that could never happen to me. After all, I am invincible, aren't I? Of course, nothing could ever happen to me--I have my whole life ahead of me. So I am not afraid. Yet. Not yet, but little prickles of fear are niggling at my neck and starting to make themselves at home.

So I yell anyway. What else can I do? I should have gone with my gut because I now know that yelling was a mistake. I don't hear any answering yell from above, but whatever is here with me gets suddenly louder. A lot of something. Hissing. No. More like squealing. Unearthly shrieks, then a loud sound like a flock of birds taking off. Chittering like a million huge ants. No. Not chittering. It sounds like a million people whispering in super-fast voices. Unintelligible. Whatever it is, it's coming closer...

The fear is real now. The sound is getting even louder. I don't know which way to go in the dark so I just stand there. Awaiting whatever is coming. I feel a small breeze, then the noise becomes unbearable. Loud. So loud. I cover my ears but I can still hear it. Millions of voices. All around me. Then I feel it. Them. All around me. Untold numbers. Buffeting me all over with their wings. I can feel some of them land on me. Crawling. A leathery feeling as they brush my face. Almost like skin but a little hairier. They are crawling on me and I can't even move. My heart is pounding like a jackhammer but the rest of me is paralyzed. Will it never stop? Is there no end to these creatures? It seems like I have been down here for hours! My brain is starting to close down, when something inside me finally breaks loose and I can scream. And scream. And scream. And all of a sudden I am alone again. They are gone and I am alive.

***

There is no pain except for my already injured leg so I know they didn't hurt me. At least not physically. My heart rate slows down and my hyperventilated breathing slowly begins to return to normal. I no longer hear anything but my breathing. I am alone, but any relief I feel is diminished by the fact that I am still down here with no way out. Then another sound. Shouting. From up above. Someone outside heard my screaming. I start yelling again and they find me! I am saved.

***

It was bats. Of course. But I was just a ten-year-old kid in the dark so I didn't know. Until they told me. Then it was obvious. Dumb kid. But not for long. It was time for me to learn all I could about bats. They say what you don't know can't hurt you. That is a bunch of garbage. It can hurt you. So I want to know. Everything about them. I learn that vampire bats feed on blood, but they don't drink it from their victim like Dracula. They find a warm spot on their victim, take a small bite with their teeth and then lap up the blood. An anticoagulant in their saliva inhibits clotting so they can continue to feed. But there are no vampire bats here; they are only in South America. I learn other things about bats, too, including the fact that there can be thousands of bats in one cave. There is even a cave in Texas that is believed to have as many as twenty million! Once you experience a bat swarm, it is very easy to be afraid. No matter what your logic or what's in an encyclopedia or what the experts tell you. It is a primordial fear of the unknown. So I keep learning.

***

Something is making me go back down there. Back into the cavern to show I am not afraid. Finding my way in through the dark woods is no problem--I remember the way. I climb down into the hole and find my way into the cavern. Bats are everywhere. On the walls, on the ceiling. Staring at me. Hissing at me. I decide to run but they have other plans. Thousands of them attack me. They rip me with their claws and me bite with their teeth. I go down to one knee. I feel blood running down my face. I try pushing them away but there are too many. I feel a chunk of my ear ripped off. There are bats biting my fingers and I feel part of one finger fall off. I scream and a bat crawls into my mouth, silencing me. I can feel his teeth in my tongue. I am losing my mind. No one knows I am here. I made a mistake, a big mistake. My right eye is the next target they are starting on. The world goes dark as the bats feast.

***

I wake up. In my bed. At home. Another dream, another nightmare, just like all the others. Haunting me. Someday soon I must find a way to be rid of them.

***

I am now a teenager--no longer the young boy who was trapped years ago. I am old enough to know that I can't live with this fear. With these nightmares. Old enough to be able to do something about it. I have prepared to go back into the caves--for real. I have read everything I can find about the bats in this area and know they are intelligent, gentle creatures that are beneficial because they eat insects. One bat can eat between six thousand and eight thousand mosquitoes and other insects in one night. Imagine how much a swarm can eat. I know what it feels like to be an insect in a bat swarm. I have experienced it. But unlike the insects, I survived. It makes no difference to me that I found out bats are not evil or particularly dangerous. My terror is real and overrides the conscious and logical brain. Fear dwells within the primitive "lizard brain" inside our heads. It is a primal fear; born of the caveman days of desperate survival--the fight or flight instinct. They say "What doesn't kill you makes you stronger," and "Face your fears." Sounds likes so much psychobabble to me; only platitudes to drum up business for the therapists. Yet there is truth in those words. However, I will visit no psychiatrists. I will conquer this fear on my own. I have the will to do it. Nothing could happen to me. I have the rest of my life ahead of me and I will conquer this. So I am not afraid. Yet. But I know I will be. This phobia runs deep and I have to exorcise it.

***

I am back where it happened years ago--where I fell in. The difference is now I have a rope and a flashlight. And I know what awaits me. I should have told someone where I was going but I am a loner and it is something I have to do myself. As I lower myself down into the cavern, I am glad I am wearing gloves; my palms are sweating so much it feels like a swamp in my gloves. My hands would slip off the rope without them. My heart is pounding again even though my logical brain says I will be fine. Sometimes the body overrules the brain. I am fully covered in overalls, with a hood and safety goggles to protect my head and face. My feet touch bottom and I switch on my flashlight. Even though it is bright and sunny outside, it is again pitch black in here. The light from above doesn't make its way down here. The flashlight beam doesn't illuminate too far and all I can see is a small tunnel leading off to my right. This must be where the bats came from so I must go that way. I must venture further in--toward the source of my terror. I hear the noises again. The noises that tell me again that I am not alone--they are still here. I notice things now that I didn't notice before. The air is cooler with a faint smell of ammonia. The walls and the ceiling of the tunnel are close to me--about three feet wide and six-and-a-half-feet high. They are damp, with some trickling water, and are of unforgiving rock. The floor is uneven and seems also to be mostly rock. Not that I care that much about those things. I just want to find the bats. I think I do. Yes, I do. Based on my studies of bats, I begin to whisper my memorized litany:

"Bats in this cave are not harmful. They are only harmful if they have rabies. Less than one percent of all bats have rabies..."

As I continue to go forward, the tunnel gets smaller. Now I am bent over and the walls are scraping against my shoulders. I don't really have claustrophobia, but this is still not a comfortable feeling. The smell of ammonia is getting stronger. I am stepping in something. Something that I don't even want to know what it is. The sounds are more pronounced. Just when I think that I can't go any further because the tunnel is getting too narrow, I step into the open. My flashlight doesn't even begin to dispel the gloom of the cavern. I can hear them--all the rustlings from far above. I take a deep breath to calm myself down, but now my entire body is sweating even though the cave is cool. I continue my litany: "Bats are only mammals, like people or primates. They are not rodents. They are the only true flying mammals. They live about 40 years and are afraid of people. It is only their fear that makes it seem like they are attacking. Bats are our friends..."

The bats don't seem concerned yet. I must not pose a threat. Time to change that. I pull an old shotgun out from where it was strapped to my back. I do not want to kill any bats, just startle them so they are disturbed and start flying. I aim the shotgun toward the wall instead of the ceiling and shoot off both barrels. The sound shocks me as it reverberates within the cave walls. So much that I don't even hear the bats at first. The feeling of the cave changes and it is only a second later that I feel them. All around me again. They are fleeing for the tunnel and the exit to freedom. I am buffeted by their passing and they keep coming. And they still keep coming. Will they ever stop? How many are there? My legs go weak and I suddenly find myself lying on the floor. I cover my head and I can still feel them. I am not afraid. Not afraid. YES. I. AM. I scream...

***

My previous attempt to conquer my fear stays with me. I failed miserably. I screamed like a baby even though I knew they were not hurting me and probably wouldn't. Phobias are not easy to overcome. Try locking a claustrophobic person in a small box and see how they react. Or take a person with acrophobia up onto a tall building and see if they can even get close to the edge. It is not easy and I knew that. If it were easy, it wouldn't be worth doing. So I plan on going down there again. And again. Until I am completely comfortable being with the bats. Then hopefully my terror will fade.

***

So a few months later, I am going down again. I am prepared in much the same way, but I bought the strongest flashlight I could find and I dressed in a couple of layers for more protection. I also found an old beekeeper's mask to protect my face. Hopefully this will make me feel safer. My hands are still damp as I descend, but I don't think they're as bad as they were before. I am not afraid of the small tunnel anymore as I know I can get through it now. I enter the cave. Nothing has changed. I can still hear them skittering around overhead. With the better flashlight I can actually see some of them. Hanging upside down like little creatures of the night. Eyes glowing like embers in the light. Wings folded up and wrapped around their furry bodies so they look like old Egyptian mummies. Obscene things. Repeat the litany:

"Bats are more afraid of me than I am of them. They are just trying to get out..."

Time for the shotgun. This time I have cotton stuffed in my ears so the shotgun blast doesn't disorient me right off the bat--yes, pun intended. I shoot off both barrels and ready myself for the stampede. I don't have to wait long. It is the same experience. Heart pounding, and irrational fear. Well maybe not irrational. Bats flapping, flying, darting everywhere. I notice that I actually am a bit less affected and I start to think I can actually get through this. My legs get weak but I don't fall. I open my mouth to scream, but all that comes out is a yell. Progress.

***

Attempts three and four are even better still, but I have not yet conquered my phobia. Bats have a thumb with a claw on the top of their wings and have long finger bones in their wings as well. When they crawl on you, they look like demons. All bunched up and using those thumb claws as fingers to pull themselves up. If you have ever seen a bat walking, you know what I mean. Creepy things. Small beady eyes and fangs in their mouth add to their demon-like appearance. That is the part that I don't have a handle on: the little demons crawling on you. The disjointed way they walk. I am not afraid exactly. More like creeped out. Well, maybe creeped out and slightly afraid. That is not good enough. I have to "own" my fear, not just control it. Bats must have no hold over me. If I can cure this part of my uneasiness and be totally comfortable, I will be fearless. Fearless enough so that I can go out in the world and do what I was destined to do. Wreak havoc. Incite fear. Be the avenging angel. Or is that avenging devil? Some people will think me a devil. And maybe they are right.

***

A young man at last. After so many trips down in to the cave, the bats no longer scare me. I have been in the middle of innumerable mass exoduses, I have had bats crawl on me and have never been hurt. They can crawl on me and stare me down with their glowing red eyes, even hiss at me with their fanged mouths, but I no longer fear them. I no longer think they are creepy. I have cured my phobia but I need more. I need to banish any doubts that bats have any power over me. This will hopefully be my last visit to the place of my childhood terrors. I no longer have any need for extra clothing; just jeans, a T-shirt, baseball cap and boots. I have a makeshift ladder to get in and out of the cave and my hands no longer sweat on the way down. This time I won't even use the shotgun. I have another idea. I enter the cave and the smell isn't even that bad any more. The fact that I walk in three inches of guano doesn't even bother me. This time I stand in front of the exit tunnel, effectively making them go through me to escape. I light a few firecrackers and throw them away from me. They explode and the response is immediate. Again the bats stream for the exit, but I am in the way.

A bat finds its way with an inner radar; what is called echolocation. It emits very high frequency vocalizations through its mouth and nose and its ears pick up the bounce back from objects. That is how it finds insects and avoids trees, buildings, or other things--like people. Or, in this case, me. So the bats know I am there, but the huge number of bats trying to get out through the small portion of the opening I am not covering makes it very difficult for them to avoid me. I spread my arms wide and welcome their touch. I am not stupid enough to face them head on as their claws could do damage to my face if they couldn't avoid it. They swarm all over me in their frantic race to freedom. I feel their panic; their heat as they land on me. Let them crawl. Let them swarm. No fear. I talk to them and let them know I am not afraid, that I am their friend. Perhaps some are less panicked. Perhaps some listen to my voice and know that I won't hurt them. After all, we have been through this together numerous times. But they all still seek escape, and after they are gone, I still feel like an invader. I do not feel part of them... yet. I am going to need one more visit.

***

Am I insane? Indeed not--I am quite sane and normal in other aspects of my life. Of course they say insane people don't know they are insane, but no one has ever intimated that they thought I was crazy. Batty maybe, but not crazy--yes, pun intended again. Am I obsessed? Perhaps to this one degree; no normal person would go to the extremes that I have to cure a phobia. Any rational person would consider my last visit as proof enough that I have accomplished the cure. Am I driven? Indubitably. Driven with the need to become one with the bats. I must. I started out just to cure my phobia, but in doing so, my life's mission has become clear to me. I cannot succeed in my calling with anything less. So, call me driven, but not insane.

The world will soon form its own opinion of me. Am I evil? I don't think so, but my victims might think I am. Good and evil are often subject to interpretation. Insane? Driven? Obsessed? Evil? Maybe I do deserve to be called a little bit of each.

***

Back down in the cave and the bats are again swarming. I feel no fear. I grab one and stare in its eyes, and just to show it who is boss, I bite its head off. Others I fling into the walls in my disdain. I crunch many under my feet.

Of course, I wake up and realize it was another dream. Not a nightmare, just a dream. I am in control, not the bats. I am their lord and master. They will do my bidding…

***

It is time. Valuable time is being wasted. There is so much to be done. I need to finish my trial now. I head back into the cave for the last time. No flashlight. It is not needed. The darkness is part of me. Also, my eyesight has gotten excellent in the dark after all the times down here. I enter the cavern of the bats and open up my pack. I pull out the siren. I pull out a net. I pull out some telescoping poles. I pull out my lunch and a small folding cot. I put the poles around the cavern exit, the tunnel that the bats must use to escape. I affix the net to the poles so that the exit is partially covered. This way many of the bats can get out, but others will become entangled in the net. That is where I will be. This must be the ultimate test, so I undress. Now there is no protection from the bats. I stand in the net and ready the siren. Goosebumps break out on my arms but that is only due to the coolness of the cave, not apprehension. I am at peace with this. I need this. I take a deep breath. I set off the siren…

***

The siren is a new sound, so the response is immediate. Thousands of bats streaming toward the exit. Some get out, but many are ensnared in the net. Where I am. I hold out my arms and stand there with the bats covering me. Any chiropterologist might call me insane, but I know there is nothing here to harm me. No rabies. No infections. No disease. They cover my entire body, sometimes two or three deep as they try to escape. I reach down and turn the siren off. I talk to them. I pick up one after the other and stroke each one gently for a second, then reach around the netting and let them out. Is it my imagination, or are they calming down? I continue my ritual. Stroke and talk. Talk and stroke. They are definitely getting calmer. Some just hanging on the net or on me. Not trying to escape. I get my lunch out and start eating. Not insane. I just want to be totally at ease with my new friends. I share my lunch with many of them. Some eat a little, some don't. They are not used to this type of food but, when I carefully put little bits into their mouths, they chew. Some swallow. I keep talking. Talking and stroking and releasing. The bats are settling in on the netting and a few are still on me. They have accepted my presence. I sit down and continue my mantra. Most are going back to sleep, no longer trying to escape. The only sounds are a few bats scrabbling and my own voice. Soothing. Reassuring. Now I lie down on the cot and close my eyes. My breathing is normal, my pulse slow and steady. My voice starts to drift off. I sleep. With the bats.

My internal clock wakes me up after about fifteen minutes--I dare stay no longer as bat guano can create a mold, which when inhaled in large quantities can lead to a fatal respiratory disease. Makes me wonder why women's mascara can contain bat guano.

Everything is pretty much as it was when I fell asleep. I no longer have any bats on me. They are all hanging upside down. Many are on the net still, but most must have settled back on the cavern ceiling. I gently whisper to each bat as I pull it off the net and send it on its way. Soon the net is clear and all is quiet. No more trips down here will be needed. I am at peace. I feel like I belong to the family of bats and they belong to me. I don't want to leave and go back to the upper world. But I must. Too much to do. I send them a telepathic thank you and a telepathic goodbye. Who knows if they hear me or understand?

***

Nothing could happen to me now. I have too much to do with my life. I have no fear. I have done it. It took years, but the fear of bats no longer controls me. Now I control it. Now it is time to get to work. Time to make others afraid. Make them pay. Let my strength become their fear. But I can't do my work as myself. No one would be afraid of me. I need to inflict them with fear as great as my former terror of bats, so I need to become someone else. I need another persona. That will be easy. I can wear a mask. Then they will fear the mask. I need the disguise. No one would be afraid of Bruce Wayne...

11
THANTOPHOBIA

FEAR OF LOSING SOMEONE

THOMAS F. MONTELEONE

Your children are not your children.
For their souls dwell in the house of tomorrow,
which you cannot visit, not even in your dreams.
—Kahlil Gibran

I'm not sure how much longer I can hold the son-of-a-bitch off.

For the past few days, I've seen more signs of his arrival. Each time I enter Becky's room, I think I smell the faintest of scents--a grim, olfactory wake of his passage.

He's so bold, coming here flirting with my daughter, thinking I have no sense of it. And yet, it is the driving force in my life. There is nothing that will give me more strength than to have the chance to beat him. He knows now that I keep an old Little League aluminum baseball bat in the pantry, but he also knows I am not afraid to use it.

It began the day Rhonda and I brought her home from the hospital. There is nothing more fragile than a newborn child--something I had never realized till that moment. I admit, being a cost accountant for Proctor & Gamble all my adult life, had perhaps kept me somewhat removed from the mainstream of life. When I brought a new life into the world, it was like getting slapped in the face.

The very first night, Rhonda kept her in a bassinet in our bedroom. I questioned the need for it until darkness fell over everything and the house had shut down to the point of the occasional creak of an old foundation. I could hear my wife's breathing at my ear, a signature of her exhaustion and a final release of tension, anxiety, and fear.

Little did I realize that mine had just begun.

I never slept that first night. An endless stretch of black time wherein I lay listening to what seemed like breathing of the most labored sort. I had no idea a tiny, living human could make such scary noises and survive till morning. Wheezing, coughing, rattling, mucous throttled sucking were only a few of the horrible sounds through which I suffered that night. It was so intensely awful, I became quite certain we would lose Becky before dawn.

But we didn't.

The bassinet remained in our bedroom another three or four weeks before I allowed my wife to have the baby sleeping in a crib so far away from us--her own bedroom down the hall. I had grown accustomed to the travail of her breathing, and it measured out the nights as a metronome of life itself.

It was just about that time when I was watching the Game of the Week (the Orioles against the Blue Jays, I think), and I saw the commercial. Actually, it was probably one of those Public Service Announcements, and what it was doing shoehorned among the endless array of beer and razor commercials I could not imagine.

(Of course, I now know the message was placed there by Divine Intercedence. It was important that I receive the message when I did.)

The message? Oh yes, it was important all right. Have you ever heard of SIDS?

Neither had I! Imagine my shock as I sat there in my Laz-Z-Boy to see that there is this hideous phenomenon known as Crib Death or Sudden Infant Death Syndrome. Newborns, up to the age of six months, are suddenly found dead in their cribs, and no one has the foggiest notion as to how or why.

How come I've never heard of this? I ask myself. How come

I've never seen anything about this terrible syndrome until now, until the very moment I have my own little baby who may be victim to this horrible thing?

This was positively incredible to me. But stunned though I may have been, I remained lucid enough to realize I had been given a Sign, a celestial memorandum so to speak, to be ever vigilant.

As the months ticked past, I took it upon myself to nightly approach the crib and listen for Becky's sweet breath. When my wife discovered my habit, she chided me for being so overprotective, and for a moment, I became suspicious of her. Surely, she could not be in league with any forces that would harm my daughter. In short order, I banished such thoughts from my head.

Well, at least I tried to...

Time continued its work, and Becky not only escaped the critical period of SIDS frequency, but she weathered bouts of commons colds, influenzas, chicken pox, measles, and mumps. It seemed like I blinked my eyes and she was four years old. She had been such a healthy baby and toddler, that I think I became lulled into a false sense of security during those years. We rarely allowed her to leave the house, other than to roam about our fenced-in yard. Whenever other children came over to play with her, I always watched them with a careful eye. I saw this movie once about a six-year-old serial killer...

When it came to protecting your daughter, you couldn't be too careful.

It wasn't until Becky started pre-school that I began to realize how foolish, how lax I had actually been. There were so many ways she could be in danger, at first I had a hard time tracking everything-- until I took a page from my accountant's training and logged everything in a wonderful ledger with cross-referencing column and rows. Once I inflicted some order on the situation, I began to feel better about everything.

I didn't allow her to ride the school bus until I'd completed a dossier on the driver and had the vehicle inspected. The dossier thing worked so well that I used the same P.I. to work up files on everyone at the pre-school, my neighbors, and even Louise Smeak, the Sunday school teacher at St. Albans Episcopal. I wanted to have total control over everyone who would have any contact with my daughter.

You could never be too careful...

I heard his radio talk show where this guy who called in had postulated that many fatal diseases were actually transmitted by those plastic "sporks" they give out at fast-food eateries. I had never thought much about this, but it certainly made sense if you stopped to consider everything.

And then somebody told me that peanut butter is a major killer of small children. People feed it to them on the end of spoon and it gets lodged at the intersection of the esophagus and the bronchial tubes or something like that. It's so dangerous that even the Heimlich maneuver doesn't work, and of course there is always the truth that a spoon is pretty damned close to a spork. But can you imagine, that Death hides even in a peanut butter jar?

Well, you can bet that my Becky didn't eat any more of that stuff.

The years slipped away from me; I had risen through the ranks at P&G until I was the Chief of the entire financial division. Sure, I had plenty of time on my hands, but still not enough to administer to Becky's needs as well as I would like. Retirement was still many years off and my wife did not seem to share my over-riding concern for my daughter's welfare.

In fact, I was beginning to realize that perhaps Rhonda was not the ally I'd always supposed.

Becky turned ten, and that meant a whole new ledger, a whole new set of variables that I would have to start tracking. She was a very pretty girl and despite my efforts to discourage contact with other people, lots of the kids in her class wanted to be her friends. More dossiers. More money. But what did I care? I was being a good parent.

It was also around this time that Rhonda actually turned against me. It started slowly and with much subtlety, but I recognized it early on because I'd sensed it coming. She told her sister I had too much pressure at my job--which I was not adjusting well to Becky's pre-teen years, and worst of all, that I needed a hobby. Can you imagine such foolishness? I could have gotten very angry, but I knew how outward displays of domestic unrest can be harmful to children. An article in the International Enquirer said depression and teen suicides tended to be caused by bad parenting, so by remaining tranquil, I was being a wise and caring father.

I knew that I would eventually discover a solution to the

problem Rhonda was becoming. If I remained patient and vigilant, I would be given a sign, an answer. And it came to me the day I realized that Mr. Death had changed his tactics. I mean, it was no secret he'd been after Becky since we'd brought her home from Cook Memorial Hospital. It was only through my stalwart efforts she'd remained as safe as she had.

But Mr. Death is slick and he took to impersonating regular people that might come in contact with Becky. That's why I had to cancel all her dental visits and of course there would be no more examinations by Doc Wilson. The biggest problem were those unexpected situations that could not be planned. For example, when Becky answered the door one after-school day to admit the meter reader for the local gas and electric company, I almost lost my usual composure.

(Where was her mother? you might ask--as I certainly did. How could she allow the child to do something as dangerous as answer the door? The answer lay ahead, as you shall see.)

You can already imagine how horrible it could have been if the gas-man had actually been The Gas-Man--if you get my meaning...

Yes, I realized I must learn from this experience. And learn I did indeed. After pulling Becky from her school, I arranged to have her education continued at home under the care of a carefully checked-out tutor. The young boys who had already begun sniffing around the hems of my daughter's skirts received stern warnings from me to simply Stay Away. I reinforced my messages with letters to all the boys' parents.

That seemed to help matters very much until a man in a charcoal suit with a red tie knocked on the door. He said he was from the State Department of Health and Mental Hygiene, and that he wanted to ask me a few questions. He also said he had a warrant to inspect my premises. He showed me some ID that said his name was Silverstein and some papers with official seals and notary stamps on them. He didn't know I recognized his true identity, and therefore misinterpreted my smile as I led him into the kitchen. I directed him to a chair at the dinette where I offered him a cup of coffee. He said yes and asked him what kind of questions he had for me. I was going to grab my aluminum baseball bat right away, but I was curious as to what Mr. Death would want to ask me. Didn't he already Know

Everything? And so I poured two cups of Maxwell House and sat down to listen.

He said a few things right up front about Becky that made me very angry. I almost reached for the baseball bat twice, and both times, I thought maybe I should listen a little longer, even though it was making me very angry.

"After reading copies of the letters you sent the Wizniewski and Harrison boys, I decided to contact you directly," said Mr. Death. "Initially, I spoke to your wife, and she told me about your... tendency to... ah, go on at length about your daughter." I asked him what exactly Rhonda had said.

"Exactly? Well, sir, she said that she is very much afraid of you. Did you know that?"

I told him no. Anything else, I asked.

"She said that she had decided a long time ago she would tolerate your behavior--"

"Tolerate?"

"Yes, as long as it remained within the family, she figured it was safer, better for everyone involved."

Safer... yes, I see, I told him. But then, why are you here, Mr. Silverstein? (I needed to allay any suspicions he might have that I knew his true identity.)

"Well, it's hard to explain, but we've received a petition to have your case examined by a state psychiatrist," he said. "We have statements by neighbors and relatives and parents at Holbrook Elementary, plus an interesting letter from a private investigator, Lucius Mallory. It was forwarded to us from Lieutenant Karsay at the 3rd Precinct."

I moved away from the table, close to the pantry door where my aluminum buddy awaited my touch. "And what do these statements and letters have to do with me?"

Mr. Death almost chuckled. Can you imagine his audacity? "I think you know what this is all about. Your daughter, Rebecca, is dead, sir. She died when she was three months old from SIDS. More than nine years ago."

I think that's when I lost it--when he mouthed such a cruel lie, a heinous blasphemy in my house. I screamed something about what a liar he was and how I knew his true identity and how I would stop him from taking my daughter away from me.

He went down like a dumb palooka from the first impact to the base of his skull. As his life fluids seeped across the tiles of the kitchen floor, I realized I'd made a mistake. This man, Silverstein, was a mere mortal. Another of Death's clever tricks, no doubt. I checked my watch, and knew I had little time. Rhonda would be due home from her part-time job at the neighborhood library at any moment.

There was no need to clean up the mess, however. None at all.

It has been a long weekend. The scent of death I mentioned earlier is getting heavy in here. The crowds of neighbors and police cars that have surrounded my little bungalow have been a terrible distraction, and I fear that Mr. Death will get in while I am forced to deal with the foolish meddling of those outside. The television says there is a dangerous hostage situation here. I think it is a good thing they don't know about Silverstein and Rhonda. They probably think I might do harm to Rebecca, which reveals them to be the *fools* they are.

Don't they know I'm her *father?*
And a father can't ever be too careful…

~~NEVER~~ FEAR - PHOBIAS

12
LOGIZOMECHANOPHOBIA

FEAR OF TECHNOLOGY

HOLLY PRENTISS

Her husband always said she played computer solitaire way too much.

In spite of the fact they had been married to each other for over 20 years (or perhaps because of it), Dennis and Liz were very much in love. They were high school sweethearts and got married right out of school. They were a little bit old-fashioned for their generation, but they were perfectly suited to each other. So much so, in fact, that each often knew what the other was thinking and could finish the other's sentence. They were never blessed with any children but they loved travel and sightseeing. They loved museums and mountain wildernesses. They loved the tall buildings and hustle-bustle of the big cities just as much as quaint, quiet, picturesque little hamlets. They loved to try interesting restaurants. They loved to go to the movies, concerts and the theater. They really enjoyed new sights and sensations and especially enjoyed them together. Dennis and Liz just really enjoyed each other's company and spending time with each other.

Dennis and Liz had such full lives that they had no need of

gadgets and technological toys. In fact, they had no PC, DVR, GPS or other "frippery." Dennis said they didn't need anything that was computerized or an acronym. They did have a TV, which didn't seem to be too technical or complicated and their one concession to *modern* technology was their cell phones, which were quite practical, given their love of road trips.

That's why it was so unusual when Liz came home with a laptop.

It started out innocently enough. Liz convinced Dennis that it was only for keeping in touch with her brother overseas and some of their far-flung friends. Sure, she could write letters and send them "snail mail" (that term always made her giggle.) But her letter writing took forever because the letters always went on and on, so she often laid them aside to do other things and then they were never finished or were forgotten. A computer would be a much easier, faster way to communicate. At least that was her reasoning. What's more, all their friends and family--in fact everyone they knew--had at least one desktop or laptop computer, tablet, iPod or smart phone. "Besides, we need to join the modern age, don't we?" What Liz wouldn't admit is that it was really a sudden impulse buy. What she *couldn't* admit, even to herself, is that she almost felt compelled. So she bought the computer.

That was only the beginning. Liz surfed the web and clicked on all the news "bits and bytes" as well as the human interest stories. She joined a social media site to keep in touch with friends and family and she "friended" dozens of people, even some she didn't know. She watched kitten videos and listened to music. She also loved showing Dennis her favorite videos and internet jokes.

"Dennis, check this out."

"Hey Dennis, you should read this. You'll like it. It's really interesting."

"This is a really good how-to video. You should watch this. We can replace that window ourselves. It looks really easy."

He dutifully watched all the videos and read all the news and human interest stories she showed him. She was right. Most of them were entertaining or instructive.

Liz researched anything and everything, spending enormous amounts of time on the computer. (At least that's what Dennis thought.) Any time a question came up, trivial or not, she would fetch the computer to look up the answer. "Whatever did we do before computers?" she wondered. This computer thing was amazing! It was fun!

In the beginning, she taught Dennis how to use the computer. After that, she would sometimes "allow" him to use it, but he always seemed to have problems with it. At first it wasn't too bad; it was merely inconvenient or annoying. Then the computer started acting more erratically; slow downloads, freezes, crashes and multiple errors became the norm. He would throw his hands in the air and shout, "I give up!" It seemed, however, that Liz never had any trouble. In fact, every time Liz took over after Dennis surrendered, the computer worked just fine. One time Dennis said jokingly, "Your computer doesn't like me, I guess." He only half believed it at the time.

Then Liz discovered the many and myriad computer solitaire games, both online and off. She reasoned that playing these games would sharpen her mind. She was a little afraid of Alzheimer's disease and had read somewhere that playing cards and doing puzzles kept the mind active and could help ward off the onset of dementia. She soon became addicted. At first the games were easy and she won most of the time, but then the games changed. It was as if the computer watched and made it more and more difficult to win which only kept her coming back for more. She had to better her time, her score. She would play the same game over and over until she won and then move on to another game and do the same thing over again.

It became her consuming obsession.

She rarely left the house now.

Dennis couldn't remember the last time they went on a day trip together. He loved their day trips. They would be-bop down the road, just enjoying life, listening to the radio and playing their own version of "Name That Tune." He smiled to himself, remembering one particular trip when Liz was singing along to the oldies at the top of her lungs until he groaned, pretending that her singing was really bad and he changed the station.

"Hey! I love that song," she protested.

"I know you do, but do you have to sing so loud every time it comes on?" He secretly loved her singing. He knew that when she was singing, it meant she was happy. *She doesn't sing anymore*, he thought sorrowfully.

That trip had been really fun. In fact, it was one of his favorite trips with her, although they all were pleasurable and memorable. They could discuss anything and everything in the car or at home. They talked about current events, going to Europe someday, their dreams of remodeling the house or the best pizza or ice cream they ever had. They even talked about such mundane things as home maintenance and gardening.

"I want to plant a vegetable garden," she announced one day last year. "I want to know where my food comes from. Besides, I read that locally grown food is much healthier for you. It can even help alleviate allergies."

"Where will you put it?" Dennis tended to be the practical one.

"Oh, I don't know. Maybe in that sunny corner of the back yard."

"You can't even take care of your flower garden," he pointed out and then they planned what vegetables to plant when they got around to it. It wasn't an exciting life but it was a happy life. A good life.

But now, Dennis and Liz didn't talk much anymore. She was always typing or "mousing" away on her laptop. He missed her.

He was becoming a little anxious about this computer situation. Liz seemed so… absent. She had always been his rock; was always there. She had an inner strength. Except where spiders were concerned. She wasn't afraid of snakes, worms or mice; but she was *terrified* of spiders. Big ones, little ones, hairy ones, even the beautiful colorful ones; it didn't matter. If it had eight legs, it sent her running. Dennis would hear a screech followed by, "Honeeeeeeeeeey! There's a spider in here! Please come kill it! Pleeeeease!" Dennis wasn't particularly crazy about spiders either but he knew he couldn't resist her summons. "Fear not, fair maiden. I shall fly to your rescue. "And he did. Every time. When Liz was satisfied that the monster had been slain and she could safely re-enter the room, she would throw her arms around his neck. "My hero," she would cry. He was her knight in shining armor and always would be.

She always said, "Drive careful. I love you," and kissed him when he left to go somewhere. Every night they would rub noses Eskimo-style, tell each other "I love you," and kiss each other good night three times. It was their little nightly ritual. Now all he got was a hasty peck on the cheek because she was so engrossed. Night after night she sat in front of that "Great Unblinking Eye" until the wee hours of the morning when fatigue overtook her. Dennis was dismayed.

She would occasionally leave the computer to do necessary things, but was always drawn back for some reason or other. It was as though she was tethered to the computer; like it had her on a leash. Whenever she strayed away too long, it jerked her back. There always seemed to be some reason she had to return to the machine with that glowing blue screen. She was mesmerized. Captivated. Captive.

Dennis remembered hearing one of his professors in college singing the praises of computers, saying what a blessing they were. How computers have helped mathematicians solve enormous complicated problems, how they helped launch us into space, how they have helped us communicate with each other and even simplified our lives. If computers were *really* such a blessing then why were so many people becoming increasingly isolated, alienated by all that time spent on their cell phones, online or playing computer games? *Television might be the opiate of the masses, but computers are crack cocaine.*

After a while, Dennis noticed that Liz started to look a little rough around the edges; a little haggard. She looked like she hadn't eaten in a week; in fact, he couldn't remember the last time he saw her in the kitchen. She used to cook the most amazing meals, but now she didn't have time. She was always on that infernal computer. She used to make great chicken dishes. She would announce, "We're having 'experimental chicken' tonight." She called it experimental chicken because she used her imagination along with whatever was at hand. Dennis would make a face and say "Maybe I'll order Chinese," and she would whack him with the dish towel. She also made amazing omelets, delicious meatloaf, quiches and she made 'killer lasagna'. He also recalled how she would yell, "Come and get it" when dinner was ready and how she laughed when he came in with his arms wide open, ready to embrace her, saying, "I came to get it." And then, trying to look disappointed, "Oh. You meant dinner." Then he would wrap his arms around her and give her a big bear hug. He heaved a sigh, wondering when those days might return; when things would get back to normal and he would have his Liz back again.

He was really worried about Liz and he tried to coax her to come with him to restaurants for dinner, but she either turned him down--too busy--or told him, "In a few minutes, sweetie. I'm right in the middle of something," and hours would go by, so he gave up and fixed something to eat and put a plate on the table next to her. Most times, he would check on her before he went to bed and the plate would be untouched. She wasn't getting enough sleep either. He could see the dark circles under her eyes. Why couldn't she tear herself away from that wretched monitor? Dennis was dismayed and disturbed.

One night, when he came home late from a baseball game (Liz used to go with him, but not anymore), he heard her talking. At first he thought she was on the phone, but she wasn't. She seemed to be mumbling to herself, but then he realized she was conversing with the computer. This really spooked him, but he passed it off as a onetime thing. Maybe she was half asleep? Maybe she was just anthropomorphizing this machine? Either way, it probably wasn't good for her and he suggested she try to spend less time on the computer.

"I'm really worried about you, Liz. You're going to make yourself sick unless you get more sleep and eat more. That computer is taking up way too much of your time. You need to take a break. Maybe you should shut it down for a whole day. Let the computer rest and you can too." He thought it was a reasonable request.

"Oh, don't be silly. I don't spend *that* much time on it." She smiled coyly at him and added, "Maybe you're just a little bit jealous."

"Just try, won't you? Please?"

She didn't do it. Or maybe she just couldn't. Dennis was even more dismayed and disturbed.

Dennis was starting to feel a bit uneasy around the computer. He began to despise that unnatural blue glow from the monitor and the tick, tick, ticking of the keys on the keyboard as Liz typed away. He started avoiding Liz whenever she was on the computer and would offer some lame excuse that seemed to satisfy her. He stopped watching TV. There was no enjoyment in it, not only because he and Liz had always watched their favorite shows together (he really missed that), but also because the TV made him a little jumpy now. That big blue screen and the little red power light were vaguely unnerving. Of course! The TV looked too much like a computer and probably was one. It was digital.

Then it dawned on him that there were other gadgets in the house with "computers" in them. It seemed that everywhere he looked there was something with a computer chip in it. Staring back. Mocking him. Even the LED digits of the clock on the kitchen stove looked almost like little red blinking orbs that seemed to say, "I've got my eyes on you." It gave him the creeps.

Eventually, he couldn't even sleep because the clock radio seemed to be watching him, as if he were its prey. Those red numbers again. He smashed it. When Liz asked him about it, he said he accidentally dropped it. "I can replace it with a second-hand, wind-up alarm clock."

One day she asked him, "Where's the coffee maker?" He had actually thrown it out but said he let a neighbor borrow it. "Besides, we can make coffee the old way--on the stove." Liz was dubious. He also sabotaged the microwave and told Liz that he forgot to take the fork off the plate and it shorted out. He could tell by the look on her face she didn't really believe him. He said he would shop for a new one. Of course, he had no intention of bringing another one of those watchful, waiting, devious, digital machines into the house.

Everywhere he went, there were those blinking red digits, "I'm watching you." Those glowing blue monitors, "I'm watching you." He couldn't get away from them. They were everywhere! He began to feel like he was being stalked by computers because, of course, there are computer chips in everything. "We're watching you."

Then, one awful fateful night, as Dennis passed the doorway to the living room where Liz sat in the dark with the computer screen's blue light casting an eerie glow on her face, he saw slimy black tentacles slithering out of the laptop, winding around her wrists, pinning them to the keyboard and twisting around her neck. Liz seemed not to notice. Dennis squeezed his eyes tight in disbelief, shook his head, looked again, and it was gone.

He decided that he had to end this madness and he advanced toward the wall, intending to pull the plug on this fiendish machine, this slayer of happiness, but from the corner of his eye he saw the flicker of movement; a menacing dark shadow. It seemed poised to strike his throat. He jumped back to safety. He went wild with fear for Liz and tried to pull her away. She snarled, turned toward him and her face was contorted with such red and purple fury that it frightened and horrified him. Her eyes looked positively demonic. This was not his wife. This was some hideous, malicious, underworld creature: a monster. What had happened to her? This woman who had been so full of life and joy, humor and adventure, was now some sort of dark, twisted, malevolent, foul--only one word came even a *little bit* close to describing what she had become--troll.

His beautiful wife, his lifelong companion, his very breath of life, was gone. He couldn't live like this... with this... thing. He couldn't bear to see what was happening to her. He was horrified. The sickly blue light from the computer monitor seemed to grow brighter, mocking him. He was terrified. His heart lurched in his chest and seemed to burst. He was shattered, split asunder. He knew he had to get away. Flee! Flee from this monstrosity that was both his wife and computer.

He dashed to the bedroom and threw some clothes into his old duffel bag. Then he went into the bathroom for his toothbrush and razor and a few other toiletries. He decided not to take his credit cards. "Better not. They have computer chips in them." He didn't have much cash, but he would take some out at the ATM. "Another one of those computerized acronym things," he thought in disgust. Oh well. It couldn't be helped. The last thing he did was toss his cell phone into the toilet. "That's exactly where it belongs."

When he left her, she was surfing travel websites and reading about London, Rome, St. Petersburg and Vienna--all places they dreamed of exploring together that, sadly, she would never see in person and he wouldn't either, because she couldn't tear herself away from that blasted computer. He wanted desperately to kiss her, but he was afraid. This time there was no "Drive careful" or "I love you." She didn't even look up when he said good bye, she was so intent. *Don't look back*, he told himself, but he found it almost impossible not to look back at this shell of a woman he loved so much, bathed in that vile blue glow.

He turned and darted out of the house and into the garage. He slung his duffle bag into the back seat of the shiny black Jeep Cherokee. Then he got into the driver's seat, put the key into the ignition and turned it. Nothing. It wouldn't start the first two tries. He was puzzled. "I just had it in the shop and they said everything was fine." And then, "Duh... I forgot that they hooked it up to a computer to read the engine status." Computer again! This thought made him apprehensive, but he needed transportation. On the third try it started. He backed out of the driveway and drove down the street toward the city.

He stopped at the first ATM he saw. He pulled a baseball cap down low over his eyes and hunching over, he approached the machine. "Can't be too careful. Security cameras and chip readers." He was nervous, fidgety. He tried to calm himself and act as casual as he could. Wouldn't do to raise suspicions. He cringed as he followed the instructions on that hateful monitor. For a brief moment he thought he caught a glimpse of a message: "We're watching you, Dennis." He shook it off, grabbed the cash--he had requested the maximum--crammed it into his pockets and then fled to the Jeep. His card was still in the machine and the receipt was dangling from the slot.

"I need to lose myself in a crowd," he thought frantically. "And I need to trade this car in for an older model without a computer or a GPS tracker." Once he was safely in the city, he located a used car dealership and found just the type of car he wanted. He would do a straight up trade; no cash. A smiling salesman approached him and offered him a seat inside at his desk. There was a computer on it. Dennis told him, "No thanks. We can do business out here in the lot."

Just his luck, though. He got an honest, decent car salesman who suspected something was wrong.

"Sir, am I hearing you right? You want to trade your 2014 Jeep Cherokee for this old clunker?"

"Yes, that's what I want."

"But your Cherokee is worth more than twice as much as this vehicle. Are you *sure* you want to do this?"

"Yes."

"But why?"

"That's none of your business. I have my reasons." Where were the shady salesmen when you needed them?

The stupid man was so uneasy he wanted to call Liz to be sure the trade was okay. Dennis fled the car lot, abandoning his Jeep and his duffle bag.

He somehow found his way on foot into the middle of the

city. It was almost rush hour and people were hurrying and scurrying everywhere. He looked around at all the faces of the pedestrians in the crowd. So many of them had cell phones plastered to their ears. So many had iPods and smart phones. They seemed to be oblivious to their surroundings and all of them were *walking with monsters!* All of them had slimy, black, writhing tentacles that twined around their necks and wrists and snaked into their ears. Why? Why did they allow this abomination? Could they not see what was happening to them?

He spotted an attractive young teenage girl walking with a friend. She was engrossed; ignoring her friend and texting someone on her smart phone, the loathsome black tentacles twining in her hair, around her ears. Fear shook him. Fear for this innocent young girl. He couldn't stand it. He had to warn her. He couldn't save his Liz. It was too late for her, but maybe it wasn't too late for this girl who still had a lifetime in front of her. He rushed toward her, his eyes wild, shouting at her, "Wake up!"

He wanted to grab her by the shoulders and shake her till she saw what was happening around her. See that computers were invading her soul, cutting her off from real people. Making her, for all intents and purposes, into a zombie. Instead, he seized her phone and dashed it to the ground.

She jumped back. "Hey! What's the matter with you, you creep?!? You broke my phone!" Dennis saw the beginning of the red and purple rage in her face.

"Don't you know what's happening to you? Can't you see the evil? I'm trying to help you. Trying to save you," he stammered. Her friend started to advance toward him and the girl was screaming for the police at the top of her lungs.

Dennis' eyes went wide in panic and he started to babble a bit. "Don't cause a scene. Don't alert the authorities. They'll haul me in to a police station or worse, take me to a hospital. I'll be at the mercy of computers and machines." He spun around and ran as fast as he could. When he thought he had lost them, he ducked into an empty alley and hid, cowering and shaking, behind a dumpster to catch his breath and try to think of what to do next.

He tried desperately to remember the "Y2K" scare back in 1999. Details. He needed to remember details about what was supposed to happen in the coming great computer crash and chaos that never came to pass. There was such a hue and cry back then that ended in a whimper. He and Liz really hadn't paid much attention at the time. They thought it really wouldn't affect them since they didn't own a computer. He wracked his brain, trying to remember the alarmist news stories about all the possible consequences. He couldn't go to the library and look it up since all the information was digitized and accessed by computer.

The digital age, he thought with a mix of fear and revulsion. "*Everything* is digitized. Newspapers, documents, books, music, movies... How soon before *people* are digitized; turned into zeroes and ones in a computer? Can they digitize a mind, a soul? How soon before people can be printed out--manufactured--with the new 3D printing technology?" That thought almost threw him into another state of utter panic, but he closed his eyes and took several deep breaths to calm himself and concentrate on the issue at hand.

He needed to remember: when the clock ticked over to the year 2000, what devices would have been affected? Obviously, home and business computers, but what about transportation? Trains and planes, traffic signals and... what else? He already knew about appliances like televisions, microwaves and coffeemakers. But banks and hospitals and medical equipment would have been affected as well. Telephones, too. Not just cell phones, but even land lines. Almost everything has a computer chip in it. He remembered reading somewhere that tiny computer chips were even being implanted in newborn babies at the hospitals. And why didn't people worry more about artificial intelligence? Maybe they've been fooled into thinking we're light years away from that. "Hah! It's here. I've seen it."

Dennis was becoming agitated, again. He was desperate. *I have to get away. But how to get away from computers? Where can I go? I need to run, to hide. Away from machines and computers.*

I can sleep in church pews maybe. For a while. If the churches don't have security cameras. Can't do that for very long, though. Not safe. Maybe up in the mountains; in the wilderness, like the old-time pioneers. Why didn't I ever take survival training? Why don't they teach these things in school? Math and science; those are for machines, computers. Survival training is the only useful subject. The only important one.

His thoughts were becoming a bit chaotic. In fact, he began to realize they were almost like computer bits and bytes. Terror rose anew in his mind and blocked out all rational thought.

Have to keep going. Find a safe place; a place where there are no computers. No computer chips.

Keep going.

Credit cards. Cell phones. Cars. Traffic cameras. Security cameras. Have manufacturers started putting smart sensory webbing in clothing yet? Don't know. Don't want to be tracked. Better not buy any new clothes. Need to stay out of stores. Security cameras, the eyes of the machine, will be watching. Maybe I can ransack a clothing donation box without getting caught.

I can find food in restaurant and grocery store dumpsters. I can slink in the shadows. I can avoid the eyes and ears of the infernal computers. I have to stay hidden, avoid people, cell phones. I can find glorious freedom from computers in the safety of the wilderness. No computers there. I can be safe there.

Keep going.

***

Some weeks later, Liz answered the door to find herself face to face with a uniformed police officer.

The young policeman seemed nervous. She could tell he was attracted to her; thought she was very pretty. She studied him noncommittally while he spoke. He was talking about Dennis.

"I'm very sorry, ma'am. He was found in the woods by some hikers. It seems your husband died of exhaustion and exposure."

She stared blankly at the handsome young police officer on the doorstep. She seemed not to comprehend his words. He felt pity for her. So pretty; so young to be a widow. Then, from the corner of his eye, he thought he caught a bit of movement inside. It almost looked like a big black snake writhing around the computer desk in the corner, but when he turned to look at it directly it was gone. *It was probably just a shadow from the blowing curtains,* he thought and dismissed it.

"One more thing, ma'am," He added. "We found this piece of paper in his hand. Do you know what it means?"

He handed her the small scrap of paper and she read the last words Dennis had written.

"I haven't the foggiest," she murmured.

As she turned away, she let drop the warning note and the corner of her lip curled up just a little.

The paper fluttered to the ground and landed face up. The officer bent down to pick it up and again read the baffling words:

"I know for a fact that the devil does NOT have horns and a pitchfork. The devil has a USB port.

"Beware!

"Diabolus ex Machina."

NEVER FEAR - PHOBIAS

13
NECROPHOBIA

FEAR OF DEAD THINGS

LAURA HARNER

Chapter One

I dreamed the dream again last night, so the episode on my way to work shouldn't have been any surprise. And yet, as always, the reality of the situation and the speed with which it overtook me caught me unaware.

"I can't breathe--" My words faltered, along with the oxygen that had stopped feeding my lungs, somewhere between Schofield Hill Road and Chambers Street--predictably, one block shy of the Juniper Springs Cemetery. Jerking the wheel to the right, I pulled from the road--not that there was any traffic at this ungodly hour, but I'd always found it best to pull over before passing out.

My heart thundered, sending my pulse skittering, the blood pumping so fast I couldn't hear anything except the roaring in my ears. I slammed my palm against the gearshift and pushed it into park as my vision started to fog around the edges and the claws tightened around my neck.

"God, no…" My plea came out as a strangled whisper. A

nameless, shapeless creature crept toward me, darkening the periphery of my vision even further, blocking out the meager pre-dawn light.

"No…" I rasped again. Gathering every bit of my remaining strength, I struck out, uselessly slapping away the nebulous blackness. As my arm dropped heavily onto the center console, my numb and shaking fingers landed on a familiar object. Fighting against the inevitable unconsciousness, I pushed the button, praying Siri would understand.

"Call Monica…" The words wheezed out on my last panicked breath.

The last thing I heard before the darkness took me was a rich contralto voice assuring me she was "Calling Monica."

* * *

I blinked slowly back to consciousness as my best friend and boss leaned into my ten-year-old Land Rover, her long, graceful fingers slapping gently against my cheeks. Judging by the change in light, I'd been out a lot longer than usual.

"Hannah? Come back, girl. Come on, Hannah, you're okay. It was just a little panic attack." Her reassuring words were undermined by the slight waver to her voice. I knew I'd scared her. That made two of us.

"M'kay," I said at last. My mouth felt like I'd been sucking on paste. "Wh-what time is it?"

"Seven. Good thing you had the location share activated on your phone. Why are you out so early?" Monica asked. She looked at my outfit then back at the road and the direction I'd been heading. I could practically see the pieces fall into place.

Monica owned a jewelry boutique in the cutesy tourist section of Sedona and I was scheduled to work today. In addition to helping her at the counter, I was one of the many artists whose work she featured. Whenever I was in the store, I needed to appear "put together" so our clients could see how a unique piece of jewelry could complete an outfit.

This morning had started out well enough. Determined to put a confident face forward, I'd selected my favorite work outfit: a black and white bandana handkerchief skirt, a white tank, and a nubby gray and white open knit cardigan. When I'd left the house my outfit was perfect--from my chin-length bob to my extravagant-but-worth-it Jimmy Choos. My coordinating jewelry and subtle makeup were perfect accents. Now black and white beads were scattered around the front seat from when I'd clawed at my neck, and no doubt I had a serious case of raccoon eyes going on.

"You left at the ass crack of dawn in case you couldn't drive past the cemetery again, didn't you?"

Heat crawled up my cheeks at the disappointment layering her words. Since my answer was evident on my face, I said nothing. She would never understand anyway.

Apparently not expecting an answer, Monica shook her head. "Are you okay to drive?"

"I-I think so." Then a sudden fear swept through me and I began to tremble. "Wait. Where? Where do you want me to drive?"

Monica rolled her eyes. "To my house. I haven't had breakfast yet and the store doesn't open for two more hours."

"Oh... uhm... I was going to eat breakfast at the Canyon View. We could meet there in an hour?" I said, eyeing Monica's sweat pants and Red Dirt T-shirt.

"An hour." Monica's voice was as dry as the Sonoran desert. "So you can drive out to the interstate and come into town from the south end?"

"I think maybe today--that's for the best," I said, my voice low and ashamed. "It's either that or I'm going to go home and try again tomorrow."

"Fine," Monica said on a sigh. "An hour. Make sure they put a pot of coffee on the table. I'm going to need it."

As Monica stalked back to her Tahoe, I started to pick up the small glass beads, dropping them into the cup holder on the console. I would have to restring my necklace once I got to the store. A quick glance in the rearview mirror confirmed my makeup was equally in need of repair. I took a few minutes to wipe away the black and wasted another minute wishing the rest of the shadows would disappear as easily.

Finally, having delayed as long as possible, I put the Rover in gear and executed a three-point turn to come perpendicular to the road. I looked both ways. Repeatedly. A left turn would mean a fifteen minute drive east to the interstate, another twenty minutes south and back west, then ten minutes north through town to the Canyon View Cafe. Forty-five minutes to the next cup of coffee. Or I could turn right and be there in five.

With my foot on the brake, I took a deep shuddering breath then dragged my palms over my skirt before taking a white-knuckle grip on the wheel.

I closed my eyes briefly and prayed for strength to any passing gods or goddesses, as if that might help. When no flashes of lightning appeared signaling the arrival of divine intervention, I sighed and turned left.

Because this is how I go on. Gripping the wheel and driving forward-- even if it appears to others as if I'm headed in the wrong direction.

It was how I imagined all mad people act when confronted with the truth of their lunacy. When the clouds mix with the morning sunlight to create shadows in the images of dead people—one says nothing. Because really—what would there be to say?

Just continue to drive, pretending only to see that which was visible through the front windshield--counting the next breath, the birds, or trees… anything to keep from noticing the very thing I sought to leave behind. The raised arm, the grasping hand, the breath cold and damp on the back of the neck.

This is how I go on.

Chapter Two

Canyon View Cafe was the local's choice in a part of town full of tourist traps. Tucked two blocks behind the Old West facade and wooden sidewalks of the shopping district, the small restaurant avoided most of the foot traffic, even at the busiest of the season. Which made it a logical choice for those who worked the galleries and boutiques. Talk often centered around the latest rude customer or the drag of always working the tourist trade. Not that Sedona was ungrateful for the income infused into the local economy. It was just that the tens of thousands of annual visitors to the majestic red rocks region made it hard for the citizens to enjoy the serenity for which their town was famous.

Gulping in one last deep breath of the crisp fall air, I looked around, smiling as usual when I caught sight of Cathedral Rock. I'd only been in Sedona for a year, but the place felt like the home I'd always wanted. Feeling more settled after my drive, I pushed open the door to the diner and stepped inside.

"Hey, Hannah," said the cheery redhead behind the register. "Sit at the counter?" She nodded in the direction of my usual stool when I came in alone.

"Can't today, Dot. I'm meeting Monica in a few minutes."

Dot gave me a grin. "Hope the boss is buying." She winked and waved her arm toward the two remaining empty booths. "Take whichever you want. I'll bring a pot of coffee."

I laughed. Dot knew us well. Monica would be ready to scold me the minute she arrived, so I selected the smaller booth tucked into the back corner and sat with my back to the door. Maybe I could keep half the people in town from learning about my most recent "spell."

As soon as the coffee arrived, I grabbed the sugar jar and a spoon. I deserved several teaspoons worth as a treat for the morning I'd had so far. Then I remembered I didn't like sweets, so slid the sugar next to the condiments and promised myself a double side of bacon instead. Sometimes life *was* fair.

Cradling the white ceramic mug in a two-handed grip, I breathed deeply of the rich aroma, then blew little ripples across the deep dark surface. Finally, having paid the proper homage, I took the first life-sustaining sip.

"I hope that was as good for you as it looked..." an unfamiliar deep baritone said from my right.

Coffee sloshed when I jumped slightly at the unexpected comment.

A man in his mid-thirties, wearing gray slacks and a long-sleeved button front blue and white striped shirt stood practically at my shoulder.

"Mind if I sit?" he asked, although he slid into the seat opposite me without waiting for an answer.

This was a small town and an even smaller diner. Dot would have her foot up his ass in a nanosecond if I so much as made a squeak, so I was more annoyed than frightened by his presumptuousness.

"Sorry, that seat's taken--"

"By me," he agreed. He reached for the pot of coffee and filled the second mug while I watched with my mouth hanging open. *The nerve of some people.*

Up close and personal, his brown hair was a mass of loose curls on top--the kind people with straight hair like me always envied. It was his best feature, if you didn't count the green eyes behind the horn-rimmed glasses. And maybe the dimple in his chin.

He looked up and smiled and I had to add perfect lips and straight white teeth to the list.

Dammit.

I took another sip of coffee, intending to wait him out. He seemed equally content to sip coffee and stare back.

"Hey, Stu. Long time no see. You two want to order or are you waiting for Monica?" Dot asked, making me jump again.

Sitting with my back to the door had definitely been a bad idea. Dot seemed to know the man, so that made him local. Or at least not a stranger-danger.

I started to answer her question. "We're not--"

"Waiting for Monica," Stu finished for me. "She called and said she couldn't make it. Some emergency at the store. Since Hannah was going to be here, I decided to come anyway."

I blinked in surprise. Stu and Dot continued to chitchat, but I pulled out my phone and immediately texted Monica.

214

WTF? I typed and hit send without elaborating. She would know exactly what I meant.

Trust me. Her reply was so fast I wondered if maybe she had already typed it in anticipation of hearing from me. I was framing a response that didn't include the five-letter word I was thinking, when I realized they'd stopped talking.

"Did you want something, Hannah?" Stu asked politely.

"Oh, she'll have the special. It's what she always gets, right, honey?" Dot said.

"Uh… sure. But maybe…" I glanced at the sugar jar then back to Dot. "Could I get an extra side of bacon today?"

"You got it, doll. Two specials and a side of bacon, coming right up." Dot tore the order from the pad and whisked off to the kitchen.

"I'm sorry. That was a little unfair to ambush you like that," Stu said, by way of an apology, I supposed.

"You think so?" I murmured, determined to play it cool until I knew what was going on.

Stu's laughter spilled out, and my mouth twitched in an automatic need to smile.

Damn. Now I had to add *'really great laugh'* to the ever-growing things-to-admire-about-Stu list.

He held out his right hand to shake. "My name is Stu Maxwell."

I accepted the handshake--nice and firm, and in no way condescending. Resisting the urge to add it to the list, I smiled in return.

"I'm Hannah Bosch. No relation despite the initials."

"Is that so? Too bad, I love Michael Connelly."

Oh sweet Mary Sunshine, this man got obscure Harry Bosch references and liked my favorite author. If this was Monica's idea of a setup, the woman hit a serious home run. I immediately took back the pending insult.

He released my hand and smiled again. "I'm a clinical psychologist. Monica thinks we should talk."

"Well, fuck."

Stu's smile widened. "Not on the first date and never with a client."

The laughter was forced from me--I couldn't help it. The

man was totally outrageous.

When I finally regained my composure, I shook my head. "That won't be a problem, since I'm definitely not going to be your client. So… should we plan the second date for tomorrow night, then?"

"Oh, very nice deflection. Okay… not a client. Definitely not a patient," he said, his mouth turning down as he shook his head. "How about we hold off on the second date discussion until you tell me about this morning. Strictly as a friend, of course."

"Seriously, Monica might have stepped in it a little here. There's nothing to tell, and I'm not looking for counseling. It doesn't--" I grabbed my coffee cup to keep from completing my sentence, but I needn't have bothered. It seemed Stu understood my point.

"It doesn't work?"

I met his steady gaze with one of my own and waited.

"I don't want to jump to conclusions based on anything Monica may or may not have told me--because unless it comes from you, it would only be her interpretation of events anyway. But, Hannah, if a person rearranges her schedule or routine in order to avoid going near a certain place, it might signify a perfectly normal fear has morphed into something unmanageable."

"Look, Stu-- *Doctor Maxwell…* this stuff just doesn't work for me. I'm non-compliant when it comes to medications, I refuse to be hypnotized, and I--"

"You hate being out of control. I can see that. And it's Stu."

Before I could respond, Stu's head whipped up and he flashed a killer smile at something… someone… over my shoulder.

Following his gaze, I sighed in relief when I saw Dot approach with a tray of food. Now we could get down to business and eat. No matter what Monica had told Stu, neither of them could ever understand. Besides, other than the cemetery, there really wasn't anything that bothered me. Not much anyway.

"So, what do you say?" Stu asked as he forked a bite of eggs into his mouth.

"I say yum. I'm hungry, but I'm kind of in a hurry."

"Oh, Monica said to tell you not to worry about coming in today, she's got it covered."

"Oh good," I said, struck by a sudden brilliant idea. "That

works perfectly. I thought I might look for a place in Sedona instead of driving in from Juniper Springs. If I got a place a little closer, I wouldn't have to--"

"Pass the cemetery? You seem like a very intelligent woman, Hannah. I'm sure you realize driving an hour out of your way or moving are extreme responses. A fear of death isn't unusual, but allowing it to control your life--"

"I'm not worried about dying, Doctor. I'm… It's about…"

For a moment, I was back on the road leading to the cemetery. A shudder twisted through me, racing along my backbone as if someone had tugged on a cold wire threaded through each of the thirty-three bones in my spine. I didn't want him to notice and draw some erroneous conclusion. I tried to smile to deflect any simmering concern, even as a pale face with wide eyes and a screaming mouth appeared in front of me waving her arms for me to slow down.

"Dead things?" Stu said, dragging me back from the edge of an unseen precipice.

"Exactly," I said, relieved he understood and that his steady voice caused the image to fade.

Stu smiled his killer smile and snagged a piece of bacon from my side order. He used the bacon like a pointer and waved it at my nearly full plate. I was surprised to see his food was almost gone.

"Perfect. Now that we have that cleared up, I think we can figure out a plan to have you functioning more comfortably in just a few visits. Eat up."

Chapter Three

"Okay, tell me again how we got here?" I asked. "Why am I standing at my kitchen counter, brewing a cup of coffee for a relative stranger who expects me to share my innermost secrets after an hour together at breakfast?"

"I see you have me confused with someone else. I'm not your relative--it's Monica who is my cousin, remember?"

"Hmm... I remember that's what she said on the phone. It makes me wonder why I've never heard of you before though."

"Probably because she didn't think you would take too well to knowing her favorite cousin is a psychologist. She's spoken about you ever since you first met. What was that, about a year ago?"

"Fourteen months." I finished brewing the second cup of coffee and brought both mugs to the table and set them down before I took my seat. "Why? Is that important?"

"I have no idea what's important. At least not yet. This is called small talk. It's the part where we exchange information and get to know each other."

"And how much an hour do you charge for this part, Doctor?"

Yes, I realized just how bitter I sounded. But if Stu knew the number of doctor offices I'd sat in over the years, he might understand. It was the fundamental difference between us. Stu believed in the value of what he did for a living. I knew from personal experience just how futile the effort could be. Still... Monica was my friend, so I suppose that made him family.

"Oh, wanna be a wise guy, huh?" Stu narrowed his eyes and made *nyuk nyuk* sounds that made me want to bop him on the head. "Come on... give me a try. What's it going to hurt?"

This time the smile wasn't nearly as blinding as the one in the restaurant, but somehow it seemed all the more sincere because of the subtle curve of his lips. When I realized I'd been staring, I quickly scrambled for something sensible to say.

"I-I'll try. But if it doesn't work this time, I swear, I'm moving."

"It's a deal. I'll help you pack." He reached into the briefcase he'd brought with him and retrieved a pencil and a steno pad. Opening to the first clean sheet of paper, he slid them across the table to me.

"The scene you described to me from this morning... do you have any objections if we classify that as a panic attack? It's a rather overused term, but I think in this instance it works to give us a focus for our discussion."

I shook my head, so Stu continued.

"We're going to talk about events and objects known to trigger panic attacks in people who fear dead things..."

"Necrophobia." I said the word matter-of-factly to show I could be as dispassionate about the subject as he could. Which of course, I couldn't be. Especially not once he started asking about my past. I pushed the unwelcome thought aside. Stu had questioned me deftly enough about the morning's panic attack--amazing how easy it could be to talk to someone over a meal. And now here we were over my kitchen table.

Clever man.

"Sure... necrophobia. When we break down the word itself, we have *nekros*, the Greek word for corpse, and *phobos*, which is the word for fear."

A roaring started in my ears. My heart rate accelerated rapidly and my palms moistened. This was it. He was going to make me tell him, and I couldn't. I just couldn't.

"Hannah," Stu said sharply. My gaze flew to his, my mouth already open as if preparing to scream. "Hannah," he said again, his tone gentler. "Look around you. Do you see where we are?"

Blinking against the bright morning sun reflecting on the gleaming white cabinets, I slowly nodded my head as where we were settled around me.

"My house," I said, my voice a little huskier than normal, but strong enough. I cleared my throat and tried again. "We're at my house, in my kitchen."

"Yes." Stu smiled as if I'd solved some particularly difficult equation. "You need to try to stay with me, stay in the moment as much as possible." He stretched his arm out across my small dining room table and squeezed my hand. "Don't worry, I'll bring you back before you get too far away."

I swallowed hard, and damn if it wasn't dusty or something

because my eyes started to sting. "Yeah. Okay, thanks. Uh… what should I do?"

He pushed the pencil and paper closer. "I want you to write the word necrophobia and then the two root words."

"But--"

"Go on, you can do this. It's just letters. Add dashes between if it helps."

I scrawled necrophobia in my usual messy cursive, but the point of the pencil seemed to freeze. Biting my lip, I did as he suggested.

C-o-r-p-s-e

"It has six letters," I said. "Why does that surprise me?"

"Because it's become larger than anything else in your life. Six letters, huh? Can you make any other word out of those six letters? Like an anagram?"

I started to write.

Crops e

Scorpe

Corps e

I couldn't find a way to use all the letters, but I could make multiple short words. Stu scooted his chair closer and brought out his own pen.

Copers

"Oh, good one," I said. "Oh, wait, it would need two p's."

We went at it a few more minutes, but couldn't come up with anything useful. It dawned on me finally what he'd done. I swapped my pencil for his pen and scrawled in big, bold letters.

CORPSE

"Atta girl," he said softly. "Nothing but letters. Did you ever notice how old people read the obituaries?" he asked, seemingly apropos of nothing.

"My parents used to read them every day," I agreed. "Out loud over breakfast. I think it was an Italian thing."

"You're Italian?"

I laughed. "Can't you tell by the coloring?" I pointed to my dark brown hair and eyes and olive skin.

"The last name threw me off. I think I'm going to demand proof."

"Proof? You want to see my mother's name on my birth

certificate? It was Del Vacchio."

Already shaking his head, Stu sat back and crossed his arms over his chest. "Prove it. Make lasagna for dinner tonight. Don't worry, I'll wait."

I burst out laughing. "It's not even ten in the morning. And what makes you think I have the ingredients?"

His mouth opened then snapped shut, and I could see he fought his own laugh.

"Monica told you--"

"Maybe," he cautiously agreed. "But I think it's safe to say we have time. And since the kitchen seems to be a comfortable place for you, I think it's a win-win."

"You really plan to keep at this... therapy all day?"

"Therapy? I prefer to think of it as two friends uncovering a mystery. If you like Harry Bosch, you can't tell me you don't like a mystery."

The room seemed to dim around me and there was a tell-tale flutter of my heart as my pulse rate started to rise. Refusing to let another wave of panic envelop me, I stood suddenly, tipping my chair in the process. Without looking at Stu, I stomped over to the freezer.

I tossed a package of bulk sausage on the counter, enjoying the solid thunk of frozen meat versus granite. I grabbed a package of ground beef and threw it down too. Next came jars of tomatoes and sauce, onions and peppers, garlic and fresh basil from the pot on the windowsill.

Once the ingredients were spread all over the counter, I put the meat in a skillet to start thawing before I browned it, muttering to myself the whole while. "Who the hell does this man... this *Stu Maxwell* think he is to come in here and tell me this is a mystery? What happened to me isn't a damn mystery. It's not a goddamn book."

"I worded that poorly, Hannah. Of course, your history isn't a mystery to you. The only mystery is why--"

"Why? You mean why it causes this... this..." I waved my arms wildly. "Why it's ruined my life?"

"We can start there," Stu said evenly. His reasonable tone made me sorry I'd already added the meat to the frying pan. I heard they made good weapons.

Sensing my mood, he raised his hands in a peace gesture. "I don't mean to downplay whatever it is that happened in your past, Hannah. I hope you'll become comfortable enough to tell me--but the truth is--it may not matter."

"May not matter?" The words came perilously close to a screech. I'd seen dozens of doctors and every single one of them had insisted the accident was the root of all my problems. They'd wanted me to relive every agonizing moment, as if once wasn't enough for a thousand lifetimes. I opened my mouth to tell him so, but he cut me off again.

"Not really. You see, whatever your initial trigger event is-- I've no doubt it was something terrible. The death of a pet, losing a loved one, seeing a dead body, accidentally causing the death of another... whatever the source of ground zero... that situation was long ago. You dealt with it. Locked it away.

"Bad things happen to a lot of people, Hannah. Most people cope and eventually move on. But some of them get caught in a loop--just like you. Most everything in their lives is absolutely normal--until it isn't and then a trigger sets off a panic attack.

"So do we *have* to dig into your past? Only if *you* want to. You are in control of which path we take. What's it gonna be? Do you want to tell me what happened? Or shall we continue with games and exercises to work our way up the fear ladder? You are familiar with the term?"

Hell yes, I was familiar with the term... The theory was, you would list key words, objects, and actions--in order from least to most disturbing.

One by one, starting with the easiest, you conquered each fear, until voila, you were cured.

Yes, I might have traveled that road a time or two, but the therapist du jour always insisted the list had to contain elements from that long ago night--which I steadfastly refused.

Thank you, no.

Still--Stu's method entertained, and if he was true to his word that reliving the past wasn't required--then I was *game* to give it a try.

Chapter Four
Four weeks later...

I walked through the house, double and triple checking the locks on the doors and windows. The ADT security panel was a reassuring green and the night-lights in each room glowed softly. Not that I was afraid of the dark... because I wasn't. But having one anxiety often led to others, so this was my proactive approach to monster-in-the-closet repelling techniques. Finally assured the house was locked down for the night, I went to my bedroom and pulled on my silk tank and boxers before washing the makeup from my face.

As I crawled into bed, my gaze settled on the blue readout of the digital clock on the dresser. *11:07.*

Sighing, I turned onto my side and punched the pillow a few times before settling into my favorite position with a piece of foam rubber tucked between my knees. Tomorrow was a big day, and I'd planned to go to bed earlier than this, but as usual, thoughts of Stu Maxwell filled my brain.

I had no idea what he planned for our regular meeting tomorrow, nor could I pinpoint exactly why my anxiety had been increasing the last two days... maybe it was tied to the approaching full moon. Or maybe it was the realization this would be our fourth official meeting--and he'd made a point to tell me many phobias could be managed in as little as four weeks with the right strategy. I didn't feel anywhere close to capable in that arena.

My first meeting with Stu had ended well--and surprisingly early. We'd actually stopped on the positive accomplishment of the corpse anagram and my admission it was the dead that I'd feared, not the comforting blackness of my future death. I couldn't have told him how the two were different, but in my muddled world, they just were. The rest of that first day had been spent in a companionable getting-to-know-you sort of way as we'd cooked lasagna and talked over world events. If the psychologist in him had been excavating any deep dark clues into my past, he'd hid it well. In fact, I'd spent many pleasant moments in the weeks since then fantasizing about our future relationship...

Even though I continued to take the scenic route to work, we quickly established a regular pattern to our not-quite-doctor-patient relationship. Stu would arrive at my house each Wednesday evening with a new activity to move me along the psychotherapy ladder of success--as he called it--while I focused on making homemade pasta of one sort or another.

The second meeting, we'd read the obituaries... which sounds oddly morbid, but turned into quite an entertaining couple of hours. It gave me an opportunity to act out some of the more memorable conversations from the kitchen table of my youth.

"Did you see Shirl died?" My mother had stabbed at the newspaper with a marinara-coated finger.

"Shirl who?" my father had asked with his bushy eyebrows scrunched together and a tell-tale flush crawling up his fleshy cheeks.

"What, you know more than one Shirl? The skinny blonde bimbo with big bazooms you took to your junior prom--" Mom wiped her finger on the towel hanging from the waistband of her stretch pants.

"Ack with the junior prom, already. For Christ's sake, I was sixteen..."

"Yeah, well, it was the boobies that got her in the end, you know..."

"What are you talkin' about, Livia?"

"Breast cancer. It's what got her. Such a shame... six kids and a fat ass, and it was still--" She cupped her breasts and pushed them up until they quivered under her chin.

"Ma! Don't ever do that again," I'd said.

Stu had laughed until his eyes sparkled with unshed tears over my impressions. It gave me a chance to talk about my past without going into specifics of the event every other psychologist had wanted me to dwell on. There was no reason--that wasn't the root of my problem.

The next week, Stu had shown up wearing an old pair of sweat pants, running shoes, and a Gold's Gym T-shirt.

"Are we going for a run?" I'd asked, frantically calculating how to change the timing on the seafood risotto.

With a grin, my not-a-date-not-a-doctor guest produced an old VHS tape and player. He'd said it was just a quick workout, starring Linnea Quigley.

"Linnea Quigley? The scream queen from *Night of the Living Dead?*" My voice had risen and my breath immediately became erratic. It had been a near disaster--because, no, I didn't do zombies.

In fact, I couldn't even say zombie--which made my entire argument something more like a ridiculous pantomime.

Stu had made all the right therapy noises--*hmm... I see... how does that make you feel...* even as he shoved my furniture aside and set up the VCR. Before I knew it, I was watching the most ridiculous, campy clip of Linnea leading a bunch of not-scary-at-all zombies in an exercise class.

I might still have problems with the word--and I wasn't about to let Stu convince me to watch *The Walking--The Walking D-e-a-d--* that show on AMC--but the *Horror Workout* was closer to horrible than to horror. We'd laughed, and after a while, I'd even tried a few of the heavy arm shuffles and shambling twists. And just like the previous week, we'd ended with a new list of words and activities for me to work on, as well as a note about celebrating milestones--such as being able to spell or say a certain word that I'd avoided for more years than I cared to admit.

Lying in bed, thinking over the past few weeks should have kept me awake, but my lids finally grew heavy. Despite the progress we'd made, I felt myself drifting straight into the dream. I knew what was coming--what always came--yet the dream pinned me to sleep, a paralysis so complete I was helpless against the pull.

***

I didn't drive in the dream... I never drive. That would be too close to reality for the dream to maintain its surreal quality. I walked through trees and brush as tall as any high-rise. They closed around me, leaving little more than a slit for the night sky to look down upon the small and insignificant woman tripping along the path. Crickets and tree frogs chirped merrily, at odds with the choking sensation of doom that crept along the ground like a fog, turning the whole world gray, ready to swallow me whole. Still I walked... footsteps quick, light, rapid. Almost running.

The water called to me, raising her voice to roll like a minor chord, at harmonic odds with the other night sounds. Still, I followed her as beckoned, for she was my siren song. As I tripped along the uneven path, I tried to peer through the gathering darkness, doing my best to avoid the roots and branches that reached for me, as if they sensed the danger I was bolting toward and would hold me back, if only I would slow this mad, headlong rush.

The tumbling madness of the river as she raged south toward the lake drove all other sounds from the night now--just as the trees closed in around me, obliterating all signs of the stars and moon. It was dark and still except for the pounding current that raced along the riverbank and pulsed through my veins. Like the smell of stepping into your childhood home after a long visit away, the scent of pine and dirt and water filled my nostrils. I was nearly there.

The wind brushed over me and I shivered in the sudden chill, and realized I was sweating. My hair stuck unpleasantly to my neck and forehead and all I could think about was diving into the cool swirling depths of the river. And then I was there.

Face first, I tumbled into the breath-stealing cold. Water closed around me, the torrents tossing me as if I were nothing more than an autumn leaf, my showy color a too-brief final moment of glory in my season of life. Then there was no room for anything else in my mind except the water as I was plunged deep, the slight metallic and dirt flavor of the river washed over my tongue and forced its way down my throat. My nostrils filled and my lungs spasmed, as they desperately fought against the rising tide. Sinking. Drowning. Dead.

Only I wasn't. Not me. I blinked against the watery depths and stared into a black face that no longer resembled anyone I could have ever known. Not in life. Not in death. Black flesh, swollen and waterlogged, floated in watery ribbons from the gray-white skull. Glowing eyes, blue as robin's eggs met my gaze. Blinked.

I opened my mouth to scream and more water rushed in. The world grew blacker. Fingers clawed at my throat, and I thought they might have been mine.

With the suddenness of dreams, my eyes opened and I saw I wasn't in the water anymore. I was back in my room, only this time I knew I wasn't alone. I lay on my back, damp from sweat and fear... heart thundering at an unsustainable level, like a bullet train approaching a dead man's curve.

No, I wasn't alone in the room... not anymore. I could sense the presence of another... being. Not something alive... something d-e-a-d.

Moving as quietly as possible, I kicked and twisted to free myself from the tangled sheet and in the process knocked my cell phone to the floor.

Don't look under the bed. Don't look under the bed. Don't look…

Hanging my head over the side, I reached down, my hand patting into the deep shadows under the bed and coming up empty. I leaned farther, my eyes squeezed tight, against what I couldn't say. Or maybe I could, but I wouldn't. Not now.

When the top of my head touched the carpet, I sucked in a deep breath and popped my lids open.

A body was lying there, caressed by a cobweb and caught between a dust bunny and a lost sock. Wet, stringy hair framed a face shriveled and black, like old leather left to the elements. My fingers scrabbled for the phone, just as the face turned toward me. Once-familiar blue eyes glowed coolly from pus-filled lids, then a gap opened where his mouth should have been and the creature hissed.

I awoke with a muffled scream. Really woke, not the faux wakefulness that allowed the dream to pull you under again. I kicked free from the covers and fell to the floor. Crawling on my hands and knees, I made it only as far as the bedside wastebasket before the gagging turned into vomiting. I vomited until I thought my eyes might be bleeding and my lungs would turn inside out with the force of each non-productive spasm. When it was finally done, I stayed on the floor, too weak to move.

Leaning back against the bed, tears fell from my eyes because that was all biology allowed, but I wept from my soul, great shoulder-shaking sobs that robbed me of breath and left me as nothing more than a bag of bones propped against the mattress. I stayed there long past the tears, until the faint gray of the pre-dawn pulled me to my feet to face another day.

This is how I go on.

Chapter Five

That evening, when I opened the door to Stu, he stood on the porch studying me for a long moment before finally stepping inside. I caught a look in the mirror when I'd first come home from work--and the circles under my eyes would do any raccoon proud. My complexion was pasty, and no amount of blush and foundation would be enough to bring it back from the lifeless gray of a sleepless night. My clothing wasn't quite workday-put-together... more like blue jeans and a loose T-shirt--my normal after-work attire, but not something that I'd worn around Stu so far.

As soon as I shut the door behind him, he drew me into his arms, and I was enveloped by a spicy ocean spray scent. It was the first true physical contact between us, and surprisingly intimate. Stu's heart beat against my cheek... I tightened my arms and sucked in a ragged breath. For a moment, my breasts pressed against his abs, then he pulled his hips back before the contact turned to something more than comfort.

"What is it? What's happened?" Stu asked as he broke our embrace and wrapped an arm around my shoulders. He steered us to the kitchen--the site of all our Wednesday night meetings so far.

Without answering right away, I allowed him to fuss over me for a minute. He pulled out a kitchen chair, then turned to the bottle of wine I'd left breathing on the counter. He poured two glasses, then joined me at the table.

"Tell me what happened, Hannah," he said, removing any hint of a question.

Sitting there in my brightly lit kitchen, I could still feel the tendrils of the dream, calling me like a lover, begging for me to return. In my heart of hearts, I knew something was badly out of alignment between my waking and sleeping self. It was disheartening that after so many years of trying and a cross country re-boot, I wasn't any better than I was the day they let me out of the hospital. The progress I'd thought we'd made the last month was illusory. I wasn't just necrophobic... there was more to it. There had to be.

Didn't there?

"Am I mad?" I blurted the question that had haunted me my

entire adult life. Oh, not in a debilitating oh-poor-me sort of everyday way. That wasn't my style. But I couldn't deny asking myself the question whenever the next doctor in line prescribed a new medication or talked about in-patient therapy options. I was an educated woman with excellent internet skills... I could look up treatment options as well as the next person. Phobias responded to short term cognitive behavioral therapy--they shouldn't require more hospitalization than I'd already had.

Stu leaned back in his chair, his eyebrows crawling nearly to his hairline.

"Mad? What on earth would make you think that? Having a fear that gets out of control isn't a symptom of *madness*." He made finger quotes to emphasize his point. "Besides, the term madness is hardly a clinical diagnosis, as I'm sure you're aware."

"I wanted to get better, Stu, really I did. For a time, with you--I had hoped we were on the right track." I pressed my fingers to the table and studied the backs of my hands, as if there might be an answer there. "So far, every week... I felt better after we met. Lighter. Almost re-energized. But this week--at first it was the same, you know?" I looked up to find him studying me through narrowed eyes.

"Then..." he prompted.

"It seemed to get harder and harder to remember any progress. And last night's dream was more vivid than ever. It was as if..."

Cocking his head to the side as if he were listening to more than just my words, Stu frowned. "As if you were being pulled back," he said slowly. Stu sighed. "This is the first you've told me about dreams. I think maybe it's time you tell me all of it. "

"*All of it?* You mean the dream?"

"I mean everything."

"I thought you said I wouldn't have to relive my past," I said through a throat that suddenly felt very tight.

"Hannah, you *are* getting better--can't you see the progress? Feel it? But something is holding you back, pulling you under. Unless you are willing to go that last step with me..."

"Are you asking me to go all the way?" I quipped, the joke a reflex attempt to lighten the mood. Or maybe such was the nature of our relationship, that even in the times that felt most desperate, Stu brought a joke to my lips and a smile to my heart.

He was right. I did want this--I wanted to get better because once I was, we could take that next step in our relationship. I sucked in a big breath.

"His name was Vance Carter and we were seventeen."

"Your first love?" Stu asked, a curious expression crossing his face for an instant before he schooled his features back into the professional interest he usually wore when we talked about d-e-a-t-h.

"Not hardly. Just a friend. I'm not sure I could even classify us as good friends--although I think we might have been, had things worked out differently." I tapped my fingernails lightly against the edge of the table.

"We lived in a small town, just outside Allentown, Pennsylvania. Not much happened there beyond football and the steel mill, but it was what we knew. Only I wasn't into the whole sports scene, and Vance was new to the town--I always thought it was a special sort of cruelty that his parents moved him in his senior year of high school. Anyway, he arrived a few weeks shy of the end of the season--and the school was all excited about the upcoming homecoming game. We were undefeated with visions of a state championship, riding high. Vance was too new to fit into any of the cliques and I suppose I was too oblivious to care."

"You seem like you'd be a popular girl..."

A smile tugged at one corner of my mouth. "Why? Because I have big bazooms, as my momma would say?"

"Do you? I hadn't noticed," Stu said, feigning indifference. "I was more thinking of your confidence. It's a trait I often associate with people who have natural charisma."

The conversation was less difficult for our attempts at humor, but no re-telling would ever be easy. I smiled tightly and continued.

"To the outside world, I probably did look like one of the popular kids--I just never really cared. When Vance stepped into my American government class, the teacher took one long look at his button-up shirt, and assigned him to the seat next to mine. A few weeks later, it seemed the most logical thing in the world to take him to homecoming."

Leaning forward, Stu grabbed the wineglasses and handed one to me. He raised the glass in a silent toast then took a sip. I had a feeling he was waiting for me to continue, but when I didn't, he tried a little conversational nudge.

"So what happened?"

I gave a casual shrug of one shoulder and ordered my thundering heart to slow. I took a sip of wine, but the Bordeaux turned to vinegar on my tongue. After setting down my glass, I folded my hands on the table.

"Nothing. We went to the dance and had a fun time. Turned out Vance was gay and we had a great time dissecting everyone's outfits and poofy hairstyles. We danced a little--he could replicate every Kevin Bacon move from *Footloose*. When it was time to go, we got in his ancient Chevy Vega and drove off." My hands started to shake so violently I had to put them in my lap and twist them together.

Stu scooted his chair closer and reached for my hands, his grip firm, the touch grounding me so that I could continue.

"I never even saw what happened. Or if I did, I don't remember. One minute we were singing along to "It's Raining Men," and the next, we were nose down in a small creek that flowed under the road. They told me later we'd gone off the bridge and floated a ways before we stuck, but I just don't--" My voice started to rise, but Stu squeezed my fingers tighter, pulling me back into the here and now.

"That was a long time ago, Hannah, you're safe. Take a good look around your kitchen. See all the lights? Know where you are?"

I swallowed hard, then nodded. "Yeah. Okay. I'm okay," I agreed.

"Is there more? How long were you there?"

"According the accident records, it was more than fifty-six hours before they found us. Another three before they cut me free."

"And Vance?"

"I tried to save him. To hold his face up out of the water so he could breathe, only… he never took a breath. They said later he died on impact." With most of the story told, I looked up at Stu and caught the pity in his eyes.

"Oh, Hannah… of course this was a tragic event no one should have to endure, let alone a teenager. Losing someone you were close to has to affect how you feel about death."

"It wasn't that," I said, my voice sounding like a plea. "It really wasn't that. We were friends, but nothing more."

"Hannah--"

"I watched him," I whispered, telling him what I'd never shared before.

Stu went very still. "Tell me what you mean," he whispered back.

"I watched him. The first night, there was a glow from the headlights for a while, and I could see Vance, his face just below the surface of the water. There was no light in his eyes, though. They just stared at me. Blue and flat and... d-d-dead." I forced the word out between wooden lips.

"He began to... melt. His face... the skin... pieces floated away. But nothing changed his eyes. Not until the third day. They sort of... glowed. Then they began to watch me back."

Chapter Six

Before I could gauge his reaction, other than to note the unnatural paleness that settled over him, Stu grabbed my hand and tugged me to my feet.

"Come on. Let's get out of here." His words were urgent and completely out of context from anything we'd discussed.

I barely managed to lock the door behind me as he hustled me outside and toward his big Ford F-150. I was fairly certain this rushed departure was another one of Stu's unconventional approaches to getting me to face my fear. What he didn't know yet, was continuing the act might be... unnecessary. At least, I hoped it was.

Despite the rapidly rising anxiety that had nearly crippled me, I'd finally told someone what had happened. Or at least what I had believed happened when I'd been a seventeen-year-old girl, trapped in the water for days with a dead friend, watching as his skin putrefied and sloughed away... *Jesus.*

Every day since--in every memory--every vision--every dream--the eyes seemed more alive. Always watching.

In the telling, the story finally shifted into place and I realized just how impossible that vision truly was.

This was nothing short of an epiphany.

Could I finally be ready to let it go?

I'd managed to say the word d-dead. *Dead--Dead--Dead.*

"Is that what the dreams are? What you've been seeing?" Stu asked, startling me from my thoughts.

It took me a minute to think back over our conversation and place his question. "You mean seeing a d-dead boy and thinking his eyes were somehow glowing? Yes--that's where the dreams always go. The other things--what I see when I'm awake--" A shudder raced up my spine. "Like when I would try to drive past the c-cemetery... it was more... obscure. Like catching movement from the corner of your eye, but turning and finding nothing there. Only sometimes there were... faces. Faces like--" I gagged, then sucked in a deep breath, trying to maintain my hard-fought control.

"Faces like your friend Vance." Stu's voice sounded flat.

Grim.

"Do you think I'm mad?" I asked again, my voice a harsh whisper in the dark.

"I think there are realities and--" He gripped the wheel tighter, then slowed for a turn. My head whipped around as I peered into the dark, trying to get my bearings.

"Have you ever seen a zombie movie, Hannah?"

I looked back at Stu to judge his seriousness, but he didn't meet my gaze. "You mean other than that stupid exercise video you made me watch? Are you kidding? No. Just... no. I understand about the whole exposure theory--you keep exposing me to incrementally more challenging elements of my phobia until I learn to cope, but seriously, Stu... this isn't like a fear of flying where my goal is to be able to fly without having a panic attack. I have necrophobia... an unnatural fear of the d-dead. I told you in the beginning--for me, a cure means I can drive past a cemetery without having a panic attack. It means I can sleep through the night-- It doesn't mean I want the ability to watch B-grade movies where monsters have to eat brains in order to keep their body parts from dropping all over town."

Stu snorted a laugh. "That's only the low-functioning zombies, you know. They need brains to survive, shed body parts, and generally can't function as sentient beings."

"Don't know--don't care."

"You should. Those are who you've been seeing. They want access to the light of your soul, but they don't realize eating you would also kill the light within you--thereby making you one of them and no longer a desirable source of healing energy."

I sighed. "Really not funny, Stu." We passed a familiar sign, and my stomach did one of those elevator-down-the-shaft sort of dives. I rubbed suddenly damp palms against my thighs. "Where-- Whatever you have planned for tonight... I'm thinking I've had enough breakthrough. I'd like to go home."

"There's a whole other level of zombie that also wants access to the energy that fairly hums off you, Hannah. But they can get that energy through proximity. These high-functioning zombies can engage in pretty much every activity and manage polite society virtually undetected."

"Is that what that American Z-z-zombie movie--wait. You know what? I don't care. Stu, I'm not joking. Turn around. I don't want to do this tonight. I-I'm not ready for this level of exposure yet."

Relief flooded me as Stu braked, and I thought he was going to turn around. Then my hands started to shake as he ignored my request and turned right into the cemetery.

"The thing is, most sources of light and energy--like yourself--never realize they're surrounded by the high-functioners," Stu continued. "And for the human, there's not a noticeable energy drain because the high-functioning zombie can use simple proximity to regenerate--although, physical contact is even more effective. The energy sources go on about their charmed lives, relatively safe from the feral zombies once they are claimed by the high-functioners."

"I don't want to hear any more about the stupid plot, Stu." I was really getting pissed. I wanted to give the man credit for the earlier breakthrough, but I needed a minute to breathe, to sort through my thoughts and the implications. To maybe see if I couldn't actually get a few hours of sleep without dreaming for a change.

"Take. Me. Home."

"Soon," he agreed. "First, we need to send a message. Make it clear you are not a source of brain food." He gave a soft laugh. "This was certainly not how I thought this would play out."

Stu pulled to a stop just inside the cemetery gate, then reached for my hand. Threading our fingers together, he heaved a sigh. "I didn't expect to be here so soon."

I heard the smile in his voice and smiled in return. It was as if that simple touch melted away my frustration and the edge of fear. Stu had made it clear that we wouldn't date until he considered my necrophobia gone. Tonight I'd told him things I'd never shared with another, had made more progress in a matter of a few hours than in a lifetime of counseling. Now he was holding my hand and I considered that a very good sign.

"Kiss me?" he asked, his voice soft and warm, like a heated caress against my heart. I leaned in, drawn by this man like no other. His laughter and smile, his quick wit, and quirky way of dealing with my anxiety. Everything about him fit me perfectly--and if we were about to take our relationship to a new level, then maybe it was exactly right we start it here. There wasn't another person on the planet who could've convinced me to come through those gates.

My tongue flicked out to moisten my lips, then I closed the

distance between us, appreciating Stu's patience in letting me set the pace. When our lips were just a hairbreadth apart, I whispered an answer.

"Yes."

Ever so softly, Stu brushed his lips against mine. Once. Twice. On the third time, I parted my lips in invitation, and Stu deepened the kiss. His tongue invaded my mouth, sliding against mine. Exploring. Claiming.

Stu twisted his fingers into my hair and changed the angle of our kiss, barely giving me time to breathe and amping up my need. When he finally pulled back, the sound of our breath was harsh in the quiet of the night.

"Want you, Hannah..."

"Yes," I agreed. I started to pull my T-shirt over my head, but Stu stilled my hands.

"Here?" he asked, with more than a hint of laughter in his voice.

I blinked as I looked around, belatedly remembering where we were. I laughed with sheer joy at the absurdity of the situation. Two hours ago, I couldn't say d-dead... now I was seriously considering having sex in a cemetery. What a way to tell my fear to fuck off.

"I'm game if you are..." I jerked my shirt the rest of the way over my head, toed off my sneakers, and gave him a long look.

Stu started to unbutton his shirt and his slow smile was all the answer I needed. We both unfastened our jeans, then Stu scooted toward the middle of the seat so I could straddle his lap.

"You make me crazy, Stu Maxwell," I whispered against his mouth when he was finally buried inside me.

"And you, my love, make me feel alive."

His words took my breath away. He'd called me love. My lips curved into a smile I thought might be permanent. I leaned my head back far enough to focus on the face I was growing to love... and met his glowing green-eyed gaze.

14
AGATEOPHOBIA

FEAR OF INSANITY

MATHEW KAUFMAN

"Welcome to Laurel Mountain Sanitarium, Mister…? " the man said, reaching out to shake his hand.

"Daggets. Frank Daggets," Frank said, accepting the hand. His arm quickly soaked with rain.

"I'm Frederick von Haussen, Superintendent of the facilities. Please, come inside. The rain can be most unpleasant," von Haussen replied.

Just then a flash of lightning shot across the storm-filled sky. It illuminated the tall stone building in a bluish white hue. The lightning flashed several more times. Thunder cracked through the air. It filled Frank's ears as he hunched at the sound and glanced up.

"Are you all right, Mr. Daggets? Surely you are not frightened of a bit of thunder. Laurel Mountain gets storms three-hundred plus days a year. Goodness. Let's get inside. "

Frank felt ridiculous after von Haussen caught his reaction to a bit of thunder. He tried his best to regain his composure. He climbed the thirteen stone steps that led to the large wooden doors of the entry way. Above the doors, carved in stone, read *"Laurel*

Mountain Sanitarium. "The door was cracked; a guard watched the interaction and waited for von Haussen's return.

Once von Haussen reached the top step, the large wooden doors creaked open. Frank stepped inside, glad to be out of the downpour, but not glad to be inside this place. It was dark inside. Small yellow lights slightly illuminated the sanitarium walls. Frank looked at his new surroundings.

The welcome area was not much more than a red area rug bordered with gold embroidery. Large patches of fringe along the edge were missing. A small tube radio sat atop the table, an orange glow emitting from the dials. The opening of "The Lone Ranger" played quietly. Several well-worn wooden chairs surrounded a table that had seen better days. It was close enough to Frank that he could see gouges in its top, near where the radio sat. His eyes widened and he gasped. *Those look like fingernail gouges.*

The gasp drew von Haussen's attention.

"Ah, yes. I see you have noticed our table. Some of our patients enter the facility in a less-than-willing manner. Please, pay it no attention. None of our patients are dangerous anymore. The ones that would be considered as such are kept well sedated. "

"What the hell happened to the carpet?" Frank inquired.

Von Haussen laughed, "Ah yes. It seems to be something of a tasty treat to a few of our ward. "

Frank forced a smile. His knees felt weak and his stomach turned. He did NOT want to be here. Psycho-crazy-insane folk scared the hell out of him. They just looked dead and broken. He had argued with Mr. Wainwright, the owner of Wainwright Plumbing, for over an hour about doing a job here. Frank had only been with WP for a few months and was in no position to turn down a job. Mr. Wainwright had made that absolutely clear.

"Mr. Daggets? Mr. Daggets!" von Haussen snapped.

"Oh, I'm sorry. I--" Frank started to speak.

"Mr. Daggets, I know a sanitarium is not the most comfortable place to be, but you must keep your focus. We need these repairs done and my staff's time is very limited. We do not have time to hold your hand. Is that clear? " von Haussen said, obviously irritated.

"My apologies, Mr. von Haussen. Please show me to the areas that need the work," Frank said, flushed with embarrassment.

"This way," von Haussen directed.

Both men and the guard walked down a long cinder block-lined hallway. The walls were painted a putrid green; not a lime color, not an avocado color. Something in-between. The paint clung loosely to the walls. Years of moisture had taken its toll on the paint. Large flakes of the hideous color hung, folded over, off of the walls.

The hall ended at a large steel door. The guard stepped to the front. His keys jingled as he grabbed them. He selected the correct key and inserted it into the lock. The guard gave it a turn and with a metal on metal clang the lock released and von Haussen pushed the door open.

"We are now in the disturbed patient wing of the facility. Most of these patients are here due to some sort of disorder that was too much for their families to deal with. A handful of them are here for crimes against humanity. As I mentioned earlier, you needn't worry about our patients. Those in the violent wards are kept in a constant state of sedation. Should one of the wards bother you, please let a guard or a nurse know. Now, to troubles at hand. Nixon, would you mind? "

The guard, Nixon, stepped forward and again searched through his keys until he found the one he was looking for. He inserted it into the lock and gave it a turn. Again, the familiar metallic clang broke the silence and the door unlocked.

Nothing could have prepared Frank for this.

The smell was atrocious. It assaulted every one of his senses. EVERY ONE! The foul smell of human shit filled the air. It hung so thick that Frank could taste it.

They stepped inside the small room. Despite the shit smell, Frank's attention immediately went to the woman in the corner of the room.

She sat on a metal bed that was bolted to the wall. A paper thin mattress lined the bed. She wore white pants and a white shirt. The woman looked to be in her early thirties. She sat staring at Frank. No sound. No movement. *Is she even breathing?* She looked like a mannequin.

Just then, the sound of a flushing toilet was heard from somewhere down the corridor. The toilet in the cell began to gurgle.

"Step back, here is goes again," Nixon said, and took his own advice.

Feces spewed from the throat of the toilet. It looked like thick brown toothpaste. Air was also forced through the pipe. That made things even worse. As the air, a horrendous smelling breeze, was forced through the fecal paste, it popped like a bubbling cauldron. Specks of feces shot into the air. Frank watched as Nixon and von Haussen retched.

"The whole--west side--is like this. It is-- Please, just fix it," von Haussen said

Frank nodded and turned back toward the door.

"Jesus Christ, HOLY FUCK!" Frank yelled, and lost his balance on the slippery sludge-covered floor. He fell on his ass directly through the door and landed back in the corridor. "What the fuck is--"

Frank, now on his back, stared up into the doorway. There she stood. The woman from the room, her blank stare locked onto Frank. Again, no movement, no sound. Frank's heart pounded, his eyes wide.

Then blackness.

***

Frank awoke to von Haussen's voice. "Are you ok? Frank? Can you hear me? "

"What the fuck just happened?" Frank interrupted as the memory of the woman's face returned.

"I should have warned you. Sometimes our patients exhibit behaviors that are completely normal for them but not for sane people. Like Claire; she's a sniffer. She smells everything. Doesn't talk, doesn't move much, just sniffs," the guard interjected. "We're so used to her and she already knows what we smell like and uh...I was distracted by all the crap. I'm very sorry. "

"Jesus," Frank said, laying his head on the ground. He brought his hands up to his face and wiped the moisture off. *This job is going to be--worse than awful.* Frank wiped his sweaty hands onto his dark blue uniform trousers. Nixon extended his hand. Frank latched on and was pulled to his feet.

"Thanks," Frank said. He brushed the muck off his back and pants.

"You fainted real good there," Nixon said. "You need a few

minutes to pull it together?"

"No! I want to get this done as fast as possible. I need to get my tools. " Frank said to von Haussen.

"I'll leave you in the care of Mr. Nixon. He will escort you in and out of the main door. You will be provided a key that opens the individual cells as we do not have the staffing to post someone with you all of the time. I ask that you open only one cell at a time please. We would not want any escapees," von Haussen said.

With that, Frank nodded and together he and Nixon walked back to the doorway that secured the corridor. They passed through and Frank heard the clang of the door being locked.

"I'll be back in just a few minutes," Frank said as he glanced back at Nixon.

Nixon nodded and Frank proceeded to the front door. He grabbed the handle, a cold brass lever, and pushed it down. The wind had picked up significantly since Frank had arrived. It shoved the heavy door into him as he opened it. Once outside it took two hands for Frank to pull it closed.

The rain had died down slightly but the sky was still lit with lightning and cracked with thunder. Anxiously, Frank descended the stairs. His boots splashed into the puddles that soaked the now muddy driveway. Rain splattered his face. He wiped at it furiously with his already wet sleeve. The wind gusted as Frank leaned into the back of his pick-up. He lifted the blue tarp that covered his tools and began to look for what he needed.

Shhhh, the wind seemed to speak to Frank. Goosebumps sprang out of his arms. He ignored the noise and continued to rummage for the required tools. *Fraaank*, the wind spoke again. *Behind you, Fraaank.* This was too much for him to ignore. He was flooded with nervous energy. A gust of wind caught the tarp and whipped it out of the truck bed and over Frank's head.

He panicked and began violently writhing inside the tarp. He fought against the wind. It wrapped the tarp around Frank. He stumbled in a struggle to get the tarp off. Something pushed into him. Through the tarp the wind spoke again. *You will die here, Fraaank.*

Frank ripped at the tarp. He pulled it in one direction and then in the other, fighting to find the edge. Finally, after several more seconds, he found the edge of the tarp. He pulled and pulled until it slipped off his head. Quickly, he looked around for the person that had said those terrifying words to him. He was alone…

As fast as he could, Frank grabbed at the tools. His arms filled with the drain snake, plunger, and a tool box, he made a run for the steps. The tools clanged in their metal container. His boots splashed through the puddles, spraying his pant legs with mud.

He ascended the stairs expeditiously; the wind pushed at his back. With his elbow, he pushed down on the handle as a bolt of lightning illuminated the sky. It was followed shortly by a crack of thunder. He heart pounded in his chest. His elbow slipped off the door handle. The wind's voice returned and whispered to him, *Go inside, Fraaank.*

His elbow caught on the latch as the voice spoke. The wind gusted and shoved the heavy door open. It slammed into the wall from the force. A loud thud filled the air. In a panic Frank's tools crashed onto the hardwood floor. Nixon rushed back into the room from the patient wing.

"You all right, Frank? "Nixon asked, with a concerned look on his face. "You are white as a sheet."

"Yeah, I'm fine. I'm just cold and wet," Frank lied.

"Shut that door would ya? I don't want to catch my death in here. "

"Yeah. Sorry, damn wind is vicious," Frank said.

"Sure is," Nixon replied. "Grab your tools; I'll let you in the wing again before I head to lunch."

Frank picked up his tools and walked to where Nixon was standing.

"Who is replacing you while you go to lunch?" he inquired.

"We ain't got that many guards, so I just go to lunch and come back. It's only an hour or so. The nurses go at the same time so as they ain't gotta worry 'bout bein' let in and out," Nixon said matter-of-factly.

"Wait. Let me get this straight. You are going to lock me in there with a bunch of psychos? ALONE? You can't do that. What if I need to get out? What if something happens and I need help? " Frank pleaded.

"Listen Frank, they ain't gonna do nothin' and you'll be fine. The nurses just finished their rounds and medicated the ones who need it. It's gonna be quiet as a church in there. It's nap time," Nixon said with a smile.

They walked back down the hall to the door at the entrance to the disturbed patient wing. Nixon fumbled with his keys, unlocked and opened the door. Frank stepped in and set his tools down by the first door on the west side of the hallway. Frank, still holding his keys, located the one that opens the patient doors and spun it off the key-ring.

"Here ya go. 'Member, only one door at a time. Don't want a hall full of coo-coos," Nixon laughed and handed Frank the key.

He took it and slid it in his pocket. Nixon backed out of the corridor and fingered through his keys. Frank heard the clang again and said his goodbye to Nixon.

"See ya in an hour," Nixon said.

Nixon's footsteps faded as he walked away, leaving Frank cold, wet, and alone. He leaned back against the steel door next to where he set his tools. *You'll be fine. It's not that bad. Nothing bad can happen to you in here. Just do your job.*

Thinking that all is fine and well–in the presence of the sun– on a well-lit day. But it's hard to swallow your own bullshit in a hall of crazy people, where the lights are barely lit, and sounds of moaning and whispering filled the air. *I hate this fucking job! And I hate these fucking psychos!*

He knelt and opened his tool box, then selected a handful of tools he thought he may need. He also secured the snake and the plunger. This was going to be messy. He slipped his hand into the pocket, removed the key, and inserted it in the lock. Frank took a deep breath and gave it a turn. Clang. The door opened.

Frank took a moment to evaluate the room before entering. The foul smell was significantly less in this room. *It must be past the blockage.* There was no overflowing mountain of fecal paste. That was a relief. He decided that this was a good room to start in since he wouldn't have to lie in any shit.

Frank anxiously entered the room and scanned for the patient that lived there. He gave it a once over but saw no patient. He looked again, more frantically. No one was in the room but him, it appeared.

This room was set up exactly like the last. The metal bed against the far left wall. The toilet bolted to the wall near the door. And the cabinet in the far right corner. Frank walked in and set his tools down. He was relieved that he started in this room. There was a distinct possibility that he may not have to be in an occupied cell. If he could manage to snake and plunge out whatever the clog was then maybe, just maybe--

Frank reached behind the toilet and found the water shut-off and twisted it. It squeaked closed. Frank gave the toilet a flush in hopes that the water would clear out of the bowl. It partially worked. He laughed to himself as he heard a toilet gurgle down the corridor and imagined the flow of shit pouring out of the toilet.

This was the best it was going to get so he located the half inch wrench and went to work loosening the bolts. Several minutes later the nuts were off the bolts and all there was to do was pull the toilet up. Frank knelt and grabbed onto the bowl. He pulled. The bolts creaked as the bowl slid off. A small trickle of water leaked out of the back of the toilet. *That wasn't so bad.*

Frank grabbed the snake. It was nothing more than a round metal cable that you pushed into the drain. On one end it had an auger bit and on the other there was a handle with a crank on it. As you turned the crank, the auger spun, chewing away at the blockage. This was usually the most effective method of clearing a drain.

He pushed the snake into the drain. This particular one had fifty feet of cable that you could feed in. Frank fed the line in and felt the pipe curve. There was no blockage yet so he continued to push. Eighteen or so feet in, the snake stopped. He gave it a push. *Nothing. This must be the blockage.* Frank began to crank the auger.

Outside the thunder continued. It was much louder that it had been. He could hear it inside the building now and it sounded as loud as it had been when he was standing outside. Thunder cracked again. Frank could hear movement down the corridor. *They must be scared.* He continued to crank the auger.

Whatever this is, it is one hell of a block. He cranked the auger faster and put more pressure on the cable. More thunder cracked. The walls rumbled from the concussion. A blood curdling scream pierced the air. Moans increased as the screams intensified. The patients began banging on the doors. Nonsensical chatter filled the air. Frank could occasionally make out words.

One patient relatively close was screaming and intermittently yelling, "They're raping me! They're raping me! Jesus' baby is dead! I have the devil's baby in me now!"

Frank stood, his body full of nervous energy. He stepped into the hall and looked down the corridor. It was empty. He listened closely to the woman rambling.

"Fuck me with your devil cock!

I'll have your demon seed!

Now put your dick inside of me and we'll begin to breed!" she intoned.

"Jesus Christ," Frank whispered to himself. *This place is crazy.* Frank had heard enough and walked back into the room and knelt next to the toilet. He grabbed the snake and cranked. The blockage dislodged. There was now a pushing force on the end of the snake. *It must be water backup.*

Frank began to re-spool the snake. Again, thunder cracked. There was a bang at the end of the corridor. Frank jumped at the noise. He clamped the snake to the side of the drain and stood. *What the fuck is that?* The banging echoed down the hall again. He walked to the hall. Thunder cracks continued to rumble against the walls. The lights flickered.

"Holy fuck… This is not ok," he said. He glanced at his watch. It had only been twenty minutes since Nixon had left for lunch. The lights flickered again as the banging continued. He slowly crept down the hall toward its source. His arms filled with goose bumps. From the cell next to him a blood curdling scream blasted into his ears. He jumped and ran several cells further down the hall toward the banging.

Half a minute later he found himself standing in front of the cell with the pounding. On the doors there were circular portholes with metal covers. Frank had seen one of the nurses using one when he first arrived. He reached for the cover and slid it to the left. The banging stopped. Curious he leaned forward and peered in.

Nothing.

The room looked empty. He pressed his face into the glass peephole.

Nothing.

Frank slid his hand into his pocket and felt for the key. *Shit, it's in the other cell.* He was glad that he didn't see anything inside the cell and that he didn't have the key. *These people are fucking terrifying. What the hell was I thinking?*

He hastily returned back to the first cell. His snake was lying on the ground, completely out of the pipe when he entered the room. *What the fuck? Must have been some kind of pressure in there, to push out six feet of snake.* Frank grabbed the snake and fed it back into the pipe. Exactly at the same point, he ran into the blockage again. This perplexed Frank. *How did the pressure blow out my snake but not the block?*

He reluctantly began to crank the auger again. The blockage moved and he began to pull out the block once more. With about two feet of snake left in the pipe, the block got caught. *Damn, almost there.* He cranked the auger. The clog moved. He pulled the snake free of the pipe just as the thunder cracked again.

This time the lights went out.

Water and several solid, wet objects flew from the pipe, striking Frank mid-chest. He emitted a guttural howl and scrambled to wipe off whatever struck him. He stood, knees shaking. A wail broke into the silent darkness. Frank screamed again.

"FUCK!"

The banging resumed down the hall. Thunder roared in the atmosphere. Frank heard something move in the room behind him. He sprang to his feet. He stuck his arms out and searched for the doorway. He had a flashlight in his tool box. He had to get it.

Another noise, a creak, came from directly behind him.

"Who's there?" Frank yelled.

Footsteps padded across the floor inside the room. Frank felt a quick breeze of air rush past him.

In a frenzy, Frank grabbed the wall and pushed his way to the doorway. He felt the steel door and rushed into the corridor, slamming it shut behind him. Quickly, he dropped to the floor and searched for his toolbox. He found it and removed the top tray, spilling its contents onto the floor. Ratchets and wrenches clanged against the cement.

There, at the bottom of the toolbox, Frank's hand found it. The familiar cylindrical shape of his flashlight. He grabbed it tightly with two hands. His thumb searched for the switch. He flicked it.

"AGH!!!!AGH! AGH!" filled the air. Frank turned the flashlight toward the sounds.

"OH FUCK!" he yelled. There, in his beam of light, stood a pale-skinned woman with ratty brown hair. She was dressed in a white and blue nightgown and was clutching her hair, pulling it out from her scalp.

She screamed again, pulling out more gnarled hair from her scalp, "WHA! WHA! RHOA!"

She continued to scream and pull her hair out, but now she began to walk toward him.

"GET BACK!" Frank yelled.

He grabbed the metal tool tray from the floor and swung it at the woman as she advanced. Her face was sunken in like starving Ethiopian's.

Frank shook as he swung the tray at her, but missed. She wouldn't stop. Finally close enough, Frank took another swing. This time it connected. The tray made a sickening thwack as it collided with her head. Immediately Frank saw a gash open in her forehead. It wasn't enough to put her down though. It was merely a glancing blow.

Another scream pierced the air. She extended her hair-filled hands out at him, then lunged. He swung the tray and it connected. Firmly. The woman fell to the floor. Frank stood and swung the tray at her head. He struck her over and over until she stopped moving.

He ran to the door at the end of the corridor. The door where he had last seen Nixon. He grabbed the handle and shook it, all the while he was yelling.

"Let me out! HELP! I need out! They are going to fucking kill me!"

His eyes blurred with tears. He felt them rolling down his cheeks.

No one came.

They could not hear his screams. *What am I going to do? Oh, God. Oh, God. Oh, God.* He shook the door again, pulling as hard as he could. He pushed. And kicked. And shoved. And punched, until his sobs overcame him and he slunk to the floor.

He sat with his back against the steel door. His flashlight shined on the feet of the woman he had just clubbed with a tool tray. Other patients could be heard milling about but each was locked in their room. *Where did she come from? How?*

Several minutes passed as he sat there sobbing. Frank checked his watch. *Fifteen more minutes until Nixon returns. Then he can get me the fuck out of here!* The woman's feet twitched in the light. He couldn't sit in the hall and watch this for fifteen minutes. *What if she woke up?* He grabbed the flashlight and stood. Overwhelmed with fear, he bolted into the now open cell.

Frank entered the cell. The room's cabinet was illuminated by the thin beam of light. The doors were now open. There seemed plenty of room for a small woman to fit in there. Frank's focus locked on the cabinet. She must have been in there the whole time. He noticed some writing on the back interior wall of the cabinet. Slowly, he stepped closer to inspect the words.

"Jesus Christ," Frank murmured quietly.

Scratched into the back wall of the cabinet was a single word. HELP! He inspected it closer. It looked to have been scratched into the paint by fingernails. Frank stepped closer and examined it further. Small droplets of wet blood were smeared throughout the scratched surface. He knelt and reached forward to touch a small white object, a fingernail that protruded from the scratches. A thunder clap broke through the darkness.

The patients began to scream again. Frank jumped at the sudden noise. He jumped, and struck his head. His foot slipped on the wet floor. His body struck the cement floor with a thud. His head followed suit and cracked against the floor. Frank's vision flashed white momentarily. The flashlight flew from his hand. He grabbed at the back of his head with both hands and winced in pain.

Frank lay motionless on the floor. He stayed like this until he regained his vision. He opened his eyes. His vision still blurred. Light illuminated the area in front of his face. *The flashlight must be just above my head.* He reached for it. His hand grasped onto an object. It was wet and softer than he expected. He pulled it into the beam of light. His eyes strained to focus. As they did, something horrific appeared.

A semi-rotted rat face glared back at him. One eye was popped out of its skull and hung on by a meaty thread. Frank lost it. His body began to convulse. He turned his head and spewed vomit. It splashed onto the floor. He threw the rat carcass and pushed himself up off the floor. Tears filled his eyes. He reached for the flashlight.

As he did, he saw them. Seven…eight… No! Ten! Ten more rat bodies lay strewn on the floor. All were in various stages of decay. Frank spewed more vomit. More tears ran down his face. He grabbed his flashlight and ran out the door. He shined it at the exit door. Still no Nixon.

Then he heard it.

The sound came from the floor next to him. Where he had left the twitching girl. He directed his beam of light at the spot. Now, where there had been only one, there were two. A female form dressed in white pants and a white shirt sat hunched over the still quivering body.

Frank froze.

Where had she come from? This second woman moved her head around the neck area of the girl lying on the floor. Frank stared as she moved.

He cried out, pleading, "What are you doing? Please... Stop!"

His body quaked as she turned her head toward him. They locked eyes. Blood covered her nose and mouth. It was the sniffer! He stared at Frank. He stared back. Neither moved.

A familiar clang sounded from behind Frank. The door opened.

"Frank? You in here? " Nixon yelled.

Frank yelled incoherently, "Ugh! I gotta-- FUH! AGH!"

He ran past Nixon, and nearly knocked him down. He ran down the hall toward the entrance. Frank heard footsteps behind him. He heard thunder crashing above him. He heard his heart pounding. He heard these things until he heard them no more. His brain rang, and filled his ears with a buzzing sound. Frank grasped the handle to the exit door. He slammed his shoulder into it as he gave the handle a turn.

His body bounced off the door and he fell to the ground. He scrambled. Unable to get to his feet Frank grabbed the handle while still on his hands and knees. A gust of wind shoved the door open. He looked outside.

The sky flashed with near-continuous lightning. His ears filled only with buzzing. It felt like he was trapped in a silent picture. Frank crawled outside onto the stoop. He rolled down the steps, still unable to stand. He crawled through puddles in the drive while he made his way to his truck.

Trapped in the buzzing, Frank reached for the truck's door handle. Still on his hands and knees, he grabbed hold. He pushed the wet, chrome button in. The door opened slightly, the wind pushing against it. Frank whipped it open further and grabbed the steering wheel.

He hoisted himself in the truck. He hastily inserted and turned the key. The gauges on the dash illuminated. Frank grabbed the shifter and yanked it into drive. He mashed the pedal to the floor.

The truck lurched forward, causing the driver's door to slam shut.

Sprays of dirt and mud flew into the air behind the speeding vehicle. Frank glanced into the rear view mirror. He saw several people standing outside the Sanitarium. He could only make out Nixon and von Haussen.

His eyes went back to the road. The accelerator was still slammed to the floor. Trees whipped by the windows as the truck sped forward. Frank cried. His tears ran down his face and dripped onto his muddy shirt. *I knew I shouldn't have gone there. Fucking psychos--*

He wiped his eyes. Standing in the road, right in front of his truck, was a woman. She was soaked with rain. What remaining hair she had was matted to her face. It was the woman he had struck with the tool tray!

"NO! FUCK!" Frank screamed.

He grabbed the wheel with both hands and yanked it to the left. The truck lurched and narrowly missed the woman. He tried to correct the steering but the speed was too much. The truck leapt from the road into the woods.

Frank bounced around inside the cab until there was only blackness.

***

Frank woke up some time later. A dim yellow light glowed above his head. Von Haussen stood above him looking down.

A nurse stepped in. A needle pricked into Frank's shoulder.

"It's nap time, Frank. We gotta go to lunch. Try not to cause any trouble this time, eh? " he heard Nixon say.

"Welcome to Laurel Mountain, Mr. Daggets," von Haussen said with a crooked smile. "Enjoy your new home."

15

MERINTHOPHOBIA

FEAR OF BEING TIED UP

JASON POZZESSERE

Boston

Traditionally when he received what he liked to refer to as "his inspirations," Vitale had a complete vision of what the finished subject would look like. This time it was different, and that unnerved him. It wasn't because he didn't have complete confidence in his skills. He was a grand master of his craft after all, and his work was highly sought after worldwide, but no matter what he tried material-wise, nothing seemed right.

Unsure of what to do next, the craftsman decided to put down his tools and take a break. He took a look at an old grandfather clock behind him and saw that it was only 2:43 in the morning. The sun wouldn't be out for at least a few hours he understood, and maybe a walk would clear his head. He pushed himself up from his workspace and grabbed for his coat from the back of the chair. As he exited through the old wooden door of the workshop, he took a glance back at the marionette's sad and unfinished countenance. It seemed to stare back at him pleadingly, with unfinished, hollow eyes.

This was to be one of the special ones, he realized with a sigh. "This fantoccini" he thought, "must be just so".

Lexington

Nicholas woke with the taste of copper in his mouth and the sound of an odd, rasping voice whispering into his ear. He didn't recognize the words, but knew there were indeed phrases being spoken. It was odd; this rough sounding voice seemed almost beautiful, both rhythmical and melodic. He tried to open his eyes and realized he couldn't. He tried to open his mouth, again realizing that he could not. Panic began to settle in when he understood clearly that he wasn't going to be able to do anything at all. Anything that was, except to listen. To make matters worse, he had absolutely no idea where he was. Where were his parents? "Mom?" he tried to scream "Where I am? What's happening? Please…" He wanted to sob, understood fully that he couldn't.

The musically vocal rasping seemed to be reaching a crescendo. The boy realized to his mounting horror that it wasn't actually musical in nature, it was more of a chant. It was an unnatural sounding and horrible culmination of words that he did not understand, but knew deep in his soul was evil. He knew this because he had read about dark rituals and rites in his favorite "Time Life" book series. He basically loved anything having to do with witches and wizards, warlocks, sorcerers and more. But in his readings he also ran into stories of demons and rituals meant to appease the Devil. Maybe this was his punishment for "Delving into subjects that God had never intended for decent human beings". That was what his Catholic school teacher, Sister Angela, said to him when she discovered him trying to hide one particularly interesting pamphlet on the modern day witches or "Wiccans" as they liked to be known, of Salem.

He considered for a moment and began trying to piece the most recent events of his day together. This must be a prank put on by some of his friends. Was he with them earlier? He must have been. Was it Randy, or possibly Levi? It had to be one of them he decided, probably both. "Ha ha, very funny you douchenozzles. Epic fail on my part not recognizing it sooner, but whatever you all did to knock my ass out really fucked me up. I can't move!" He tried to move again, and failed. He was going to kick those fuckers' asses when this was all over. He enjoyed pranks as much as the next guy, but this was just not cool.

Thinking of cool, he hoped to God no one was filming this. He had seen the videos of people coming to from their dentists visits and didn't want to be one of those pathetic assholes on YouTube. He didn't know what his friends had used to fuck him up, or how they did it, but he knew the shit was really strong. Not X, or acid, nothing like that, probably just a bunch of ground up over the counter PM pills. "Fuckers," he thought again. He had just worked up the nerve to send a "friend" request to Marissa Kyle on Facebook and she'd accepted. If he was made to look like an idiot and she saw it he knew that...

Agony, fear, and confusion enveloped him as what seemed like a thousand fire ants tore into his flesh all at once. Blisters felt like they were beginning to form and burst suddenly and randomly throughout his body, the ooze dripping over the few areas of his skin that were not on fire. And still, he could not scream, still he could not move, still he could not cry.

Nicholas would not remember exactly how long he endured his torment. It felt like he had been boiled in oil, thrown into a fire, flayed and could do absolutely nothing to end it. All he wanted to do was scream, and he couldn't. The worst part was that he didn't know why. Why oh God why was he being put through this? He wasn't a bad kid, he knew, as far as teenagers go anyway. He never spoke back to his parents or teachers, even when he really wanted to. And aside from reading up on the macabre when getting a little bored during lectures and catechism classes, never really did much of anything to get into trouble. Who was doing this to him, and why wouldn't they finish it already? He was not resisting, and he knew he wasn't screaming, although he dearly wanted to. "Please make it stop... just... please."

Sometime later it did, but not before he heard the voice speaking to him again, soft and sympathetic. This time the boy did indeed understand the words, and they did nothing to reassure him that everything was all right. They told him of more pain to come, but that it would be brief. He knew then that he was going to die, and he accepted that. Then, in a language that he thought might be Latin, the voice was chanting again.

Nicholas saw something other than darkness when a misty green color began to coalesce in his mind. He felt a sharp blade invade the area of his chest where his heart was located. He felt his ribs being cracked and torn, and then the valves around his heart being slowly sliced through. He felt hands entering into his chest, and then the heart itself being carefully lifted and removed from his body. Afterwards he felt those same strong hands reposition his head. A cloth wiped away debris his eyes. As the skin was methodically and precisely peeled away from first the left and then the right eye sockets he got to see the world one final time. A green light, an aura really, surrounded everything faintly in his line of vision. There were hands just above his head now and he could still not turn either his head, or his eyes. They looked to be strong and covered in gore, his gore, he understood. He tried to whimper. Still he could not.

A man's head then lowered close to his. Two faintly glowing eyes looked down on him from within a stern, elderly face. The man was holding a small knife delicately in his left hand, while the other hand held his face still. The old hands did not shake as they held the boy still. They did not shake as the man proceeded to remove Nick's blue. When the task was finished, the old man kept his promise to put an end to the boy's pain. With a wave of his hand he released more of the green mist, and Nicholas was finally allowed to drift into oblivion. "Sleep sweetly, my precious piccolo" Vitale said as he looked down upon the mangled body of the boy and kissed him gently on the forehead. It was an unnecessary part of the ritual, but he insisted on doing it anyway. He took a handkerchief out of his breast pocket and delicately wrapped the two bloody blue eyes inside. "Che bello," he thought depositing the precious bundle into his pocket. As he finished packing his tools a melody came to him, one he hadn't thought of in quite a while. Gabrieli's *La Spiritata* began to take hold in the mind of the old craftsman. The rise and fall of the fiffaro in this piece always put him in good spirits. It was time to go he decided, the sun would soon be out and he wanted to be sure he was home before morning had fully broken.

Salem

For Mona, Sunday morning began as Sundays mornings generally usually did. She went into the into the kitchen, pulled out a bag of green tea, poured water into the metal boiler and turned it on. She was in a foul mood. Yesterday had not gone as planned. She was supposed to have received the package she had ordered for the wax museum so that she could put the final touches on her newest and greatest exhibit: Alexander the Great! She had worked long and lovingly for months to perfect his scarred and yet undeniably beautiful physique. He would be the epitome of male masculinity and perfection. And she should know. Mona had had plenty of experience with men. She had enjoyed them greatly throughout her forty-plus years, and she would continue to enjoy them as long as she could, but she knew she was older, and she was more particular about her men and the endowments they needed to possess if they wanted to make it into her bedroom. She had never met a perfect man, and believed that in the world there were no perfect men. But in her museum, she had almost finished creating her own perfect man, her Adonis. Well, she would once she received that fucking package.

Mona poured herself a steaming cup of tea, grabbed a cereal bar out of her cupboard and headed downstairs. Even if some of the other locals didn't want to admit it, she felt that her wax museum was the true pride of Salem. It was more popular than even the witch museum or the Old House. Seventeen glorious rooms were filled with all sorts of wonderful scenes out of history and literature. None of the others came close to hers in either detail, charm, or beauty. However, she felt her greatest achievement up to this point was her Chamber of Horrors. Her attention to detail provided guests with unequaled repulsiveness and an unapologetic assault on their senses. She had taken pride when members of one of the local church groups told her that her Jesus on the cross was a disgrace to not just Christians, but to any human beings with a sense of morality. She received a letter stating her work was a "blasphemy" which needed to be" dismantled and destroyed." Knowing that simply reaffirmed that she was a true artist. For is not the purpose of art to delve into the true feelings of the soul?

Her store, while small compared to others in the city, made more money in a week during the regular tourist seasons than most of the others in a month and in the off months she still had the doors opened at least four days a week. Sure, she sold some of the typical knickknacks found throughout the town, but she was also good at following trends and knowing her typical client base. Take a few herbs, package them up in an authentic looking cheap leather bag and you have a love potion. Go on a hike and pick up a few interesting twigs leaves of different colors and you have yourself a wand of the Green Man or the Great mother. Sell traditional candies that you can pick up at any bulk supermarket and a parent usually caves into the demands of their little brats whining for a sugar fix. Life was there and for the taking, and at this point in her life she knew how to get what she wanted, and when she wanted something she always got it.

Knowing that made her mind start to reel at the thought of that egotistical and ironically dimwitted Carl. Where the hell was he with her order? She was becoming impatient and she hated having to wait too long for anything. The unveiling was only five days away and she needed the hair. She took solace in remembering that he had always followed her details explicitly and had never failed when he had promised that he would get for her the perfect specimen. He was a dimwit, but had impeccable taste, and was one man that had never fallen too short of her expectations, as long as she kept those expectations minimal.

As Mona took her morning walk around the galleries she decided to get a few errands done before opening. She made her way briskly through the rooms, then headed back upstairs to her living quarters. Before she could leave she needed to take a shower and make sure to take out the trash from the night before. She could hear him snoring in her bed.

Boston

If someone had asked him, Nicholas would simply have said he felt he had gotten lost in a terrible dream. He relived his last visit to see his grandfather over and over again. The old man lay sick and dying from lung cancer in his hospital bed, coughing and wheezing so violently that Nicholas was sure he would see Pop Pop Joseph literally cough up a lung. He remembered his mother clutching him tightly, weeping softly while she spoke to him. She made him promise over and over again that she would never catch him using tobacco, ever. She told him how she could never lose him, and if she did, she wouldn't want to go on living. He loved his mother dearly, and hated seeing her in pain. He promised her she would never lose him, and believed she never would.

As he sat motionless on the worktable where he had been placed, Nicholas wondered how many of the other puppets lining the shelves contained trapped souls trapped like as his. He wondered if they were as terrified as he was. He wondered if they had promises they could no longer fulfill, loved ones who were probably desperately looking for them. He wondered how many parents might be begging to God for them to just be alive, not understanding that to do so was pointless.

And all for what? What future torments awaited him at the hands of that old devil? He didn't remember much about how he got here, but what little he did remember was enough to convince him that the sick fuck wasn't done using him for some foul purpose.

Making everything worse was that Nicholas knew he was absolutely powerless to do anything about it. He couldn't move, he couldn't weep, he couldn't scream. He couldn't do anything but sit there, staring silently outward in the same direction. He would be the plaything of a devil, and would probably be used to entice other children into the clutches of this sick and twisted monster.

Nicholas began to think of the unmentionable and disgusting acts a degraded old man might do to a child and fell into an even deeper state of despair. He hoped that he at least had put up a fight. He wanted to think he made the ass-munch bleed, but in truth, all he remembered was pain and a green mist. Had he been raped? Jesus no, he would definitely remember something that twisted, wouldn't he? Those ideas and more floated through his mind for hours.

Sometime later that day, his consciousness retreating in on itself, Nicholas drifted back into a state of hibernation.

When he emerged from his trance, Nicholas found himself repositioned and looking up at the countenances of two individuals. Even though the room wasn't particularly well lit, Nicholas saw enough of the first one to immediately recognize the old man, his tormentor. The madman was rubbing a damp cloth directly into his immediate field of vision. Surprisingly he didn't feel any pain, or the need to recoil away from someone pushing something directly toxic into his exposed eyes. The man took a small step back to admire his handiwork.

"Gli occhi, sono cosi belli," the old man murmured to himself as much as anyone else present. Nicholas didn't need to understand Italian to know that the elder craftsman was making some sort of reference to his eyes. Looking back helplessly at the old man, he took in all the details of his face. He would never let himself forget the bushy eyebrows, the sharp beak of the nose, or the deceptively kind eyes, which had housed the glowing demon eyes of a madman, despite the fact that there was no illumination in them now.

The man situated next to the old devil was larger, much younger, and hauntingly pale. In stark contrast to his skin, the man's hair was the color of night. He possessed a pronounced and dimpled chin, prominent cheekbones and startlingly beautiful eyes. Interestingly, they were almost golden in color. They observed him almost sympathetically, and Nicholas' gut feeling told him that the expression was genuine. "Please help me" he tried to scream. "Please tell me you can hear me! I know you can sense that something is wrong here, why else would you be looking at me like that? Please... I just want to go..." Go where? He didn't know, but felt anywhere would be better than here.

The spectacular and beautifully pale gentleman nodded as if in understanding and said, "Soon, young man, all will be made clear." He turned to look at the old man. With a resounding sigh he nodded and said, "Master Vitale, you have my permission to finish your work." Vitale simply nodded his agreement adding, "It must be just so."

The pale man moved in closer and looked directly to Nicholas. "Fear not young one, for soon you shall enter one final slumber." The boy heard the words, although the man hadn't seemed to have spoken, "When next you awaken you shall be released from your prison." Two massive hands then appeared from seemingly out of nowhere. They reached down to cradle the boy by each side of his face. The man inhaled deeply, lifted Nicholas gently, and proceeded to lower his lips to the puppets. Nicholas saw the man close his eyes and then heard him exhale slowly. As he slowly drifted back into oblivion, Nicholas was happy to realize he was no longer afraid. He didn't feel as if he were anything at all.

Salem

Package in hand, Carl strutted confidently into Mistress Mona's Museum of the Mysterious using one of its main entrance's double doors. He had hoped that Mona's new greeter Dominick *a fancified word for cashier*, he mused, would be at the front desk today. He enjoyed toying with the young man, making some subtle and some not so subtle remarks about the boy's good looks and how he'd make a true man out of him if only Dom would let him. In truth, the adolescent was pudgy, a little slow, and to Carl's taste, a little too easy to make uncomfortable. It's not that Carl wouldn't follow up on any of his promises to teach him what pleasure truly was, but the boy had proven more dense than reluctant up to this point, and Carl wasn't sure if he felt the gimp was really worth his time.

When he was done with his male conquests in particular, he liked to feel as if he had achieved a state of total domination. True domination required not the just breaking of the body, but the mind as well, and this boy seemed like he didn't possess much of either, quite unlike that delicious young man he had enjoyed just two nights prior. Now that boy, he was a fighter! It was a shame that he eventually had to bind him up one final time, and watch him sink quietly into the Cambridge Reservoir. Even after scalping the teenager, he heard the boy struggling to breathe as he placed him into the large construction grade trash bag.

Thinking of that beautiful young face brought a philosophical tear to Carl's eye. He knew he was a true sociopath as well as psychopath, and would never feel any real remorse for anything he had done. He would have enjoyed keeping that boy and breaking him over and over again, but the Mistress needed his services and had always paid well, and on time. Carl was just a working man after all, and as most true blue workers, he had taken great pride in his reputation. The fact that she was a great piece of ass as well was another reason he continually strived to keep himself in her good graces. "Yes," he mused, "for you Carl, life is truly a smorgasbord of pleasures."

As he entered the main lobby he was a little surprised to see no one there. "Hello, anyone home?" he called to no one in particular. He saw that the rope that sealed off the counter to the register was up and latched, and that the door leading up to the second story apartments was closed. A sign hanging from it declared "Employees Only." The museum traditionally closed at 9PM, and seeing as how it was already 9:13 Carl shouldn't be too surprised to find no one in the lobby. Usually the process of tidying up after business hours took at least half an hour. Realizing that he had exhausted all but one He decided to head into the museum proper.

In the world outside, Carl knew without a doubt, he was a brave man. To be involved with the people he associated with and employed him, he had to be. Yet he always hated walking through this place at night. Even with the air on in the summers or heaters on in the winters when the tourists left, it was unnaturally quiet. Mona said she had purposely arranged her rooms and displays that way. Her museum was not just a wax museum, after all, but a gallery full of masterpieces. And like the Louvre in Paris, the Met in New York, or the Vatican museums in Venice, she insisted on maintaining as serene an environment as possible. What Mona found serene, he found creepy.

He entered first into the Hall of the Americas. Within were displays of some of the great colonial leaders. Adams and Jefferson were debating over some bill or other with supporters and loyalists alike showing signs of concern and/or distress. Civil War buffs would be in awe as they could see Lee surrendering to Grant in front of the Appomattox Court House. There were several more historically significant moments on display which interest didn't Carl, so he proceeded to the hallway that would lead him to the next section of the museum. As he left, he had the suspicious feeling that a particularly lifelike figure of J.F.K. was watching him walk by. He hoped he found Mona soon; this place gave him the willies.

Shaking off the creepy feeling by reminding himself that nothing here was real, *well really breathing in any case,* Carl decided to turn down the hallway displaying a sign with an arrow announcing that the Chamber of Horrors, Hall of Heroes and Storyland Station were all located just ahead. It dawned on him that of course that's where she would be! She'd sent him on his errand specifically for a new project she was working on the in the Hero room. He would just have to move on through the Chamber of Horrors and be there in a snap. While the figures themselves made Carl a little uneasy, that room in particular always had a different effect on him. Filled with thought provoking methods and special tools he only dreamed of, Carl had actually spent more than a few hours daydreaming about situations he'd enjoy finding himself in. Returning to his usual state of relative ease, Carl continued down the hall towards the Chamber of Horrors, *No wait, Chamber of Pleasures,* he considered as a sinister smirk made its way across his face.

After traversing the short and dimly lit hallway leading from the Hall of the Americas, he entered into the Chamber of Horrors. The room was darker than the rest, with studio quality lighting professionally placed to create both focal areas for the pain found on the faces of the unfortunate along with menacing shadows and crevices where undoubtedly more insidious devices and monsters waited to jump out at unsuspecting victim! Carl took a sort of grim satisfaction in knowing there were truly terrible things that went bump in the night, and he was one of them. Believing that Mona was here somewhere, he called for her as he entered the room. "Heya Sweet-cheeks, come out come out wherever you are! I've got something packaged special and it's waiting just for you! Oh, and I got your order too! "

Receiving no response, Carl decided to take a look about the room. There were two displays where he felt the lighting had a particularly gruesome effect. The first and largest of them was the two-story "Hell on Earth" arrangement This particular exhibit displayed not just people, but demons and animals as well interacting with one another in different states of debauchery, depravity, and ultimate violence. Some of the participants had expressions of the purest ecstasy, while others looked to be in the throes of agony.

The second was The Trial of Christ. Located in the center of the gallery, this exhibit alone was responsible for at least half of the wax museum's notable popularity. On one side an angry mob dressed in biblical robes looked to be cheering on three Roman soldiers. One stood vigorously, arms crossed with one hand resting comfortable upon the hilt of his sword. He was watching the crowd, daring anyone to approach. A second soldier stood in a similar fashion, yet the look on his face was one of pity. He seemed to be staring into the eyes of the pitiful and pathetic creature with outstretched arms tied at the wrist to an ornate table. The third soldier was the most interesting to Carl. He wasn't sure how Mona had done it, but she had captured a look of maniacal glee on the face of the man delivering lashes with a barbed cat o' nine tails. He knew that look, was sure he had worn it on one or more occasions when on his "errands."

There were two other Romans positioned behind the standing guards, but they seemed either disinterested or in a state of disappointed acceptance. He looked at the focal point, the naked and bloodied shell of what had obviously been a beautiful man. The confusion and acceptance in its eyes rang true of the victims of such atrocities. Mona had even given loving attention to the long, gore crusted hair hanging in matted tatters around the Messiah's head. He remembered the MIT student he had collected it from and smiled.

As Carl stood admiring the scene before him, he got an even stronger sensation that was indeed being watched. Scanning the room again he noticed something in the Hell on Earth exhibit he had inexplicably not seen before. How had he missed it? It was spectacular!

In place of the thin, robed, traditional skeletal reaper used to stand, there was something entirely new. Black wings stretched out six feet to either side of a pale skinned, angelic figure that was crouching on one knee. With golden eyes that seemed to glisten randomly from beneath a beautiful mane of hair darker than the deepest midnight, Carl saw the mannequin's eyes turn to focus directly on his. It was then that Carl realized there was strange music coming from the hallway leading to Storyland Station. What was going on here? Had Mona finally taken his advice and gone electronic without telling him? He hadn't actually been in this part of the property in months, but he was sure he would have seen the workers coming and going. Those kinds of upgrades not only took a great deal of money to get started, but time as well. Mona would probably have needed to shut the place down while it was happening, and he had heard of nothing like that at the museum.

Curiosity got the better of Carl and he decided to investigate this wonderful addition to the display. He was just about to reach the velvet rope barrier designed to keep out the tourists when he suddenly felt as if he wanted to vomit. An explosion went off in his mind, followed by a voice offering a warning. "Only a fool presents oneself to the Angel of Death before he has been summoned. Continue down the chosen path, knowing well we shall meet again."

Confed and nauseous, Carl dropped the package and decided he no longer wanted a closer look at the angel. He no longer wanted to be in this room. Truth be told, he wanted nothing more now than to be out of this fucked up place. Fuck Mona, fuck the package, fuck it all; and yet ,the sound of a sad, slow waltz coming from the room ahead seemed to beckon him forward and he found himself heading towards the next gallery.

As he entered another hallway leading from his current gallery to the next, Carl noticed a light green mist on the floor around him. He tried to get his feet to turn him around, and realized he couldn't. Panicking, he yelled for Mona. "Jesus Christ, you fucked up bitch what the hell are you doing to me? This isn't fucking funny! I'll fucking kill you!"

He entered the Storyland Station gallery and saw Mona standing in the center of the dark an empty room. Standing underneath a red spotlight Carl saw that she had what looked to be long green wires attached to the back of her head, her wrists, knees, and small of the back. Her arms to her side and forearms positioned so that her hands were covering her face, the woman seemed to be laughing at him. "I'll kill you, you cunt, I'll fuc--"

Carl stopped mid rant as a piercing pain exploded just inside the fleshy part of his jaw. Something had entered from underneath his mouth and lodged itself beneath his tongue. A taste like rotten food mixed with copper began to fill his mouth and he gagged. When he tried to open his mouth to spit out the blood, he found he could not. "I will not be broken!" he tried to say, but could not. More strings like the ones that seemed to be supporting Mona descended from directly above him. He found himself involuntarily raising both of his hands and spreading his fingers and thumb wide. Fresh agony introduced itself as two of the phantom strings bored their way through the backs of his splayed hands, bonding solidly to his palms when they had finished pushing through.

Carl tried to scream again and found that he couldn't. He was facing Mona now. She had an odd mix of expressions on that pretty, miserable face of hers. For one, her green eyes were wide with the shock and confusion of the horror she had just witnessed, tears streaming down her makeup muddled cheeks, and yet her head was tilted at an angle which suggested she was trying to look coy. Her lips were pulled back tightly in a smirk.

Carl started going through the traditional rationalization process as more of the strings attached themselves to his body. When one dug itself into his spine he told himself that none of this was real, it couldn't be. He would wake up soon to find out it was all just a dream. When two strings needled their way through the top of his knees and out through the joints behind, he rationalized that he was on a bad high. When the final string dug into the back of his head, Carl found himself trying to give in to the demands of his body and go to sleep, only he couldn't.

***

A small, elderly gentleman with bushy white eyebrows and a stern look on his face appeared from the mist. His eyes were aglow with the same ghostly green color as the fog and as he approached the couple, Carl noticed that he was pulling a large wooden wheeled trunk behind him. Stopping at the woman first, he checked her bindings, appeared satisfied with the way they appeared, and continued on to Carl. The old man then grabbed the human marionette's hand roughly, pressing firmly around the entrance wounds, and then proceeded to check the remaining bindings in the same fashion. When he was finished with his inspection he returned to the trunk.

Vitale reached into his coat pocket for the key and unlocked the latch to open the lid. Looking upon the burattino inside, he took a moment to admire he most recent creation. He said, "Precious Piccino, you were not deserving of a fate such as this." He reached down into the trunk and carefully extracted the exquisitely crafted and detailed marionette.

"You know" Vitale said to the man and woman staring terrified in his direction, "I haven't put onna de show inna years, might be a'needing somma volunteers! "

An unseen hand pulled on the strings attached to both Mona and Carl, and Vitale clapped. "Thanka you, thanka you! It's always nice having sucha' captive audience!" Carl and Mona then both put one hand on their bellies and started laughing. "But first, I shalla' introduce de star of tonights'a performance, everyone give'a de big round applause for Nicholas!" He looked at the puppet, put a hand over its face and released the enchantment keeping the boy asleep.

***

Carl watched in renewed terror, knowing that the puppet was modeled after the young man he had raped, scalped, and watched drown earlier in the week. How did the old man know? How could he have depicted the boy in such a lifelike manner? His attention to detail had been astounding. The eyes! He could clearly remember those same eyes expressing shock, anger, and pain. He delighted in it then, and yet the only emotion he could feel now was fear. Had he made a mistake when getting rid of the body? He never had before. He had made double sure that the trash bag he disposed the body in had disappeared out of sight in the deepest part of the reservoir. He had made double sure to secure the construction blocks he had used to weight down the body with industrial wire, the same wire he used on all of his victims. Carl tried to move his body, any part of his body. He couldn't.

***

Nicholas awoke to see his captor looking at him as his grandfather used to before he got sick. He stared into the old man's eyes and realized that the man was speaking directly to him. "If'a you can hear'a me boy, then nod'a your head." Believing this to be another twisted game Nicholas just sat and stared blankly into the man named Vitale's face. "I know you have'a very good'a reasons not'a to believe'a me, but'a try you must. Your mind will soon'a be clear."

Vitale stepped back away from Nicholas and proceeded behind the two living marionettes. He began to tell a story of an evil woman and a sadistic man who felt they were above the laws of human decency. The marionettes acted out the scenes as the man narrated a sad story of sex, greed, depravity and murder. The man was a special kind of sick, for he delighted in the taking of young men and boys against their will and breaking their spirits and bodies into nothing. The woman didn't mind the use of the man's special talents in either the bedroom or in his ability to provide her with the purest of materials for her museum. She pretended that since she didn't active take part in the deeds that she should be absolved of any guilt.

When Vitale began to describe the last murder, Nicholas began to remember. He remembered wanting to walk to Leo's Pizza as he always did on Friday nights. He remembered seeing a man in distress asking if someone would help move his dog. It had just been hit by a car and the man said he hadn't wanted to try to move the poor thing without help. He remembered being led to a mostly abandoned lot with a motionless mound of fur next to a brown van.

Watching the story unfold before him Nicholas remembered starting to walk away and then getting hit on the head. He remembered coming to, not knowing where he was, scared, and in pain, cold and naked. He remembered pleading with the man, the same man hanging now from the green, glowing strings, to just let him go. He wouldn't tell anyone, he promised. He remembered the man removing his own clothes, and he remembered the worst of it. In the beginning Nicholas fought back, and he fought back hard. Eventually the man tired of it and broke one of Nicholas's arms. Nicholas was too injured, too tired to fight back any more. That's when the man truly violated Nicholas. When he was finished he pinned the boy's head down using his knee, reached for a sharp blade he had stored in a bag, and took Nicholas's scalp.

After the macabre presentation, Nicholas stood up on his wooden legs and rummaged through the craftsman's trunk until he pulled out a saw and a screwdriver. Afterwards he quietly closed the lid and approached the still hanging man and woman. Fully intending to take advantage of the opportunity for vengeance, Nicholas was surprised to find he truly hadn't wanted to kill anybody. He dropped first the saw, then the screwdriver. "What would be the point?" He announced to everyone. "I'd just end up a monster too." For the first time since this nightmare had begun, Nicholas realized this.

"Did'a you see my friend?' Vitale exclaimed to seemingly no one. "I'a told you, una speciale!"

The pale man appeared to manifest suddenly from the surrounding darkness. "Una special indeed," he said as he continued towards the puppet. "Are you prepared to return home?"

"Home" Nicholas repeated slowly. "I think I'd like that." Stepping towards the old craftsman he said, "I don't understand what has actually taken place since this all began. Part of me still believes it's been a dream or really a nightmare. Either way I feel as if I should thank you Mr…"

"If you want to truly thank him, call him by using his proper name, isn't that right Signore Geppetto? Geppetto smiled. "Be'a you on you way now! I have work to do. Arrivederci," said the pale man as he ushered the boy into the shadows.

The old man looked back at the couple still hanging in their ghostly prisons. He picked up both the saw and screwdriver that Nicholas had dropped upon the floor. Returning them to the case, he considered for a moment. Reaching back in, he pulled out a carving knife. He looked towards Mona and Carl and smiled. No, he thought, he would have no shortage of inspiration for some time.

16
CYPRIANOPHOBIA

FEAR OF VENEREAL DISEASES

ED DEANGELIS

Thunder rumbled along the darkened sky. The alley I had chosen was well hidden. Many of the alleys in New York City were filled with various clutter that blocked the view of any who passed them. It made it easy to take her to a secluded spot. The concrete was wet from an earlier shower, and the smell of trash filled my nostrils, but that was not what made my hands shake: it was the aged hooker before me. I spent hours searching from one whore to another until I found one I knew was tainted, and also did not have a pimp watching her. Pimps cared a lot for their property, and had proven themselves to be very dangerous. The hooker I eventually picked had just spoken to me, something about hurrying up, but I could care less what she said.

My mind was focused on my goal, my mission, to rid the city of filth, to protect the unknowing and the ignorant, to save the innocent. These thoughts, these ideals, helped to quell the gnawing fear that writhed in my gut. I watched as she leaned against the wall, thrusting her hips toward me. Fifty dollars exchanged hands, along with the expressed desire to go down on her, and indeed, down I was going, but for reasons she would never guess. And would never ever understand.

She raised a worn skirt up and draped it over my head. The feel of the worn and filthy cloth made me shudder. Who knew what was on it. But this filthy rag was in truth a blessing. Her line of sight to me was blocked by her own clothing. That made the sleight-of-hand I used to retrieve the knife that lay hidden within my windbreaker so much easier. I leapt up, startling her. Her eyes were focused on mine, a look of shock and confusion filling them. She did not see the knife coming, but she certainly felt it as it punctured her throat. I heard a soft wet pop, and I knew my aim had been true. I had punctured her trachea.

Her eyes grew wide and her body jerked as my knife pushed deeper until I felt the tough resistance of bone. All that escaped her mouth was a bubbling sigh. Oh, how I love that sound. My other hand came up and slammed her head back into the brick wall she had been leaning against. I knew it was over, but she didn't understand that yet. Her eyes crossed, dazed for a moment from the impact and the trauma. I only needed a moment. The knife slipped free of her neck so easily. The wound closed, but bubbling blood soon began to leak out. I brought the knife lower, just under her breast. My hand guided the blade into her pliant flesh. It parted so easily, I hardly had to push at all. Then I began to penetrate her, over and over again, for the last and final time, a fitting way for her to end. Fear and revulsion fueled my anger and hate.

She struggled for a bit longer, but her strength began to ebb rapidly, and defeat ultimately settled into those dimming eyes. I removed my gloved hand from her mouth. Dropping the knife, I grabbed her body as it began to slump, making sure not to draw it to myself. It was already bad enough that I had to touch her in the first place.

"Shhhh, it's almost over, there is no need to fight anymore, just relax. It's almost over."

I whispered words to calm the fear in those eyes as I squatted once more, lowering her to the ground. She was scared, and I did what I could to ease her fear of the darkness encroaching upon her sight. It would be cruel to allow someone to die alone and scared; I was no monster.

A few moments passed, and I watched as the light left her

eyes. Her chest rose and fell in short irregular spasms until finally it settled. I let out a sigh of relief before my gaze gave the surrounding alley a quick glance. I knew no one would be out this late, or at least in this alleyway, but better to be safe than sorry. I had learned long ago awareness of my surroundings was needed at all times. Without that awareness, innocent people could get hurt, and that thought was one I did not wish to linger upon. The area was secure for now, and my righteous task was not yet over.

I turned my gaze back to the cooling body. My gloved hands reached out, grasping her ankles. I began pulling her body flat, dragging her in a pool of her own blood. My hands shook a bit as I saw all the fluids. But I calmed myself, remembering under the leather gloves there was a second level of protection, surgical gloves, they would keep me safe from infection. I gazed at her blank face, searching for the signs I knew were there. My body quaked as I found them. Small, fluid-filled lumps painted over with thick layers of lipstick bunched around the corner of her mouth. The very sight of them made my stomach twist, and my hands, which had begun to calm, once more began to quiver. But I stilled the shaking with the knowledge of my purpose. I even chuckled slightly at my own thoughts. *Still afraid, even after years and over a hundred cleansings.* Yes, I was still afraid, but sometimes fear was a good thing, it kept me sharp, and reminded me, my goal was one worth fighting for.

The knife cut quickly across her mouth, a simple X shape. The blade slid down through the soft tissue of the upper and lower lips until the tip pushed through her gums and scraped across her teeth. Then moved lower. I breathed in deeply, steadying myself before peeling up that skirt. Gray lumps of warty, cauliflower-looking flesh greeted my eyes.

She was infested! My insides coiled, my chest no longer rose and fell, and fear at least for moment stole my desire to breath. The fear that by drawing breath I was going to catch her filth. But I had seen this foul thing before and had conquered it, and I would do so again this time. I had to; I needed to. I cut across her hairy, diseased-covered snatch, marking her, warning those that would find her.

With that done, I grabbed her side. Despite her small size, I grunted with the effort required to roll her over and expose her backside. Her skirt was already bunched up and I could see the filth had traveled there as well. Three large growths ringed her anus. I made quick cuts, marking this area as well. My work was done, I stood and gazed around, making sure I had dropped nothing, making sure I was not stepping in any blood. No trace, no sign left, other than her. I bent down to clean my knife on her skirt, then stopped. Her eyes: they were staring at me, accusing me.

"Stop staring at me," I snarled. "I didn't want to do this. You *made* me. Your choices, your actions, and your... filth!"

Rage overcame caution, and my knife slashed out over and over, the razor edge tearing through the soft, wrinkling flesh of her face. The attack was savage and short, ending with trickles of blood mingling with the mixture of liquids that oozed from her ravaged eyes. I stumbled back, my breath ragged. I should have learned to control my anger, but sometimes it got the best of me. Quickly I reached down, wiping my knife off on her skirt before sheathing it again inside my windbreaker. It was time to hurry home. The walk to my car would take a while, but that was ok. I had done my research and knew all the back ways to go to keep my interactions with others to a minimum.

It rained hard that night, and rain always helped me sleep. The droplets of water drummed out a soothing beat. The knowledge of what had been achieved sent a feeling of satisfaction throughout my entire being, the kind of feeling a solider gets when he returns from a successful mission and is once more safe and sound. Feeling proud, I drifted off into a deep, peaceful sleep.

The gentle rays of the sun kissing my face woke me. I wanted to lie in my bed a little longer, but there were still many things to do, precautions to take. My knife looked clean, but it was not. And I knew something about being clean. My mother had made sure of that. A couple hours soaking in a jar of bleach should make sure that even if blood somehow had seeped into the cracks and crevices, it would be removed or degraded to the point where any DNA that had gathered would be useless. The clothes I had worn consisted of a simple pair of black Crocs, cheap Walmart pants, a black short-sleeved shirt, my windbreaker, and a New York Yankees' baseball cap. These things were all very common in New York City. They were stashed inside a thick plastic bag. I had undressed before getting in the car, switching to some simple running shorts, white tank top, and sandals. The Crocs were simple. Some bleach on them, followed by a wash would make them clean. The clothing, on the other hand, well, those could always be washed, then scattered around town, far away from my home or where I did my work. There was also a giant furnace that the old apartment building still used, conveniently located next to the apartment's laundry room in the basement. That furnace had handled many clothing-related problems for me.

I placed my knife in its bleach bath alongside its bleach-stained sheath, letting them soak and allowing toe bleach to eat away the invisible, tainted blood. The rest of my morning went fast: only a quick shower, since I had not gotten any fluids on me from the filthy beast. The urge to fully cleanse my body was suppressed. I stared into the mirror after I was clean, looking over myself. I was nothing special, almost six feet tall, with trimmed, short brown hair and blue eyes, which tended to switch from gray or green depending on what I wore. Stocky was a term I chose to use to describe myself, weighing in around 230–240 pounds. Most of the weight was carried in my gut. Little fat was carried on my arms and legs, a modicum of muscle instead showing on them. I flexed in front of the mirror, giving a sly smile and a wink.

It had been hard to look at myself in the mirror in the early days, the weight, the guilt of what I had done almost destroyed me. But after a while, after days of self-doubt and worry and countless hours of making myself sick at what I had done, I came to the realization that I did what *needed* to be done. There were so many evils in this world, but the world and the system that people create are flawed. By doing what I was doing, I made the world safer, less scary. To remove as much filth as I could, I had to remove those who carried and transferred it. The world was cleaner. I was cleaner by doing what I was doing. People were being saved.

Afterward, I was able to mail a bunch of transcripts I'd typed up for the local public broadcasting station, something I did often to put some extra change into my pocket. My main job was writing for one of the local papers, nothing special, just various ads and other such things that people paid the paper to have listed. Simple work: no headliners for me, but it was easy and paid all right. Most importantly, it allowed me to focus on my true purpose: my higher calling, as I liked to think. I strolled out of my apartment on the third floor and was instantly assaulted by a small, twiggy teen named Susie.

"Hi, Mr. Connor." She skipped over to me. Her gangly frame was dressed in some jeans and a T-shirt with some cartoon figure on

it.

Susie O'Neill was a spunky, young teen who lived in the apartment across from mine. I think she had turned thirteen this year, and her mother and father, Liam and Lindy O'Neill were great people who always invited me over for dinner. But then again, the entire apartment complex invited me over, many of them attempting to find me a woman. I was blessed to have found this complex. Not only did it have amenities that aided me in my purpose, but the people living here were right out of a movie. Everyone knew and liked everyone. I was constantly enjoying community events in the small fenced-in backyard of the complex. It was the closest thing I had ever had to a real, loving family. Well... my mother loved me, but that was different, and not something I wished to dwell upon.

"Hey, Susie, what are you doing?"

"Not much, Mr. Connor. My parents want me to go get the mail. Are you going to the cookout today? I know Mr. Guter is gonna make his beloved brats, and I am sure everyone else is going to bring something. My mom is even making her seven-layer dip."

Susie hopped back and forth on her pink sneakers as she spoke. She always had so much energy. The cookout had been forgotten. My mind had been focused on last night's task, so much so that I did not even remember that someone had slid the flyer under my door a few days ago.

"I'm not sure I can attend. I've been busy the last couple of days and am rather drained. But you know how much I like Mr. Guter's brats, and your mother's seven-layer dip. I guess I could pick something up and make an appearance, but I need to get some things taken care of. I'll see you later tonight, Susie."

"Bye!" Susie called out to me as I headed down the stairs, favoring them to the elevator in a small effort to make my gut shrink a bit more.

I first headed down to the basement, where I happened to run into a few other members of my apartment complex: Mrs. Lansky from 4A and Tommy from 2B. We made small talk for a while as I did some laundry. Our conversations revolved around the upcoming community cookout tonight, and, as always, with Mrs. Lansky nagging about needing to find me a nice woman. Her jabbering was tolerated because I knew she meant well. But a woman would only complicate things, in my already complicated life.

Thankfully, they soon left, allowing me to take my small, plastic-sealed bag of goodies and enter the furnace room. The lock had long ago been broken. The items were disposed of quickly enough. A simple pair of black cloth gloves I had stuffed in my pocket made sure I never left fingerprints on the furnace door or anywhere inside.

Once all my laundry was taken care of in one way or another, I dropped it off in my apartment before heading out to run a few day-to-day errands. My last stop was to grab a couple bags of chips and two twenty-four packs of various sodas to bring to the cookout. It was approaching 7 p.m., and the sun was almost down. The days were getting warmer, and I was enjoying my stroll back to my home. The streets were busy. The sound of traffic and humanity filled my ears. A smile spread across my face, while my mind wandered. Looking around, I saw families walking, smiling, all types of people milling about. Single men and women going about their own business, and my chest swelled with pride. Because of me, the streets were clean. The whole city was cleaner, and these people could go about their day, ignorant of the filth that had been removed from their home by yours truly. They were safe. No one was afraid. But then again most people were shielded from that fear by ignorance. They did not have the knowledge I did.

In a way, they were lucky. They did not know what prowled the streets: loose, diseased women, ruining families and killing men, women, and even children, striking all indiscriminately. Whole families were ruined by the horrifying diseases. Mostly, the diseases were spread by women-of-the-night, and it is why I searched for them, because I knew that they did not care about the blight they hid within their bodies. They, and the various infestations of diseases they carried, were a horror that needed to be cleansed. I shook my head, clearing my mind. I was sweating profusely, and felt nauseated, but years ago when I began my quest I trained myself never to vomit. I could not afford to allow my fear, no matter how bad, to make me do such a thing. I breathed deeply, reassuring myself in soft whispers that everything was good. And that is when I heard the man calling out:

"Modern day Ripper strikes again! Brutal slayer of prostitutes, claims another victim!"

My head snapped toward the small newsstand and focused on the scrawny middle-aged man who had called out. I knew the papers, as well as the man, were referring to me. Once the cleansings I had done were exposed and linked, I had been deemed a modern-age Jack the Ripper by the press.

A beeline was made toward the newsstand and its vendor. My eyes narrowed and a large vein on my forehead began to visibly throb as I read the banner headline.

"New York Ripper strikes again!" Before I could read more of the article, the vendor once more caught my attention.

"The madman killed another one. This one they found in a park in the worst area of Queens. But I hear from a friend that works for the *Times* that they just found another one in some alley today. What a frickin' sicko, going around murdering hookers left and right."

Sicko? Madman? I was none of these. I was helping people! And this ignorant asshole was slandering me and my deeds, making all my hard, horrifying work into nothing more than the chaotic deeds of a lunatic! My fists clenched, ripping a bit of the cardboard container of the soda I was carrying.

"He is not a *sicko,* nor a *madman!* Perhaps he is doing us a favor removing filth-mongers from the streets. I personally think he is a *frickin'* hero. It's about time someone did something to clean up this city. God knows the cops only deal with the violence. They never stoop low enough to really see the cancer spreading throughout this city. And when they do finally run into those horrifying creatures responsible for a majority of its spread, no substantial action is taken."

My voice had picked up in my short rant; my face burning as blood rushed into it, as anger filled my voice. The vendor stepped back behind his small stand, his eyes growing a bit wide in surprise at the acrimony that had crept into my voice.

"Whoa there, son, think whatever you want. I'm... I'm just trying to sell some papers. If you wanna think of him as some kind of masked vigilante going around at night and cleaning up the city, that's fine. I just don't want any trouble." His voice, unlike mine, had filled with fear. I felt a chill enter my body, cold and calming, leaving me numb but focused. My face was slack, lacking in emotion and yet it exuded cold, pure malevolence. It was the look of someone who had taken a life, and seemed like they would again with even the slightest provocation.

But as quick as it had come, my rage melted away, his words and my own mind telling me to calm myself and shut my mouth.

"I... I am sorry." My chest rose and fell rapidly, my shirt soaked with sweat. "I did not mean to be so rude and speak with such anger. Had a bad day at work. I am sorry, sir."

I quickly turned and continued my walk back home. My breathing began to slow, and my profuse sweating abated, but relief and confusion soon settled in my mind. The news vendor had clearly not been a native New Yorker, otherwise I would have had a fight on my hands. No true New Yorker would have taken the abuse I had thrown at him, but confused I was nonetheless. I never understood, and still don't understand, how people can't see the good that I am doing, the selfless service I provide for the city. For Christ's sake, I am risking my own life to give the people of the city peace of mind.

But my internal rant was interrupted by the grumbling and rumbling of my gut, demanding one of Mr. Guter's brats, which I knew he was just breaking out to put on the grill. A barely visible smile appeared and the once prominent vein on my forehead had vanished, as my thoughts now drifted toward the cookout, and the peace and joy I would experience there. Those people had become more than just neighbors to me--they were my *family*.

I approached my apartment. My pace quickened, while my stomach grumbles and rumbles had begun to assert their desires louder and more forcefully. I passed one of the side alleys between my apartment complex and the now closed-down Mexican restaurant that bordered it. I was tempted to head down the alley, as our complex's tiny yard was surrounded on three sides by a tall oak fence. The side of the fence in this alley had a door we had built into it. It was bolted from the other side, but they would open it once I bribed them with soda and chips. I turned into the alley, intent on getting some food and having a fun night. I deserved it.

"Hey there, sweetie, you look like you're going to have a fun night. Wanna start it off with a bang?" The voice was sweet. It carried a slight tone that pushed the idea that it belonged to an innocent little girl.

As I gazed toward the source of this sweet voice, a chill of horror swept across my body. The woman who had emerged from the alley, and now stood before me, was young, perhaps in her twenties. I could tell that just by looking at her. The word innocent would hardly describe her. Large black heels ran up moderately toned legs. Her skin, the majority of it, was the color of moonlight. Much of that exposed flesh came from those legs. She wore a mini-skirt, which covered little and showed off much. Her upper body was clothed in a thin, transparent fishnet shirt, small rips and tears showing its age. It covered much, yet still exposed her slender waist and perky breasts, which were covered with a simple black bra. What once had been a lovely face was now covered in a barrage of makeup, making her look like some kind of whorish clown. Short, and obviously dyed, red hair added to the horror show before me. But it was none of that which made me break out in a cold sweat, made my pulse skyrocket. My heart started to race until it felt like it would explode from my chest. I saw the small, rough-looking, reddish-brown dots that appeared to be various rashes all over her body, Many of them were healing, and the color was fading, but I knew well what this creature had syphilis.

My eyes shot down to her hands, and even though they were clenched, I could see there was a massive congregation of those reddish-brown dots. It was in the secondary stages, which normally occurs two to eight weeks after being infected. She was new to the infection. She probably assumed it was something else. I knew from my research that the sores are painless, and she might not have even noticed the initial chancre, the small, painless, disgusting wound that forms around the infection area.

But in a way only I would understand, this was excellent news. She had been corrupted recently; the filth spreading inside of her had not had enough time yet to go into hiding, to be able to conceal itself from the prying eyes of those who would know and understand what it was and what it meant. But I knew, and my righteous purpose was once more confirmed. It was almost divine, as if God himself had sent her here to my home to cleanse her, testing me, seeing if I would once again overcome my fears so the people of New York would be safe. Distant laughter snapped me out of my daze. I heard the loud infectious laugh of Susie come from down the alley. My family--they were in danger. This creature was not only endangering the random strangers in the city, but now she was after my family.

I smiled, although it must have looked more like a sneer from a madman, as she took a step back.

"That would be wonderful. Why don't you go to the alley next to us? The building's Dumpster is there. Go wait for me. I need drop to this stuff off." I could tell she was nervous, as her eyes became hesitant. She stared at me for a second.

She was right to be nervous. That cold look I had given the news vendor had entered my eyes once more. My fear had been replaced with an urgency to deal with this filthy beast who had dared to come close to my home and my adopted family. She was going to pay for her audacity. I turned, heading toward the front door of my apartment complex. No one from my complex would see. They were all at the party in the back.

"Hey!" she called out a little louder than I preferred, my body wincing for a moment. "We never discussed price. It's one hundred if you want..."

I cut her off, my voice snapping. "Price is not an issue. Now shut up and go where I told you."

"Fuck, you!" she snapped back. "You got ten minutes to get the fuck down here, cash in hand or I am *gone*."

She looked pissed, her pale face flushed in anger, lips drawn tight together. She stormed past me, heels clicking loudly upon the concrete. I thought she was going to leave, that she had changed her mind. But as I saw her disappear into the side alley I had told her to go to, I knew she must be desperate. Most hookers that I snapped at left, their instincts telling them something was wrong. Before I had learned to control my revulsion and anger toward them, many escaped to spread their filth and ruin lives of countless people. It had been hard to change, but lives were on the line. And her eagerness, despite my anger, showed how much she must have needed the money.

I headed inside, for once taking the elevator. My fat gut could wait, people were in danger. When I got into my apartment, the chips and soda were discarded on the floor. If they were crushed or popped, I could claim they had been dropped them on the way over. Quickly, I changed my clothes. I tossed on a black windbreaker. I had a closet full of them. My gloves and knife were still soaking in bleach. I would need to use one of my other instruments I had hidden in my apartment. I quickly rummaged through my closet, pulling out a simple pair of black cloth gloves, not what I wanted, but they would make do. I hurried into my bedroom and opened the bottom drawer to my dresser. My fingers slid under the dresser drawer until I reached a flat, inconspicuous area. My finger pushed up, and after a second, a soft click was heard as the bottom of that dresser drawer popped up, opening the hidden cache. I reached inside and quickly pulled out a length of metal wire, each end having a solid, simple metal grip, which the wire had been threaded through. I rarely used the garrote. It was cruel, but this filthy whore had besieged my home and my family. She needed to suffer. From the hidden cache I also withdrew a smaller knife, the blade a few inches shorter than its larger bathing brother. The hilt was heavier, made of a composite material I had chosen because it was non-porous, like the garrote handles. Both of these items I concealed in my windbreaker. Focusing my mind onto the task ahead, I moved toward the door. My home was under attack, and not only I, but my family, was in danger.

I cannot fail, I thought before I gently whispered, "I won't fail." And with those words, I began my hurried trek outside.

She was waiting for me behind the Dumpster. I could sense her wariness grow when she saw my gloved hands.

"What the fuck is going on? Why do you have gloves on?" She took a step back. She was tense, and if I was not quick, she would flee.

I raised my hands, showing her the simple gloves.

"Just some gloves. I saw you have a rash, and I wanted to be safe." I slowly lowered my left hand and gently reached into my windbreaker jacket and pulled out a crisp, one-hundred-dollar bill. There was a stack of them in my apartment, and they were only ever handled when I had gloves on. Her eyes focus on the bill, her tense posture relaxing. She must have assumed that if I was going to do something I would not have brought the money. She was *terribly* mistaken.

"Hundred bucks enough for a quickie?"

A curt nod was given before her hand snatched the bill from mine. It was like watching a snake strike. Her hand was a blur. In the blink of an eye, she was stuffing the bill into her bra.

"Where do you want me?"

My head jerked toward the Dumpster. "Just grip it and bend over."

Pale shoulders shrugged in indifference before she complied, hiking up her skirt. She exposed a bony pale bottom. I moved behind her, and then suddenly stopped as a question formed in my mind. It was not one I needed to ask, but I felt compelled to do so.

"You have a condom, sweetie?"

Her head turned, lips, and eyebrows narrowed. "Do I look like a drug store to you? Do it or don't, you already paid." Head turned back to face the Dumpster, her boney behind giving a little shake.

"Ok, just checking." My hands reached out gripping her ass. I rubbed gently, attempting to calm her more, fingers slowly spreading those pale cheeks. I saw it then around her small clenched sphincter: the round open sore, the point of infection. She must indeed be freshly tainted if this painless chancre was still an open wound. But the filth must be spreading fast through her if she was also showing the secondary signs. The oozing sore looked raw and infected, but she likely had no idea it was there.

She giggled. "Calm yourself, hon, it's ok. I promise my pussy will make you cum fast. I am nice and tight." She reached down between her spread legs, fingers gently finding her pussy and spreading it, showing me her pink, slick insides.

I realized after her comment that she had felt my hands shaking. The sight of the open chancre had unnerved me. I knew this was most likely the sight of the initial infection. She mistook it for nervousness. It was the last mistake she would make. I pulled the garrote from my right-side jacket pocket. It was quick. I looped it around her neck, and before she could utter a word, I had crossed the cords over one another and spun myself around, my hands tight on the grips as I pulled it over my shoulder. Her body rose and slammed into my back. She struggled.

Oh, how she struggled. I could hear the gurgles and other frantic noises as she tried to fight. I felt her twisting and pulling. That only made it worse for her, made her suffer more. I was glad she was twisting and pulling. She needed to suffer for coming to my home. I leaned forward, tugged hard. I could feel her shaking. I could almost feel the life draining from her as her struggles began to lessen, her kicks becoming less pronounced. Soon, her hands dropped to her side, and I looked over my shoulder. A smile of delight crept onto my face while I saw her fingers twitching gently. They were bloody. She must have ripped at her throat in an attempt to remove the wire.

Light spasms shook through her body, but that was ok, she was dead. I released the wire, and with a heavy thud, her body slumped to the ground. I looked down at her, then quickly gazed around to make sure no one had wandered by and witnessed the struggle.

I saw no one and heard nothing but the normal city sounds. But just in case, I reached into my jacket and pulled out a large pair of sunglasses and put them on. It was night already, so these would conceal my features better if someone decided to walk down the alley.

It had happened once, before I moved to New York, before I trained myself to be aware of my surroundings. A young man had wandered below the overpass I had been working in. He found me crouched over the girl. He had raced over to see if we needed help. I had hated to kill him, but he would have never understood my task. So when he came close, I had called out for his help. Luring him in, the same knife that was now soaking in bleach had been used to end his life. It had been quick, a lucky strike had pierced his heart on the first thrust. That death had come with a price, I had been sick for days with the knowledge that I had killed without purpose, without proper reason--beyond saving my own hide.

My head shook, there was work to be done. With a soft grunt, I flipped her over. Her glazed eyes had rolled back in her head. Her pale, once beautiful throat was torn by the wire, bloody rakes furrowed her delicate flesh where she had clawed her skin off in an attempt to get her fingers around the wire, a futile and painful last act of desperation.

Reaching down into her bra I pulled out the hundred-dollar bill she had stashed there. I knew it was clean, but I always played it safe if I could. Something else fluttered out from her bra, a small square piece of what I thought was paper. I reached down to pick it up and place it back inside her bra, when I saw it was actually a picture: the girl without the rash holding what looked like a young, little male toddler--her son. My body rocked, as if hit by some unseen force. The pictured slipped from my fingers, fluttering to the ground. Memories flooded into my mind, and with those came emotions, ones I tried to keep locked down, but struggled with constantly. Now they overwhelmed me. My sight went red. Rage welled up inside of me. Without thinking, without thought or logic, I took my knife out and leaped upon her like some savage beast, the knife rising and falling as I plunged it in and out of her flesh. With no rhyme or reason to where the blade fell, the thrusts became slashes as I carved off hunks of her flesh. I removed her nose, slicing it off like a fisherman removed shark fins. I sliced at her mouth, until her bloody teeth grinned at me. Ragged lumps of flesh lay everywhere. I don't remember ripping her bra off, but I must have, as I carved off those perky pale breasts, leaving the ragged bloody hunks of breast-flesh upon the ground, one on each side of her. Massive gapping wounds now replaced what had once been soft white breasts, the remains of which laid next to her, now longer recognizable. My knife continued to work over her in a frenzy. I plunged the knife into her stomach. Wet, delightful pops greeted my ears with each plunge of the blade into her gut. The red rashes on her skin were soon camouflaged by the blood that oozed out. Her heart had stopped, thankfully, so it was not spurting. And when I try to think back to that time, I don't think I would have cared if it was.

I stood over what once was a person, gasping. My body trembled. I ached as the adrenaline-fueled rage wore off, and I gazed down, beholding in horror what I had done.

I stumbled back, blinking. The fog of rage had befuddled my thoughts, but they were coming back now. With haste, my shaking hands jammed the knife and garrote into my windbreaker pocket. I should have gone over the scene, but the mutilated corpse below me stared back with vacant, bloody, oozing eye holes. Her bloody, lipless smile was now a constant rictus of repulsion. The sight of her mutilated chest, the countless other wounds where I had removed so much flesh, and the wet bone that shone back at me, made me sick. I gagged twice, but my jaw clenched till it hurt, and I kept myself from being sick.

I made my way back toward the corner of the building as my feet tore through the dirty puddles that lined the alley. The sound of my racing heart was all I could hear at first, till my thoughts finally broke through my panic. *Calm yourself!* I screamed to myself right before I ran out of the alley. At the corner, I lowered my head, my hand braced against the brick wall. I gulped in deep breaths of air for just a few seconds while I waited for the street to empty for just a few moments, allowing me to slowly, albeit unsteadily walk back into my home. Once inside my apartment, I slammed the door and collapsed against it. I gazed down at my hands. I saw and felt the blood had soaked through my gloves. The wool did not protect me like my leather ones did. I knew I was dirty. In my rage, her filthy blood had gotten on me. I could feel it: the corruption in her blood attempting to find entrance into my body, to make me what I had so long strived to destroy. I needed to be clean. Clean meant safe. I could almost hear my mother speaking those words to me again.

I stood, my clothes were removed quickly. I grabbed the small trash bin by my door and dumped them inside. I went into the bathroom, my body still quaking; I was terrified, and just wanted to curl up and cry. But one desire overwhelmed even my fear: I was dirty. I needed to get clean. I had to *be* clean.

The pounding of water filling the tub made me wince, I knew what was coming, but had no choice but go onward. As it warmed, I went under the sink, grabbing two of the many gallons of bleach I kept. Then I poured the bleach in the trash bin where I had stuffed my diseased-covered clothes. I filled it to the brim and let them soak.

I gazed into the mirror and what stared back was horrifying: a pale scarred, hollow creature, so very different from what I had seen this morning. But this morning I had been confident, and that confidence had fueled my delusion. It had strengthened the barricade I had placed around my past memories that kept me from seeing the truth. The truth was disturbing and something I hide from all others. Much of my pale body was covered in smooth scars where the flesh had been scrubbed off. Other than upon my head and in sparse patches around my groin, I was smooth. But this mutilation of my body was proof I was, and would remain clean. My mother had shown me this truth; she had forced it into my mind.

I stepped into the tub and hissed at the heat. But the heat was cleansing. Burning made all that was bad, clean. My skin grew reddened, but this was just the start. I reached for the pumice stone. I began to scrub. Tears rolled down my cheeks as my hands methodically scrubbed along my body, tearing away the old, corrupted layers of skin, baring the new flesh to the searing kiss of hot water. I rocked, closed my eyes, and remembered.

* * *

"Come on, baby, stop crying, Momma needs to get you clean!"
I was nine, and my mother was kneeling next to me while I sat in a

small cast iron tub with the hot, steaming water filled to the brim. My skin was red and raw, the water a pinkish color from the parts of my skin that were bleeding. And yet my mother scrubbed across my body, scouring almost every inch with that pumice stone. It hurt, but it was my mother. I glanced up at her with wide tear-filled eyes. She looked sick--in more ways than one. Her painted-up face did little to hide the massive, open, boil-like sores that covered the right corner of her mouth. They had popped earlier today, whether on their own or by her hand I was not sure, but I really didn't care. I had come home from school and found my mother preparing herself for company. She always had company come over: strange men and women coming day and night and at all hours. They stayed for a while, and Mommy made me stay in the second guest bathroom.

She had been acting funny today, talking funny and wobbling. It happened when she drank her adult juice. She had given me a kiss when I came home. But then my mother had started screaming about how she was sick and asked why I let her kiss me. It happened often. Mommy was sick often, and sometimes, she scrubbed me even if we hugged or sat close to one another.

"Clean, baby, gotta get you clean before company comes!"

She scrubbed hard at my face, mostly upon the cheek she had kissed. My cheek was starting to bleed. I didn't understand why Mommy was so sick. I had mentioned her going to a doctor, and she just laughed and told me that her sicknesses would not go away, regardless of what any doctor did. She reached up and turned the faucet handle. I let out a little whimper and tried to get out of the water. It was getting too hot. But she just gripped my shoulder and pushed me down.

"Burning is cleaning. Heat will kill the sickness before it can get into you!"

Her words were loud and slurred; her eyes had a feverish tint to them. She coughed. It was a deep cough that rattled in her chest. She dunked me under the water and held me there. I lay still. My chest began to burn and I began to feebly struggle, but she held me down still.

"Almost done, baby. Gotta let the heat kill the germs. Gotta let it vaporize the filth!"

She let me rise, and I gasped for air. I shook. I was afraid of her. No-- not of her, of the illness that had done this to her. She had not always been this way. I remembered fun times. But then she had changed. She started working with men. Some of them scared me. Some had said things about me, or looked at me funny. That's why I had to hide in the spare bathroom whenever the people came over.

I was spared more vicious scrubbing by a loud knock. My mother jerked up, and I looked up to her with half of my face raw and bleeding slightly. She adjusted her skirt and the small blue top she had on.

"Stay in here, baby. Keep the door locked and don't come out till Mommy comes to get you." She cleaned herself quickly in the mirror, before a loud knock was heard again, this time making her jump.

She called out hastily, "Coming, honey, hold on for just a second. I am getting myself ready!"

My mother moved to the door. She was halfway out it before she stopped and glanced back at me. She touched her lip, and for a moment the look upon her face was one of sorrow and sadness--but there was something else. There was fear.

"Keep cleaning yourself, baby. I know it hurts, but you're my baby and you have to be clean, I need you to remain healthy and not get the sicknesses that Mommy has." That look upon her face vanished as she turned and slammed the door, making sure it was locked before she went to work.

My mother died a few months later. The police told me it was a bad man that had come into the house, but I knew she had died because of the illness. The diseases she had are what killed her. They made her drink her adult juice, which then made her act bad. I loved my mommy, and she died because of the sickness she had been given by someone. The illness ruined my mother. It ruined my family and my life. It was a horrid thing. Only when I was older did I understand the names of the sicknesses and what my mother really was. Once I was on my own, I vowed I would protect people from this hidden horror: this destroyer of families and lives.

* * *

But I had to be clean to do that.

So here I sat in the almost scalding water, scrubbing and washing my body. I now had an array of soaps and other cleaners that I used to make sure my body was clean.

An hour later, my body burned. I felt clean once more. All the rage, all the bad memories had been scrubbed and burned away.

I was suddenly startled by a knock at the door followed by a sweet voice that instantly lifted my mood, a slight smile spread across my face.

"Mr. Connors, are you home? You missed the cookout and everyone is wondering where you're at."

Susie, of course, had not even bothered to wait to see if I answered and was indeed home before she went on delivering her message.

I stood, not bothering to wrap myself in a towel. I stumbled out of the bathroom, my body shaking as if I were a newborn animal.

"I'm home, Susie. Just not feeling well. Tell your parents and the others I'm sorry I couldn't make it. I needed to get home, take a nice long shower, get clean, and relax. It has been a long, messy day."

"Ok, Mr. Connors, I hope you feel better. I will let everyone know. Expect Mrs. Guter to come by some time with her chicken soup!"

"Thanks, Susie, I look forward to it. Have a good night." I heard her skipping or running down the hallway. She always had so much energy and an infectious smile. I never minded or feared that kind of infection.

I had stayed inside for the next few days, writing a bunch of transcripts and giving myself time to compose my thoughts. I made sure my apartment was cleaned and my tools were sanitized properly and hidden away. The clothes soaking in bleach were dry now and stored in a plastic bag ready for disposal. The police, of course, had found the latest victim of "The Ripper," but when they questioned our complex, everyone vouched for everyone, saying they overheard nothing and everyone was accounted for--even me. Everyone swore I had been sick and had been in my apartment, which was what I told the cops. My neighbors were wonderful, sweet people. They gave me a solid alibi because, in their mind, how could Allen Connors, the young single tenant from 3B, harm anyone?

Finally, I was ready to go out. It was about 2 p.m. After I tossed some clothes on, and grabbed a bunch of transcripts I needed to mail off, I headed out to check on my, no doubt filled, mailbox. Once outside my apartment door, I heard the tell-tale signs of Susie, the thumping of sneakers hitting the floor. The door across the hall opened.

"Mr. Connors, you're all better!" She skipped over and gave me a massive, unexpected hug. She stopped when I did not return her hug. She frowned and stepped back. "Are you still sick? You're shaking."

My eyes were focused on her, and I indeed was shaking. Her eyes were wide, pupils dilated. I managed to push a few words past my lips, my voice almost failing me. "Wha... what is that?" A shaking hand lifted pointing toward her.

Susie instantly pouted, her little brow furrowing. Her hand snapped up to cover her mouth. "It's just a cold sore." Susie's voice took on a sad, almost whiny, pitch. "I must have gotten it from someone at school." I could tell she was upset and hurt for having noticed it, and for having reacted in the manner that I did.

"No, Susie, I am ok, just... a little off. What are you doing? Where are your parents?" My voice was distant and hollow, shock and horror overwhelming my normal ability to banter.

Susie slowly removed her hand, exposing the swollen, large blister upon her lip.

"They are out for a date day. So I get to stay home all by myself! I wanted to go to the park, but with what happened with that lady in the alley, my parents said I have to stay in."

I knew Susie loved to go to the large public park a few blocks south of our apartments. I had gone there with her and her family and many of the other tenants who lived here. She loved to play soccer or just go exploring in the moderate patches of wooded area the park had. She was very talented at finding spots that were hardly tread upon by other park-goers.

I could almost see it pulsating upon her once pretty face. It could pop at any moment, allowing its liquid filth to dribble on, and infect, others. "I... see. Well, I can take you to the park, Susie. I will make sure you are taken care of. We can even go exploring."

Her smile returned a bit at my suggestion, but only for a moment. "I would love that, Mr. Connor. But you seem... sad. Are you sure you're ok?" She sounded truly concerned for me. It made me want to cry, for I was indeed sad. "No, I am ok, Susie. Something sad happened today, but I will explain it all to you... at the park."

I turned to walk back to my room, then looked back to find her sad concerned gaze still upon me. I forced a small smile. "Trust me, Susie, everything will be fine."

She nodded and her smile returned. "Ok, I'll go get changed, after I get the mail."

She moved to go back inside, but I spoke out, halting her for a moment.

"Susie sweetie, don't tell your parents. They will be too afraid, and don't tell anyone else either. You know how gossip spreads."

Susie nodded before entering her apartment. Her door closed at the same time as mine did.

Tears fell freely down my face as I dropped my packaged transcripts. My purpose, my path was clear, despite the tears that were blurring my vision. Tonight my righteous duty required a great and terrible sacrifice. But for the good of all people. I would endure, and stand firm, once more in the knowledge that what I did served a greater purpose. God forgive me.

I moved to my room, and in a few moments returned. As I sat on the sofa, free falling tears dripping on the whetstone, I began sharpen my knife. Whispered words of strength passed my lips over and over in an attempt to bolster my wavering resolve.

"Nevertheless, the righteous will hold to their ways, and those with clean hands will grow stronger." Job 17:9

Poor Susie.

Her energy would be missed.

17
CHRONOPHOBIA

FEAR OF TIME

CRYSTAL PERKINS

Chapter One

I feel it coming on again. The panic. It's always this way when I wake up. I've been in this cell for 1,856 days. I've marked them on the walls. A hash mark for every day. It's the only way I can keep track of what day it is, and keep myself sane.

I look to the side, needing to touch those marks and know that another day has passed. Wait...where are they? Where are the marks? They're all gone. No. They can't be gone. They can't.

I'm pulling at my shirt, as I feel it suffocating me. It's not enough, and I start to scratch my arms, digging long grooves into them. I need to get out of this cell, out of this prison. Yes, I killed two people, but I should still have a chance to get out. I'll die in here if I don't. Not when it's natural, like my sentence demands, but by my own hands. I can't live like this. Who could live like this?

"Good morning," a guard I've never seen before says, walking up to my cell. "How are you adjusting to your first day here?"

"First day? I've been here over five years."

His face hardens. "Piece of advice, honey. Don't fuck around and maybe, just maybe, you'll survive until the end of your sentence."

"I'm not. I swear it! Please tell me this is a joke. Please?"

"I don't joke," says the beautiful Asian woman before she walks away.

The walls are closing in. I can feel them, they're physically getting smaller around me. I start scratching my arms harder, digging in as the blood starts to flow down them and onto my hands. I stand up, running to the cell door, attempting to will it open. It's not time for my hour in the yard yet, but I need to get outside. I need to. I need to…

***

I wake up on the floor with my own blood smeared on the concrete in front of me. I start to stand, but freeze. The hash marks are back on the wall. That's impossible? They were gone. I look down at my arms, and know that it was real. It *is* real.

"Guard," I yell.

"What did you do to yourself?" my normal guard asks me, looking at my arms. "We need to get you to the infirmary."

"What day is it? What year?"

She tsks at me. "You know the answer. We've let you make all those marks on the wall. Now back up so we can open your door."

I stand back as another guard joins her. Once the door is open, they come in and put the restraints on me, then motion me out. They stand on either side while leading me to see the doctor. It's a long walk from my cell in solitary, and I walk as slowly as possible, relishing this small piece of freedom. I killed those people, and nearly destroyed the other one, too, but my punishment doesn't fit the crime. I shouldn't be kept alone for the rest of my life. Everyone deserves human contact, and I'll take advantage of whatever I can get.

"Hello," says the doctor, a voluptuous Latina woman. "What have you been doing to yourself?"

I shrug, since it's obvious that I scratched myself. "I guess I had a panic attack."

"And what caused that?"

I look around at the guards as I fight the urge to start scratching again. "I-I thought it was five years ago all of a sudden."

"I see," she says, patting the examination table; I climb on. "That's rather common for prisoners--losing track of time."

"I keep track. I have hash marks on the walls. They were gone, though. Now they're back."

"It seems as though your imagination was playing tricks on you."

"I scratched my arms when the marks were gone. And I saw a guard I've never seen before," I say earnestly, trying to make her understand.

"There are no new guards," the one I see every day tells me. "You must have been dreaming."

"I wasn't," I protest. "I scratched myself. You can see that."

"Calm down, my dear." After the doctor has finished cleaning and bandaging my arms, she looks at me with this condescending fake concern. I can see that it's fake--it doesn't reach her eyes.

"No," I tell her, feeling another panic come on. I know I wasn't dreaming. I couldn't have been. "I'm not crazy."

"Let me give you something to calm you down," the doctor tells me, carrying over a syringe with some amber liquid in it.

"I don't need it. I don't."

"You do. You're obviously suffering from delusions, and I want to help you. I will have the guards hold you down if you're not willing to cooperate."

Her entire face has hardened, and she's practically sneering at me. I don't want this shot, but I also don't want a repeat of what happened earlier. I hold out my arm. "That won't be necessary."

Chapter Two

I wake up thinking today has to be better. The doctor gave me that medicine, and it made me feel calm all day yesterday. Today is a new day, and I just have to mark that on my wall. That will keep me calm. It has to. I'm too strong to rely on some drugs.

I start to reach for my marker, but my body stops. My hand looks old and wrinkled. The bandage is gone from my arm, and there's just wrinkled, spotted flesh in its place. No scratches, just loose flesh. The kind you see on people who have lost a lot of weight. I haven't lost weight. I'm still as beautiful as ever. Only I'm not.

I jump out of bed and run to the reflective surface on my wall. I'm covered in wrinkles; my hair is thin and white. It hangs limply around my face, accentuating the fact that my beauty is gone. Some of my teeth are gone, too. I look horrible. No. No, no, no! I am not ugly. I'm not. This isn't me. It can't be. It's a trick.

I touch the plastic surface in front of me, and then touch my face. I can feel them. I can feel the wrinkles, and as I move my tongue, it hits the gaps where teeth used to be. This isn't right, I'm not old. I'm not even thirty yet. I glance to my left and let out a blood-curdling scream. The left wall is covered in hash marks from about two thirds up, all the way to the ground.

"What is it," a guard asks, running up. I don't recognize her. She has chocolate brown hair, and the body of a centerfold.

"Who are you?"

"Not this again," she says with a sigh.

"Again?"

"You've been forgetting me at least once a week for the past five years."

"I've only been here for five years, and I've never seen you before."

"You've been here fifty-five years," she says all too calmly, like she's said it a million times.

"No. This is a dream. Just a dream. I'll wake up from it and be okay again. I will."

"Calm down. You'll remember once you calm down."

No. I won't remember. This isn't real, and I'm not old. Even if I was old, I wouldn't look like this. I run forward and try to rip the plastic mirror from the wall. I pull and tug, tearing what's left of my nails to pieces. I can hear the guard yelling, and threatening, but I don't care. I scratch and pull, tearing it half off the wall before she and another guard enter the cell. She tazes me and then it all goes dark.

***

I'm happy to wake up again, because that means my nightmare is over. As I shake my head, I realize that I'm on the ground. I look down and see that my nails are shredded, and pieces of metallic plastic are stuck to them. My side hurts, and I feel disoriented. I'm scared to look up, but I do.

The plastic mirror is torn half off the wall. I look right and see my hash marks, just the ones that should be there. I slowly look left, and see that the wall is bare. Leaning on my left hand to get up, I almost fall under the weight of myself. I look down and scream.

My left hand is old and wrinkly, just like in my dream. Or was it a dream? I lift my top to find the marks from the Taser. What is going on?

I stagger to my sink and splash cold water on my face. As I rub my eyes, I notice that my face feels different. I chance a look in what's left of my mirror; another scream. My face is half normal, half old and wrinkled. I continue screaming until the guards come, and then I fall to my knees.

"What are you screaming for?" one of them asks.

"Look at me. Look at my face. My hands," I say, holding them out.

"You look the same as you did yesterday," says the other.

"I don't, I don't. Please make it stop. Make. It. Stop."

"Make what stop?"

"Whatever's happening to me? What *is* happening to me?" I ask, sobbing.

"We need to get you to the shrink."

They come towards me, and I lash out. I don't trust them--I don't trust anyone right now. Not even myself. It doesn't take them long to get me to the ground and cuff me. I'm losing my strength along with my mind.

They pull me to my feet and start walking me towards the medical wing again. I can feel the difference as I walk--me left side is considerably weaker than my right, and my left knee feels like it's cracking as I walk. How can the guards not see this?

I'm led into a room with soft lighting, and big, comfortable chairs. There's a very young woman with glasses sitting behind a big desk. She smiles as we walk in. "Hello. How can I help you?" she asks the closest guard.

"She's hallucinating. Been doing it for two days now. She scratched up her arms pretty bad yesterday, so we took her to the doctor. She's removed the bandages, and we found her yelling about being old just now. It looks like she tore half of her mirror off the wall with her hands."

The woman looks down at my hands, takes one in her own, and frowns. "Please have a seat, and tell me what's upsetting you so."

"Upset? Look at me? Half of me is old, wrinkly, and *ugly*. I've never been ugly. I'll never *be* ugly."

"You do know that ugliness *inside* can sometimes manifest itself, making you feel ugly on the outside."

"I don't just *feel* it. I look like an ogre. Can't you see it?"

"No."

"What do you mean, 'no'?" I ask, jumping out of the chair. "How do none of you see it? I have no scratch marks on my arms, and half of me looks like I belong in a retirement home."

The woman looks at me curiously, and then pulls a hand mirror from one of the drawers in her desk. "There *are* scratch marks on your arms, and none of you looks old."

I look at my arms and see the healing scabs that have all of a sudden reappeared. My hands look almost identical to each other, and when I force myself to look at my face, there are no wrinkles anywhere. "How? I don't understand how this happened."

"Being locked up all day, every day, can make people a little..."

"Crazy? You think I'm crazy?" I think *I'm* crazy, but shrinks aren't supposed to say that.

"I think you're disturbed. Troubled. Do you regret what you did to be confined here?"

"No. I don't regret it. I'd do it again in a heartbeat, only this time I wouldn't get caught." I smile at the thought of killing those two perfect people.

"I see," the woman says, her eyes turning to steel. "I'll need to place you on medication, to ensure that you don't hurt yourself or others."

"What others? I'm in lifetime solitary."

"You go out into the yard with your guards for one hour per day. *They* are who I'm concerned for."

She pulls a syringe out of a mini-fridge and sets it on the table. The contents are green and don't look like something a person should have injected into their body. "I'll pass, thanks."

"I wasn't asking you," she says, pulling on latex gloves and smirking at me. "Is this going to be easy or hard for you? Either way is fine with me."

I know I have no choice, so I hold out my other arm this time and hope for the best. I'd pray, but I doubt God is listening. I'll never repent, and I'll never stop laughing every time I think of what I did to *him*. Not the two I killed, but that stupid man I almost destroyed. I would've succeeded if *she* hadn't come into his life, but at least I watched him fall before she caught him.

Chapter Three

I wake up feeling more like myself than I have in the past couple of days. My panic is at a low level, and I tell myself that today will be a good day. Today needs to be a good day. I'll be me--the me of today. No more imagining that I'm old, or anything else.

That feeling lasts until I look at my wall. Only about half of my hash marks are there. I look down at my arms and see the new bandages that had been put on are gone. My arms are smooth, with no scabs or scratches. I should be happy, but I'm not. Especially when I look over and see that my mirror is intact. It looks just like it did before I tried to tear it off the wall. My nails are nice and tidy, filed down and not ripped to shreds.

I drop to my knees, covering my mouth with my hands to muffle my scream. I don't want to see what guard will show up. If it's not the ones I've seen for the past two years, I may lose my mind. Unless I've already completely lost it.

How is this happening? How am I moving in and out of time? It's literally my worst fear come to life. I've kept my sanity in here by keeping those hash marks, by knowing what day it is. Now I don't, and I feel the panic engulfing me.

It's seeping into my bones, into my brain, willing me to succumb to the horror of what's happening to me. I fight it, but it's no use. My body starts to shake, and I can't get the scream I now need out of my mouth. I need to scream for help, but I can't.

I pull at my hair, yanking it hard enough for clumps to come out. I know my scalp is bleeding--I feel the hot liquid sliding down my face and back. I don't stop, though. I keep pulling and pulling, until I know I have more hair on the floor in front of me than I do on my head. Seeing the physical manifestation of my inner turmoil finally allows me to release the scream from my throat.

"What the hell did you do?" I hear from above me.

I don't recognize the voice, and I don't want to look up, but I do. I was right to be afraid. Another guard I've never seen is standing above me. She looks like a brunette Barbie doll--without the big rack--and I can't stop myself from laughing out loud.

"You're a Barbie."

"A Barbie with a gun, a big knife, and a Taser. You'd do well to remember that, bitch."

I crawl backwards as she opens the door and walks in. Guards aren't supposed to enter our cells alone, but this one doesn't seem to care about the rules. The look in her eyes tells me she's going to hurt me, and the smile on her face confirms it. I hold up my hands, but she just knocks them away. I don't have a chance to see the knife before it slices my cheek, but I definitely feel it.

I try to hold onto time, and how many minutes are passing, but I can't. After that first cut, the rest that follow are shallow, almost like whispers over my skin. None of what she's doing will kill me, but I feel like I'm dying a slow death anyway. The cut to my cheek will scar. I know it will. I also know that when I wake up again, no matter what time in my life it is, I'll have that cut. I should be thankful that she only uses the Taser to keep me from struggling, and doesn't use the gun at all. I should be, but I'm not.

"My boyfriend taught me well, didn't he?" I hear her ask before I pass out.

***

I'm curled in a ball with my hands in front of my face. It's too late to protect myself. I know that now. Whatever is happening to me is not stopping, and I need to try and accept it. Try and wrap my head around it. I can't, though. I did well in school, but there is nothing in my brain that could prepare me for this. For these time hops that steal a little bit more of my sanity with every passing day.

"Oh my God," I hear from the side of me.

It's my regular guard, and so I know I'm back in the "present." I've already lost sense of the days, unable to mark them on the wall without getting confused, but I find some comfort in the guard's voice.

The door opens, and I feel myself being pulled up. "Stand over there while we check your cell. What did you use on your cheek?"

"I didn't do this to myself."

"You've been alone in your cell all morning," the other guard says.

They search my cell, but can't find anything. There's nothing to find. That Demonic Barbie hurt me, and took her knife with her when she left.

"The warden's going to want to see this," the first guard says, as they cuff me once again.

I stumble to the door, a guard on each side. They're both holding onto one of my elbows. It's not tight enough to help me walk, but they have just enough pressure on me to keep me moving. I don't really need any encouragement. I had to get out of that cell before I succumbed any further to my madness.

We go up in the elevator, instead of down, and I'm led into a part of the prison I've only been in once. When I arrived here, I was taken to meet the warden. He's a stern man who warned me that my years in solitary would pass by very slowly. I could feel the disgust for me rolling off off him, and was surprised when he showed me a small bit of kindness. He gave me my first marker, and said that one would be available for me as long as I was here. He explained chronophobia, and how prisoners tend to panic when they can't tell what day or time it is. He said that time throughout the day may still be hard for me, but at least I could count my days.

It's not him I see when the door opens but it's a woman around my age. She's gorgeous, but also throws off a vibe that warns you to never mess with her. "Where's the warden?" I ask.

"I'm the warden here now. As long as you behave, you can call me Reina. If you don't, you'll be calling me the Devil. Not to my face of course, because that would be a *very* bad idea."

I get the feeling that she doesn't want me to behave, and that scares me almost more than this crazy time thing. "Why did you want to see me?"

"You've been causing the guards some trouble these last few days. Scratching yourself, trying to destroy prison property, and now look at you today? You're missing clumps of hair, and there's a large cut on your cheek. Where did you hide the knife?"

"I-I didn't."

"You didn't what?" she asks, her eyes narrowing.

"I didn't cut myself."

"You're in solitary. No one but the guards see you. You're not suggesting that one of *my* guards hurt you, are you?"

I know that if I tell the truth, she's going to hurt me. I know it deep in my bones. "No. Of course not," I say, swallowing hard. "I... I used the metal on the edge of my bed to do it."

"Honesty is the best policy. Especially where I'm concerned," she tells me, twirling her pen around her fingers. I relax a little. "I'm afraid, in your case, this little bout of honesty is going to make your life a lot harder."

"Reina?" I ask, starting to tremble.

"If you're able to hurt yourself on the bed, we'll need to remove the bed. I also think allowing you to mark up your walls was a bad idea."

No. I can handle sleeping on the floor, but she can't take away my marker. "Please, no. I have chronophobia."

"Oh, I'm sure you do. That's really not my problem though, is it?"

"Please," I beg again in a small voice.

"Did the two people you killed beg for their lives?"

"Yes," I admit.

"That didn't stop you, did it?"

"No."

"Then why should your plea of mercy stop me?"

"I don't know."

"Take her down to Audrey and get her patched up. We're done here."

I'm taken back to the doctor, who injects me with something else before stitching up my cut, and treating my scalp with some ointment. After, I'm led to a new cell. There's an iron door instead of bars, no bed, and just a thin blanket and pillow on the floor. The small light fixture is high on the ceiling--too high for me to use the blanket for anything other than warmth. The walls are bare, and I know they'll stay that way for as long as I live. I pray to the God who won't hear me that my death will come sooner, rather than later.

Chapter Four

I feel things as I slowly wake up. Crawly things. I swipe my hand across my face, and feel parts of it missing. I sit up, and see the bugs crawling all over me. Not just bugs, but maggots. Pieces of my pants and top are gone, along with pieces of my flesh. I start to open my mouth when I feel one start to crawl in there. I knock it away with a hand that's devoured down to the bone.

I try to stand up, but what's left of my legs can't hold me. I look like half a skeleton already. I feel them crawling all over my scalp, and push as many as I can off, realizing that I have *no* hair left. None at all.

I swat at the maggots, displacing as many as I can, but they just seem to multiply. I'm not dead, I know I'm not. Why are they eating my flesh? And why doesn't it hurt? Maybe I *am* dead.

I watch in horror as another piece of my flesh is ripped from the bone on my arm, consumed by what seems to be hundreds of these insects. I swipe my hand across my mouth, and then scream. I swipe and scream, over and over again, making sure that none of them go into my mouth.

They go into every other part of me--my ears, nose, and other places I don't care to mention. I watch in morbid fascination as my calls go unanswered, and what's left of my body continues to disappear. I don't have any sense of time as I watch, and while that panics me, knowing that I'm being eaten alive has taken precedence over my other fear. I watch, and watch, up until the moment that my chest is completely opened to me, and I see my heart beating too fast. It's then that I succumb back into the darkness.

***

I don't open my eyes right away when I wake up this time. I know without a doubt that at least some of the damage I felt from the maggots will still be evident. I don't know how much, but there will be some. No matter what time it is.

I feel a coolness on my cheek where I was cut, and on my arms where I received my shots. Those areas are cooler than the other parts of my body, and I know I'm missing skin in those places.

I *know* it. I move my tongue inside my mouth, and I feel it meet no resistance as it moves past where my cheek should be. I notice belatedly that my head is also cold, meaning my hair really is gone.

I try to move my arm, but I can't. It won't move. Neither will my legs when I try them. I don't feel any bindings on me, but I'm stuck anyway. Paralyzed, I realize. I'm paralyzed.

"Hello, Amber," I hear a voice from my past say to me, and then Maggie Griffin is standing over me.

"Wh-what are you doing here, old woman?"

"You didn't really think I'd let you get away with killing my daughter and son-in-law did you? Or trying to destroy my son?"

"Erin wasn't your daughter," I say.

"In every way that matters, she *was*, and you took her from me. From us. Her daughter has had to grow up without parents. That's can't go unpunished."

"How did you do this to me? *What* are you doing to me?"

She shrugs. "All that's important right now is for you to understand that you will never again know what time it is. *Never.*"

"You can't do this to me," I cry, struggling to move.

"We already have," Yasmin Griffin says, joining her mother-in-law to stand over me, a smug smile on her face.

"On behalf of me and my crew, I'd like to thank you for making this ride so entertaining. Don't worry, you'll be seeing some of us again. When you least expect it," Reina tells me as she also looks down on me with a smile.

"Yes, it could be any time. Any *time* at all," the doctor-- Audrey--tells me with a laugh.

They're all still laughing as I scream. I scream until I can't scream any more, passing out once again.

When I wake up, they're gone, but I'm not alone for long. Another doctor comes in and hooks me up to an I.V., telling me I'll be receiving my nutrition from this from now on, since I've had to be restrained. She says she's never seen a prisoner hurt herself the way I have, especially with nothing but a blanket and pillow in the room with me.

"It was them," I tell her.

"Who? You're alone in this cell."

"Maggie Griffin, and someone named Reina. Please. You have to stop them."

"Why on earth would someone like Maggie Griffin come here?"

"To do this to me. She's torturing me. Her and the new warden."

"New warden?" the man I'd met years ago asks, entering the room. "I've been here for twenty years, and I don't plan on leaving anytime soon."

"But I saw them... I saw her... she told me!"

"I don't know what you think you saw or heard, but I can assure you that no one who doesn't belong here ever entered this prison. Maybe you should give her a sedative, Doctor. A little bit of sleep may do her some good."

No. I can't go to sleep again. I can't ever sleep again. "I'm fine. I don't need to sleep."

"Oh, but I really think you do," the doctor tells me with a scary smile on her face as she injects something orange into my I.V.

I feel myself going under, and I try to fight it, knowing I'll wake up in yet another time. I'll never regret what I did in my life, but I do regret not paying more attention to time as it flowed around me--and not realizing that it's something to be afraid of. I might have been better prepared for what is happening to me if I had. Then again, you never fear something you're not aware of--until the phobia overtakes you, and fear is all you have left.

18

IATROPHOBIA

FEAR OF DOCTORS

AIDAN RUSSELL

November

The sunset was beautiful. It always was, but the weather was a bit colder than Jeff was used to. Had he remembered to grab a jacket on his way out of the house, he may have actually had to wear it. The news even called for rain the next day, and though San Diego wasn't doing so badly, California needed every drop of rain it could get, otherwise people were going to be really pissed about the increases in price to get avocado on their foot-longs.

There were downsides to living in San Diego, however. Sometimes traffic would back up for no reason other than that's how California traffic works. Sometimes the Padres would lose. The snow at Big Bear usually sucked, which meant twelve hours stuck in a car listening to whatever one-hit wonder band caught his daughter's attention at the moment for the annual family ski trip. Then they would finally make it to Park City and she would spend half the weekend in the lodge ogling all the penniless snowboard instructors who looked like they were one bong hit away from contracting dyspraxia.

Then, of course, there were the cross county drives when he'd get called out on a Sunday afternoon. The wife and he finally made plans to get out of the house and go hiking the hills outside Temecula, but then some observant Border Patrol agents had found a body a mile east of San Ysidro.

Jeff took a bite of the chipotle veggie burger he picked up from the brewery and wiggled his toes in the Coronado beach sand as the sun slowly dipped lower. Lisa had already eaten at home, so he figured he would stop and enjoy the sunset and the Coronado Brewery had some pretty good vegan options. He just didn't feel much like dining in. On a Sunday, there was bound to be at least one group of SEALs or Basic Underwater Demolition/SEAL (BUD/S) and Special Warfare Combatant-craft Crewman (SWCC) candidates getting tipsy and reminding Jeff of shattered dreams.

As he swallowed down his food, the flip phone holstered next to the Glock 43 inside his waistband began to vibrate and let out the factory-installed jingle that Motorola thought would sound good back in whatever decade the sheriff's department had bought the things.

"Bukowski," he answered, as if the lieutenant didn't know who he was.

"Is it going to be related?" his boss' boss asked.

"Tough to say already. Her throat was slit, hands duct taped behind her back, and she worked at Pure Platinum, so same M.O. (Modus Operandi) but we'll have to wait on the coroner before we start connecting dots."

"Pure Platinum? She must've been classy. Look, Jeff, you've been a homicide detective for ten fucking years. The media isn't going to wait for the coroner's report and neither is the Captain. Is this going to be part of the series or not?"

Jeff listened to the BUD/S candidates calling cadence in the distance. How any of these rich tourists ever got a moment of sleep with the Navy always blowing something up or tearing up the beaches at 5am, he could never figure out.

"Yeah, it's our guy," he said.

"Ok," Lieutenant replied. "I'll let the brass know before they do the briefing. Tell Lisa I said 'hi' when you get home."

"Will do, Lieutenant."

Jeff flipped the phone shut and snapped it into place on the cheap plastic holster the department had issued him. He almost shivered as the breeze picked up. He took a sip from his water and a final bite of his veggie-burger before crumpling it up in the paper wrap and tossing the leftovers into the trashcan next to the picnic bench. He sighed as he thought about all the report writing that awaited him in the morning and began to brush the sand off his feet before pulling his socks back on.

***

"Hi, Dad. Bye, Dad," Emma said as she grabbed the keys to the Corolla she had inherited from her mother when they bought the Explorer last year and ran out the door.

"Where's she off to?" Jeff asked his wife.

"Who knows?" Lisa answered in the thick Jersey accent she still carried after twenty-five years in SoCal. "She's eighteen now. She could be running off to buy crack and marry one of the Mexicans hanging out in front of the landscaping store for all I care."

"You say that now," Jeff said as she fell into his arms and he planted a peck on her lips, "but when she's running around campus next year with all those blue-eyed Brigham Young Mormon boys, we'll see what your attitude is."

"Oh, Lord. I am not raising a bunch of Jack Mormon grandkids and I sure as hell ain't sitting through a dry wedding reception." Lisa was the sweetest, most caring woman Jeff had ever met, but she started more sentences with "I'm not racist, but…" than anyone he knew.

"So, how many does this one make?" She filled a mug from the filter pitcher in the refrigerator, placed it in the microwave, and pressed the beverage button, knowing her husband would need a cup of chamomile before heading to bed.

"Six. Another young girl."

"A hooker or a stripper this time?"

"Stripper."

"At least this sicko's consistent. Three hussies paying their way through nursing school giving out hand jobs and three guys with enough money to blow on hand jobs. Just have every doctor, lawyer,

307

accountant, and slut barricade themselves at home until Detective Bukowski and the San Diego Sheriff's Department can string the bastard up and drag him through the streets." Jeff eyed the Our Lady of Fatima prayer card hanging by a magnet on the refrigerator door. Only his wife could get away with talking about hussies and sluts in front of the Virgin Mary and still be considered a sweetheart.

"Yeah, well, they have to pay their way through nursing school somehow. Navy ain't taking every old Jack and Jill off the streets like back in our day."

"Oh, heavens, if they had the same recruiting standards back in our day, I'd have had to have met you giving out handies behind a dumpster instead of having poor, laid up, Seaman Bukowski coming into the clinic with his bum ankle."

Theirs was the love story every uninspired romance author dreamed up: Sailor gets hurt training and discovers he has a thing for foul-mouthed Italian girls when the corpsman comes walking in to wrap up his ankle. It takes a special talent to look good in camouflage utilities and Lisa had that talent. Somewhere, beneath everything Jersey and Italian about her, she had just enough Irish in her genes to make her fertile enough to get knocked up the first time they fucked in her barracks room after a fancy date to McP's.

The microwave chimed and Lisa dropped a tea bag into the steaming mug before taking a seat beside Jeff at the table. The tea bag bobbed in the water as he pulled on the string, waiting patiently for the tea to cool.

"You hear from Sam at all today?" Jeff asked.

"No, I think he and Melissa had plans today."

"Well, at least you won't have to worry about those two having a dry wedding, the way her family is."

"Speaking of which, you need to talk to your son. I'm not saying they need to pop out a kid right away like we did with him, but with Emma out of the house next year, it'd be nice to have some grandkids come out and visit."

Jeff chuckled as he lifted the mug to his lips and slurped up more than he intended. The hot liquid burned at his esophagus before lighting a fire within his stomach. He grabbed at his chest and the edge of the table, trying to fight away the dizziness and tightening within his chest.

"Oh, for fuck's sake, Jeff! Will you go to a doctor already?"

"I don't need to see a doctor, Lisa," Jeff squeezed out between his clenched teeth.

"No, you never see the fucking doctor. How long are you going to keep doing this? It's been, what, four, five months you've been fighting with this? I'm sick of eating kale and fucking tofu because you're scared every doctor's got it out for you just because one shitty Navy doc messed up. I'm sorry you never got to see your dream of becoming a SEAL, but I'm not going to tell my grandkids stories about their late grandpop because he was too scared to go see a doctor."

Jeff tried to think of a comeback, some way to keep himself out of a doctor's office, but he was too busy holding himself up by the table's edge.

For as long as he could remember, Jeff had wanted to become a Navy SEAL. He had spent his whole life surrounded by the Navy until his father retired as commander in charge of an aviation squadron Jeff's junior year of high school. On every base they had been stationed, Jeff would get as close as a dependent could to watch the SEALs training or watch the BUD/S candidates getting the shit kicked out of them when his dad pulled a tour at Naval Air Station North Island.

Jeff shipped to basic training the day after high school and, after he saw Charlie Sheen's cheesy action-flick of Naval Special Warfare's elite fighting terrorists in Lebanon a week after graduating his A school (advanced training school), he dropped his BUD/S paperwork. The day after Hell Week started, Jeff found himself laying on a hospital bed in Balboa having his ankle getting wrapped up by none other than the gorgeous Hospital Nurse Lisa Marrazzo. It was supposed to be a quick surgery to fix the tear in his Achilles tendon caused by falling off the spider wall during a run of the obstacle course. The doc cut too deep and Seaman Bukowski was handed medical discharge paperwork. Luckily, Lisa was still covered medically when it came time to deliver Sam and Jeff taught himself how to walk so as to cover up the injury in time for the sheriff's academy.

"You going to go see a doctor so we can finally go out to dinner for once without having to wonder if they put cheese on their soy burgers?"

"No," Jeff grunted, grabbing his chamomile and stomping off to bed.

December

Clairmont Mesa just off the 805 wasn't the most upscale neighborhood, but it wasn't one prone to having a body found in a dumpster behind a taco shop either; let alone two bodies.

"They got any ID on these two yet?" Teddy asked.

"No, they're letting the crime scene guys do their thing before we start digging for pocket litter," Jeff replied to his partner. He took a sip from the coffee cup to warm up a tad. He had remembered a jacket this time. The weather was being as obnoxious as San Diego weather could be; rain, cold, and fog hung around until almost midday.

"I got the patrol guys running all the cars in the parking lot."

"So, what's the deal?" Teddy said. "Taco shop guy's closing up for the night and finds these two while he's taking out the last load of garbage?" Teddy shot a thumb in the direction of the dumpster. A pool of clumpy, congealed blood mixed with kitchen grease beneath one of the dumpster's corners. The killer was usually pretty good about draining the bodies before he dumped them. Two bodies must have been too much work. Jeff hoped, somewhere in the bloody trash heap, they could find something resembling a clue.

"Pretty much."

"How much you want to bet she works at the Cheetah's up the street and he's a big shot lawyer with a fast car and tiny dick? Any surveillance?"

"Taco shops ain't working," Jeff said. "We'll have to wait until morning to see if anybody else's works."

"Taco shops are getting 211'd every other night and they can't bother to have a working surveillance system. Who the fuck's running these joints?"

"It's a taco shop, Teddy. It's not exactly like they have a security manager checking the thing every morning to make sure they didn't get held up the night prior. Somebody's got to have working surveillance around here and, the way the crime scene techs are working, we'll still be here when the furniture store and the bank across the street open up."

"Yeah, they didn't pull any punches on this one," Teddy said, patting the side of the crime lab truck Jeff had been leaning against and stealing coffee from.

"Look! Two homicide detectives on a homicide scene standing around with their thumbs up their asses while the sheriff's got his whole fist up my ass. I guess it's not a party unless everyone's getting fucked."

"Ah, shit," Teddy said under his breath.

There wasn't a thing in the world Assistant Sheriff Thompson wouldn't do to get another two stars on his shoulder, and he sure as hell wasn't going to get elected the next year with a serial killer on the loose.

"Morning, Boss. Look, we're not even setting foot in the scene until the lab gets done turning over every rock and crumb inside the tape. As soon as patrol gets back with all the plates and their owners, we'll start digging on them. There's no video to review until the other businesses start opening up." Jeff took a sip from his coffee cup so his mouth would be too busy to tell the assistant sheriff all the other things he wanted to.

"Where's your sergeant and lieutenant at, while we're at it?" their boss asked.

"Should be on their way, Sheriff," Teddy answered, while Jeff busied himself with another sip of coffee.

"This makes eight victims in case you all forgot how to count," the assistant sheriff reminded them. "If your squad doesn't get this asshole, Christmas is getting fucking cancelled for your whole section. The sheriff's department has the lead on this case because our perp's been dumping the bodies all over the county, but so help me God, if we have to turn this over to the Fucking Bunch of Idiots (FBI), I'll have you all back in black and whites the next day."

"Sir," Jeff said, finally having had enough of listening to the assistant sheriff's threats, "the guy's fucking smart and we've been following up every lead we can. Unfortunately, there's only so many of us with only so much time to spare. Just because this asshole's on the loose, husbands aren't going to stop shooting their wives, wives aren't going to stop stabbing their lazy-ass husbands, and the gangsters sure as fuck aren't going to stop smoking each other, so the case loads are stacking up, nut-job murderer or not."

"Listen here, Detective!" It was when the assistant sheriff stuck his finger in Jeff's face that caused Jeff's blood pressure to shoot through the roof. He didn't hear the ass chewing that came after it. He was on his knees a second later pulling at the tightness in his chest. By the time the world stopped spinning, he was already being loaded into the back of the ambulance.

"Lisa? It's Teddy," he said into the department issued flip phone. "It's about Jeff…"

April

"Adult Congenital Heart Disease," Dr. Rosenthal said as he sat down behind his desk. Lisa squeezed Jeff's hand to remind him she was there.

"Heart disease?" Jeff furled his brow, the confusion overwhelming him. "Doc, I've been watching what I eat for twenty years, exercising, and haven't touched a cigarette since the last time my dad whooped my ass. How the hell do I have heart disease at forty-six?"

"Well, that's just it, Jeff. You were born with this. Since the day you were born, it's only been a matter of time before it was bound to surface. Regular check-ups can sometimes identify it early if there are heart murmurs." Jeff could feel Lisa's "I told you so" glare on his face. "Even then, sometimes there are no warning signs. Stress at home, stress at work, physical stress, these can all trigger the symptoms."

"So what now?" Lisa interrupted.

"Well, luckily Jeff has one of the least serious kinds of the disease and his heart hasn't deteriorated much. He has Aortic Valve Stenosis; a leaky heart valve," Dr. Rosenthal explained before they could even ask.

"What does that mean for me from here on out?" Jeff asked.

"We need to get a catheter inside that ticker of yours. Now, there are two surgery options."

"I'm not doing any fucking surgery," Jeff blurted out. He felt his blood pressure raising and the dizziness that came with it. Dr. Steinberg, one of the doctors who worked in the ER at Sharp Memorial with Lisa, had taught Jeff a series of breathing exercises to help out whenever he got too excited. In for a four count, hold for a four count, out for a four count. It was amazingly simple and always seemed to work.

"Jeff, relax. Listen to what Dr. Rosenthal has to say. We haven't been driving all the way here so you can go back to being scared of doctors and telling them how this is all going to work," his wife scolded him. They had been making the drive to Scripps Memorial in La Jolla because Lisa said they were the best.

Lisa had finally had enough after Jeff lost it behind the taco shop. He was either going to go to the doctor and get fixed up or she was going to kill him herself. It didn't leave him much of a choice in the matter.

"Jeff, I know you haven't had the best opinion of medicine and doctors since the incident in the Navy, but I assure you this isn't some government circus show. Medical procedures have come a long way since the early nineties. I'm even going to give you some options."

Jeff sighed as he realized he didn't have much of an option, especially with Lisa knowing the combination to the gun safe. "What're my options, Doc?"

"Well, the end result is all the same, we get a catheter into your heart to stop that valve from leaking. It won't make you bulletproof. You'll need to get regular check-ups to make sure no murmurs have started back up and make sure you're in working order and I don't see you running anymore marathons.

"The two options are how we get the catheter into your heart. The first way is to insert the catheter into one of your arteries through your arm, your leg, the groin, wherever, and then thread it up the artery to your heart. It's minimally invasive and you can be awake through the whole procedure."

"The last thing I want is to be awake while you're all sawing away at me," Jeff said. Dr. Rosenthal ignored him.

"The second way is to insert the catheter directly into the heart. We make a small incision between the ribs and go right in, no need to do some gruesome open heart surgery where we have to crack your sternum open. A quick cut, we're in, we're out, and we sew you up."

Jeff sat there for a moment. A few months ago he had been counting his calories and browsing for a new treadmill to put in the basement just to avoid having some quack touch him with a stethoscope. Now he was listening to one of those quacks talk about cutting his heart open and sticking tubes into it. In for a four count, hold for a four count, out for a four count.

"What's the quickest and easiest way to get this done with?" Jeff asked after two breaths brought his heart rate back under control.

"To be honest, the surgical option is the easiest. Like I said, we make a small cut, we're in, we're out, and you're on the road to recovery. The other way is less invasive, but we have to map out your arteries ahead of time, pumping dye into your veins, and even then it's still a process getting the catheter up to your heart."

"Yeah, the last thing I want is for you guys to be pumping me full of chemicals right before you start shoving plastic tubes into my heart."

"I guess it's settled then," the doctor said. Jeff didn't want to say it, but he didn't have much of a choice at that point.

"I guess that settles it then," Lisa said for her husband. "When can we schedule it?"

"We're looking at about six weeks for the pre-surgery and we should be able to have him in a week after that. Until then, keep the exercise light, don't let the boss stress you out, and keep eating right. Honestly, the whole vegan diet isn't really necessary, nor do I really recommend it to…"

The doctor's words trailed off in Jeff's ears as he began to realize the gravity of what he had just agreed to. A four count in, hold for a four count, and out for a four count.

May

"Asshole's not even trying to hide the bodies anymore," Teddy said as he held up the crime scene tape for Jeff to duck under. Five months with no new cases, but it was also five months with no new leads.

The bank and furniture store had no surveillance coverage of the taco shop's dumpster area and cars were in and out of the shopping center's parking lot non-stop from the time the cook took the trash out midday until he took the last bags out after closing.

The demographics on the victims perplexed them the most. Three of the four female victims were strippers and Sasha Donnelly had been posting ads all over the nether parts of the internet offering to let a john put it wherever he wanted if he had the right amount of money.

The males were where things made it confusing. The first victim had been a doctor, the second a tax lawyer, the third owned a few pool stores, and the one found in the dumpster had been a corporate accountant. Besides all of them being successful professionals in their late thirties to early-forties, there was nothing to relate them. One Jew, two Protestants, and one with no religious affiliation whatsoever. Three were white and the tax lawyer was black. Two were San Diego natives, one was from Boston, and the other from Montana. None of the male victims had any relationship with each other and it was a daunting task just to find the next of kin to notify for the female victims. Between the victims and methods, even the psychologists were having trouble putting anything together.

"Who called in on this guy?" Jeff asked.

"Some woman out walking her dog for the morning," Special Agent Morgan answered. The feds had been called in to help out on the case and Assistant Sheriff Thompson was pissed. Luckily for Teddy and Jeff, they didn't get in on the case until after Christmas.

"Good thing she found him, I guess. Could you imagine if some family on their way to Sea World stumbled across this shit?" Jeff said. With the weather warming up, tourists started their annual flock to Mission Beach. Another month and the beach would be full of tourists, surfers, sorority girls, and all the bums there wasn't enough room for in Ocean Beach.

"The media's going to have a shit storm either way with this one," Sergeant Campbell answered with his heavy Kentucky accent. "What kind of sick fuck ties a guy up with duct tape, slices his throat open, and then lays him on a fold-out chair on the beach, toes in the sand, and a piña colada in the cup holder?"

"That's the question we've been trying to answer for almost a year now, Sarge," Teddy said.

"There's got to be surveillance footage on this one. Has to be with all these hotels around," Jeff said.

"No drag marks either. Son of a bitch must've pulled him out of the trunk and carried him all the way from the parking lot. Victim's no Tiny Tim either," Morgan said.

"You get a look at him?" Jeff asked.

"Yeah. Lab took pictures, but not a whole lot to process until mortuary gets him down to the coroner. Go ahead and take a look, no shoe prints to fuck up anyways."

Jeff nodded and plodded into Mission Beach's soft sand, hoping he wouldn't wind up in any of the cellphone pictures all the looky-lou's standing outside the crime scene tape were taking. The patrol cops had taped off a large part of the beach, but there was only so far back you could push the public before taking over the whole beach.

Sure enough, a piña colada sat in the chair's cup holder; paper umbrella, pink straw, and all. Jeff walked around the beach umbrella to study the wound. There was one precise, razor-thin slash right across the throat, severing the trachea and carotid arteries. Their killer had done a better job draining out all the blood here than back at the taco shop. The crook had even tried to clean his victim off a little before sitting him out for a day on the beach, but the human body held a lot of blood and Jeff knew their bad guy was smart enough not to load a body in the back of a pick-up and run it through the car wash.

The arteries had sucked into the flesh as a last ditch effort to preserve themselves, but with how much blood those arteries pushed out, it would do little help. Wherever the killer did his dirty work, there had to be a wall freshly painted in bright red arterial blood. The head of the wound, the part where the cut was deepest because the killer had to apply more pressure to initially cut through the skin, was on the left side of the throat and had the biggest mess of half-cleaned blood from the initial bleeding. That helped confirm their suspect was probably right-handed, which didn't help them much at all. The victim had no bruises or signs of struggle and Jeff already knew what the toxicology was going to find: just enough propofol intravenous to keep the victim from screaming as their throat was cut open.

One would think the sedative's presence in every victim's bloodstream would give the investigators a place to start, but it was so common and the list of people authorized to be around the stuff was too long for one homicide section to sift through. That list also didn't include all the junkies and kleptomaniacs who took whatever they could get their hands on when they went for a stroll through emergency rooms. There wasn't even a guarantee their bad guy was getting the stuff from within San Diego county.

Special Agent Morgan was right. The victim wasn't small by any means. A pot belly hung over a pair of Hawaiian flower-print swim trunks; arms and legs that hadn't seen a gym since college days were laid out like the victim had just gone out for a day at the beach, which Jeff guessed he had... just not willingly. Duct tape bound the victim's hands to the chair's arms. He was sure the guy had been dead well before being put into the chair, but the suspect apparently didn't want to change his calling card too much for the morning's display. Jeff eyed the victim's body once more and then went on to study his facial expression, looking first into Dr. Rosenthal's open, lifeless eyes.

Jeff didn't get to count to two on his breathing exercises before he was doubled over in the sand, vomiting up the coconut yogurt and oatmeal he had sucked down for breakfast after getting the phone call. Teddy steadied his partner by the shoulder. His partner was probably asking what was wrong, but Jeff couldn't make out any of the words. A few minutes later, Jeff found himself once more in the back of an ambulance.

***

"We're going to have to move surgery up, Jeff. We can't take any chances. I'm going to clear some space up and get you in next week." Dr. Henry slammed Jeff's chart closed with his beefy arms and dropped it back into the slot on the end of the hospital bed. Judging by the high and tight haircut he still carried since retiring from the Army Medical Department a decade ago and his straight-shooting, Dr. Henry wasn't about to fuck around. Despite everything going on, Jeff actually kind of liked the doctor's no-nonsense approach. Jeff figured there probably wasn't much room for nonsense treating soldiers in a tent on the Iraq/Kuwait border as a battlefield surgeon during the opening days of the war.

Jeff didn't answer at first. He breathed in, held it, and let it out. Dr. Rosenthal, along with Lisa's prodding, had finally put Jeff's fears of having the same mishap that had taken place on his ankle happen to his heart. Jeff had never bought much into Lisa's catholic practices, showing up for Christmas and Easter so she could prove to the priest she did in fact have a family. However, seeing Dr. Rosenthal there on the beach, Jeff had a sudden realization that there were forces at work in the universe and those forces did not want Jeff to have a healthy heart.

"You tell us when, Doctor," Lisa said with no regard for the fact it wasn't her heart that was about to have fingers and scalpels shoved into it by some complete stranger.

"Next Wednesday. We'll do it at Scripp's like you all intended to from the get go. Same instructions as before, nothing to eat twelve hours prior and pack an overnight bag. I have us marked down to start prepping at 10am, so be there an hour prior to check in."

"Thank you, Dr. Henry," Lisa said.

The doctor nodded and walked off to check on his next patient, and just like that, Lisa had once again made the big decision for Jeff before he ever got to say a word.

***

"Jeff, go the fuck home," Sergeant Campbell ordered as he threw his blazer around his shoulders and headed out the door himself.

Jeff didn't look up and kept dragging icons around the screen while Agent Morgan looked over his shoulder. Lines connected all the icons, pictures of the slain victims, like tire spokes to a big question mark in the center. Morgan and Jeff had been working all day on a link analysis for all the victims' relatives and close friends.

"All this crap will still be here when you get back," Teddy said as he plopped into chair next to Jeff's desk.

"We just got the subpoena approved to dig up the records for one degree of separation from the victims," Morgan said.

"I faxed it over to the county recorder and they're going to dig everything up and send it over next week," Jeff said.

"One degree? We might as well have swung for the fences on this one and just 'deep dived' everybody on their social media and phone contacts," Teddy said.

"You really think any of these liberal-fuck 9th Circuit judges are going to approve anything more than immediate family and close friends?" Morgan asked.

"If we asked for any more than that, we'd wind up making case law legalizing recreational heroin somehow," Jeff said as he continued to create icons of the persons whose records they had subpoenaed and attach them to the victims. He would copy their driver's license photos from the DMV's database and paste them to the link chart. Juries loved pictures, probably because most jury members never made it past the second grade.

"Hey, imagine all the caseloads that would clear up if the heroin addicts could pump themselves up with all the shit they wanted." Teddy reached over and took the mouse from Jeff. He dragged the cursor up to the save icon, clicked, and then logged Jeff off the computer.

"Go home," Teddy told his partner. "You just got out of the hospital yesterday and you're going back in on Wednesday. Sarge and L.T. gave you the rest of the week off and you start FMLA next week. Morgan and I can handle the case until you get back, and I assure you it will still be here when you get back."

"I'm going to be out for a month," Jeff said, conceding and grabbing his car keys from the desk. "You guys better give me a call if something big pops up. And, if you do get this asshole ID'd, you better have someone pick me up before you have S.E.D. (Special Enforcement Detail) pick him up."

"Why's it got to be a guy? How do you know it's not some hooker taking out her competition and some johns who didn't tip enough?" Morgan joked.

"Because we already worked that angle before you got on the case," Jeff called over his shoulder as he walked out the door.

Wednesday, 8:30am

Teddy's desk looked like the Enola Gay had done a fly-by, dropping the Library of Congress instead of a nuclear weapon out of its bomb-bay doors. Jeff had subpoenaed the records of twenty-nine individuals. The recorder's office needed to borrow a van from the department to transport all the files.

"Where do you want to start?" Agent Morgan asked as he loosened his tie.

"I'll take the first victim. You take the second?"

"That was Christine Johnson?"

"Yeah. That stack right there," Teddy pointed.

Morgan grabbed up a stack of manila folders stuffed to capacity and carried them over to his desk. Then he came back for the rest of the stack and an oversized three-ring binder. Teddy grabbed the first folder from Dr. Jeremy Pitter's stack.

Dr. Pitters had a private optometry clinic in Solana Beach. He had almost lost his license on one occasion when he had been stopped by Carlsbad PD with an unnecessary amount of medicinal cocaine in his convertible. Lucky for him, he had gotten the blood test thrown out of the criminal court and the state medical board lost the grounds to strip him of his license to practice, although it did keep a closer eye on the medications he was ordering.

Dr. Pitters had three children with his first wife. Two were grown and the ex-wife had custody of the fifteen year-old. His second wife had had a messy divorce of her own from her first husband. Andrea Pitters, formerly Andrea Henry with a maiden last name of Filipov, her father having emigrated from Bulgaria during the opening days of the Cold War.

Andrea Pitters' first husband had deployed to Kuwait as a trauma surgeon in early 2003, treating soldiers wounded during the Iraq invasion before they were evacuated out of theater. It must have been those Eastern European good looks that kept landing her in the arms of doctors. She had taken to various internet pages to find the company of other men while Lieutenant Colonel Henry was deployed. He came home earlier than expected and found she was in San Francisco with one of her liaisons. The internet browsing history was all Dr. Henry needed to secure a swift and secure divorce with no alimony. A month after the judge signed the divorce decree, Andrea married Dr. Pitters. It didn't take any of Teddy's years of investigative experience to figure out the two had probably had several romantic encounters prior to her husband discovering what she had been up to.

**

The anesthesiologist shook his head as the heart monitor beeped rapidly.

"Jeff, listen to me, I know you're scared, but I need you to trust me," Dr. Henry said as he leaned over his patient.

"I'm sorry, Doc," Jeff said in between his fast breaths.

"Jeff, take my hand." Jeff reached up and took hold of the cardiologist's hand. "Lisa is right outside. I know you have some reservations and worries because of what happened to Dr. Rosenthal. It's tragic and terrible, but for the sake of your health, I need you to trust me like you trusted him."

Jeff's heart rate dropped slightly and the anesthesiologist kept an eye on the numbers displayed on the heart monitor.

"Do the breathing exercises for me, Jeff. I'll count for you. In, two, three, four. Hold, two, three, four. Out, two, three, four. There you go, just like that." The beeping slowed.

Jeff had told Lisa they would go have a steak dinner at one of the fancy places in Hillcrest once he recovered and got the thumbs up to eat whatever he wanted. Lisa was ecstatic at the idea of being able to leave the house for the first time in years and not have to worry about whether or not there was kale or black-bean burger patties on the menu.

The anesthesiologist nodded and handed the respirator mask to Dr. Henry while he checked the gas levels.

"Keep it up, Jeff. Just listen to the sound of my voice and keep up the breathing. As soon as I put the mask on, I want you to count backwards from ten with me. Okay?"

Jeff nodded.

"Are you ready?"

Jeff nodded again as he held his breath for a final four count.

Dr. Henry placed the respirator mask over Jeff's mouth and nose.

"There we go. Now count with me," the doctor whispered into Jeff's ear. "Ten. Nine. I killed Dr. Pitters. I killed Christine Johnson. I killed Joseph Washington. I killed Sasha Donnelly. I killed..." Jeff's eye's fluttered shut. He tried to understand Dr. Henry's words, but the whole world felt heavy as his body forced itself to sleep. The drowsiness overcame him so suddenly he could barely comprehend where he was, let alone where he had heard those names before.

"...And now, I've killed you," the doctor whispered an instant before Jeff drifted off to sleep.

NEVER FEAR - PHOBIAS

19
TOXIPHOBIA

FEAR OF POISONS

HEATHER GRAHAM

I knew that the woman hated me.

I knew she meant to kill me.

I knew it the moment she laid eyes on me.

Really. I'm not mean in any way, but, the way that she looked at me, mouth pursed in a knot, eyes bulging out--all I could think was, wow! What a paranoid *bitch!*

Killer-crazy bitch!

We shared living space, you see, and she should have appreciated the wonderful things I could do to help her around the complex and even her apartment.

She didn't. She was oblivious.

I did my best to stay out of her way, to be entirely obscure. I went about my life and my business being almost completely silent, staying out of her way at all times. I was alone; the love of my life had died young, and it was just me.

And I was afraid.

If she was headed to the laundry room, I made sure that I was not.

If she came out to the front steps, I kept far away!

The thing is, the house was now an apartment complex. There were four apartments, two upstairs, and two downstairs. It was an unusual and charming place, once a gracious old plantation, and now a home owned by a man named Stephen Lee. Stephen as a nice guy; I was a kid when he renovated the place. He lived upstairs and rented out the three apartments he had created--a great way for him to maintain the expensive property.

The house was out in the country; beyond the sweeping lawn were rolling green hills and beautiful forests. The house itself had fabulous gardens--he often worked outside, to Stephen Lee's delight. She was, I must admit, an excellent gardener.

Stephen Lee himself worked in the garden, growing things. He was huge on the ecology and passionate about growing his own vegetables.

So, there were flowers and what-not, beautiful neat rows of growing vegetables, and then, beyond, beautiful grasses and forests with lovely thick trees.

In short, it was all perfect and breathtaking. And the house was delightfully old; it was filled with dark crannies and secret corners and wonderful and mysterious trunks. It was historic and perfect for me.

I sat sometimes--making sure she was nowhere near!--and just looked through the window and loved the view. It should have been peaceful and wonderful.

It had been great--beyond great!--before she moved in. Once she did, II should have just given it all up and left.

But, I didn't. Like I said, I loved it, and whether she liked it or not, it was just as much mine as it was hers--I was there first--I was actually born there. Still, I'm not stupid. Once she saw me, and I saw her face--I was afraid.

I was just stubborn.

I really did my best to disappear. But, still, sometimes, I could hear her talking about me. She'd be on the phone, arguing with this one or that one. Yes, she understood the house was old. Yes, she understood that she was in the country, she'd chosen to live where I was...

I'd hear her whisper; I'd hear her say that she just didn't care. She'd smile and go through life--knowing I was there--but she'd sleep with one eye open, certain that I would murder her in her sleep.

Me! All she had to do was ignore me and I'd stay so far away she wouldn't even know that I was there.

But, here's the thing. The woman was nuts. I mean, totally on the far side. Insane--paranoid. She outright said at times that she'd like to torture me--burn me!--and then cut my head off! I heard all this, mind you, but, she didn't really scare me.

She was a "beautiful woman, stunning, really!" I'd heard Stephen say to Mrs. Sandusky--second floor, apartment B--when my nemesis moved in.

Yes, she was beautiful, I guess.

But, she wasn't at all coordinated--she'd never catch me.

For a while, it went on. We both lived in the house--we carefully watched one another.

Her friends and relatives would come by now and then, mostly a young nephew named Frank.

Frank knew I was there. He would shake his head and smile and bring his fingers to his lips when he would see me. Nice guy--I liked Frank. Sometimes, he'd even talk to me. "Hide, my friend, hide. Don't let her see you," he would say.

And I would hurry away.

One night when Frank was there, I heard her talking to him. "I'm going to hire someone to take care of the situation," she said.

Frank groaned. "Hire someone? Oh, please, Aunt Belle. Please, please, you're being ridiculous. You're being absolutely ridiculous."

"Ridiculous! Why, I could die, Frank!"

"Aunt Belle, you're not going to die. She doesn't give a wit about you--you're just obsessed with her."

"I will hire a killer!"

"Really? Don't even talk like that! Someone might get wind of it. Stephen Lee could hear about it. Oh, my God, truly, you're talking crazy!"

"Shush! Don't be ridiculous. I'm not crazy--Stephen Lee is a bit crazy. He doesn't see that *she's* the one who is a killer!" she said.

Frank tried to explain that I was harmless and that it was all in her head, but none of his words were to any avail.

"Don't do it!" Frank insisted. "Don't even talk this way-- you'll upset Stephen, he'll refuse to renew your lease, and you'll be very upset! Honestly, Auntie, this is crazy."

I thought it was cute, the way he called her "Auntie." He was the son of her oldest brother--not more than four or five years younger than she was.

He gave her one of his great smiles--he'd assumed that he'd talked her out of doing something so ridiculous that it wasn't worth talking about. Something, of course, that she didn't really mean.

When he left, she walked around muttering. "I'll do it myself--by God, I'll do it myself!"

She had that crazy look in her eyes. The woman was a menace. I needed to be afraid.

She meant to kill me--herself.

And so, I warily kept an eye on her.

A few days later, I was down in the laundry room, minding my own business, causing no harm or foul to anyone.

It was a beautiful day, truly beautiful. Not too hot, a few puffy clouds in a sky that was unbelievably blue. The air was moving, just a touch cool.

But the laundry room was delightfully warm.

She came in.

I hadn't been watching for her--I wasn't expecting her. She usually did her laundry on Tuesdays and it was a Monday.

But, in she bustled with her wicker basket filled with her delicate little "unmentionables." I really should have been smarter; she wasn't seeing a man at the moment--she was extremely ambitious and creating "the world's finest tour company."

Still, she did her sexy little pieces of lingerie separately--on a different day every couple of weeks.

How had I been so remiss!

There she was--there I was!

And it was just her, and me, there, in the laundry room.

I can remember the hum and whirl of the washers and dryers, the sun dappling through the windows. Mrs. Sandusky--from the second apartment upstairs--had been doing her husband's work shirts. They were piled upon one of the empty dryers. An old wooden bookshelf between the washers and the dryers held detergents and water softeners, and, actually, books!

I didn't say a word. I stared at her. And she looked at me with that crazed, serial-killer gleam in her eyes.

I froze for a moment.

"You! They don't you like I know you!" she cried. "You heinous creature!" she said.

And then, she took her shoe off and ran at me like a truly crazy person.

I think I mentioned that this was not a coordinated person. Nor did she seem to have much depth perception--lucky for me.

She charged; she charged as if she were a maddened bull. I moved--and quickly, I do assure you!

She slammed into the washer, banging it hard enough with the heel of her shoe to leave a crack in it. Again--she came after me, this time slamming into the dryer where Mr. Sandusky's shirt had been set, neatly folded.

They all went flying in a pile of white tailored cotton.

I swear, the woman went entirely insane. Next she spun around and slammed at the book case. Bottles of *Tide* and *Arm and Hammer* went flying. Thick bluish liquid flew all over the floor, the walls, and the machines.

She hit the boxes of fabric softening sheets--they seemed to explode into a million pieces.

War and Peace went flying next. A gossip magazine blew into confetti.

I'd had enough--I knew I had to escape.

I started for the door.

As I did so, I heard her scream. When I slowed in my own maddened scurry to escape, I saw that she was on the floor.

She'd slipped in the blue liquid--and apparently hit herself in the head with her shoe.

I just ran.

Then, of course, for the rest of the day, I worried. I stayed hidden, and I listened and fretted.

She was insane; she needed to be reported by someone to someone as being totally, completely, certifiably insane.

And yet...

If she'd hurt herself, *I* could be blamed. She was beautiful; she could be charming. She could lie her way out of just about anything.

On pins and needles, I waited.

And then, I began to hear the others talking.

"Something terrible!" Mr. Sandusky said, wearing a new shirt since his old shirts were quite ruined.

"And how crazy! A break-in to destroy a laundry room!" his wife said.

There was more; I heard Stephen Lee talking on the phone. Police came! The police.

I kept my peace, staying far away and I slowly realized that *she* had never reported what had really happened. She'd gotten up and run herself--and pretended she'd had nothing to do with the wanton destruction in the laundry room.

I did have to laugh when I saw her. She was sporting a big bruise on her forehead. Yes, the crazy woman had apparently hit herself really hard with her own shoe!

The experience must have rattled her. There were long days then when she seemed to settle down, when she came and went--and I came and went--and she either didn't see me, or she pretended not to see me.

I thought that maybe she had come to a state of peace with me. While she might have lied to everyone else and told them that there must have been a break-in that terrorized the laundry room, I knew the truth.

I would so carefully hide myself and try to watch her as she came and went. Days went by; we seemed to be okay.

And then, on the third day of watching her, I saw her eyes again. Now, they had this glazed look that was no less crazy than the bulging look.

She wasn't at peace. She hadn't accepted me.

She was plotting.

She didn't say a word to nephew Frank again. And when she saw Stephen Lee or Mr. or Mrs. Sandusky, she was all pleasantries and smiles.

The Sandusky couple remained perplexed.

Who the hell broke into a laundry room and simply tore it to pieces?

A high school kid just pissed off because he had to read *War and Peace?*

The police, of course, had put it down to a gang of wandering would-be toughs from the local high school. The same kind of kids who liked to deface gravestones and rip up gardens or knock down garbage cans.

While most of our residents remained baffled, that certainly seemed to be the logical explanation

Not that the gentle, intelligent, industrious, and gorgeous young woman living on the ground floor had totally and completely lost her mind and gone on a killer rampage!

She was letting time pass, and that was it, and nothing more.

And then, she'd be coming to kill me again.

I thought about the things I could do to her in revenge. But, of course, if I hurt her, she might well develop some kind of proof that I was the one who was evil.

I reminded myself that the best defense was often an offense.

Ah, yes. There were many sayings I could go by.

Revenge is a dish best served cold.

That was one that stuck with me as the days went by and I thought of the way she had looked at me while trying to attack me with her high heel--stone-cold whacked-out-institution-able-dangerously crazy.

Downright terrifying.

Revenge. Get her--before she got me.

The thing is, I'm not mean, and I'm truly not evil. Honestly, all that I wanted was to live in peace--and let her do the same.

Move, I told myself. Just move! Find another place to live!

But, as I said, it was my place. I'd been there longer than her. Why should I give up a place I loved because this woman was deranged?

I was actually starting to feel okay--weeks had gone by since the shoe incident.

Then, she changed her approach.

Like many obsessed people, she couldn't help talking about what she was doing.

She talked to herself.

She started to wander around the house and garden and grounds--carrying on long conversations with herself.

Her next mode of attack, I learned, was going to be poison.

She argued with herself.

What kind of poison? How would she set it out? If she cooked it into something, how would she get me to eat it?

Decisions, decisions!

But, I knew the day she bought the poison--I could tell by the giant smile on her face the day she came home from the store with it.

I saw the bag.

I knew what it was.

It was summer and hot and while Stephen Lee had seen to that most of the house--except for the laundry room and the storage in the basement--was nicely air-conditioned.

But, when she was cooking, she opened the window above her stove.

Naturally, I snuck around to watch her.

Amazing! It was like the woman had transformed into an animated fairy-tale witch!

She was humming and singing, and I swear, she *cackled* now and then. She was putting the poison into some kind of muffins.

"You're dead now!" she said over and over again. "Dead, dead, dead! Ah, my pretty! My pretty, pretty, pretty--pretty dead!"

And then she'd cackle and then she'd sing...

But, when the muffins were done, she set them to cool on the windowsill.

Naturally, *I* knew not to touch her cursed muffins.

I didn't think that she'd gone insane enough to try to kill Stephen Lee, her nephew, or the lovely Sandusky couple. But, still, a whole batch of muffins...

Well, what happened was this. Her nephew Frank did come by. When he knocked on the door, she told him to come on in. And Frank did. He went into the kitchen and saw the muffins and he called out to her. "Wow, Auntie Belle! Who knew? A modern, working woman who can cook like this! These look phenomenal! I'm going to have one, all right?"

I wasn't close enough--I was outside. I couldn't stop him.

He reached for a muffin.

Luckily--for Frank!--she came tearing into the kitchen, flying at Frank.

The muffin was nearly in his mouth.

In fact, he paused in the action of putting it into his mouth because she had that absolute crazed look in her eyes as she ran at him and slapped his hand so hard that the muffin went flying out the little area of open window above the stove.

"Auntie Belle, what in God's name?" Frank demanded.

She didn't have to answer.

A large black crow swept down and nipped off a piece of the muffin and went flying up into the sky.

Five seconds later, the crow crashed down to the earth.

Its little clawed feet slashed at the air.

Its wings flapped insanely.

Then it was dead. Stone cold dead. And for the longest time, Frank just stared at it in horror.

Then, of course, he turned to his aunt.

Oh, Frank went on and on that day. And she was cowed. And she cried.

And she swore, swore to him, a dozen times over, she would cease and desist.

I was so disgusted I wanted to spit! But, that was the thing about her--the reason I was so wary and careful of her. She was so lovely that even when she cried, she was beautiful. Her eyes became so big; her words so soft. She charmed everyone.

I didn't stand a chance against her wiles. And, trust me, they were wiles! She made people believe; she twisted them around her finger.

So Frank--who might have died himself!--listened to her cry. And he soothed her. He suggested that she talk to me; befriend me.

She looked at him as if he was the crazy one.

She tried to get him to stay for dinner. But, Frank, as I said, was a nice guy, a good guy--and not at all stupid. She might make him believe that she was truly penitent.

He still wasn't staying for dinner.

He looked out the window at the dead crow and declined, telling her that he was really busy, he and his girlfriend had a date with one of his real estate clients.

I looked at the dead crow for a very long time myself that night. I realized how far her deadly mania would take her.

But, while she was insane, she was also amazingly devious.

Once again, while I contemplated revenge--someone had to act on behalf of the poor dead crow!--she lay low. She was careful.

Luckily, Frank had made certain that the poisoned muffins-- and the deceased crow--were carefully discarded, wrapped in plastic and put in a tin. Frank didn't want any animals digging around a landfill to fall prey to her insanity. I was very glad--I had been fearing greatly for the Sandusky family poodle. Who knows? The little pest might have decided to chew up a dead bird.

Once again, a few weeks went by in which she came and went about her business, smiling and pleasant. I never let up my guard, though. I saw what others did not--the complete depth of her insanity. All they saw was the beautiful woman. People always smiled when she spoke with him; their smiles remained after she had gone.

I wanted to vomit.

And, of course, I quickly realized that, even in killing the crow, she had not realized the error of her ways.

She was as nuts as a pound of roasted pecans.

And still, somehow, I was the only one who saw it. Frank knew, but maybe he just couldn't admit it to himself.

Days went by; weeks went by.

A whole month went by.

To the best of my knowledge, I avoided her completely. I kept an eye on her carefully--but I kept myself hidden as I did so!

I was in the storage room, completely minding my own business, when I heard her come in.

I hid. I hid behind a pile of boxes that held family treasures belonging to Stephen Lee's family.

I thought she was drunk at first. She seemed to stagger in. I heard her as she clumped her way through boxes, around a dressmaker's dummy, through the path between an old wheelbarrow and a bucket of baby toys.

She stopped, and she started to talk.

"I know you're in here. You think you can hide, but I know that you're in here. I know!" She almost screamed the last. "You're watching me. You think I don't see you, but I do! I feel your eyes--I feel your wretched eyes on me. I lay awake at night...you have to die. You have to die! The others don't see it...they think you're just good and helpful, but I know the truth!"

I wished I could have shouted back at her that she was off the charts loco, but...

I had to stay hidden. I had to move furtively. I had to get away, but I couldn't let her see me.

Because this time, she had a massive lighter with her.

It was one of those things that people bought to light candles or barbecues of whatever; the torch at the end created a searing blue flame, but kept the person wielding it a foot or so from the fire they intended to create.

She wanted to burn me alive!

She thought that she saw me; she did not. She raced toward a dressmaker's dummy, screaming and cursing, and swearing that I was dead!

As I'd mentioned, coordination was not her highest asset. She tripped over a pile of old computer gadgets on her way to the dummy. She'd already lit the barbecue match or whatever the flame-thrower in her hand was called.

The flame soared blue and gold toward a stack of old newspapers and magazines.

They burst into flames.

Sobbing incoherently, she jumped to her feet. She grabbed an old horse blanket and tried to tamp out the flames.

Well, paper was burning. Old, dried-out paper. Bits and pieces leapt to into the air as if they were alive.

The sparks flew about the room.

The dressmaker's dummy burst into flames.

The flames jumped to one of the cardboard boxes.

She knew what she had done.

She wasn't coordinated, but--other than her obsession!--she wasn't stupid.

She grabbed her flame-thrower and ran.

And while the fire burned around me and my eyes smarted with the smoke, I waited--waited until I knew she had cleared the place.

I had just one window of opportunity to get out after she had gone--and before Stephen Lee came racing down with a fire extinguisher and the sound of the fire engine sirens could be heard blazing through the night.

Again, I contemplated the truth.

Again, I determined that, if I was seen, she would lie. She would lie like crazy. She would somehow make it all my fault.

Sometimes, the truly crazed are able to do such things, they are such deep believers in the insanity in their own heads.

Well, it was sad, that's what it was. No crows or animals died, but it was sad, nonetheless. Poor Stephen lost valuable family antiques.

Worse, he lost pictures that couldn't be replaced; little bits of the memories of his life that could never be restored.

Of course, they never discovered what had caused the flame. Summer's heat? Some kind of combustion caused by that heat? Even the fire marshal couldn't say. He was able to determine where the fire started--old papers--but not exactly what caused the fire to start. They were all very lucky that it had been contained to the basement, but then, the basement was dark and dank--it was really the stone foundations for the house.

Thankfully--oh, truly thankfully!--it had been quickly contained and the house itself hadn't caught fire. That would have been a disaster.

Once again, she got away with it.

And while I pondered so many possibilities, there was nothing I could really do about it.

She commiserated with Stephen Lee, trying to bake for him, trying to tell him how sorry she was about the loss in the storage area of the basement.

I wondered then if Stephen had some inkling he was harboring a madwoman. I saw him hesitate--and then I saw him thank her, tell her that he appreciated her thoughtfulness, but he already had plans for the evening.

I thanked God. Stephen is, like Frank, a good guy.

Well, of course, she began her quiet period again. Her fear of being caught period, perhaps--or her renewed plotting stage.

I'd hear her murmuring to herself, but her stage of mental instability had become so serious that I couldn't understand her half the time when she was speaking.

But, as time went on, I began to recognize a few words. *Hire a professional.*

She began to talk to herself. She'd get money from the bank. She'd pretend the killer was a friend; she'd even have him over to dinner.

(With any luck, she'd feed him bran muffins, and he'd be gone before he could do me in.)

She wouldn't tell Stephen Lee what she was doing, because he would be horrified. In fact, he'd ask her to leave or have her arrested!

She knew that. She knew that she had to be incredibly careful. So careful that she didn't say a word to Frank.

In fact, when her nephew was over, she told him that she'd grown to like me! Frank was so pleased. He seemed to think that she had really found knowledge and understanding. When he left, he was cheerful.

I wanted to go to him when he left; I wanted to find a way to tell him that she was a liar, a paranoid, maniacal liar.

He was gone before I could reach him.

I watched, and I waited.

And then came the day.

I began to understand her a bit that day, oddly enough. Because, the man she brought in scared me as no one had ever scared me before.

In fact, I was almost frozen with fear.

He went to the kitchen. They spoke very matter-of-factly.

Oh, he was "professional" all right!

He told her what he could and couldn't do--he didn't intend to be caught, no matter what her fear and determination.

He even suggested that she move!

But, you see, she was beautiful, and she could be very persuasive. She smiled; her eyes grew huge with tears she didn't quite shed.

She begged; she pleaded.

She cajoled.

Such a woman could make a man forget about danger.

And the man--that huge fellow, that hired professional!--fell for her, hook, line, and sinker.

He was hired; he was going to kill me.

Well, this time, there was nothing left to do.

Run?

Oh, no.

Now I was so angry that, come hell or high water, I was going to fight back.

I listened to her talk. I listened to her tell him about *me*, about my schedule, about where I tended to be when. She told him how I seemed to like the darkness--that was where I skulked, watching her! I didn't mind being alone in the dark in the least. I seemed to see better there--I seemed to watch her with evil intent from the darkness at all hours.

He was a little mystified. He asked her if I'd come after her--

she said no. He asked her if I kept to my own space--she said yes.

"Really, I don't understand," he told her.

But she began to cry again. No one understood. She knew--she just knew!--that I was there, pretending innocence, biding my time, waiting...

And then I would get her.

Of course, within minutes, his arms were around her shoulders and he was reassuring her, and telling her that yes--he would kill me for her, no matter what the consequences.

She told him about me and the laundry room.

He prepared; I watched him gather his weapons.

But, unknown to either of them, I was the wiser. I wasn't in the basement waiting to be taken by surprise.

I was ready to follow.

He headed down--carefully--lest Stephen or Mr. or Mrs. Sandusky come upon him.

He entered the laundry room.

I'd never moved more cautiously, more carefully myself--or with greater anger.

He came down whistling.

"Where are you?" he sang softly.

First, he looked about everywhere. He moved just about everything down there. He swore and swung around--as if he knew then that he had been followed.

I ducked behind the door.

He didn't see me. He began to breathe more slowly, shook his head as if he'd imagined something, and returned to his search.

Apparently, he thought I might be hiding in a washing machine. How dumb.

He had no idea that I was behind him!

He bent low, his head all but completely in a dryer...

And it was my moment.

I told you, honestly, I'm not mean. But this man had absolutely terrified me. Left me frozen to such an extent that I almost understood *her* terror of me.

And, it truly was life or death.

In a maddened, insane rush of my own, I jumped, going straight for the back of his neck.

Well, for a big man who should have been somewhat

intelligent and coordinated--being a professional and all--he behaved like an idiot child. He screamed. He tried to slap at me; his arms and hands flailed and the idiot struck his head hard on the rim of the dryer.

So hard that he fell to floor in a dead thump.

And...

Well, as it turned out, it really was a "dead" thump.

I never even hurt the man--I didn't get a chance. He did himself in, catching the back of his head in just the right place to do something to his brain.

It was a while, of course, before I figured it all out. I ran like a chicken myself after he fell--I ran and found a dark corner and waited there, shaking and afraid. I didn't know at first that the man was dead.

Sadly, it was nice Mrs. Sandusky who found him.

She went screaming; Mr. Sandusky came, and then the police and, eventually, everyone figured out that *she* had hired him, a professional, to kill me.

She might have been beautiful, but no amount of tears would change things then.

Stephen Lee grew organic vegetables; he was passionate about ecology. And she'd hired him to come and plant poison everywhere...

And the man had died! On Stephen Lee's property!

She was out, of course. Not only was she out, but, her nephew Frank had to have her put away for a while.

She had gone completely mad. She turned me into a truly horrible monster in her mind, bigger than a great blue whale, more cunning than a fox, more vicious than a wolverine. She talked so crazy that there was no way out of it--she needed help.

So, she was gone...

And I was fine; I was there.

Silly woman. Such a pity.

A spider's lifespan is three years at best.

I know I'm not going to make that. Tonight, my eggs will hatch. I'm so pleased that I was able to have my offspring here, where I was hatched myself, where--for most of my life!--I protected others from mosquitos and the bugs that would have ripped the beautiful gardens apart.

It was a good life, except for her.

And the man. The man who terrified me so much that I was terrified.

They all say that she suffered severely from arachnophobia.

I almost felt sorry for her. I felt that same kind of debilitating fear once she'd brought in the exterminator.

That must be a phobia too?

I wonder what they call it.

Exterminator-phobia?

ABOUT THE AUTHORS

13Thirty Books, LLP Author Collective includes: *New York Times*, *USA Today*, Amazon Top Ten bestselling and award-winning authors, as well as new, unique and upcoming writers.